Praise for *New York Times* bestselling author DEBBIE MACOMBER

"Full of unexpected delights."
—*Publishers Weekly* on
There's Something About Christmas

"A tale as joyful as the season itself."
—*Booklist* on *When Christmas Comes*

"Readers looking for a holiday fairy tale
will find plenty of reasons to cheer."
—*Publishers Weekly* on *When Christmas Comes*

"Perfect fireside reading."
—*Library Journal* on *The Snow Bride*

"A fast, frothy fantasy for those looking to
add some romance to their holidays."
—*Publishers Weekly* on *The Snow Bride*

"Ms. Macomber provides the top
in entertaining relationship dramas."
—*Reader to Reader*

"Sometimes the best things come in small packages.
Such is the case here."
—*Publishers Weekly* on *Return to Promise*

"Macomber's storytelling sometimes yields a tear,
at other times a smile."
—*Newport News, VA, Daily Press*

Dear Friends,

You're going to require two things to enjoy this holiday volume.

1. A sense of humor.

2. An open mind when it comes to fruitcake.

As it happens, I love fruitcake, and because I do, I'm sharing three special fruitcake recipes with you. One comes from my mother-in-law, Marie Macomber; it started out as an applesauce cake that I adapted through the years into a moist fruitcake. (The rum certainly doesn't hurt!) The others are from two readers, Cindy Thornlow and Penny Raven, who have become friends of mine through the years.

The second story in this set is a romantic comedy I wrote in the early 1990s. It's long been a favorite of mine. You'll see that I've updated it a little.... I hope that, just like Maryanne and me, you'll fall in love with Nolan.

Both stories feature heroines who work for newspapers. The title, *Glad Tidings,* refers to that— and, of course, to the good news of Christmas.

My wish is that these stories will make you laugh. If you enjoy them as much as I hope you do, please consider your laughter my gift to you this Christmas.

Debbie Macomber

P.S. I love to hear from readers! You can reach me at www.debbiemacomber.com or P.O. Box 1458, Port Orchard, WA 98366.

DEBBIE MACOMBER
Glad Tidings

MIRA

ISBN-13: 978-0-7783-2355-6
ISBN-10:   0-7783-2355-2

GLAD TIDINGS

CONTENTS

THERE'S SOMETHING ABOUT CHRISTMAS

To Emma Ingram (the real Emma) and her mother

Chapter One

On that cold day I was born, in February 1955, my great-aunt gave me a classic fruitcake for the celebration of the occasion of my birth. Every year during the holidays I pull it out of the attic and take a look at it and it still looks great, and every year I try to get up the nerve to take a slice and try it.

—Dean Fearing,
chef of The Mansion on Turtle Creek

This job was going to kill her yet.

Emma Collins stared at the daredevil pilot who was urging her toward his plane. She'd come to Thun Field to drum up advertising dollars for her employer, *The Puyallup Examiner,* and wasn't interested in taking a spin around southeast Puget Sound.

"Thank you, but no," she insisted for the third time. Oliver Hamilton seemed to have a hearing problem. However, Emma was doing her best to maintain a professional facade, despite her pounding heart. No way would she go for a ride with Flyboy.

The truth was, Emma was terrified of flying. Okay, she white-knuckled it in a Boeing 747, but nothing on God's green earth would get her inside a small plane with this man—and his dog. Oliver Hamilton had a devil-may-care glint in his dark blue eyes and wore a distressed brown leather jacket that resembled something a World War Two bomber pilot might wear. All he needed was the white scarf. She suspected that if he ever got her in the air, he'd start making loops and circles with the express purpose of frightening her to death. He looked just the type.

Placing the advertising-rate sheet on his desk, she turned resolutely away from the window and the sight of Hamilton's little bitty plane—a Cessna Caravan 675, he'd called it. "As I was explaining earlier, *The Examiner* has a circulation of over forty-five thousand. As you'll see—" she gestured at the sheet "—we have special introductory rates in December. We serve four communities and, dollar for advertising dollar, you can't do better than what we're offering."

"Yes, yes, I understand all that," Oliver Hamilton said, stepping around his desk. "Now, what I can offer *you* is the experience of a lifetime…."

Instinctively Emma backed away. She had an aversion to attractive men whose promises slid so easily off their tongues. Her father had been one of them.

He'd flitted in and out of her life during her childhood and teen years. Every so often, he'd arrived bearing gifts and making promises, none of which he'd kept. Still, her mother had loved Bret Collins until the end. Pamela had died after a brief illness when Emma was a sophomore at the University of Oregon. To his credit, her father had paid her college expenses, but Emma refused to have anything to do with him. She was on her own in the world and determined to make a success of her career as a journalist. When she'd hired on at *The Examiner* earlier that year, she hadn't objected to starting at the bottom. She'd expected that. What she *hadn't* expected was spending half her time trying to sell advertising.

The Examiner was a family-owned business, one of a vanishing breed. The newspaper had been in the Berwald family for three generations. Walt Berwald II had held on through the corporate buyouts and survived the competition from the big-city newspapers coming out of Tacoma and Seattle. It hadn't been easy. Now his thirty-year-old son had taken over after his father's recent heart attack. Walt the third, the new editor-in-chief, was doing everything he could to keep the newspaper financially solvent, which Emma knew was a challenge.

"Hey, Oscar," Oliver said, bending to pet his dog. "I think the lady's afraid of flying."

Emma bristled, irritated that he'd pegged her so quickly. "Don't be ridiculous."

He ignored her and continued to pet the dog. She couldn't readily identify his breed, possibly some kind of terrier. The dog was mostly white with one large black spot surrounding his left eye. Right out of that 1930s show *Spanky and Our Gang.* Wasn't that the name? She shook off her momentary distraction.

"I'm here to sell you advertising in *The Examiner,*" she explained again. "I hope you'll reconsider."

Oliver straightened, crossing his arms, and leaned against his desk. "As I said, I'm just getting my business started. At this point I don't have a lot of discretionary funds for advertising. So for now I'll stick with the word-of-mouth method. That seems to be working."

It couldn't be working that well, since he appeared to have a lot of time on his hands. "Exactly what is it you do?" she asked.

"I give flying lessons and I've recently begun an air-freight business."

"Oh."

"Oscar and I haven't crashed even once."

He was obviously making fun of her, and she didn't appreciate it. Nor did she take his alleged safety record as an incentive to leap into the passenger seat.

"But then," he added, "there's always a first time."

"Exactly what I was going to say," Emma muttered. "Well, I'll leave the information with you," she said more pleasantly. "I hope you'll think about our proposal when it's financially feasible."

Retrieving her briefcase and purse, she headed toward the door—which Oliver suddenly blocked with his arm. His smile was as lazy as it was sexy. Hmm, funny how often *lazy* and *sexy* went together. Considering all that boyish charm, plenty of other women had probably melted at his feet. She wouldn't.

She met his gaze without flinching.

"Are you sure I can't take you up for a spin?" he asked.

"Absolutely, positively sure."

"There's nothing to fear except fear itself."

"Uh-uh. Now if you'll excuse me, I have other calls to make."

He moved aside. "It's a shame. You're kinda cute in an uptight sort of way."

Unable to resist, she rolled her eyes.

Oliver chuckled and walked her out to her car, his dog trotting behind him. Normally Emma would've taken time to pet the terrier, but Oliver Hamilton would inevitably read that as a sign she was interested in him. She was fond of animals, especially dogs, and hoped to get one herself. Unfortunately, her apartment complex didn't allow pets; not only that, the landlord was a real piece of work. As soon as she had the chance, Emma planned to find somewhere else to live.

Using her remote, she unlocked her car door, which Oliver promptly opened for her. She smiled her thanks, eager to leave, and climbed into the driver's side.

"So I can't change your mind?"

She shook her head. The one thing a ladies' man could never resist, Emma had learned from her father, was a woman who said no. Somehow, she'd have to get Oliver to accept her at her word.

She reached for the door and closed it. Hard.

Oliver stepped back.

After she'd started the ignition and pulled away, he smiled at her—a mysterious smile—as if he knew something she didn't.

As far as Emma was concerned, she'd made a lucky escape.

Her irritation had just begun to fade when she returned to the office and walked down to her cubicle in the basement, shared with half a dozen other staff. The area was affectionately—and sometimes not so affectionately—termed The Dungeon. Phoebe Wilkinson, who sat opposite her, glanced up when Emma tossed her purse onto her desk.

"That bad?" Phoebe asked, rolling her chair across the narrow aisle. She was one of the other reporters, a few years older than Emma. She was short where Emma was tall, with dark hair worn in a pixie cut while Emma's was long and blond. Most of the time, anyway. Occasionally Emma was a redhead or a brunette.

"You wouldn't believe my afternoon."

"Did you sell any ads?" Phoebe asked. It'd been her turn the day before and she'd come back with three brand-new accounts.

Emma nodded. She'd managed to get the local pizza parlor to place an ad in the Wednesday edition with a dollar-off coupon for any large pizza. That way, the restaurant could figure out how well the advertising had worked. Emma just hoped everyone in town would go racing into the parlor with that coupon. Badda Bing, Badda Boom Pizza had been her only sale.

"That's great," Phoebe said with real enthusiasm.

"Yes, at least our payroll checks won't bounce." She couldn't restrain her sarcasm.

Phoebe frowned, shaking her head. "Walt would never let that happen."

Her friend and co-worker had a crush on the owner. Phoebe was the strongest personality she knew, yet when it came to Walt, she seemed downright timid—far from her usual assertive self.

Emma sighed. Her own feelings about men had grown cynical. Her father was mostly responsible for that. Her one serious college romance hadn't helped, either; it ended when her mother became ill. Emma hadn't been around to help Neal with his assignments, so he'd dropped her for another journalism student. Pulling out her chair, Emma sat down. She hadn't worked so hard to get her college degree for *this*. Her feet hurt, she had a run in her panty hose and no one was going to give her a Pulitzer prize when she spent half her time pounding the pavement and the other half writing obituaries.

Yes, obituaries. Walt's big coup had been getting a contract to write obituaries for the large Tacoma newspaper, and that had been her job and Phoebe's for the past eight months. Emma had gotten quite good at summarizing someone else's life—but that hardly made a smudge on the page of her own.

She hadn't obtained a journalism degree in order to persuade the local department store to place mattress sale ads in the Sunday paper, either. She was a reporter! A darn good one…if only someone would give her a chance to prove herself. Emma longed to write a piece worthy of her education and her skills, and frankly, preparing obituaries wasn't it.

"I don't think I can do this much longer," she confessed sadly. "Either Walt lets me write a real story or…" She didn't know what.

Phoebe gasped. "You aren't thinking of quitting, are you?"

Emma looked at her friend. She'd been hired the same week as Phoebe. The difference was, Phoebe seemed content to do whatever was asked of her. She loved writing obituaries and set the perfect tone with each one. Not Emma. She hated it, struggling with them all. The result was always adequate or better because Emma took pride in her work, but it just wasn't what she wanted to be doing. She had ambition and dreamed that one day she'd write feature articles. Eventually, she hoped to have her own column.

"I don't *want* to quit. I've been waiting six months

for Walt to offer me something more than funeral home notices."

"Sleep on it," Phoebe advised. "You've had a rough day. Everything will seem better in the morning."

"You're right," she murmured. An ultimatum shouldn't be made on the spur of the moment. Besides, it wasn't the obituaries or even drumming up advertising dollars that depressed her the most.

It was Christmas.

Everywhere she went, there was holiday cheer. But not everyone in the world loved Christmas. She, for example, didn't enjoy it at all. Christmas was for families and she didn't have one. Yes, her father was alive, but that was of little comfort. Since her mother's death, he always invited Emma to his house in California and she always took a certain grim satisfaction in refusing him.

Almost everyone she knew had family and shared the holidays with them. Emma was alone. But she'd rather be by herself than spend it with her father and his new wife. Last year she'd ignored the season entirely. On Christmas Day she'd gone to a movie and had buttered popcorn for dinner and that had suited her perfectly.

"You don't want to quit just before Christmas," Phoebe told her.

Emma sighed again. "No, you're right. I don't." But she said it mostly to avoid upsetting Phoebe.

* * *

"You're actually going to confront Walt?" Phoebe peered at Emma across The Dungeon aisle the next morning.

"Yes," Emma murmured. She'd decided that after almost a year, she wasn't any closer to writing feature articles than the day she was hired. It was time to face reality. She'd reached her limit; she was finished with working in the bowels of the drafty building, tired of spending half her week traipsing around Bonny Lake, Sumner and Puyallup searching for advertising dollars.

"What are you going to say to him?" Phoebe's brown eyes regarded her carefully.

She didn't know what she could say that she hadn't already said a hundred times. If Walt refused to listen, she would simply hand in her notice. She wouldn't leave until after Christmas; that was for strictly financial reasons. Where she'd apply next, however, was the question.

"Walt won't want to lose you," Phoebe said confidently.

"You mean when he isn't yelling?"

"He has a lot on his mind."

Emma narrowed her eyes. Phoebe's infatuation with Walt blinded her to the truth.

It was now or never. Emma stood, squaring her shoulders. "Okay, I'm going to talk to Walt." She motioned at the stairwell. "Do I have the *look*?" The one that said she was serious.

"Oh, yes!" Phoebe was nothing if not encouraging.

"You'll be stuck writing all the obituaries," Emma cautioned.

"I don't mind," her friend said.

"Okay, here goes."

Emma marched up the stairs and toward the back of the first floor, where Walt's luxurious office was situated. Well, perhaps it wasn't as luxurious as all that, except when compared to the dank basement where Emma and Phoebe were relegated.

Walt glanced up, frowning, as she planted herself in the threshold to his office.

"Do you have a minute?" she asked politely.

His frown slowly transformed itself into a smile, and for the first time Emma noticed her employer had company. She opened her mouth to apologize, but Walt didn't let her finish.

"I was just going to ask you to step into my office." He waved her inside. "I believe you've met Oliver Hamilton."

It was all she could do not to ask why he was here. "Hello again," Emma managed to say as her stomach lurched. She should've known; Oliver wasn't a man who took no for an answer.

He stood when Emma came into the office and extended his hand. "Good to see you again, too."

Emma reluctantly exchanged handshakes, not fooled by his friendly demeanor, and avoided eye contact. A weary sensation came over her. The man was up to no good. At this point she didn't know *what* he wanted, but she had a feeling she was about to find out—a sinking feeling, which was one of those clichés she'd learned to excise in journalism school.

"Sit down," Walt instructed when she remained frozen to the spot.

She did, perching on the chair parallel to Oliver's.

Walt leaned back in his seat and studied her. Despite the free and easy style typical of the office, Emma chose to dress as a professional, since that was the way she wanted to be perceived. Her hair was secured at the base of her neck with a gold clip. The impression she hoped to create was that of a working reporter with an edge. Today's outfit was a classy black pinstripe suit with a straight skirt and formfitting jacket.

"You've been saying for some time that you'd be interested in writing something other than obituaries," Walt began.

"Yes, I feel—"

"You say you want to write what you refer to as a 'real story.'"

Emma nodded. She glanced out of the corner of her eye at Oliver. "However, if the story's about planes and such, I don't think—"

"It isn't." Her employer didn't allow her to finish.

Emma relaxed. Not completely but enough so she could breathe normally.

"It's about fruitcake."

Emma was dying to write a human interest story

and after months of pleading, Walt was finally giving her an assignment. He wanted her to write about *fruit-cake*. Surely there was some mistake.

"Fruitcake?" she repeated just to be sure she'd heard him correctly. Emma didn't even like fruitcake; in fact, she hated the stuff. She firmly believed that there were two kinds of people in the world—those who liked fruitcake and those who didn't.

She'd once heard an anecdote about a fruitcake that was passed around a family for years. It was hard as a brick and the fruitcake shuffle finally ended when someone used it as an anchor for a fishing boat.

"*Good Homemaking* magazine ran a national fruit-cake contest last month," he went on to explain. "Amazingly, three of the twelve finalists are from the state of Washington."

He paused—waiting for her to show awe or appreciation, she supposed.

"That's quite a statistic, don't you think?" Oliver inserted.

Still leery, Emma slowly nodded once more.

Walt smiled as if he'd gotten the response he wanted. "I'd like you to interview the three finalists and write an article about each of them."

Okay, so maybe these articles weren't going to put her in the running for a major writing award, but this *was* the chance she'd been hoping for. There had to be more to these three women than their interest in fruitcake. She'd write about their lives, about who they were. She had her first big break and she was grabbing hold of it with both hands.

The professional in her took over. "When would you like me to start?" she asked, trying not to sound too eager.

"As soon as you want," Walt told her, grinning. Judging by the gleam in his eyes, he knew he had her. "The magazine's going to announce the winner on their Web site in three weeks, and then do a feature on her in their next issue. It could be one of our ladies. Flatter them," Walt advised, "and get permission to print their recipes."

"All right," Emma said, although she had the feeling this might be no small task. A niggling doubt took root and she shot a look at the pilot. "I assume all three finalists live in the Puget Sound area?" Oliver was in the newspaper office for a reason; she could only pray it had nothing to do with fruitcake.

Walt shrugged. "Unfortunately, only one lives in the area." He picked up a piece of paper. "Peggy Lucas is from Friday Harbor in the San Juan Islands," he said, reading the name at the top of the list.

A ferry ride away, Emma thought. Not a problem. It would mean a whole day, but she'd always enjoyed being on the water. And a ferry trip was definitely less dangerous than a plane ride.

"Earleen Williams lives in Yakima," Walt continued. "And Sophie McKay is from Colville. That's why I brought in Mr. Hamilton."

Emma peered over her shoulder at the flyboy with his faded leather jacket.

He winked at her, and she remembered his smile yesterday at the small airport. That I-know-something-you-don't smile. Now she understood.

A panicky feeling attacked her stomach. "I can drive to Yakima. Colville, too…" Emma choked out. She wasn't sure where Colville was. Someplace near Spokane, part of the Inland Empire, she guessed. She wanted to make it clear that she had no objection to traveling by car. It would be a piece of cake. Fruitcake.

"A woman alone on the road in the middle of winter is asking for trouble," Oliver said solemnly, shaking his head. "I don't think that's a good idea, do you?" While the question was directed at Walt, he looked at Emma. His cocky grin was almost more than she could bear. He *knew*. He'd known from the moment she'd refused to fly with him, and now he was purposely placing her in an impossible position.

Emma glared at him. Hamilton made it sound as if she were risking certain death by driving across the state. Okay, so she'd need to travel over Snoqualmie Pass, which could be tricky in winter. The pass was sometimes closed because of avalanche danger. And snow posed a minor problem. She'd have to put chains on her tires. Well, she'd face that if the need arose. In all likelihood it wouldn't. The interstate was kept as hazard-free as possible; the roads were salted and plowed at frequent intervals.

"I wouldn't want to see you in that kind of situation," Walt agreed with Oliver. "In addition to the risk of traveling alone, there's the added expense of putting you up in hotel rooms for a couple of nights, plus meals and mileage. This works out better."

"What works out?" Emma turned from one man to the other. It was as if she'd missed part of the conversation.

"We're giving advertising space to Hamilton Air Service and in return, he'll fly you out to interview these three women."

For one crazy moment Emma couldn't talk at all. "You…want me to fly in that…little plane…with him?" she finally stammered. The last two words were more breath than sound. If she started to think about being stuck in a small plane, she might hyperventilate right then and there.

Walt nodded. He seemed to think it was a perfectly reasonable idea.

"I—"

"I've got a flight scheduled for Yakima first thing tomorrow morning," Oliver told her matter-of-factly. "That won't be a problem, will it?" His smile seemed to taunt her.

"Ah…"

"You *have* been saying you wanted to write something other than obituaries, haven't you?" This was from Walt.

"Y-yes."

"Then what's the problem?"

"No problem," she said, her throat tightening and nearly choking off the words. "No problem whatsoever."

"Good."

Oliver stood. "Be down at the airstrip tomorrow morning at seven."

"I'll be there." Her legs had apparently turned to pudding, but she managed to stand, too. Smiling shakily, she left the office. As she headed down to her desk, Emma looked over her shoulder to see Walt and Oliver shaking hands.

Phoebe was waiting for her in The Dungeon. "What happened?" she asked eagerly.

Emma ignored the question and walked directly over to her chair, where she collapsed. Life had taken on a sense of unreality. She felt as if she were watching a silent movie flicker across a screen, the actors' movements jerky and abrupt.

"Aren't you going to tell me?" Phoebe stared at Emma and gasped. "You quit, didn't you?"

Emma shook her head. "I got an assignment."

Phoebe hesitated. "That's great. Isn't it?"

"I…think so. Only…"

"Only what?"

"Only it looks like you're going to be writing the obituaries on your own for a while."

Phoebe gave her a puzzled smile. "That's all right. I already told you I don't mind."

"Maybe not, but I have a feeling that the next one you write just might be mine."

Chapter Two

The first thing Emma did when she got home from the newspaper office that evening was check her medicine cabinet. Her relief knew no bounds when she found six tablets rattling around in the dark-brown prescription bottle. A few months earlier, she'd twisted her knee playing volleyball. Phoebe had conned her into joining a league, but that was another story entirely. The attending physician in the urgent-care facility had given her a powerful muscle relaxant. Her knee had continued to hurt, as Emma vividly recalled, but thirty minutes after she'd swallowed the capsule, she couldn't have cared less. All was right with the world—for a couple of hours, anyway.

Knowing how potent those pills were, she'd hoarded them for a situation such as the one she now faced with Oliver Hamilton. For the sake of her career she'd accompany him in his scary little plane, but it went without saying that Emma would need help of the medicinal variety. If she was going to be flying with Oliver Hamilton she had to have something to numb her overwhelming fear at the prospect of getting into that plane. She clutched the bottle and took a deep breath. For the sake of her craft and her career, she'd do it.

Emma simply couldn't survive the trip without those pills. One tablet to get her to Yakima and another to get her home. That left four, exactly the number she needed for the two additional trips.

Thankfully, Phoebe had agreed to drive her to the airport and then pick her up at the end of the day. Emma was grateful—more than grateful. Once she'd taken the muscle relaxant, she'd be in no condition to drive.

At six-thirty the next morning, Phoebe pulled up in front of the apartment complex. Carrying her traveling coffee mug, along with her leather briefcase, Emma hurried out her door to meet her friend.

"Don't you look nice," her landlord said, startling her. She was sure that was a smirk on his face.

Under normal circumstances Emma would've taken offense, but in her present state of mind all she could do was smile wanly.

Mr. Scott leaned against his door, this morning's *Examiner* in his hand. He was middle-aged with a beer belly and a slovenly manner, and frankly, Emma was surprised to find him awake this early in the day. After moving into the apartment, she'd stayed clear of her landlord, who seemed to be…well, the word *sleazy* came to mind. He didn't like animals, especially cats and dogs, and in her opinion that said a lot about his personality, all of it negative.

"Good morning, Mr. Scott," Emma greeted him, making a determined effort not to slur her words. The pill had already started to take effect and, despite the presence of the loathsome Bud Scott, the world had never seemed a brighter or more pleasant place.

"It's a bit nippy this morning, isn't it?" he asked.

Emma nodded, although if it was chilly she hadn't noticed. In her current haze nothing seemed hot or cold. From experience she knew that in three or four hours the pill would have lost most of its effect and she'd be clear-headed enough for what she hoped would be an intelligent interview.

"I don't suppose you know anyone who needs an apartment," Bud Scott muttered. He narrowed his gaze as if he suspected she wasn't sober—which was a bit much considering she rarely saw him without a can of Milwaukee's finest.

"I thought every unit in the complex was rented," Emma said.

"The lady in 12B had a cat." He scowled as he spoke.

He'd underlined the *No Pets* clause a number of times when Emma signed her rental agreement. Any infraction, he'd informed her, would result in a one-week notice of eviction.

"Mrs. Murphy?" Emma cried when she realized who lived in 12B, two doors down from her. The sweet older lady was a recent widow and missed her husband dreadfully. "You couldn't have made an exception?" she asked. "Mrs. Murphy is so lonely and—"

"No exceptions," Mr. Scott growled. He shoved open his door and disappeared inside, grumbling under his breath.

"What was all that about?" Phoebe asked when Emma got into the car.

"He is truly a lower life-form," she declared righteously. "Doesn't possess an ounce of compassion." She stumbled a bit on the last word.

Phoebe gave her an odd look. "Are you all right?"

Emma smothered a yawn and then giggled.

"What did you do?" Phoebe asked, eyeing her suspiciously.

"Remember the pain pills I got last August?"

"The ones that made you so…weird?"

"I wasn't weird. I was happy."

"Don't tell me you took one this morning!"

In response Emma giggled again. "Just one. I need it for the plane ride. Can't leave home without it."

"Emma, you're supposed to be doing an interview."

"I know… The pill will wear off by then."

"But…"

"Don't worry, I'm fine. Really, I am."

Phoebe didn't look as if she believed her. When she

stopped at a traffic signal, she cast Emma another worried glance. "You're *sure* you're doing the right thing?"

Emma nodded. All at once she felt incredibly tired. Closing her eyes, she leaned her head against the passenger window. In her dreamlike state, she viewed a long line of circus animals parading down to Bud Scott's office and protesting on behalf of Mrs. Murphy. The vision of elephants carrying placards and lions ready to rip out his throat faded and Emma worked hard to focus her thoughts on the upcoming interview. Fruitcake. Good grief, she hated fruitcake. She wanted nothing to do with it.

Yesterday, once she'd received her assignment, Emma had phoned Earleen Williams, the Yakima finalist, who was a retired bartender. Earleen had seemed flustered but pleased at the attention. Emma had made an appointment to talk with her late this morning. She'd spent much of the night reviewing her questions when she should've been sleeping. No wonder she was exhausted.

"We're at the airport," Phoebe announced.

Emma stirred. It required tremendous effort to lift her head from the passenger window. Stretching her arms, she yawned loudly. The temptation to sleep was almost irresistible, especially when she realized that all too soon she'd be suspended thousands of feet above the ground.

"Flying isn't so bad, you know," Phoebe said in a blatant effort to encourage her.

"Have you ever flown in a small plane?"

"No, but…"

"Then I don't want to hear it. See you back here tonight," Emma murmured, hoping to boost her own confidence. People went up in small planes every day. It *couldn't* be as terrifying as she believed. But this wasn't necessarily a rational fear—or not completely, anyway. It didn't matter, though; fear was still fear, whatever its cause. She reminded herself that in a few days she'd be able to laugh about this. Besides, writers across the centuries had made sacrifices for their art, and being bounced around in a tin can with wings would be hers. By the end of this fruitcake series, she might even have conquered her terror. Even if she hadn't, she'd never let Hamilton know.

Oliver and his dog were walking around the outside of the aircraft, inspecting it, when she approached, briefcase in hand.

"You ready?" he asked, barely looking in her direction.

"Ah…don't you want to wait until the sun is up?" she asked. She hoped to delay this as long as possible. The pill needed to be at the height of its effectiveness before she'd find the courage to actually climb inside the aircraft.

"Light, dark, it doesn't make any difference." He walked toward the wing and tested the flap by manually moving it up and down.

"There hasn't been a problem with the flaps, has

there?" she asked, following close behind him. Too bad he was so attractive, Emma mused. In another time and place... She halted her thoughts immediately. This man was dangerous and in more ways than the obvious. First, he was intent on putting her at mortal risk, and second... Well, she couldn't think of a second reason, but the first one was enough.

No, wait—now she remembered. Since he was a good-looking, bad-boy type, she probably wasn't the only woman attracted to him. Tall, dark, handsome and reckless, to boot. Men like Oliver Hamilton drew women in droves and always had. He was far too reminiscent of her father, and she wasn't interested. Emma preferred quiet, serious men over the flamboyant ones who thought nothing of attempting ridiculous, hazardous stunts like flying small rattletrap planes.

"You're worried about the flaps?" he asked, and seemed to find humor in her question.

"Haven't they been working properly?" While Emma actually had no idea what function the flaps played in keeping an airplane aloft, she was sure it must be significant.

Something in her voice—perhaps a slight drawl she could hear herself—must have betrayed her because Oliver turned and gave her his full attention. Frowning, he asked, "Have you been drinking?"

"This early in the morning?"

"You didn't answer my question."

"No," she returned with an edge of defiance. "I don't drink."

"Ever?" His eyebrows rose as if he doubted her.

She shrugged. "I do on occasion, but I don't make a habit of it."

His dog sneezed, spraying her pant leg. This was her best pair of wool pants and she wasn't keen on showing up for the interview with one leg peppered with dubious-looking stains. Oscar sneezed again and again in quick succession, but at least she had the wherewithal to leap back. "Yuck!" she muttered. "Oh, yuck."

"You wouldn't happen to be wearing perfume, would you?" Oliver demanded in a voice that suggested she was attempting to carry an illegal weapon on board.

"Yes, of course I am. Most women do."

He grumbled some remark she didn't hear, then added, "Oscar's allergic to perfume."

"You might've told me that before now," she said, wiping her pant leg a second time. Thank goodness she'd brought gloves. And thank goodness they were washable.

He raised his shoulder in a nonchalant fashion. "Probably should have. It slipped my mind." He continued his outside inspection of the plane. "Oh, yeah," he said, testing the flap on the opposite wing, "I need to know how much you weigh."

"I beg your pardon?" There were certain things a man didn't ask a woman and this was one of them.

"Your weight," he said matter-of-factly.

Despite her drug-induced state of relaxation, Emma stiffened. "I'm not telling you."

"Listen, Emma, it's important. I'm loaded to the gills with furnace parts. I have to know how much you weigh in order to calculate the amount of fuel we're going to need."

She scowled. "You expect me just to blurt it out?" A woman didn't tell a man anything that personal, especially a man she barely knew and had no intention of knowing further.

"If I miscalculate, we'll crash and burn," Oliver said, apparently assuming this would persuade her to confess.

She glared at him in an effort to come up with a compromise. With her mind this fuzzy, it was difficult. "I'll write it down."

He didn't seem to care. "Whatever."

Emma set her briefcase on the floor inside the plane and extracted a pencil and small pad. The only time she weighed herself was when she suspected her weight had fallen. She certainly wasn't overweight, but a desk job had done little to help her maintain the figure she'd been proud of back in college. A few pounds had crept on over the last five years. She penciled in her most recent known weight, according to a doctor's visit last year, and then quickly erased it. After a moment's hesitation, she subtracted ten pounds. At one point in the not-so-distant past, she'd weighed exactly that and she would again, once she got started with an exercise program.

Tearing the sheet from the pad, she folded it in fourths and then eighths until it was about the size of her thumbnail.

Oliver was waiting for her when she'd finished. He held out his hand.

Emma was about to give him the folded-up paper, but paused. "Swear to me you'll never divulge this number."

He grinned, increasing his cuteness a hundredfold. "This is a joke, right?"

"No," she countered, "I'm totally serious."

He grunted yet another comment she didn't understand and grabbed what now resembled a paper pellet. "I can see this is going to be a hell of a flight."

Oliver stepped away, and Emma didn't see where he went, but he came back a few moments later. He casually told her it was time to board. She stood outside the aircraft as long as she dared, summoning her courage. Maybe she should've swallowed two tablets for this first flight.

Oscar was already aboard, curled up in his dog bed behind the passenger seat. He cocked his head as if to say he couldn't understand what she was waiting for.

"You got lead in your butt or what?" Oliver said from behind her.

With no excuse to delay the inevitable, she hoisted

herself into the plane and then, doubling over, worked her way forward into the cramped passenger seat. Her knees shook and her hands trembled as she reached for the safety belt and snapped it in place, pulling at the strap until it was so tight she could scarcely breathe.

Oscar poked his head between Oliver's seat and Emma's, and she was left with the distinct impression that she'd taken the dog's place. Great, just great. She'd arrive for her first interview with her backside covered in dog hair.

Oliver handed her an extra set of earphones and pantomimed that she should put them on. "You ready?" he asked.

She forced herself to nod.

He spoke to someone over the radio in a language she didn't understand, one that consisted solely of letters and numbers. A couple of minutes later, he taxied to the end of the runway. And stopped there.

Emma didn't know what that was about but regardless of the reason, she was grateful for a moment's reprieve. Her head pounded and her heart felt like it was going to explode inside her chest.

Oliver revved the engine, which fired to life with an ear-splitting noise. The plane bucked as if straining against invisible ropes.

Despite her relaxation pill, Emma gasped and grabbed hold of the bar across the top of the passenger door. She clutched it so hard she was convinced her fingerprints would be embedded in the steel.

Without showing a bit of concern for her well-being, Oliver released the brake and the plane leaped forward, roaring down the runway. Emma slammed her eyes shut, preferring not to look. She held her breath, awaiting the sensation of the wheels lifting off the tarmac.

For the longest time nothing happened. She opened her eyes just enough to peek and realized they were almost at the end of the runway. Despite the speed of the aircraft they remained on the ground. In a few seconds of sheer terror, Emma realized why.

She'd lied about her weight.

Hamilton had miscalculated the weight on board. In her vanity, she'd shaved ten pounds—well, maybe fifteen—off the truth. Because of that, she was about to kill them both.

Unable to restrain herself, Emma dragged in a deep breath and screamed out in panic, "I lied! I lied!"

No sooner had the words left her mouth than the plane sailed effortlessly into the sky.

Chapter Three

Fruitcakes are like in-laws. They show up at the holidays. You have no idea who sent them, how old they are, or how long they'll be hanging around your kitchen.

—Josh Sens, freelance writer in Oakland,
California,
and food critic for *San Francisco* magazine

The fear dissipated after takeoff. Emma kept her eyes focused directly in front of her, gazing out at the cloud-streaked sky. For the first while her heart seemed intent on beating its way out of her body, but after a few minutes the tension began to leave.

It wasn't long before the loud roar of the single engine lulled her into a sense of peace. No doubt that was due to the pill, which was exactly the reason she'd taken it. When she did find the courage to turn her head and look out the side window, she found herself staring Mt. Rainier in the face. She was so close that it was possible to see a crevasse, a giant crack in a glacier. Had there been hikers, she would've been able to wave.

Gasping, she shut her eyes and silently repeated the Lord's Prayer. Talk about spiritual renewal! All that was necessary to get her nearer to God was a short flight with Oliver Hamilton.

Forty minutes later as they approached the Yakima airport, Oliver made a wide sweeping turn with a gradual drop in altitude. Emma felt the plane descend and nearly swallowed her tongue as she reached for the bar above the side window again, holding on for dear life.

"You okay?" Oliver asked when he noticed how she clung to the bar with both hands.

How kind of him to inquire now. These were the first words he'd spoken to her during the entire flight. He'd glanced at her a number of times, as if to check up on her, and whenever he did, he started to laugh. She failed to understand what was so funny.

"I'm okay," she said with as much dignity as she could. A little the worse for wear, but okay, she mentally assured herself. Her head was beginning to clear.

She felt every air pocket and bump as the plane drew closer to the long runway. When the wheels bounced against the tarmac, Emma was ready for the solid thump of the tires hitting concrete, but the landing was surprisingly smooth. She slowly released a sigh of pent-up tension; she'd lied about her weight and lived to tell the tale. Now all she had to do was make it through this interview and find something noteworthy about Earleen Williams and her fruitcake recipe.

Oliver taxied the plane off the runway. He cut the engine and as the blades slowed, he unbuckled his seat belt and picked up his clipboard.

Emma was just starting to breathe normally again when Oscar sneezed.

"You might want to leave the perfume behind for the next flight," Oliver said matter-of-factly.

Emma wiped her cheek although most of the spray had been directed elsewhere. She resisted the urge to tell Oliver he could leave his dog behind, too. At this point, she didn't want to risk offending the pilot—or his dog. And, she supposed, it wasn't really Oscar's fault....

Crawling behind her, Oliver opened the door and climbed onto the airfield. Emma followed, bent double as she made her way out of the aircraft, feeling a sense of great relief. He offered her his hand as she hopped down. She was hit by a blast of cold air, which she ignored. Staring down at the ground, she was tempted to fall on all fours and kiss the tarmac.

A white van bearing the name of a local furnace company pulled up to the plane. Oliver spoke briefly with the driver, then walked over to where Emma stood.

"How long do you think the interview will take?"

"Ah…" Emma didn't know what to tell him. "I'm not sure."

He stared out toward the Cascade Mountains, only partially visible in the distance. "We've got bad weather rolling in."

"Bad weather? How bad?"

"Don't worry about it."

"I…" How could he say such a thing and then expect her not to worry? She was already half-panicked about the return flight and he'd just added to her fears.

"Do what you have to do and then get back here. I want to take off as soon as I can."

"All right." She glanced around and felt a sense of dread.

"What's wrong?"

"I…I don't have any way of getting to Earleen's house."

"Not a problem," Hamilton said, walking to the other side of the plane.

Emma assumed he was going to ask the guy in the van to give her a ride, but that turned out not to be the case. He climbed back inside the Cessna and returned a moment later with a large leather satchel.

"What's that?"

"A foldable bike."

Emma watched as he unzipped the bag and produced the smallest bicycle she'd ever seen. "You don't honestly expect me to ride this…thing, do you?" The wheels were no more than twelve inches around. She'd look utterly ridiculous. Nervous as she was about this first interview, she hoped to make up in professionalism what she lacked in experience.

"What's wrong?" he asked, frowning.

"I'll phone for a taxi." It went without saying that the newspaper wouldn't reimburse her, but she absolutely refused to arrive pedaling a bicycle Oliver Hamilton must have purchased from a Barnum and Bailey rummage sale.

"Hold on," Oliver barked, clearly upset. He walked over to the van this time and spoke to the driver. The two had a short conversation before Oliver glanced over his shoulder. "What's the address you have to get to?" he shouted.

Fumbling to find the slip of paper inside her briefcase, Emma read off the street name.

"She can tag along with me," the driver said.

"Great." Oliver flashed the other man an easy smile.

"Thank you so much," Emma murmured, grateful to have saved the taxi fare. She hurried around to the passenger side and opened the door. One look inside, and Emma nearly changed her mind. The van, which must've been at least ten years old, had obviously never been cleaned. The passenger seat was badly stained and littered with leftover fast-food containers, plus half-eaten burgers and rock-hard French fries. A clipboard was attached by a magnet to the dashboard and several papers had fallen to the floor.

"You getting in or not?" the driver asked.

"In." Emma made her decision quickly and hopped inside the van. She could just imagine what Walt would say if she announced that she'd missed the interview because she refused to get inside a messy vehicle.

Earleen Williams lived on a street called Garden Park in a brick duplex. The van dropped Emma off and drove away before she had time to thank the driver. He was apparently glad to be rid of her and she was equally thankful to have survived the ride. She'd worry later about getting back to the airfield.

Straightening her shoulders, Emma did a quick mental survey of her questions. She'd reviewed her class notes about interviews and remembered that the most important thing to do was engage Earleen in conversation and establish a rapport. It would be detrimental to the interview if Emma gave even the slightest appearance of nervousness.

Emma so much wanted this to go well. She didn't have a slant for the story yet and wouldn't until she'd met Earleen. If she tried to think about what she could possibly write on the subject of fruitcake, it would only traumatize her.

Knowing Oliver was probably pacing the pilots' lounge, Emma walked onto the porch and pressed the doorbell. She stepped back and waited.

"Oh, hi." The petite brunette who answered the door couldn't have been more than five feet tall, if that, and seemed to be around sixty. It was difficult to tell. One thing Emma did conclude—Earleen wasn't at all what she'd expected. She wore a turquoise blazer and black pleated pants with a large gold belt and rings on every finger. Big rings.

"You're Earleen?"

"I am." She unlatched the screen door and held it open for Emma. "You must be that Seattle reporter who phoned."

"Emma Collins," she said and held out her hand. "Actually, I'm from Puyallup, which is outside Seattle." There was a difference of at least a quarter-million readers between the *Seattle Times* and *The Examiner*—maybe more. The *Seattle Times* hadn't sent her a circulation report lately.

"Come on inside. I've got coffee brewing," Earleen said, smiling self-consciously. "This is the first time anyone's ever wanted to interview me."

They had a lot in common, because this was Emma's first interview, too, although she wasn't about to mention that.

Earleen looked past her. "You didn't bring a photographer with you?"

Actually she had. Emma would be performing both roles. "If it's all right, I'll take your picture later."

"Oh, sure, that's fine." Earleen touched the side of her head with her palm as if to be sure every hair was neatly in place, which it was. She smelled wonderful, too. Estée Lauder's Beautiful, if Emma guessed correctly. Just as well Oscar wasn't around or he'd be sneezing on her pant leg.

"I thought we'd talk in the kitchen, if you don't mind," Earleen said as she led the way. "Most folks like my kitchen best."

"Wherever you're most comfortable," Emma murmured, following the older woman. She gazed around as she walked through the house and noticed a small collection of owl figurines lined up on the fireplace mantel, among the boughs of greenery. The Christmas tree in the corner was enormous, and it had an owl— yes, an owl—on top.

The kitchen was bright and roomy. There was a square table next to a window that overlooked the backyard, where a circular clothesline sat off to one side and a toolshed on the other. A six-foot redwood fence separated her yard from the neighbors'.

"Sit down," Earleen said and motioned to the table and chairs. "Coffee?"

"None for me, thanks." After the pill she'd taken earlier, Emma didn't think she should add caffeine, afraid of the effect on her stomach—and her brain. She took out her reporter's pad and flipped it open. "When did you first hear the news that your recipe had been chosen as a national finalist?"

Earleen poured herself a mug of coffee and carried it to the table, then pulled out a chair and sat across from Emma. "Three weeks ago. The notification came by mail."

"Were you surprised?"

"Not really."

"Any reason you weren't surprised?"

Earleen blushed. "I know I make a good fruitcake. I've been baking them for a lot of years now."

Emma could see this wasn't going to be as easy as she'd hoped. Earleen wasn't much of a talker.

"Do you have a secret ingredient?"

"Well, yes. I have two."

Emma made a notation just so Earleen would recognize that she was paying attention. "Would you be willing to divulge them to our readers?"

Earleen rested her elbows on the table and held the mug with both hands. "I don't mind telling you, but maybe it'd be better if I showed you."

Emma frowned slightly when the other woman rose from the table. She dragged out a step stool, placed it in front of the refrigerator and climbed the two steps. Then she stretched until she could reach the cupboard above the fridge and opened it. Standing on the tips of her toes, Earleen brought down a bottle of rum and a bottle of brandy.

"Your secret is…alcohol?"

Earleen climbed off the step stool and nodded. "One of my secrets. I didn't work all those years at The Drunken Owl for nothing. I serve a mighty fine mincemeat pie, too. That recipe came from my mother, God rest her soul. Mom always started with fresh suet. She got it from Kloster's Butcher Shop. When I was in high school, I had the biggest crush on Tim Kloster. My friends used to say I had Kloster-phobia." She giggled nervously.

Emma didn't think it was a good idea to point out that "phobia" was technically the wrong term. She hesitated, unsure how this interview had gotten away from her so quickly. "About the fruitcake... Did that recipe come from your mother, too?"

"Sort of. Mom was raised during the Great Depression, and her recipe didn't call for much more than the basics. Over the years I started adding to it, and being from Yakima, I naturally included apples."

"Apples," Emma repeated and jotted that down.

"Actually, I cook them until it's more like applesauce."

"Of course." Having lived in Washington for only the last eight months, Emma wasn't all that familiar with the state. She knew more about the western half because she lived in that area. Most of the eastern side remained a complete mystery.

Come to think of it, as Oliver landed she'd noticed that there seemed to be orchards near the airport. Distracted as she'd been, it was nothing short of astounding that she'd remembered.

"Yakima is known for apples, right?" she ventured.

"Definitely. More than half of all the apples grown in the United States come from orchards in Yakima and Wenatchee."

Emma made a note. "I didn't know that."

"The most popular variety is the Red Delicious. Personally, I prefer Golden Delicious. They're the kind I use in my fruitcake."

Emma held her breath. "I hope you'll agree to share the recipe with *The Examiner's* readers."

Earleen beamed proudly. "It would be my honor."

"So the liquor and the apples are your two secret ingredients."

"That's right," Earleen said in a solemn voice. "But far more important is using only the freshest of ingredients. It took me several tries to figure that out."

Emma was tempted to remind her that one of the main ingredients in fruitcake was dried fruit. There wasn't anything fresh about that. But again she managed to keep her mouth shut.

"How long have you been baking fruitcakes?" Emma asked next.

"Quite a few years. I started in—way back now. You see, I was going through a rough patch at the time."

"What happened?" Emma hated to pry, but she was a reporter and she had a feeling she'd hit upon the key element of her article.

"Larry and I had just split, and I have to tell you I took it hard."

"And Larry is?"

"My ex-husband."

Emma couldn't help observing that Earleen seemed more of a conversationalist when she stood on the other side of the kitchen counter. The closer she got to the table, the briefer her answers were. Emma speculated that was because of Earleen's many years behind a bar. She'd always heard that bartenders spent a lot of time listening and advising—like paid friends. Or psychiatrists.

"The first time I ever tried Mom's fruitcake recipe was after Larry moved out."

"I'm sorry."

"Me, too. Have you ever been married?" Earleen asked.

"No…" The sorry state of her love life was not a subject Emma wanted to discuss.

"Larry and I were high-school sweethearts. He went to fight in Vietnam and when he got back, we had a big wedding. It was the type of wedding girls dream about. Wait here a minute," she said and bustled out of the kitchen.

In a couple of minutes, she returned with her wedding photograph. A radiantly happy bride smiled into the camera, her white dress fashioned in layers of taffeta and lace. The young soldier at her side was more difficult to read.

"Unfortunately, Larry had a weakness for other women," Earleen said sadly.

"How long have you been divorced?"

"From Larry? Since 1984."

"You've been married more than once?"

"Three times."

"Oh."

"All my husbands were versions of Larry."

"I see."

"I didn't learn from my mistakes." Earleen turned away. Then, obviously changing the subject, she said, "I imagine you'll want to sample my fruitcake." She slid open the bread box and took out an aluminum-foil-wrapped loaf. "Have you noticed that people either love fruitcake or hate it?" she said companionably. "There doesn't seem to be any middle ground."

"That…seems to be true," Emma agreed.

"Like I said, I started baking after Larry left," she said, busily peeling away the cheesecloth from the loaf-size fruitcake. "I'd never suffered that kind of pain before. I figured if you've ever been divorced you'd know what I mean."

Emma was confused. "I don't exactly think of fruitcake as comfort food."

Earleen shook her head. "I didn't eat it. I baked it. Loaf after loaf for weeks on end. I was determined to bake the perfect fruitcake and I didn't care how long it took. I must've changed that recipe a hundred times."

"Why fruitcake?"

She paused as if she'd never put it into words. "I'm not sure. I guess I was looking for the happiness I always felt as a kid at Christmastime."

There it was again, Emma mused. Christmas. It

did people in emotionally, and she wasn't going to allow that to happen, not to her. She found it easy enough to ignore Christmas; other people should give it a try. She might even see if Walt would let her write an article about her feelings. Emma believed she wasn't alone in disliking all the hype that surrounded Christmas.

"When I was with Larry and my two other husbands, I felt there must be something lacking in me," Earleen continued. "Now I don't think so anymore. Time will do that, you know?" She glanced at Emma. "As young as you are, you probably don't have that much perspective." Earleen paused and drew in a deep breath.

Emma stopped taking notes. She suspected this was it; she was about to get to the real core of the interview.

"By the time Larry and I split up, both my parents were gone, so I was pretty much on my own. I realize now that I was searching for a way to deal with the pain, although God knows the marriage was dead. That's where the fruitcake came in."

"The comfort factor," Emma said with a nod. "How long were you and Larry together?" she asked.

"Sixteen years. It's a shame, you know. We never had kids and it was real lonely after he left."

"What happened to him?" Secretly Emma hoped he was miserable. In some ways Earleen reminded Emma of her mother.

The woman sighed. "Larry married the floozy he'd taken up with, and the two of them got drunk every night. It only took him a few years to drink himself to death."

"How sad," Emma said, and she meant it.

Earleen shrugged. "I was single for nearly ten years. I thought I'd learned my lesson about marrying the wrong man, but obviously I hadn't."

"What about the other two husbands?"

"Morrie courted me for a long time before I agreed to marry him. He didn't have a roving eye so much as he did a weakness for the bottle." She paused. "Of course, Larry had both. The thing is, and you remember this, young lady, you don't meet the cream of the eligible-bachelor crop working in a tavern."

Emma scribbled that down so Earleen would think she'd given due consideration to her words.

"Morrie died of cancer a couple of years after we were married." She shook her head. "I never should've married Paul after that."

"What happened with Paul?"

A dreamy expression came over her. "Paul looked so much like Larry they could've been brothers. Unfortunately, looks weren't the only trait they shared. We were married only a year when he suffered a massive stroke. He had a girlfriend on the side but he really loved my fruitcake. I think if Larry had lived, he would have, too."

"Do you have anyone to share your good news with?" Emma asked. "About being a finalist?"

Earleen shrugged again. "Not really, but it doesn't matter."

"Of course it matters," Emma insisted. "Your recipe was one of only twelve chosen from across the entire United States. You should be kicking up your heels and celebrating."

"I will with friends, I suppose." Earleen opened her cutlery drawer for a knife and sliced through the loaf. "It's time I started baking again," she said. "This close to Christmas, I'll bake my mincemeat pies. People are already asking about them."

"When do you bake your fruitcakes?"

Earleen sipped her coffee, her fingers sparkling in the light. All ten of them. "I usually bake up a batch every October and let it set a good two months before I serve it. The longer I give the alcohol to work, the better. Then, before Easter, I bake another version that's similar but without the dried fruit." Earleen moved the slice onto a plate and brought it over for Emma to taste.

Although she wasn't a fan of fruitcake, Emma decided it would be impolite to refuse. Earleen watched and waited.

Emma used her fork to break off a small piece and saw that it was chock-full of the dried fruit to which she objected most. She glanced up at the older woman with a quick smile. Then she carefully put the fruitcake in her mouth—and was shocked by how good it tasted. The cake was flavorful, moist and pungent with the scent of liquor. The blend of fruit, nuts, applesauce and alcohol was *divine*. There was no other word to describe Earleen's fruitcake.

"You like it, don't you?"

"I do," Emma assured her, trying not to sound shocked. "It's excellent."

"I'm sure Larry would've thought so, too," Earleen said wistfully. "Even if he's the reason I started baking it."

"You still love him, don't you?" It seemed so obvious to Emma. Although she'd married twice more, Earleen Williams's heart belonged to a man who hadn't valued her. Her mother had been the same; Pamela Collins had loved her ex-husband to her dying day. Emma's father had never appreciated what a wonderful woman she was. For that sin alone, Emma wanted nothing more to do with him. He'd been a token husband the same way he'd been a token father.

When she spoke, Earleen's voice was resigned. "I've been over Larry for a long time," she explained. "Much as I loved him, all I can say is that it's a good thing he left when he did. Larry was trouble. More trouble than I knew what to do with."

More trouble than Earleen deserved, Emma reflected.

"Is there anything else I can tell you?" Earleen asked. She seemed eager to finish the interview. "I didn't mean to talk so much about my past. I never could figure out men—but I know a whole lot about fruitcake."

Emma scanned her notes. "I think I've got everything I need for now."

After snapping a picture of Earleen and collecting the recipe, she asked, "Can I call you later if I have any questions?"

"Oh, sure. Since I retired from The Drunken Owl, I'm here most of the time."

"Would you mind if I used your phone book?" Emma stood and gathered up her things. "I want to call a taxi to take me back to the airport."

"You don't need to do that." Earleen shook her head. "I'll drive you. It's not far and I have errands I need to run, anyway."

"Are you sure?"

"Of course I am. It's my pleasure."

Emma smiled her gratitude. She already knew that Walt wasn't going to reimburse her for any taxi fare, and it was too close to the end of the month for unnecessary spending on her part.

Earleen backed her twenty-year-old Subaru out of the garage and Emma got inside. The contrast between the interior of Earleen's vehicle and the furnace company van was noteworthy in itself.

Ten minutes later, Earleen dropped Emma at the airport and after a few words of farewell, drove off.

As soon as Emma climbed out of the Subaru, Oliver came from the building next to the hangar, with Oscar trotting behind him.

"You done?"

Emma nodded absently, wondering how to structure her article on Earleen. Start with her childhood or her wedding or—

"How'd it go?" he asked, interrupting her thoughts.

She stared at him, eyes narrowed. "In case you didn't know it, men can be real scum."

To her surprise, Oliver grinned. "You're going to have even more reason to think so when you hear what I've got to say."

This didn't sound promising. "You'd better tell me," she said.

Oliver buried his hands in his pockets. "Blame me if you want, but it won't make any difference. We're grounded."

"Grounded?" She blinked. "What does that mean?"

"We're grounded," he repeated. "Because of the weather. We're stuck in Yakima."

Earleen's Masterpiece Fruitcake

2 cups sugar
1 cup butter
2 1/2 cups applesauce
2 eggs, beaten
2 cups raisins
2 cups walnuts, chopped
4 cups flour
1 tsp. salt
1 tbsp. soda
1 tsp. baking powder
1 tsp. cloves
1 tsp. nutmeg
2 tsp. cinnamon
2 pounds candied dried fruit mix
1 1/2 cups chopped dates

Cream sugar and butter. Add beaten eggs and applesauce. Mix flour, salt, spices, soda and baking powder, then gradually add to other ingredients. Mix well. Blend in candied fruit, dates, raisins and nuts. Mixture will be stiff. Bake in 325-degree oven in two loaf pans for one hour.

Cool and remove fruitcake from pans. Cut a piece of cheesecloth to fit and soak in 1/2 cup rum or brandy. Pour any remaining alcohol over the fruitcake. Wrap fruitcake in cheesecloth and then cellophane, followed by aluminum foil. Store in refrigerator for up to three months.

Chapter Four

"This is a bad joke—isn't it?" Emma cried. "Oh, please tell me it's a joke."

"Sorry."

From his darkening scowl, Emma could see he wasn't pleased about this turn of events, either. He'd obviously enjoyed giving her the bad news but he wasn't grinning anymore. A delay probably affected his bottom line. Oscar sat down next to Oliver and stared up at him confidently. She'd heard somewhere that a man was always a hero to his dog; that was certainly the case with poor deluded Oscar.

"I mentioned the weather earlier, remember?" Hamilton said.

Emma had forgotten that. Her afternoon muscle relaxant was ready to be swallowed, and she was glad she hadn't taken it yet. "What are we supposed to do now?"

"Wait it out. We could find ways to entertain ourselves."

This was exactly the kind of comment she expected from Flyboy. And was that a wink? "In your dreams," she snapped.

"Do you have any other brilliant suggestions?"

Emma wished she did.

"We might be able to get out late this afternoon, but I wouldn't count on it." He raised his eyes to study the heavily clouded sky. "There's a snowstorm in the mountains and it's heading in our direction. The clouds don't concern me as much as the problem with icing."

Emma wasn't sure what that meant; she had her own problems. "I've got an article to write," she murmured, biting her lower lip. Walt had wanted the first piece written as quickly as possible. Earleen Williams had been a great interview, but Emma still hadn't decided exactly what slant she should take. She needed time to study her notes and think over their conversation.

Oliver nodded glumly. "To tell you the truth, I'm not thrilled about sitting around here all day, twiddling my thumbs."

Emma realized he could've left after making his delivery if he hadn't been waiting for her. She felt bad about that. She'd been less than gracious. "Are you hungry?" she asked.

"Why?" His voice was suspicious.

"I was being friendly." She glanced across the street at a café. Several letters in the neon sign had burned out. It'd once read MINNIE'S PLACE but now said MI...CE. This wasn't exactly an enticement, but Emma's stomach was growling. It was past noon and all she'd had to eat was a small slice of liquor-drenched—and quite delicious—fruitcake.

"Are you offering to buy me lunch?"

Emma mentally calculated how much cash she had with her. "All right, as long as you don't order anything over five dollars."

Oliver grinned. "You've got yourself a date."

"This *isn't* a date."

"Sure it is," he said. "One day I'll tell our children you asked me out first."

"One more remark like that, and you can buy your own lunch."

Oliver chuckled. "I wasn't trying to be funny."

"Yeah, right."

"You're half in love with me already."

Emma didn't dignify that with a reply. They started walking toward the café; Oscar trotted obediently beside them and seemed to know to wait by the restaurant door. Oliver patted his head and assured the terrier he'd get any leftovers.

Emma resisted reminding Oliver that it wasn't a good idea to feed people food to a dog, but she doubted he'd listen. If she had a dog, she'd feed him only the highest-quality, veterinarian-approved dog food.

Once inside the café, they slid into a red vinyl

booth, facing each other. Emma reached for the menu, which was tucked behind the napkin dispenser, and quickly decided on the ham-and-cheese omelet. Oliver ordered the club sandwich.

"How long have you been flying?" she asked.

"Why?" Once again, he sounded suspicious. For heaven's sake, did the man have some big secret?

Emma sighed. "I don't know. It seemed like a good conversation starter, that's all."

"I'm not interested in being interviewed," he said curtly. "Besides, I have a couple of questions for you."

She smiled at the waitress who poured her coffee, then relaxed in the padded vinyl seat. "Wait a minute. You can ask me questions but I'm not allowed to know anything about you? Is that fair?"

"Fair doesn't matter. I'm your ride home—or I will be."

"So you think I owe you for that? Oh, never mind," she said, suddenly tiring of the argument. "Ask away."

"How long have you been with *The Examiner?*"

"About eight months—long enough to know I'm tired of writing obituaries."

Oliver frowned. "That's the only thing Walt lets you write?"

"For the most part. A month ago he let me cover the school board meeting." Emma had written what she thought was a masterful commentary on the events. Walt hadn't agreed, to put it mildly, and had rejected her article in scathing terms. He said she was trying too hard. People were looking for a clear, concise summary, not a chapter from *War and Peace.* "What I want is a real story," she told Oliver in a fervent tone, "something I can really get my teeth into."

"Like fruitcake?" Oliver said, teasing her.

"It's a start."

"Yes." Once again, he was obviously trying to restrain a smile. "What are you going to write about Earleen Williams?"

Emma was mulling that over. "I don't know for sure. She's a complex woman. She's had a number of difficult relationships with men, and—"

"You don't date much, do you?" he broke in.

Emma stared at him. "Who says?"

"Phoebe."

"You know Phoebe?" Either her friend had been holding out on her, or Oliver was lying. If Phoebe knew him, Emma was positive she would've said so earlier.

"We've had a couple of conversations about you," Oliver admitted, nimbly twirling the fork between his fingers.

Emma found the action highly irritating. Stretching across the table, she grabbed his wrist. "Please don't do that."

He grinned; he seemed to do a lot of that around her. "You can't keep your hands off me, can you?"

She toyed briefly with the idea of getting up and walking out. She would have, too, but their food hadn't been delivered yet. Her stomach won out over her pride.

"How do you know Phoebe and when did you talk to her?"

"We met through…a friend of mine. Phoebe's a few years younger than me, but I've seen her around town. No big deal." He shrugged. "I stopped in at the office after your visit to the airfield and asked about you. Casually, you know. Phoebe sang like a canary."

Emma refused to believe it. Phoebe had never mentioned this supposed conversation.

"She said the two of you were hired at the same time and that you kept pretty much to yourself. So what gives?"

"What do you mean?"

"Where's the boyfriend?"

Emma's jaw sagged open. "You've got a lot of nerve!"

"Men are scum, remember?" His eyes twinkled. "So tell me, what's happening in the men department?"

"Nothing. I'm a serious writer—well, maybe not yet, but I intend to become one."

"Being a 'serious' writer means you don't have time for relationships?"

Emma didn't care for the direction this conversation was taking. "At present, no—not that it's any of your business."

"Why not?"

"Are you always so nosy, or is this expressly for my benefit?"

"Both." He picked up his fork and studied the tines with every appearance of interest.

To Emma's relief, their plates arrived just then. The waitress set the bill facedown in the middle of the table.

Emma spread the paper napkin across her lap, looked over her meal and lifted her fork. By the time she'd taken two bites, Oliver had wolfed down half his sandwich. She glared at him disapprovingly.

"What?" he asked, apparently perplexed.

"Nothing," she said, knowing it would do no good to explain.

He munched on a French fry, then glanced across the table at her. "If I asked you out on a date, would you go?"

"No," she said without hesitation. She didn't mean to be rude but she could read him like a book. He was her father all over again. Besides, she wasn't much good at relationships.

"Why not?" Oliver pressed.

Emma groaned. "Listen, I'm sure a lot of women would consider you charming—" she almost choked on the word "—and you're not unattractive…"

"In other words, you think I'm cute."

"No," she inserted quickly. "That isn't what I meant at all." The last thing she wanted was for Oliver to assume she was attracted to him. "I like that you're kind to animals."

"You want me."

Emma set her fork down, astonished at his audacity. "I most certainly do not!"

He cracked an even bigger smile. "Keep telling yourself that, but I know otherwise."

"This is exactly what bothers me," she said, sighing heavily. "Your arrogance is unbelievable. You assume that because you're reasonably good-looking, any woman would be grateful for the opportunity to date you. The fact is, it's simply not true."

"You're dying to find out everything you can about me."

This time Emma laughed outright. She couldn't help it. "*You're* the one asking all the questions—and making a lot of assumptions. *I* was making conversation. It seemed the polite thing to do, since we might end up spending the next few hours together."

Some women might find his smile sexy. Not Emma, of course, but others. She forced herself to look away, in case he misread her interest.

"All right then. What do you want to know about me?" he asked, leaning forward.

Emma considered his question. Anything she asked him, Oliver was bound to interpret in such a way that it would seem she was falling head over heels in love with him. Really, his attitude bordered on the comical.

"How soon before we can fly out of here?"

He frowned. "I can't answer that until I get an updated weather report. Anything else you want to know?"

Plenty, but she planned on asking Phoebe first. "Not really."

She sliced into her omelet and saw that he'd already finished his sandwich. Only a handful of French fries remained.

"Are you going to eat your toast?" he asked.

She shook her head and slid the plate across the table.

Oliver took it, slipped out of the booth and headed outside to where Oscar waited. As soon as he left the café, Emma plucked her cell phone from her bag and pushed the button that speed-dialed the newspaper office. A moment later, she connected with Phoebe.

"This is Phoebe," her friend answered in her usual cheerful fashion.

"When did Oliver Hamilton ask you about me?" Emma demanded.

"Emma?"

"You know exactly who this is."

"I take it the muscle relaxant has worn off?"

So it was true. "Why didn't you say something?"

"Because," Phoebe murmured, "it was a short conversation. Two minutes, if that."

"You knew he was coming in to talk to Walt."

"Yes," Phoebe admitted. "All right, I'll tell you. I was afraid that if I mentioned I'd talked to Oliver, you'd have all these questions about how I knew and I didn't want to get into that."

"How *did* you know?" Emma asked. It could only be one thing—Phoebe was seeing Walt. Why she wanted to keep that a secret, Emma wasn't sure.

When Phoebe answered, it was in a whisper. "Walt and I are dating."

"You *are?*" Even though she'd already guessed, Emma was shocked. "Why didn't you tell me?" As soon as she asked the question, she knew. "Walt doesn't want anyone at the office to find out." It explained a lot.

"He doesn't think it's good policy. I hated not telling anyone, especially you, but I…couldn't."

"How long has this been going on?"

"Three months."

Emma was stunned into silence. She couldn't believe that her best friend had managed to keep this from her for *three months*. Obviously, Phoebe wasn't as timid around Walt as she'd seemed.

"You can't let him know that you know," Phoebe said anxiously.

"Fine." Emma blew out her breath. "But when I get back, I want you to tell me everything, understand?"

Phoebe laughed softly. "I'll make a full confession."

"Good. Now, what do you know about Oliver Hamilton?"

"Just that…he likes you. He specifically asked for an opportunity so the two of you could fly together."

"*What?*"

"You heard me."

Oliver had done that because he knew she was frightened to death to get into his little plane. The man was a sadist, and between them, her employer and her best friend had willingly handed her over.

"He told Walt you'd done a wonderful job of selling him on advertising and he wanted to give the newspaper his business because of you."

"Did you tell Walt that if I didn't get an assignment soon, I'd quit?"

"I couldn't let my best friend quit," Phoebe said—although Emma noted that she hadn't really answered the question. "Not if I could prevent it. Then Oliver showed up and, well, it was meant to be."

The truth was out. She'd gotten this assignment thanks to her friend. Walt hadn't thought she was ready; he was just trying to keep Phoebe happy.

"I can't understand why you don't like Oliver," Phoebe said.

Emma pinched her lips tightly together. "Oliver Hamilton is accustomed to women swooning over him."

"He's not like that," Phoebe protested.

Emma knew otherwise.

"You're not upset with me, are you?"

Emma considered the question. "I guess not."

"If our situations were reversed, you'd have done the same thing for me," Phoebe said. "Now tell me what's going on in Yakima."

Emma looked out the window and noticed that

Oliver had walked across the street, presumably to get an updated weather report. "At the moment we're stuck."

"Together?" Phoebe asked with an inappropriate amount of amusement.

It figured she'd see this unfortunate situation in a humorous light. "For now, and trust me, I'm not happy about it."

"You should be. Oliver and Walt get along really well. He's a cool guy."

The problem was he knew it. Emma didn't bother to comment. She chatted with Phoebe a few minutes longer before ending the phone call.

The waitress refreshed Emma's coffee and took the money she'd left on the table. While she waited for her change, she read over her notes from the interview with Earleen Williams. But it wasn't the older woman who dominated her thoughts, it was her own mother.

Pamela Collins had wanted the very best for her, Emma knew. What she could never understand was why her mother had stayed in the marriage as long as she had. From as early as Emma could remember, she'd known her father was having affairs, betraying his wife and family. To this day, her father didn't get it. Her mother had been so forgiving; Emma wasn't. And she was too smart to be taken in by a man who had all her father's worst traits—and all his appeal.

She couldn't imagine what her mother would think

of Oliver. No, she could imagine exactly. Her mother would think he was wonderful and treat him like a king, the same way she'd done with Emma's father whenever he'd seen fit to bless them with his presence.

The café door opened and Oliver returned, his leather jacket splotched with damp. He walked across the room, sliding into the booth. He handed her a sheet of paper.

"What's this?" she asked.

"The weather report. You aren't going to like it."

Emma's heart sank. "How long are we trapped here?"

He hesitated as if weighing how much of the truth he should tell her. "Overnight."

The word echoed in her brain. "No!"

"Have you looked outside lately?"

Emma hadn't. She stared out the window now. Thick flakes of snow drifted down; already the sidewalks were covered and the sky had grown darker. No wonder his coat was wet. She closed her eyes. "What are we going to do?" she whispered.

Oliver shrugged. "It happens, especially this time of year. I don't like it any better than you do, but I try to make the best of it."

"How?"

"I don't know what you're planning, but I've already got a line on a poker game. I don't suppose you'd care to join us?"

Chapter Five

The snow fell fast and furious as the afternoon wore on. Although Emma strongly suspected Walt wouldn't be willing to reimburse her, she broke down and rented a motel room near the airfield, using her credit card since she was almost out of cash. Her knight in tarnished armor had disappeared inside one of the hangars with three other pilots for a poker game, and she hadn't seen him since.

The motel room was about what you'd expect for $39.95. The mattress and pillows were thin and no matter what she did, Emma couldn't get comfortable on the bed until she marched down to the office for extra pillows, which she propped up to support her back while she used her laptop on the bed. Her fingers flew across the keys.

Lessons from Fruitcake: Earleen Williams
by Emma Collins

For *The Examiner*

Earleen Williams of Yakima bakes masterful fruitcakes but she's the true masterpiece.

It's no surprise to anyone who has tasted one of
her fruitcakes that Earleen and her recipe have
achieved national acclaim. With a shy smile, she'll
laughingly say that her secret ingredient is stored in
her liquor cabinet. But there's more to it than that.

Now Earleen's recipe has been chosen as one of
the twelve nationwide finalists in *Good Homemaking*'s fruitcake contest. The winner will be announced December 20th on the magazine's Web
site. The January issue will feature a profile of the
winner. That winner might be Earleen Williams.

Earleen admits her life hasn't been easy, not that
she's complaining. She was married to her first husband, Larry, for sixteen years, but as she says, he
was more trouble than she could handle. They
parted, and in her pain and loss she returned to the
days of her childhood and the happiness she'd
known, surrounded by family and love.

Earleen's parents had little money for frivolous
things, but there was an abundance of love in the
home. And somehow, through good times and bad,
there was always fruitcake at Christmas. It was
this spirit of love, laughter and joy that Earleen
sought to recapture in making her own fruitcake.
Adding local apples, cooked down into a sauce, and

using only ingredients of the highest quality, she began with her mother's recipe and expanded on it. When asked, Earleen was happy to share her secrets—liquor and apples. In the years since her divorce, her fruitcake has become a holiday staple for family and friends.

The former bartender continued baking through two subsequent marriages. Discussing her three husbands, Earleen commented that none of them appreciated her. Each pursued other women—or sought escape in a bottle. Over time, Earleen says, she gained perspective on her life and learned to recognize that her husbands' infidelity wasn't due to any lack in her.

Earleen Williams creates a moist, succulent fruitcake—a baking masterpiece. But she, too, is a masterpiece, just the way she is.

This was a draft, but Emma felt it was a good start. The more she read over her notes, the more she realized that the interview hadn't been about fruitcake as much as about Earleen. Briefly she wondered if all the interviews would be the same. Lessons about life, wrapped up in a fruitcake recipe. She hoped so.

By now it was past four o'clock; dusk had begun to fall in earnest. The room had grown chilly and Emma was ready to stop work for a while. The heater below the window belched and coughed before it sent out a blast of hot air. When she turned on the television, all she got was a blank screen and some strange noise. Bored and restless, she threw on her coat and wandered out to the office to complain.

The middle-aged woman at the desk looked up when she appeared. "The television doesn't seem to be working," Emma told her in a friendly tone.

"We've been having problems with the cable," the clerk said.

"I'd really like to watch the news." Listening to the weather report was vital at this point. She wanted out of Yakima, and the sooner the better.

"I'll send Juan over to see what he can do," the clerk promised. "He's our handyman. He knows what he's doing, but his English isn't very good. I'll do my best to explain it to him."

"Thanks. I'd appreciate that," Emma told her.

Since Oliver didn't know where she was, Emma decided she'd better inform him. If there was a break in the storm, he wouldn't appreciate having to search for her.

Unsure where to find Oliver, she stepped out of the motel office and turned toward the hangar where she'd last seen him. Pulling her wool coat more tightly around her, she trudged across the snowy street. Fortunately, Oscar trotted over to her, happily wagging his stub of a tail.

"Where's Oliver?" she asked the terrier, then followed the dog as he led her to a hangar not far from Oliver's Cessna.

When she walked inside, shaking the snow from her coat, Emma found Oliver sitting at a table with his poker-playing friends. Two were dressed in beige overalls, and Emma assumed they must be mechanics. Oliver sat across from a third man who wore a leather jacket similar to his. Probably another pilot.

Oliver pulled his gaze away from his cards, glanced up and frowned, almost as though he couldn't remember who she was.

"I wondered where you'd wandered off," he mumbled, returning his attention to his hand.

"I got a motel room."

At the mention of the room, his three friends stared at her. From her, they turned as one to Oliver. All speaking at the same time, the men made suggestive comments.

"Way to go, Oliver."

"Atta boy."

"Oo-la-la."

To her dismay, Oliver played along, grinning from ear to ear as if it was understood they'd be making wild, passionate love as soon as he'd finished his poker game.

Emma wasn't letting him get away with that. If he wasn't going to explain, then she had no qualms about doing so. "The motel room isn't for him," she said coldly. "There's absolutely *nothing* between Oliver and me."

One of the mechanics laughed. "That's what all the girls say."

"I'll be back shortly." Oliver set his cards down on the table and stood, his movements casual.

"Take your time, ol' buddy."

"Don't hurry on our account."

Emma glared at the men as Oliver took her by the elbow and steered her out of the hangar. She peered over her shoulder on her way out the door, strongly tempted to put them all in their place. That would be a waste of time, she realized. Besides, any argument was only going to encourage them.

"You got a motel room?" he asked.

"That's what I said, isn't it?" she muttered irritably. Then, repenting her sharp tone—at least a little—she added in a more conciliatory voice, "You said it would be morning before we'd get out of here." She hadn't wanted to spend money on the motel, but there was only so long she could sit in Minnie's Place, otherwise known as MICE.

"That was probably a good idea." Oliver looked both ways before jogging across the street, Oscar at his heels.

"I wanted to see the weather report. Unfortunately, the television in my room seems to be on the fritz. The manager sent a repairman."

"I wouldn't mind getting a current weather update, either."

"The only reason I came to find you was so you'd know where I was." She wanted to make it clear that she hadn't gone searching for him because she wanted his company. She was being considerate, nothing more.

He nodded. "I'll see about getting a room for the night myself."

While Oliver filled out the paperwork, Emma went back to her room. She opened the door to find Juan, the repairman, sitting on the end of her bed, gazing intently at the television.

Emma took one look at the images flashing across the screen and gasped. He was watching the pornography channel. Obviously, a lack of familiarity with English was no impediment to following this kind of movie—not that there was much dialogue to worry about.

He grinned at her as if he'd managed some spectacular feat. "I fix," he said, beaming. He flipped off the television and handed her the remote on his way out. Emma stared at him openmouthed as he disappeared into the snowstorm.

Emma didn't know how long she stood in the doorway, still holding the remote, but it must have been more than a minute.

"Problems?" Oliver asked as he strolled toward her.

"The repairman was in my room watching porn." She was shocked by the other man's audacity.

Oliver followed her into the room. "Let me see the remote," he said, and took it from her. He pushed the power button; instantly the television returned to the scene she'd witnessed when she walked into the room.

"Change the channel," she insisted, whirling around so she wouldn't have to look at the entwined figures. This was so embarrassing. All she could hear were moans and groans.

Oliver made several attempts but the pornography channel was the only one that seemed to be working. Every other channel remained a snowy blur.

"Ah," Oliver said after a moment. "I get it."

"You get what?"

"You asked to watch the news, right?"

"Right," she concurred.

"Juan thought you wanted to watch the *nudes*."

"Oh, for heaven's sake." Half-laughing, Emma felt the heat radiate from her cheeks.

"I'm two doors down if you need anything." He tossed the remote onto the rumpled bed, where she'd been working earlier.

"I won't," Emma rushed to assure him. But when she closed the door she remembered that she still couldn't watch television.

Sighing, she sat cross-legged on the bed. Might as well work, she decided. Emma reached for a pad of paper and a pen, one of a dozen she kept in a special compartment in her briefcase.

She wrote down the date, then chewed on the end of her pen while she mentally reviewed the conversation with Earleen. She needed an introduction to her first article.

Life is a journey, she began, *and as with any journey,*

*a traveler will come upon unexpected twists and turns.
Sometimes a person will follow the same path for so
long that change seems imperceptible. Conversely, another will travel the shortest of distances and discover a
completely new landscape. In a single lifetime, it is possible to live both experiences, as Earleen Williams discovered.*

When Emma finally glanced up, she was surprised
to see that it was pitch-black outside, the darkness
punctuated by the lights in the motel parking lot.
There was a knock on her door.

"Who is it?" she asked.

"Who do you think?" Oliver called from the
other side.

Emma opened the door.

"My television works if you want to trade rooms."

The idea was tempting.

"I'm going back to my poker game."

"All right," Emma said gratefully. "Thanks."

"Can Oscar stay with you?"

"Sure."

"Good." They exchanged room keys and he turned
away. Then, as if he'd just thought of something, he
turned back.

"What?" Emma asked.

"Nothing," he said. Without another word he
kissed her.

At first Emma felt too stunned to react, but once
she'd collected her wits, she was furious. He was try-

ing to shock her, and she refused to give him a reaction. "What was that for?" she asked.

Oliver stopped, shrugged, smiled. "Can't say. All of a sudden, I had this urge to kiss you."

"Next time curb it."

He shrugged again. "Don't know if I can."

"Try."

Just the way the edges of his mouth turned up annoyed her. "Come on, admit it," he said. "You liked it."

Emma examined her feelings. If he wanted honesty, then she'd give it to him. "As kisses go, I guess I'd call it fair."

His grin slowly faded. "I don't think so."

Before she could take a single step back, he pulled her into his arms again and brought his mouth to hers.

Ample opportunity came and went for Emma to object. Her mind shouted at her to put an end to it right that minute but…she simply couldn't.

His mouth moved over hers with practiced ease. Emma parted her lips and moaned involuntarily. On second thought, maybe it was Oliver who moaned.

They were still fully caught up in the kiss when Emma heard someone clear his throat. Even then, she didn't make an effort to break away.

"Oliver," a man's voice said.

"Yeah, Oliver. We playin' cards or not?"

Oliver lifted his mouth from hers and slowly

opened his eyes, as if she were the one providing the answers.

"He's playing cards," Emma answered for him. She barely recognized her own voice. It didn't matter. Oliver got the message.

Chapter Six

"Emma! Open up." The words were accompanied by a loud knock on the motel room door.

The harsh sound of Oliver's voice woke her abruptly, and she bolted upright. Taking a moment to orient herself she realized Oliver had awakened her in the middle of a dream about *him*. She blamed Oscar for this. The terrier slept at the foot of her bed, a constant reminder of his master. Her face instantly went red as she tossed aside her covers and hurried to the door.

"What do you want?" she demanded without unlatching the chain. She'd slept in her shirt and her legs were bare.

"The weather's clear. We're leaving in fifteen minutes."

"Fifteen *minutes*? I don't know if I can—"

"Hurry up. I'll be waiting at the plane."

"Okay, okay. I'll be as fast as I can." Already she was fumbling about, looking for what she needed.

As soon as she heard him leave, she tore around the room, dressing as quickly as she could. Twenty-five minutes later she was strapped in the plane's passenger seat with headphones on. They sat at the end of the runway, awaiting clearance. Oscar was asleep in his dog bed in the cargo hold, oblivious to the tension up front.

Oliver ignored her and spoke to the tower, again rattling off a list of letters and numbers.

That was when it hit her. In her rush Emma had forgotten to take her pill. The muscle relaxant was wrapped in a small plastic bag at the bottom of her purse.

Her first instinct was to interrupt Oliver and insist he taxi the plane back to the hangar. She needed to swallow the pill and then wait thirty to sixty minutes for it to take effect. One glance at the intense expression on his face and she could see that wasn't the best plan. Just then, he pulled back on the throttle and the plane roared down the runway, gaining speed. Leaning against the seat, she closed her eyes and gritted her teeth. A few minutes later, the wheels left the runway and they were airborne. Okay, she'd survived.

Emma held her breath. Keeping her eyes closed, she tried to think happy thoughts. Unfortunately, her mind had other interests, drifting back to the scene in the doorway last night. In an effort to dispel the memory of their kiss, she opened her eyes. That, she immediately decided, wasn't a good idea. All she could see in the darkness was a blur of lights far below. Far, *far* below. Dwelling on exactly how far was not conducive to her peace of mind.

About twenty minutes into the flight, the Cessna hit an air pocket and bounced. She gasped and bit down on her lip. She'd grabbed a cup of coffee in the motel office; it was boiling hot, but after adding cold water, she'd managed to drink it. Now, with the slight turbulence, her stomach revolted. Feeling light-headed, she closed her eyes once more and pressed her cheek against the passenger window. It felt nice and cool against her skin.

As if he sensed her discomfort, Oliver glanced in her direction and asked how she was doing.

"I…is there any way it would be possible to land?"

"Land?" he repeated into his mouthpiece. "We can't land here."

Emma refused to look at him. "I think I might be sick."

Oliver chuckled. "Quit telling yourself that. You're going to be fine."

"Quit telling me how I feel. I've got nausea."

"Take deep breaths."

"I'm trying." He made it sound as though she had a choice in the matter.

Oliver took one hand off the controls and stretched his arm behind her seat. He appeared to be searching for something. Sure enough, a couple of seconds later, he triumphantly gave her a plastic bag.

"What's this?"

"A container for you to puke in," he said without the slightest hesitation.

Emma supposed she should be grateful, but she wasn't. "Thank you so much," she muttered sarcastically.

His scowl told her he didn't appreciate her sarcasm.

Her stomach settled down a few minutes later, and she slowly exhaled. "I think I'm going to be all right."

He nodded. "I thought you would be."

They exchanged no further conversation for the rest of the flight home.

Once they'd landed, Emma was out of the aircraft in record time, eager to be on her way. Unfortunately, her car was parked back at her apartment. Oliver offered to drop her off, and she accepted, but he certainly wasn't in any hurry. She chafed with impatience as he tended lovingly to his plane, exchanged protracted greetings with various other men, then retrieved his truck. Finally they arrived at her apartment. As she politely thanked him for the ride, Oscar took her place in the passenger seat—well, *his* place, she assumed.

Emma watched them drive away, more determined than ever not to get inside a plane with him again. Somehow, she'd persuade Walt to listen to reason. With her mind made up, she headed into her apartment. After showering, washing her hair and changing clothes, Emma drove to the office.

It seemed that every eye in the newsroom was on her when she walked through the door. Judging by the looks cast in her direction, she could easily have been the page one story.

"How'd it go?" Phoebe asked the minute Emma entered The Dungeon. She hadn't even sat down at her desk before Phoebe rolled her chair across the aisle. "I think it's wildly romantic that you and Oliver Hamilton were stranded together like that."

"It wasn't." Emma refused to elaborate. Bad enough that he'd kissed her without permission. "I didn't even have a toothbrush with me. It wasn't an experience I care to repeat."

"But you were with Oliver."

Emma sent her friend a glower that said she wasn't impressed with the pilot.

"In case you haven't noticed, Oliver's pretty hot."

"There's more to a man than his looks." Her father was an attractive man, too, but his character wasn't any deeper than the average mud puddle. Emma suspected Oliver was like that. His glibness infuriated her. He took delight in making her uncomfortable, which she considered a juvenile trait—and one that seemed particularly typical of men.

Phoebe wouldn't be thwarted. "I'll bet he kissed you."

Emma ignored the comment. She set her briefcase on her desk and removed her laptop. As soon as she could, she'd review what she'd written and go over her interview notes one final time.

Phoebe grinned knowingly. "He did, didn't he?"

Her friend wasn't going to stop tormenting her. Emma sighed. "Not that it's any of your business, but yes."

"I *knew* it." Phoebe's eyes flashed with victory, as if she were personally responsible for that kiss. "And?" She waited for Emma to elaborate.

"And nothing," Emma returned. "It was okay as kisses go, but I didn't feel the earth move or anything."

"You didn't?" This seemed shocking to Phoebe. "But everyone says—"

Emma had no interest in hearing the details of Flyboy's amorous exploits, even if it was only by repute.

"The truth is," she broke in, "that ninety percent of the time we were stranded, Oliver was busy playing poker with his cronies."

Phoebe's expression suggested that she was terribly disappointed in both of them. The only way to end this inquisition, Emma decided, was to ask a few questions of her own. "While I have your attention, I want you to tell me what's going on between you and Walt," she said. "You promised."

Phoebe glanced over her shoulder and lowered her voice. "I've probably said more than I should have already." She rolled her chair back across the aisle.

Emma followed her, and leaned against the cubicle wall with her arms folded. "I'm not sure whether I should thank you or yell at you for getting me this assignment."

"I did not," Phoebe insisted righteously. "I just felt Walt should know that if he didn't do something quick, he was going to lose you, so I...I told him what you said about quitting."

"That's practically blackmail!" Emma said in a horrified voice. "What if he'd fired me because *you* told him I threatened to quit?"

"Don't worry about that. I wouldn't have let it happen," Phoebe said calmly. "But you deserve a shot at something other than obituaries. I knew Walt couldn't afford to let you go—and he knows it, too."

"Okay, at least you used your power for good," Emma murmured. She was thankful that Phoebe had spoken to Walt on her behalf; still, she'd rather stand on her own merit. "Oliver said that when he asked about me, you sang like a canary. And that's a quote."

Phoebe laughed out loud. "Yeah, right, and if you believe *that*, then you don't know me at all."

"I thought he was exaggerating." Just then the phone on her desk rang. Reaching across the aisle, Emma picked up the receiver. It was Walt, wanting to see her. Now.

Phoebe's eyes widened in speculation when Emma hung up the phone.

"Wish me luck," she mouthed to her friend. Grabbing a pad and pen, she walked up the stairs. When she got to his office, her boss was on the phone, but he motioned her inside. He grinned in her direction, which boded well. She had no idea who he was talking to or about what—although the word "no" featured prominently—but after another moment he ended the conversation.

Emma sat in the chair on the other side of his desk.

"So. You're back."

She nodded, but resisted mentioning the motel bill.

"I understand you and Oliver Hamilton had a bit of an adventure."

She couldn't help wondering how much Walt knew about what had happened in Yakima. "You could say that." She mulled over how to tell him she refused to fly with Oliver again.

"The interview with Earleen Williams went well?"

She nodded. "Earleen was wonderful. She was flattered by the attention and excited about the article. Her recipe's terrific—I had a taste and, believe it or not, I loved it. By the way, she's already signed the legal documentation so we can print her recipe in *The Examiner.*" If nothing else, Walt should be pleased by that.

He inclined his head slightly in apparent approval. "I'd like the article about Earleen on my desk this afternoon."

Emma's mouth fell open. "This afternoon? As in today?"

Walt raised his eyebrows as if she'd contravened some kind of reporters' code by daring to ask such a question.

Swallowing hard, she offered him an apologetic smile. "It'll be there."

"Good." His eyebrows started to return to their usual position. "And be ready to leave for Colville first thing tomorrow."

So soon? She wanted to tell him she needed time to regroup after the flight from Yakima. Yes, it had gone fairly well. Other than the fact that she'd nearly vomited. The best part was that she'd survived without drugs. Her employer simply had no idea what she'd gone through just to get to the other town and home again in one piece. Then there was the problem of no transportation when they'd landed in Yakima. Not only had she risked her life for this interview, but she'd encountered germs besides.

Now all she had to do was find a way to tell Walt that she preferred to drive to her next interview. "If you have a moment, I'd like to talk to you about Sophie McKay."

Walt gave her a questioning look.

"As you know, I ended up spending the night in Yakima. In a motel room. A cheap one."

He sat back in his chair. "Hamilton said that was unavoidable."

So Walt had already spoken to Oliver. "There's no guarantee it won't happen again—being delayed due to weather, I mean."

He pinched his lips together. "True. Not to worry, the newspaper will reimburse you for the room."

Emma couldn't prevent a look of surprise at his easy capitulation on the matter of her expenses. Still, that wasn't her main concern at the moment.

"I appreciate it, but I was thinking, you know, that it'd probably be better if I drove to Colville this time, rather than fly. I realize it's a full day's drive, but—"

Walt raised his hand and stopped her. "Out of the question. I already have an agreement with Hamilton. He's got a run into Spokane tomorrow morning. He'll drop you off at Colville, fly into Spokane and then come back for you later in the afternoon."

Emma's heart shot to her throat. "You actually want me to do this again…tomorrow?"

Walt nodded. "Meet Oliver at the airfield same time as before."

"Oh." She stood, but her feet felt weighted down. In less than twenty-four hours, she was going back up into the wide blue yonder with Oliver Hamilton.

"Have a good day," Walt said, turning to his computer and dismissing her. "Remember, I want that first article before you leave this afternoon. We're already in the second week of December, and there's a time factor here." He gestured at some limp Christmas garland draped on his window.

"It'll be on your desk," she promised, relieved that she had the rough draft on her laptop computer.

More by instinct than knowledge, she stumbled back down to her cubicle in The Dungeon, preoccupied by the fact that she'd be flying again so soon.

She'd learned that—especially with the help of drugs—she *could* handle being in a small plane. She didn't like it, never would, but in all honesty, the flight hadn't been as bad as she'd feared.

Examining her reluctance to repeat the experience, she was forced to admit something she'd rather ignore. More than the flying itself, it was Oliver Hamilton she wanted to avoid.

Chapter Seven

A fruitcake is to a chef what love is to a gigolo—
an item we both desperately try to avoid.
                        —Michael Psilakis, executive chef
                        and owner of Onera, New York City

Oliver wasn't in the best of moods. He'd made a recent and rather disturbing discovery: Emma Collins wasn't good for his ego. Until he met her, he'd been doing just fine when it came to attracting the opposite sex. Better than fine.

His late-afternoon conversation with Walt had further eroded his ego. Apparently, upon their return from Yakima, Emma had attempted to get out of flying with him a second time. Fortunately, Walt had said no; a deal was a deal and Oliver didn't plan to let her kill his chances of advertising his air-freight business in the local paper.

Okay, he'd admit it'd been a mistake to kiss her, a

mistake he didn't intend to repeat. If this was how Emma felt, then he could ignore her, too.

A glance at his watch told him she had five minutes to show up. If she wasn't at the airport by seven, he was leaving without her. He would've kept *his* end of the bargain, and she'd just have to explain to her boss that she'd been late. He'd only signed this new contract a few weeks ago, flying Alaska salmon packed in dry ice to restaurants in Spokane and Portland. It was a regular job and he couldn't afford to mess up the opportunity.

Just as he was about to board the plane, Emma hurried onto the tarmac, clutching her briefcase and a large takeout coffee.

"You're late," he snapped.

"I most certainly am not." Then, perhaps to reassure herself, she stopped and checked her watch. "I've got five minutes to spare," she announced with more than an edge of righteousness. "At least by my watch."

"Well, not by mine."

This time she wasn't having trouble remaining upright because—or so he assumed—of some stupid pill.

Regardless, he was going to stick to his policy of ignoring her; he'd simply fly his plane.

He felt her scrutiny. "Someone got up on the wrong side of the bed this morning," she said in a singsong voice.

He pretended not to hear. Oscar was already in the

plane, ready and waiting to take off. The terrier poked his head out the passenger door as if to ask what was taking so long.

"Listen," Emma said, "why don't we start over, all right?"

"Fine, whatever."

She rolled her eyes and climbed into the plane with absolutely no complaints. He didn't know what had happened to get her to relax. She'd probably switched drugs and had swallowed some heavy-duty, industrial-strength mood enhancer. Nothing else could explain this cheerful state of mind.

Suddenly he wondered if she'd been drinking, although she'd denied it yesterday. He studied her and sniffed on the off-chance he could smell alcohol.

She glared at him. "Why are you looking at me like that? What's wrong with you, anyway?"

"Nothing," he muttered, returning to the task at hand. He walked beneath the wing, stepping in front of the engine to examine the blades.

Emma's headphones were in place, with the small microphone positioned by her mouth, before he'd finished his preflight check.

His faithful—or should that be faithless?—companion had obviously accepted her, barely raising his head when Oliver climbed into the plane. Oscar had settled onto his dog bed in the cargo hold.

"You didn't wear perfume this time, did you?" he asked.

"No, because I didn't want to get sneezed on again."

"Well, good for you."

Her eyes narrowed. "I don't know why you're in such a bad mood, but I wish you'd snap out of it."

As if to apologize for Oliver, his terrier stood up and poked his head between the two seats. When Emma bent toward him, he licked her ear. Smiling, she stroked his face. Traitor that he was, Oscar seemed to relish her attention. Not until the engine started did the dog go back to his bed.

"Finish your coffee," he said. "We'll be leaving in a couple of minutes."

"It's not coffee. It's latte. Eggnog-flavored." She had to argue about everything. But she obediently drained the large cup.

Oliver taxied to the end of the runway and waited for approval to take off. It wasn't long in coming. He was in the air before he realized that Emma's eyes were squeezed shut. Like yesterday, she held on to the bar above the door with what could only be described as a death grip. But at least she wasn't confessing at the top of her lungs that she'd lied about her weight. The memory produced a grin and for a moment he forgot that he was annoyed with her.

They hardly spoke the entire flight. Every now and then he felt her glance in his direction, as if to gauge his mood. An hour outside of Colville, he saw that she was squirming in her seat.

"What's the problem now?" he asked.

Emma shifted from one side to the other. "If you *must* know, I have to use the, uh, facilities."

"You should've gone before we left."

"I did," she said, not bothering to hide her indignation.

"There isn't a toilet on the plane."

She turned and scowled at him. "I noticed. Do you have any other suggestions?"

"You can do what I do," he told her. Reaching behind him, he grabbed a wide-mouth red plastic container.

She looked at it as if he'd just handed her a dead rat. "You aren't serious, are you?"

"You said you had to go."

"You don't honestly expect me to…go," she said, apparently not finding a more suitable verb, "in that."

"I use it."

"It's different for a man. There's a bit more effort involved for a woman."

"We're a little less than an hour from Colville."

She crossed her legs. "I guess I can wait."

"I thought you'd say that."

By the time he approached the Colville runway, Oliver's sympathies were with Emma. She was clearly uncomfortable, if the number of times she'd crossed and uncrossed her legs was any indication. He didn't have the heart to tell her there wasn't a terminal in Colville. The runway was next to a cow pasture, and while there was an office, that didn't necessarily mean anyone would be there to let her in. It'd been a while since his last visit and he didn't recall if there was a restroom of any kind in the hangar. For her sake, he hoped there was.

Emma bit her lower lip when the wheels touched down. Oliver taxied and parked the plane and leaped out. Just as he'd suspected, no one emerged from the office.

"There's a toilet in there," he said, helping her down. "But I'm not sure it's open...."

She had a desperate look.

Emma hurried toward the office, but no one answered her frantic knock. When she glanced over her shoulder, he shrugged, pointing at the hangar.

With that, she bolted for the large metal shed. She must have found what she needed because she didn't immediately reappear. While he waited, Oliver got on his cell and phoned the Spokane restaurant with his ETA. Someone would meet him at the airfield to pick up the salmon delivery.

When she returned from the hangar she was frowning. "The conditions in there were deplorable. Downright primitive."

"Hey," he said, holding up both hands in a gesture of surrender. "It wasn't me who gulped down that eggnog latte."

She threw him an irate look. "The least you could've done was warn me how long the flight was going to take."

"You're a reporter. You could've done the research." He was about to say something else when he saw the small black dog.

Emma had noticed the mutt, too, a curly-haired mixed breed, probably part poodle. From the matted hair and the lost expression in her brown eyes, Oliver could tell the dog was a stray.

"Where did you come from?" Emma asked, gently petting her. The dog stared longingly up at her and started to shake. "She's cold," Emma said.

Oliver felt bad, but there was little he could do. As it was, Oscar had seen her, jumped down, barking loudly, and then promptly did what dogs always do when they meet another of their kind. He sniffed her butt.

"I had no idea this town was so small," Emma commented. She looked over the cow pasture and wrapped her coat more securely around her. "Do you have anything to eat?"

"You're hungry?"

"No, but the dog is. I don't usually carry food with me." She checked the inside of her purse; the best she had to offer was a half-used package of antacid mints. Unfortunately, Oliver wasn't much help, either.

A lone car drove past the road next to the airfield. "Do you have my cell phone number?" he asked, following the vehicle with his eyes.

"You gave it to me in Yakima."

"Right." He remembered that now. "Call me when you're finished, all right?" As soon as she was picked up, he'd fly into Spokane.

"When will you be back?" she asked.

So she was going to miss him, he thought, warmed by the question. She wouldn't admit it, of course, but she *was* attracted to him. He decided it was better not to react.

"You're sure you have a ride," he confirmed.

"Sophie McKay said she'd come and get me."

She pulled out her cell and punched in a number from her little daybook. After a short conversation, she nodded in his direction, letting him know her ride was on the way.

Oliver hesitated. He didn't feel entirely comfortable about leaving her here alone, in what was virtually a deserted field.

"You can go," she said, her shoulders hunched against the wind. "Ms. McKay will be here any minute."

"How long will the interview be?"

"I'm not sure. I imagine an hour, two at the most."

Oliver estimated that he wouldn't be away more than a couple of hours himself, but it wasn't a problem if Emma required more time. The Indian casino was a few miles down the road, and if she was occupied, the gaming tables offered him ample entertainment. Emma might not want to ride his folding bicycle, but he didn't mind using it. He welcomed the excuse to try his hand at blackjack. The slot machines were pretty much a bust, but he did fairly well with a deck of cards.

"Take all the time you need."

She smiled and frankly he wished she hadn't. When she acted this pleasant, it was hard to remember what a pain she really was.

Emma wrapped the plaid wool scarf around her face to ward off the chill wind, then buried her hands in her pockets. At the moment, she looked about as pitiful as the stray dog huddled next to her feet.

"Just call my cell and I'll be back as soon as I can."

"I will," she assured him, her words muffled. "You'd better go or you'll be late."

"I know."

He hesitated a moment longer, then returned to the plane and opened the cargo hatch. To his surprise, Emma followed him.

"You're upset because you found out I didn't want to fly with you again," she said. Her hands remained in her pockets.

He shrugged as if it didn't matter either way.

"If not that, then is it because…" She stopped, her expression mildly embarrassed.

"What?" he demanded.

"Never mind."

"No," he said. "I want to know."

She looked at him hard. "Is it because I…I didn't react the way you wanted when you kissed me?"

He didn't want to answer that and climbed aboard the plane.

"I didn't see any fireworks when we kissed. Did you?" she asked, sticking her head in the cargo hold.

He snorted.

"Then it isn't any big deal, right?"

"Right."

"Friends?" she asked.

Without meaning to be rude, Oliver paused. "I guess. Why do you care?"

His question appeared to catch her off guard. "I don't know, but I do. If we're going to be spending time together for the next week or so, then I think it's preferable to get along."

"Of course. You have nothing to worry about."

She glanced nervously away. "My mother told me that when a man uses that line, I *should* start to worry."

He chuckled. "No, you don't. You're perfectly safe with me."

As if in disagreement, the little black dog at her feet snarled up at him.

Chapter Eight

Fruitcake is one of those foods that evoke lots of different feelings in people. For me it marks the holiday season that is accompanied by traditions and family. Sharing foods that you eat during certain times of the year is something that I look forward to. A warmed thin slice of fruitcake with freshly made ice cream is the way to go.

—Craig Strong, chef de cuisine, The Dining Room,
The Ritz-Carlton in Pasadena, California

Sophie McKay arrived at the airfield five minutes after Oliver left. Although Emma would never admit it, she found his reluctance to leave her somewhat comforting. She just might have to change her opinion of Oliver Hamilton.

Emma spent those five minutes alone paying attention to the small stray, whom she called Boots because she had two white paws and otherwise black fur. The poor thing shivered in the cold.

When a compact car turned off the road and onto the airfield, Emma straightened. The vehicle came to a stop not far from her, and the driver rolled down her window.

She was an elegant eighty or so, with thick white hair, fashionably styled. Her face glowed with pleasure. "Are you the reporter from *The Examiner*?"

Emma nodded. "And you must be Sophie McKay."

"I am. You seem half-frozen. Come on, I'll drive you to my house. It's warm and cozy, and I'll put on a pot of tea."

Emma looked down at the little dog. Crouching, she petted Boots.

"I see you have a friend," Sophie commented.

"Does she have an owner?" Emma asked hopefully, but considering the dog's appearance, she agreed with Oliver that Boots was most likely a stray.

"Not that I know of. The poor dog's been hanging around the area for a while. I put food out for her a few times, and I know other people have, too, but she's skittish. I think someone must've mistreated her because she doesn't let anyone get too close. Except for you, apparently."

Boots had taken to Emma right away, and she hated to leave the dog behind. "Would you mind if I brought her with me?" What she'd do with Boots after that was a quandary, but Emma didn't feel she could just walk away.

"That might be a problem because of my cats."

Emma gazed down at the dog, unsure what to do.

"Could you find somewhere warm for her to stay until later?" Sophie suggested. "Maybe in the hangar? I'll give you some food to bring back for her."

"Good idea." Emma hadn't thought of that. Boots followed her inside while Sophie dug up an old blanket from the trunk of her car. Emma folded it and placed it on the bathroom floor. Boots didn't object when Emma shut her inside the small room. At least the dog was out of the cold and out of danger. Squatting down, Emma stroked her thin sides and spoke in low, soothing tones, assuring her she'd be back soon.

A few minutes later, she left the hangar and walked over to Sophie's Taurus. A welcome blast of hot air warmed her the instant she slid into the passenger seat.

"I have to tell you," Sophie said as she slipped the stick shift into reverse and revved the engine. "You coming for this interview has really stirred up interest in town. We don't get much notice this side of the mountains. Of course, there's not much that's newsworthy coming out of Colville, so the western half of the state doesn't pay us much mind."

"Your fruitcake recipe is a finalist in a national contest," Emma reminded her.

"Yes," she agreed readily enough, "that was exciting news around here. It made the front page of our weekly paper. Still, none of us figured anyone in the Seattle area would care about my recipe."

"Why do you think yours was chosen?" Emma asked. She might as well get started with the interview now. She opened her purse and brought out her notebook and one of her pens.

"That's easy. It's different. How many recipes have you heard of for chocolate fruitcake?"

"Chocolate?"

"That's right. I created it for my husband years ago and he loved it. Christmas just isn't Christmas without it anymore. I've been baking my chocolate fruitcake every year for longer than I can remember."

"I imagine your husband appreciates that."

Sophie took her eyes off the road for an instant. "Harry's been gone twenty years."

"I'm sorry," Emma murmured awkwardly. "Um, when exactly did you create this fruitcake?"

"It all began shortly after Harry and I were married. Within a year he was off to fight in World War Two," Sophie told her. "I mailed the chocolate fruitcake to him and he got a real kick out of that because, you see, we'd had our first real fight over fruitcake. I'll explain all that once we get back to the house. He wrote to let me know how much he enjoyed it, and I've been baking it every year since. I still have all his letters. Now that he's gone, I read them every once in a while for the memories."

"You never remarried?"

"No, I never did. I found the love of my life. There wasn't another man like Harry and I knew it." Sophie shook her head as she drove down Main Street and the large clock that stood in the center of town. From there, she turned up a steep hill and past the city park.

Although Harry McKay was very different from her own father, Sophie's devotion reminded her of her mother's. Pamela had been like that, loving one man her entire life, despite his weaknesses and flaws. Bret Collins wasn't worthy of such adoration, such heartfelt affection. And Emma wasn't willing to be the daughter he seemed to want now that he was aging.

"Did you have any children?" she asked, unwilling to waste another moment thinking about her father.

"Two sons. Both live in other parts of the country. Harry was very proud of his sons. I am, too. They're good boys—handsome like Harry and smart like me." She laughed a little as she pulled into a long driveway that led to an older home with a large front porch. Sophie parked in the back and turned off the engine.

"The boys want to buy me a new car this Christmas," she said with a thoughtful look. "Lonnie wants to get me one of those old-style cars you see around. I forget what they're called—Cruisers, I think. Unfortunately, they don't come with a stick shift."

"You don't like automatics?" Emma asked.

"Never learned how to drive them and at my age, I'm comfortable with what I know."

That made sense to Emma.

Sophie ushered her onto the back porch. She stepped around pie tins filled with cat food, both kibble and canned.

"Sorry for the mess and the smell," Sophie apologized. "I feed the strays. Some of them have bad teeth, hence the soft food. God only knows how many cats I've got living under this old porch. I do what I can for them—take the sick ones to the vet and give them a bit of attention." She paused and smiled. "It makes me feel good, even when they don't appreciate it."

Emma looked out over the large well-maintained lawn and flower beds. "Your yard is lovely."

A fir wreath with pinecones and red bows hung in the kitchen window. "You should see my irises in the spring. I have them planted everywhere and the yard is full of color. Flowers, cats and chocolate fruitcakes are my passion. Harry and the boys, too, of course, but my husband is gone and my boys are living their own lives now. They don't need me the way they once did." She unlocked the back door and brought Emma into the oversize family kitchen. Three cats meowed as they entered. "These are Huey, Duey and Louey. They're the house cats. They're spoiled, ill-mannered and don't take kindly to strangers or dogs, so you'll have to forgive them."

Emma petted one, who instantly scooted into another room.

"This is the problem with living alone," Sophie said as she filled the kettle and placed it on the stove. "It's just me and the cats and we have certain ways of doing things."

"That's understandable."

Sophie walked into the dining room and returned with a large teapot. "I reserve this one for special company," she said as she measured out tea leaves. Motioning toward the table, she added, "Make yourself comfortable. Just pull out the chair if there's a cat in it and he'll move."

"All right." Sure enough, a large tabby was nestled on the seat cushion. As soon as Emma drew out the chair, the cat stretched and yawned and grudgingly vacated the seat.

"Here, let me brush away the cat hairs." Sophie brought over a whisk broom and swept off the cushion.

"Thank you." Emma sat down at the table, which was cluttered with magazines, newspapers, mail and sales flyers.

Sophie glanced at the wall-mounted clock. "Do you mind if I turn on the radio for a few minutes? It's bingo."

"Ah…sure." Bingo over the radio? Emma had never heard of such a thing.

The radio was on the table, too, next to an aged

photograph of a young man in uniform. Harry, Emma guessed. His widow was right; he'd been a handsome man. Other pictures caught her attention—framed photographs of two families. Emma assumed they were Sophie's two sons and their wives and kids.

Her hostess turned on the radio, sat down and lined up her bingo cards in neat rows. Her timing was perfect. She reached for a round blotter pen and waited for the numbers to be called. Her eyes darted back and forth over the cards after each number was announced. Radio bingo was followed by the farm report, which Sophie immediately switched off.

"Sorry about that, but I'm on a winning streak. I've won two weeks in a row," she told her proudly as the kettle on the stove started to whistle. "My friends say I'm lucky, and it's true."

"I've never heard of radio bingo."

"You haven't?" Sophie shook her head as if this was a real shame. "The local merchants sponsor it. When you bingo, you call it in to the station and then take your card to the participating merchant for your prize."

"What did you win?" Emma asked, curious now.

"Five dollars off my next haircut at Venus de Milo Beauty Salon, and the week before, it was buy one, get one free at the A & W Drive-In. If you were going to be in town longer and it wasn't so cold, I'd take you down for one of their root beer floats."

Emma smiled appreciatively as Sophie poured

the tea and brought out a dark wrapped loaf from the refrigerator.

"I thought you might want to try my chocolate fruitcake."

"Uh, sure…"

"You'll be surprised—pleasantly so," Sophie told her. Within minutes, she brought two cups of tea and a plate of the most unusual-looking fruitcake Emma had ever seen.

"Taste it," the woman urged.

Emma helped herself to a slice, unsure what to expect. The flavors came alive in her mouth and she widened her eyes. Sophie hadn't exaggerated. This was incredibly good. "Is that pineapple I taste?"

"Yup, and coconut, too."

"Oh, this is *wonderful*." Emma took another bite and licked her fingers when she'd finished. For the second time, her preconceptions and prejudices about something—fruitcake—had been tested.

"I use lots of nuts. Harry was wild about pecans. My own favorite is walnuts. Do you realize how good nuts are for you?" she asked conversationally. "Just think about it. Inside each nut is the potential for an entire tree. They're packed full of nutrition. A lot of people are concerned about the fat content, but nuts have good fat, not bad fat."

Emma smiled. Being with Sophie was such a delight that she was having a hard time remembering to take notes. "How did you come up with the recipe?"

"That's the most interesting part," she said, joining her at the table once more. "The first year Harry and I were married, I wanted to make fruitcake at Christmas. My mother always had, and I wanted to be a good wife and homemaker, just like her. Harry told me he hated fruitcake and furthermore he didn't want me wasting money on ingredients for a cake he wouldn't even eat. This was toward the end of the Depression, when money was still scarce. I told him he was being selfish and mean, and I burst into tears." She paused and sipped her tea.

"You see, to me, Christmas *was* fruitcake. It felt as if Harry had asked me to give up my favorite holiday. That was our first big fight. Telling me I couldn't bake that fruitcake was like telling me we couldn't afford Christmas."

As far as this Christmas thing went, Emma's sympathies were with Harry.

"The next morning," Sophie continued, "Harry said if it meant that much to me, I should go ahead and do whatever I wanted. So I baked fruitcake, but I used the ingredients I knew Harry liked best. When I told him what I'd done, he put his arms around me and said it wasn't any wonder he loved me as much as he did. Harry had a real sweet tooth, especially for good chocolate."

"You used the ingredients he liked?" Emma thought that was a clever compromise.

"I admit chocolate fruitcake isn't run-of-the-mill

fruitcake, but that's what got me into the finals, don't you think? I can only imagine how many recipes they received. Mine was different, and I have my Harry to thank for that."

Emma made another note on her tablet. Sophie was about to say something else when someone knocked on the back door.

"That'll be Barbara, my sister-in-law. I told her she could stop by and meet you. I didn't think you'd mind."

"Sure, that's fine."

Barbara came into the kitchen, wearing a heavy winter coat and a long hand-knit scarf with matching gloves. "Hello," she said, beaming Emma a warm smile. She removed her gloves, tucked them in her pockets, then extended her right hand. "It's a pleasure to meet you. We're all so proud of Sophie, and it's nice that the Seattle newspaper's doing this."

Emma didn't have the heart to tell her that *The Examiner* was a regional paper with a limited circulation. Of course, Puyallup was considerably bigger than Colville with its population of less than seven thousand, and compared to Colville's weekly, *The Examiner* was practically the *New York Times*.

"How was your flight?" Barbara shooed a cat out of a chair and joined them.

"Uneventful—just the way I like them." The discomfort of a full bladder was not a topic she wished to pursue.

Barbara wasn't the only visitor Sophie had. By the end of the interview, Emma had been introduced to Dixie, Sophie's next-door neighbor; Florence, her best friend; and Cathy, who cleaned her house once a week. They all gathered around the table with tea and chocolate fruitcake and told story after story. Their laughter echoed through the house. It was a party unlike any Emma had ever gone to; none of these women were close to her age but she felt like one of them.

By the time Sophie dropped her off at the airfield, it was almost two in the afternoon. The Cessna was parked at the end of the strip near the hangar, and Emma assumed Oliver was inside.

"I'll wait just to be sure," Sophie insisted.

Emma didn't want to hold up the other woman, but reluctantly agreed. She hurried over to the plane, seeking Oliver, disappointed not to find him immediately. She felt excited—no, elated—after the interview and wanted to talk about the experience. Share some of the wisdom she'd gained from Sophie and her friends.

In discussing the interview with Oliver, she might get a slant for her story. She had a thousand ideas and impressions chasing around in her head and needed to sort through them. It was important to her that she do Sophie and her friends justice.

"Oliver!" she called out. He might have curled up inside the hangar for a nap. "Oscar?"

No response.

Emma let Boots out of the restroom and bent down to feed her the can of cat food Sophie had given her. The dog would be too hungry to be finicky, Emma guessed, and she was right. Boots gobbled up the small can's contents and looked for more.

Emma found her cell phone and walked outside to make sure she'd get a good connection. She waved at Sophie, then punched in the number for his cell. The phone rang three times before Oliver responded.

"Hamilton."

"Where are you?" she asked.

"You're finished?"

"Where are you?" she repeated. She couldn't place the background noise, which sounded like some sort of circus.

"The casino. It's a couple of miles out of town."

After the poker experience, she should've known he'd be gambling. "Will you be much longer?"

"I'm in, I'm in," he shouted, obviously not to her. "Listen, I'm in the middle of a game and I can't quit. Find a way out here, will you?"

"You want me to come to the *casino?*" She couldn't believe the nerve of this man.

He didn't answer and the line was disconnected. She called again, but this time there was no answer, even after a dozen rings. Like it or not—and she didn't—Emma was going to the casino.

Chapter Nine

On the short drive to the casino, Emma brooded about the unreliability of Oliver Hamilton. She hoped Sophie didn't notice how upset she was with her so-called pilot. In case he'd forgotten, she needed to get back to the newspaper office sometime before the end of the Christmas season.

"Colville's a pleasant little town," Sophie was telling her. "I wish you had more time to look around. There's a lumber mill on the other side of town, which helps keep the local economy afloat."

Emma smiled politely, finding it difficult to concentrate. Boots was curled up next to her feet and had gone to sleep. She still didn't know what she was going to do with the stray. Maybe she could persuade Phoebe to take her until Emma moved into a new apartment that allowed pets.

When Sophie pulled up in front of the casino, Emma had to look twice. The place resembled nothing so much as an overgrown tavern. Other than a sign on the roadway, there wasn't a single indication that this was a casino. Emma had expected flashing neon lights, a fancy restaurant offering steak and lobster dinners at cut-rate prices, uniformed valets. Instead, Sophie parked on a gravel lot.

"I can't thank you enough," Emma told the other woman as she climbed out of the vehicle. Boots hopped out with her as Emma reached for her purse and briefcase.

"It was lovely to meet you," Sophie said, leaning across the front seat. "I hope you win today. I'll be out here on Sunday after church—for bingo. I won eight hundred dollars a year ago." She grinned. "Like I said, I'm just plain lucky."

The door to the casino opened and out sauntered the largest lumberjack Emma had ever seen. Not that she'd seen many lumberjacks. This man had to be close to seven feet tall and wore a red plaid shirt, dirt-smudged jeans with suspenders and a red wool cap. She glanced around, just to make sure Babe, the blue ox, wasn't following behind.

He took one look at Emma and pointed a beefy finger in her direction. "You. Be my woman."

Emma gasped.

Shaking her head, Sophie got out of the driver's seat. "Grizzly, you leave this young lady alone."

Grizzly looked crestfallen and rubbed the side of his face. "I shaved before I came into town."

"It takes more than a shave to attract a woman. Now apologize."

Grizzly shuffled from one foot to the other. "I didn't mean no offense."

"None taken." After a final wave for Sophie, Emma grabbed Boots and tucked the dog under her arm as she scurried into the casino. When she found Oliver, she intended to let him know *exactly* what she thought.

Oscar was patiently waiting for Oliver just inside the door. As soon as he saw Emma and Boots, he barked twice. This appeared to be the cue Oliver was waiting for, because he turned abruptly and faced the door.

He was at a table near the entrance playing some card game. Blackjack? It was hard to tell in the smoky haze. The entire place was shrouded in cigarette smoke, and she gave an involuntary cough. Oscar sneezed, but she managed to jump back in time.

"Won't be long," Oliver called out. "Make yourself comfortable."

"In here?" The smoke was likely to kill her first.

With a disgusted grimace, he left the table and walked toward her. "I'll be ten minutes or so."

At her horrified expression, he looked over his shoulder at the blackjack table. "You want something to eat?" he asked quickly.

"No, I want to go home. How are we supposed to get back to the airfield? And why did you make me come out here, anyway?"

He gazed at her a moment, pure innocence in his eyes. "Why, Ms. Collins, I thought you'd enjoy being introduced to another fascinating aspect of Washington state culture. Maybe you could write a travel piece. And like I said, you can get a meal here. Or try one of the slot machines. Don't worry about getting back, either. A friend of a friend said he'd give us a ride to the airfield. You'll like Grizzly. And don't be put off by his name. He's as gentle as a lamb."

"Grizzly?" That completely distracted her from the sarcastic remark she'd been about to make.

"Now, don't judge a man by his name. He's a sweetheart."

"Big guy in a red plaid shirt?"

Oliver nodded. "You know him?"

"He just asked me to be his woman," she said from between clenched teeth.

Oliver blinked. "I'm sure he didn't mean it."

Emma's eyes opened wide. "What is *that* supposed to mean?"

"He doesn't come into town often. Don't worry, you're safe."

If that was supposed to reassure her, it didn't. From the sound of it, the big guy hardly ever saw a woman. And since she was going to be stuck in some vehicle with him, he might well think he'd hit the jackpot.

"I'm in the middle of a lucky streak." For the first

time Oliver seemed to notice that Boots was with her. "What do you intend to do with the dog?"

"I…I haven't figured that out yet."

Someone impatiently shouted Oliver's name.

"Be right with you," he yelled over his shoulder. "Can't you entertain yourself for a few minutes?"

He spoke as if she were ten years old.

"Don't be concerned about me," she said. Next time she was going to insist on driving, and she wouldn't take no for an answer.

"Hamilton, you in or not?"

"In," he shouted back.

Emma watched him sprint over to the table. This was great; it was either breathe in smoke or risk facing Paul Bunyan in the parking lot. Emma decided her chances were better in the casino. But she didn't like it there. Boots didn't, either. The dog trembled in her arms, alarmed by all the lights and noise. Oscar, however, despite an occasional sneeze, relaxed in his corner by the door. He appeared to be an old hand at this, which no doubt he was.

After a few minutes, Emma couldn't tolerate the smoke anymore. She needed fresh air. She stepped outside and wasn't completely pleased when Oliver's terrier followed her into the pale wintry sunlight. She didn't like the way Oscar was eyeing Boots. Her hold on Boots tightened. No way was she letting Oscar have his way with this sweet dog.

"If you're thinking what I think you're thinking,"

she told the other dog, "forget it. Boots is off-limits. Understand?" Once she got home, there'd be a veterinary appointment for Boots—checkup, shots and spaying. She planned to be a responsible pet-owner, and that included thwarting Oscar's evil-minded intentions.

It was cold outside, and her fashionable leather boots weren't enough to keep her feet warm. Her toes lost feeling; reluctantly she retreated inside once again, determined to drag Oliver away from the gaming table if necessary.

Fortunately, he was finished with his game. Counting his money as he walked toward her, he looked up as if nothing were amiss and smiled. "I won three hundred dollars."

She ignored that. "Can we leave for the airfield now?" she asked, keeping her voice as level and even as she could manage.

"Sure thing. And considering your worries about Grizzly, I got us another ride."

"Good."

"You don't have any objection to riding in the back of a pickup, do you? It's only a couple of miles."

"*What?*"

"Just kidding."

"Ha, ha." She wasn't amused.

"Come on, Emma, loosen up. Where's your Christmas spirit?"

She didn't answer. The less said regarding her feelings about Christmas, the better. Instead she asked, "Three of us are supposed to cram into a truck cab?"

"You have a problem with that?"

"As a matter of fact, I do. I'll find my own way back to the airfield." Oliver was really starting to get on her nerves. "Why did you have me come out here, anyway?" she demanded. "Seriously. Don't give me any nonsense about culture or travel, either."

He sighed. "I was on a winning streak. I didn't know how long it was going to last. But sending for you was the stupidest thing I could've done. The minute you showed up, I started losing."

"You're blaming *me*?" Emma had to get away from this Neanderthal. "Go ahead without me," she told him. "I'll phone for a taxi."

Oliver nearly doubled over as he burst into laughter. "La-di-da. Her highness requires a private conveyance. Do you actually believe a town the size of Colville has a taxi service?"

"Oh." Emma had assumed there was one.

"Don't worry. I'm the forgiving sort. I'll still let you ride with me and if you're real nice I won't make you sit in the back of the truck."

By this time Emma was so angry with Oliver, she wanted to smack him upside the head. "Have you been drinking?" she snapped.

"Absolutely not." His smile faded. "FAA regulations don't permit it. I worked too hard for this license to mess it up over a beer."

She had half a mind to lean over and smell his breath. She didn't, for fear he'd try to kiss her again. And yet…the thought was strangely appealing.

She and Oliver clambered into a rickety old truck driven by a bearded taciturn man named Michael Michaels—known as Mike-Mike. He had remarkably little to say, which was fine with Emma. Preferable to Grizzly's idea of conversation, anyway.

On the ride back to Colville Emma reminded herself that she wasn't attracted to Oliver Hamilton. Still, if he wanted to kiss her—not now, of course, but later—she was afraid she might let him. Perhaps she was experiencing altitude sickness. There was definitely something in the air, but it wasn't Christmas and it sure wasn't love.

Emma sat between the two men with Boots, plus her purse and briefcase, on her lap and Oscar down by Oliver's feet. When they arrived at the field, Emma climbed out of the truck once Oliver had leaped to the ground. She thanked Mike-Mike politely for the ride.

Oliver handed his new friend a few dollars. With the two dogs trotting behind them, Emma and Oliver headed toward the Cessna.

"How'd the interview go?" Oliver asked as they approached the plane.

The tension left her shoulders. "I think Sophie is one of the most interesting women I've ever met."

"Really." Oliver walked around the Cessna, giving it the usual inspection.

"She's loved one man her entire life."

He nodded, although she doubted he was listening.

"Harry died twenty years ago, and she's loved him and only him all these years. I find that so romantic."

"Romantic," he repeated absently.

"Did you hear me?" she asked.

Oliver glanced back at her. "I heard you. So what's the big deal? Men and women stay in love all the time."

"They don't," Emma said. "Do you know what the divorce rate is in this country? One out of every two marriages fails. That's a fifty-percent failure rate. Men and women *don't* stay in love, and do you know why?"

He yawned.

"It's because there aren't any genuinely romantic men left in this world. Where's Cary Grant when we need him? What about Humphrey Bogart? Rock Hudson? No, wait. Not him. Although he was very romantic in all those Doris Day movies."

"Donald Duck. Daisy thought *he* was pretty romantic."

This time she couldn't resist and slapped his shoulder. "It's all one big joke to you, isn't it?" Without giving him a chance to respond, she said, "I'm serious."

"There are romantic men in this world, Emma. Lots of them, and they don't look anything like a bunch of old movie stars, either. Real romance isn't about candlelit dinners or diamonds or champagne. As for couples staying in love, my parents have been married for thirty-six years."

Suddenly Oliver Hamilton was the expert. "You know all about this subject, do you?" She let him hear the sarcasm in her voice.

"You'd probably consider my brother a romantic. At least he tried to be. Unfortunately, the whole thing backfired on him."

Emma knew he wanted her to ask what happened and she refused to. She needn't have worried because Oliver was intent on telling her, whether she wanted to be told or not.

"Jack took his girlfriend to a fancy restaurant in order to propose. He wanted to do it up big, you know. So he had the chef bake the engagement ring into a piece of chocolate cake." He was smiling as he described the details of his brother's attempt at romance. "The problem is that when Ginny ate the cake, she swallowed the diamond ring." He slapped his knee now, overcome by mirth.

"Oh, let's just get in the plane."

But Oliver seemed determined to finish his story. "I told him he was lucky Ginny didn't choke to death on that diamond. They've been married for six years now and have two little rug rats, both as cute as can be."

Emma was about to comment when a white van drove into the airfield. Boots started barking frantically. Emma bent over and picked up the dog in order to calm her. She'd welcome the opportunity to clean her up. Maybe she could sneak her into the apartment and do that later today.

The van pulled up next to the plane. Emma read the lettering on the side of the vehicle and groaned. Animal Control.

"It's the dogcatcher," Oliver said out of the side of his mouth, in case she wasn't smart enough to read it for herself.

"I can see that."

"Afternoon, folks," the tall thin man said as he climbed down from the van.

Boots growled and Oscar joined him in perfect harmony.

"Good afternoon, Officer Wilson," Emma said formally, reading the nametag on his jacket.

"Do you know that dog?"

"Ah…we only just met."

"Before you ask," Oliver said, distracting Officer Wilson. "Oscar's license is paid in full. He's not a local but he's legal." He grinned, apparently at his own cleverness.

"I'm more concerned with the stray your lady friend's holding."

"I named her Boots."

The dogcatcher nodded in a friendly fashion; he seemed to approve of her choice of names. "Do you plan to adopt Boots officially?"

"Ah…" Emma didn't know how to respond. She needed time to work something out. If Mr. Scott discovered she had a dog, he'd evict her from the apartment so fast her head would spin. She'd probably end up living at the office.

"It seems she's taken a liking to you." His expression grew somber. "You know, for some reason she's been hanging around the airfield lately. That's dangerous, for her and for the pilots."

Boots growled again and squirmed as if begging for the opportunity to nip at the dogcatcher's heels.

"This dog doesn't have an owner," Officer Wilson informed her, "and we've had complaints. That's not good."

Emma gathered Boots closer to her side.

"If I take her to Animal Control, I'm afraid she'll be euthanized."

"No!" Emma's protest was immediate. She looked to Oliver for help, although she didn't know what he could do.

"Emma wants to adopt Boots," Oliver said. "It's obvious those two have bonded. What are the fees?" Oliver pulled a wad of cash from his pocket.

Officer Wilson frowned. "Adoption isn't my department. But…" He gave Emma an assessing glance. "I'll turn the other way if you want to take her with you."

"Thanks," Oliver said, steering Emma toward the plane.

"Yes, I'll take her," Emma cried. She couldn't bear the thought of Boots going to the shelter. She didn't know how long the poor thing had fended for herself, but that was about to end. Somehow or other, she'd figure out a way to keep the dog hidden until she found an apartment that accepted pets.

The dogcatcher pulled two dog biscuits from his pocket and offered one to Oscar and the second to Boots. "No hard feelings, girl, I was only doing my job." He gently petted the small dog's head. "Glad it worked out for you."

As if accepting Officer Wilson's apology, Boots licked the man's hand.

"You'll see to buying Boots a license when you get home?" he reminded them.

"We will," Oliver promised.

Mr. Wilson seemed pleased and drove off with a "Merry Christmas" and a jolly wave.

Sophie McKay's Chocolate Fruitcake

Make 3-4 weeks in advance. Store in refrigerator.

Place into large bowl:

2 cups maraschino cherries, sliced in half
2 cups chopped dates
2 cups pineapple tidbits, well drained
1 cup coconut
2 cups walnuts
2 cups pecan halves
2 12 oz. packages semisweet chocolate chips

Beat the following ingredients on low for thirty seconds, then on high for three minutes:

3 cups flour
1 1/2 cups sugar
1 tbsp. baking powder
1/2 tsp. salt
3/4 cup shortening
3/4 cup butter
2/3 cup crème de cacao
1/2 cup cocoa powder
9 eggs

Pour batter over fruit and nut mixture. Pour into two well-greased loaf pans. Bake at 275 degrees for 2 1/2 to 3 hours. After two hours, check with a toothpick every fifteen minutes.

When cool, set each loaf on a large piece of plastic wrap and pour a jigger of crème de cacao over them. Wrap tightly and place inside a Ziploc bag and keep refrigerated for 3-4 weeks.

Chapter Ten

It was dark by the time Oliver and Emma landed back at the airstrip in Puyallup. They hadn't talked much during the flight, which was unexpectedly turbulent. Emma had white-knuckled it, choosing to close her eyes and pray. She hadn't prayed this much since grade school.

As soon as they taxied to the end of the runway, Oliver parked the plane. Emma climbed out and reached for Boots, who came willingly into her arms. The poor dog trembled, and Emma realized it hadn't been an easy flight for her, either.

"I'll be in touch," Oliver said after Emma had collected her things.

Her legs felt shaky and her stomach queasy, so she merely nodded, eager to get home. It was too late to return to the office; besides, she had more pressing concerns that had nothing to do with her job. Somehow, she had to find a way to smuggle Boots into her apartment. Even more of a challenge would be keeping the dog hidden until she located someplace else to live. Maybe Phoebe could help. Money was tight already, this close to payday, and she needed to make a veterinary appointment, plus obtain a license for Boots and buy a collar and leash. Groceries weren't necessary, Emma decided; besides, she needed to lose a few pounds. Somehow she'd make it to the end of the month, despite the unexpected drain on her cash reserves. There were real advantages to avoiding Christmas, and this proved it.

On the drive back to her apartment, Emma explained the tricky situation to Boots. She took her eyes from the road for just a second to smile at the little black dog. Boots gazed at her adoringly, but it would be ridiculous to assume the dog understood her dilemma and would voluntarily remain out of sight. And what about walks? She'd have to sneak Boots in and out for her walks.

Fortunately, when she arrived Mr. Scott was nowhere to be seen. Clutching Boots with one arm, Emma wrapped her coat around the dog. Anyone who noticed her bulging side would guess she was making a poor attempt at hiding something. That being the case, she could only hope no one suspected it was a dog.

Her mind was whirring from her afternoon with Sophie McKay and the woman's community of family and friends. Sophie's chocolate fruitcake recipe was unusual, and it didn't surprise Emma that it was a finalist. As soon as possible, she wanted to sit down with her laptop and begin drafting the article. First, however, she had to give Boots a bath.

The moment Emma entered her small one-bedroom apartment, she closed the drapes. She didn't want Mr. Scott walking past and peering through her window. Her neighbors on both sides had decorated Christmas trees on display in theirs. Not Emma.

After checking the refrigerator and discovering an open box of baking soda, two small containers of yogurt and a shriveled-up orange, she realized she'd need to go out later for dog food.

Because she was hungry, she ate the yogurt as she ran warm water into her bathtub. Boots sauntered from room to room, sniffing and exploring her new home. The dog didn't object when Emma placed her in the water and gave her a bath. Using her own shampoo, she worked up a good lather, then rinsed Boots off and repeated the process, finishing with a cream rinse that left the black fur glossy and soft. The muck on Boots's coat had deposited a dirty residue on the bottom of the tub. The dog had been completely filthy. She licked Emma's hand as if to thank her.

"You're a darling." Emma laughed as she dried Boots off with a thick towel, and then cleaned the tub.

The doorbell chimed and Emma froze. She'd barely been home an hour. It didn't seem possible that someone had already gone to Bud Scott and reported that she was in violation of the *No Pets* clause.

Perhaps it was Phoebe, who sometimes stopped by in the evening. Cautious, she locked Boots in the bathroom and checked her peephole.

"Oliver?" she said aloud, surprised to see him. She unlatched the lock and opened the door.

He stood on the other side of the threshold with a pizza box in one hand, a bag of dog food in the other.

"You said there weren't any romantic heroes left in this world," he said, balancing the pizza box on the tips of his fingers. "I'm here to prove you wrong."

Impressed by his thoughtfulness, Emma stared at him, hardly knowing what to think.

"Can I come in?" Oliver asked.

"Oh, yes…sorry." It didn't even occur to her to refuse him. She stepped aside and as he passed, the scent of warm pizza made her stomach growl. The yogurt hadn't taken her far.

With flair, Oliver set the pizza down on the kitchen table. "Deluxe, with extra cheese," he announced. "Plus two cans of Coke."

"Where's Oscar?" Emma asked as she took a couple of plates from the cupboard.

"In the truck. Where's Boots?"

"In the bathroom. I'll let her out in a minute," she said, thinking it was probably for the best that Oscar had stayed in Oliver's truck. No need to raise Mr. Scott's suspicions by letting another dog inside her apartment.

"Boots has a thing for him, you know." Oliver pulled out a chair, sat down and served her a slice of pizza.

"Don't be ridiculous." She would've argued further but she was too hungry for a full-blown argument. "You're making that up."

Oliver's mouth twisted into a lazy smile and he wiped his fingers on a paper towel.

Boots scratched at the bathroom door. When Emma opened it for her, she hurried into the kitchen. Sitting on her haunches, she stared longingly at the steaming pizza. "Look what Oliver brought us," Emma told her dog. She got a cereal bowl from the cupboard and filled it with dog food. Setting it on the floor, she watched as Boots gobbled up the entire amount and then begged for more.

She was about to refill the dish when Oliver stopped her. "Don't overfeed her," he said. "Especially now. She's been semistarved for some time. You don't want her getting sick."

Emma nodded, rinsed out the bowl and ran clean water into it.

While she did that, Oliver glanced around the apartment. "Do you have something against Christmas?" he asked.

"Not really." She didn't feel like launching into a long explanation.

"The least you could do is put up a sprig of mistletoe."

"Very funny." She rolled her eyes.

"I mean it." He gestured around him. "You have a deficit of Christmas cheer. When are you planning to put up your tree?"

"I'm not." Leave it to Oliver to press the issue. "I don't really like Christmas."

"Why not?"

"It's personal."

"You *have* to have a Christmas tree," he said. When she shook her head, he murmured, "Come on. Why don't you enjoy Christmas, Ms. Scrooge?"

She frowned at him, struggling to maintain her composure. "Not everyone lives and breathes Christmas, you know."

"Most people do. Take my mom. She's really big on Christmas, with family dinners and parties—the whole nine yards. I thought all women were."

"I'm not." He was really irritating her now. "But you, of course, know women so well."

"Hey." He shrugged. "It was just a question."

Emma realized she was overreacting. Oliver had been very kind to her this evening and didn't deserve to be snapped at. "My mother was a big fan of Christmas," she said quietly, paying a lot of attention to her pizza slice. "She used to bake cookies and decorate the house and make a big fuss over the holidays."

"So you spend the day with her," Oliver said, smoothly accepting her explanation. "That makes sense."

Emma turned away. A part of her wanted to let him assume that was true. But she couldn't, although she wasn't sure why. "My mother died several years ago."

Her announcement was followed by an awkward silence. "I'm sorry."

Emma raised one shoulder in a half shrug. "I've gotten over it."

"Do people really get over losing their mothers?" he asked softly.

She looked at Oliver then. Really looked at him. A small shiver of awareness went through her. It occurred to Emma that he was working hard to prove he could be a romantic hero, *her* romantic hero. Emma wasn't sure she was ready for anything like that, with anyone.

"What?" he demanded after a lengthy pause.

Emma blinked, embarrassed that she'd been staring at him. "Nothing."

"No," he said. "You were thinking about something and I want to know what."

"Ah…"

"I'll bet it was me." He raised his eyebrows. "You want me, right?"

"Would you stop?"

"No." Oliver smiled. "A little pizza, a bag of dog food, and you're ready to fall at my feet. Who would've thought it'd be this easy." He'd abandoned all seriousness and seemed absolutely delighted with himself. Grinning widely, he took a giant bite of pizza.

Emma could see it was going to be impossible to have a real conversation with this man.

"Come on, admit it," he urged.

She pretended to be absorbed in her dinner. "The dog food was a nice touch," she finally said.

He nodded. "Actually, it was Oscar who thought of that."

"You carry on conversations with your dog?" She didn't mention the little heart-to-heart she'd had with Boots on the drive home.

"All the time." Oliver motioned toward the apartment door. "Now that Boots has eaten, would it be okay if I brought Oscar inside? He hates being left in the truck for very long."

"He doesn't mind the plane."

"No, but he knows Boots is here."

Emma thought about warning Oliver not to let anyone see his dog, and decided against it. "Boots would enjoy the company." If they were caught, it would be easy enough to explain that the terrier was only visiting. Surely Mr. Scott couldn't object to that.

Oliver stood and headed for the door and then, as if he'd forgotten something, he turned back.

Emma glanced up, wondering what he was doing, when he leaned over and kissed her. This wasn't any peck on the cheek, either. His mouth was warm, insistent, and Emma felt overwhelmed by sensation. By excitement. His hands found their way into her hair and she instinctively opened to him. Thankfully, she was sitting, otherwise she feared her knees would have given out. Oliver was gentle, coaxing, as the tip of his tongue outlined the shape of her lips. When he pulled away, he reached for the back of the chair as if he, too, needed something to ground him.

"Nice," he whispered, not sounding anything like his normal self.

Wanting to make light of it, Emma tossed her head. "It was all right, I guess."

Oliver grinned, and she could see he wasn't fooled. "You could really damage a man's ego."

But not his, she suspected.

"I'll be right back." He started for the door again.

Emma remained where she was in order to gather her scattered wits. This man's kisses were a lot more potent than she'd been willing to acknowledge. Earlier, the first time he'd kissed her, she'd deluded herself into thinking it'd been rather pleasant but nothing earth-shattering. Wrong. *This* time, she'd experienced a response of seismic proportions.

Oliver was back and let himself in the apartment door. Oscar barreled inside and the instant Boots saw the other dog, she barked joyfully. Oh, dear, was it possible Oliver was right about that, too? But Oscar played it cool, his head at a cocky tilt. It was true, Emma thought, unable to hold back a smile. After a while, dogs and their masters began to look alike.

Emma bent down and stroked Oscar, then poured him a bowl of dog food, too.

"Was that a dog I saw just now?"

At the sound of Bud Scott's brusque voice, Emma nearly fainted. He'd opened her—regrettably unlocked—door and was peering into the apartment.

"Yes," Oliver answered gruffly. He'd clearly taken exception to Mr. Scott's offensive tone.

Emma hurried to stand next to Oliver, hoping to block the landlord's view of the two dogs. "Oscar belongs to my friend," she explained, trying to sound innocent and accommodating.

Mr. Scott's eyes narrowed. "I thought I saw *two* dogs in here."

"You did," Oliver confirmed.

Emma elbowed him hard in the ribs.

"Ouch." Oliver glared at her and rubbed his side.

"There's only Oscar," she said sweetly. Unfortunately, Boots chose that moment to bark excitedly. Oscar joined in, and Emma sagged against the door-jamb.

"You know this is a pet-free zone." Bud Scott scowled.

"Yes, but…"

"We have a no-tolerance policy in regard to pets, especially cats and dogs."

"Friendly place you chose to live," Oliver muttered.

"You aren't helping," she said furiously. It would've been a whole lot better if he'd just gone home, taking his leftover pizza with him.

He made a resigned gesture and stepped back.

Emma folded her hands. "Please, Mr. Scott," she implored. "I…only got Boots this afternoon. She was a stray—"

"You brought a *stray* into this complex?" He looked at her as if she were insane. "Do you have any idea what you've exposed your neighbors to?" He retreated a step as if he feared an infestation of some kind at any moment.

"But—"

"One week," Mr. Scott intoned. "One week and you're out."

"One week," she echoed, aghast.

"I want you and that…that mutt out of here one week from today."

Both dogs growled when she closed the door.

"Now what am I going to do?" she asked Oliver. Money was already tight, and she couldn't possibly come up with first and last month's rent in that short a time.

Chapter Eleven

I've had the honor to cook for seven presidents
of the United States here at the Waldorf-Astoria. Unless President Bush asks me to make it,
fruitcake isn't on the menu.

—John Doherty, executive chef,
The Waldorf-Astoria

"I have to move," Emma moaned to Phoebe when
she arrived at The Dungeon the next morning.

"What happened?" Good friend that she was,
Phoebe immediately rolled her chair across the aisle.

"It's a long story." Emma didn't want to explain
just now; it would take half the morning and she had
an article to write. What bothered her most wasn't the
problem of having to be out of her apartment in seven
days. That was bad enough, but it wasn't what had
kept her up half the night. Instead, all she could think
about was Oliver's kiss. By morning, with her eyes

burning from lack of sleep, she hoped she'd never see him again. It wasn't true, though, Emma admitted reluctantly. She very much wanted to be with him, and that frightened her. Maybe she wasn't so different from her mother, after all.

"I have news," Phoebe whispered.

Emma glanced up expectantly.

"Walt and I are having some…serious conversations."

"That's great." The look in Phoebe's eyes was rapturous, suggesting that the couple was on the brink of announcing their engagement.

"Unfortunately Walt's having a problem telling anyone at the office that we're seeing each other."

Even Emma hadn't known until just recently. She was astonished that they'd managed to keep their romance such a well-guarded secret.

"He wants to wait awhile," Phoebe said. She lowered her voice again as someone came down the stairs and passed their cubicles. "I don't know why, but Walt seems to think we should wait until after the holidays."

"Why?"

"I don't know."

"And you agreed?" Emma asked. Like Phoebe, she didn't understand Walt's hesitation. She doubted anyone at the office would object to his relationship with Phoebe. There might be a few raised eyebrows, but so what?

"I think Walt's concerned about setting a good example. You know—doing things the way his father would. I mentioned that, but he denies it."

"I guess this means I won't be able to move in with you if I don't have a new apartment by next week?" Emma muttered. "It would only be for a few days—until I can find a place."

Phoebe frowned. "In case you've forgotten, I only have a one-bedroom apartment and my sofa's pretty ratty. What's going on, anyway? I was so absorbed in my own news that I'd completely ignored yours."

"I have a dog now."

"A dog?" Phoebe's eyes rounded with surprise.

"Like I said, it's a long story."

"That no doubt involves Oliver Hamilton."

"How'd you guess?" Emma sighed. "Although I'd like to blame Oliver, the dog sort of chose me. Now I have to move because the landlord is dead set against animals."

"In other words, you're desperate?"

Emma sighed again; she still had six days. "Close, but not panicking yet."

"I'm sorry, but I can't have a dog, either," Phoebe said. "I'll check and see if a visiting dog is allowed, okay?"

Emma was grateful; this was a lot to ask, but she might not have any other choice. She wouldn't need to move in until next week—if at all. She'd certainly do her best to find something else before that.

"How did the interview go? The one in Colville?" Phoebe asked.

"Really well." Emma glanced longingly toward her blank computer screen. "I have all my notes, but do me a favor, would you? Don't let Walt know I'm here just yet. He's going to want this article and I haven't even started writing it. I intended to, but then… Well, it's complicated."

"Oliver Hamilton is somehow involved, right?" This was becoming a refrain.

"Isn't he always involved?" Emma said, reaching in her briefcase for her notes on Sophie McKay.

As she'd told Phoebe, she wanted to blame Oliver for her current troubles, but that would be decidedly unfair. In bringing Boots home with her, Emma had taken a calculated risk. Now she had to write this article and quickly, because she needed to spend her lunch hour making phone calls. At least she had access to the very latest rental listings, she told herself. If only she could find a decent place that allowed pets and required a minimum cash outlay…

Without wasting another moment, she began drafting her article.

Lessons from Fruitcake: Sophie McKay

Sophie McKay, the second of the Washington State finalists in the *Good Homemaking* fruitcake contest, resides in Colville, the seat of Stevens County in the northeast part of our diverse state.

Sophie believes her entry, Chocolate Fruitcake, caught the judges' interest because it was different. She first created this fruitcake with its unusual mixture of ingredients during the Depression. Her husband, Harry, claimed to hate fruitcake, but it was an important aspect of Christmas for Sophie. Her compromise was to use his favorite foods and flavors—including chocolate.

Although Harry's been dead for twenty years, Sophie continues to bake the fruitcake in his honor. And while the ingredients are indeed unusual, what makes Sophie's fruitcake special are the memories she bakes into each one.

In life, as in fruitcake, this mother of two adult sons reminds us all to use the ingredients we love. For her that includes cultivating a beautiful garden, rereading her beloved husband's wartime letters, feeding and caring for any cat that comes her way. And, of course, enjoying her family and friends.

Sophie says we shouldn't skimp on the "ingredients" that matter to us, at Christmas or any other time. Like her, we should surround ourselves with family members and friends and share stories and laughter with them. We should cherish our memories and treat all creatures with kindness. We—

Hearing someone approach, Emma looked up to discover Oliver Hamilton leaning against the partition in the narrow aisle that separated her cubicle from Phoebe's. At first, she was too shocked to respond.

"Hi," she managed, before her throat went completely dry.

"Hi, yourself. I don't suppose you've had a chance to check out new apartments yet?"

"Ah—no, not yet." As it was, Emma had barely made it to work on time. After she'd dropped Boots off at a veterinarian Oliver had recommended, she'd been hard pressed to get to the office by nine.

"Well…" Oliver wore a cocky grin. "I have good news. There's a vacant apartment on Cherry Street. The tenant got married and he's already moved out. It'll be available right away."

This was a lovely area of Puyallup and within walking distance of the office. The cherry trees that lined the boulevard gave the street its name; they bloomed each spring in a profusion of pink blossoms. Apartments there were coveted and hard to come by. "Cherry Street?"

He nodded. "If you want, I can pick you up at lunchtime and you can take a look."

"How much?" Not only were those apartments at a premium, but more than likely they'd be way out of her price range.

"Same as you're paying now," Oliver said, seeming pleased with himself.

This sounded too good to be true, and things that

sounded too good to be true generally were. But just maybe... "What about the first and last month's rent?"

Oliver shrugged as if this were a minor consideration. "A friend of mine owns the complex, and he said if your credit rating's okay, he'd be willing to waive that."

"Wow." This came from Phoebe.

"Boots won't be a problem?"

"Not at all. But Jason will want a $150 deposit in case of damage."

Only a hundred and fifty dollars—this was unbelievable. She'd expected it to be much more than that. She'd heard of apartments that asked for five-hundred-dollar deposits when the tenant owned a pet. Emma wondered for a moment whether Oliver had gotten his facts straight. No, wait. There had to be *something* he wasn't telling her. "No strings attached?" she asked with a skeptical look.

Oliver raised both hands. "None."

Emma felt as if she'd won the lottery. "How come?" She didn't want to examine this gift too closely, but she was still terrified there might be a catch.

Oliver ignored her question.

"Oliver?" she persisted.

"Oh, all right. Jason owes me a favor. I flew him and his wife to San Francisco—and I promised I'd do it again."

"Oh..."

"I put a hold on it for you, but Jason said he can't

keep the apartment off the market any longer than one o'clock this afternoon."

"I'll take it." Emma didn't want to risk losing this opportunity. She smiled at Oliver.

"Sight unseen?" he asked.

"Maybe you'd better go see the place," Phoebe cautioned. "In fact, you should go now."

Emma nodded; her friend was right. Still, she hesitated. Walt would be looking for that article and all she had was an unfinished rough draft. She was going to need several hours to work on it and to shape it into the piece she wanted it to be.

"We'll take thirty, forty minutes, tops," Oliver said. "We can run over, do a quick tour and you can make up your mind then."

"I'll cover for you," Phoebe promised.

"But Walt—"

"Don't worry. If Walt asks where you are, I'll explain the situation to him. He'll understand."

"Won't he be upset if he finds me skipping out in the middle of the morning?"

Phoebe's eyes brightened and she shook her head. "Let me take care of that."

"Okay, I will." Emma reached for her coat and purse. Although she'd never admit it—at least not to Oliver— she was delighted to see him again. She wasn't quite sure why he was being so helpful, but then she remembered his comments about ordinary men and real romance as opposed to romantic gestures. A real hero brought you and your dog a meal; he didn't worry about providing the perfect setting. He made you laugh instead of presenting you with poetic words. He found you an apartment when you needed one....

When they approached his truck, he opened the passenger door for her. Oscar barked a welcome and seemed to be looking for Boots.

Emma raised her eyebrows. "You're really taking this romantic-hero stuff to heart."

"Absolutely," he said, grinning. "If a pizza and a bag of dog food results in a kiss, I can only dream about what finding you an apartment will do."

"Don't get your hopes up." It figured—he wanted something. What all men wanted, apparently. And after she'd had all these lovely thoughts about him, too.

He chuckled. "Want to go flying with me later?"

She stared at him. "No way!"

"You're getting to be a pro at this. There was hardly a peep out of you the entire flight home."

"I was busy praying."

Oliver shook his head. "Come on. We'll have a good time."

Oliver Hamilton was *not* getting her back in the air, especially for the so-called fun of it. To her, flying simply wasn't entertainment. "No. N-O," she said, spelling it out.

"That's a pity."

Not to her. It was life preservation.

The apartment, a ground-level corner unit, was small but well-designed. The single-story complex was fairly new but beautifully maintained, and each unit had its own front door. The surrounding doors were all decorated with wreaths and pine swags and lights. Inside, Emma was thrilled to see brand-new appliances, including a dishwasher. Sliding glass doors off the kitchen led to a fenced area in the back that would be perfect for Boots. There was even space for a container garden, which pleased Emma. Her mother had always had a garden. Emma had hated weeding and watering it as a girl. She'd never believed she'd miss it, but she did.

Oscar walked around, cocking his head as if confused. He looked up at Oliver, who ignored his canine friend.

"Well, what do you think?" Oliver asked, leaning against the kitchen counter in a nonchalant pose.

"It's wonderful!"

He grinned knowingly. "I thought you'd like it."

"I do. Thank you, Oliver, thank you so much." Impulsively she kissed his cheek.

Not one to let an opportunity slip away, Oliver grabbed her around the waist and brought her into his arms. "You can thank me properly, you know."

She was tempted to do just that when there was a sudden knock at the open door and Oliver's friend Jason let himself in. Emma had met Jason when Oliver took her to the owner's unit to collect the key.

"Have you made a decision?" he asked.

Embarrassed, Emma quickly disentangled herself from Oliver's embrace. "I'll take it. Just show me where to sign."

Jason had the paperwork with him, and after reading the lease agreement, she quickly signed her name at the bottom and wrote him a check.

Jason handed her the keys, assured her she could move in anytime, and left.

"You *are* my hero," Emma said once the other man had gone.

"I know," Oliver murmured in modest tones.

She was half-tempted to kiss him again, but changed her mind. "I suppose I should get back to the office," Emma said reluctantly.

"Okay, but I need to stop at my place first."

She couldn't quibble, since he'd driven her here and, more, had arranged for her new home.

He walked out, turned right and went down two doors.

Emma followed. She didn't understand, until he inserted the key into the lock, that this was his place— two doors down from hers.

"You live here?" she asked. *"Here?"*

He nodded, opening the front door. It had the biggest Christmas wreath of all, and the front window sparkled with tiny white lights.

"It didn't occur to you to maybe mention this before now?" She'd asked him earlier if there were any strings attached and he'd promised her there weren't. She should've known.

Her tone must have conveyed the fact that she wasn't happy with this unexpected turn of events. She remained standing in the doorway, resisting the impulse to look inside, although she did catch sight of a gaily decorated Christmas tree.

"What's the matter? Don't you want me for a neighbor?"

She found it hard enough to keep him out of her thoughts as it was. Living two doors down from him would make it impossible. "As a matter of fact, no. Why didn't you tell me?"

"Didn't enter my mind. You should be grateful I found you an apartment."

"Which I wouldn't have needed if you hadn't opened your big mouth," she said, even though that was only partially true.

"So it's *my* fault?" he cried out at the unfairness of her accusation.

"Yes, yours."

Oliver glared at her. "Fine."

She crossed her arms and glared right back at him.

Jason stepped up to his vehicle on the other side of the street and raised his hand. "Merry Christmas," he shouted.

"Right," Oliver muttered back. "And goodwill to all mankind."

Chapter Twelve

Late that afternoon, Oliver joined Walt Berwald at the tavern down the street from the newspaper office. Walt sat at the bar with his shoulders hunched forward, looking as if he'd just received some piece of devastating news. His demeanor was at odds with the cheerful rendition of "Deck the Halls" playing on the tavern's crackling sound system.

Oliver shared Walt's sentiment. He had no idea what he'd done that was so terrible. There was no mistaking Emma's irritation with him, although he'd expected her to be overjoyed that he'd found her an apartment. Oh, no, that would've been far too rational. He should've remembered that there was nothing rational about most women. His mother and one of his three sisters were the exception that proved the rule.

What *really* got to him was that he hadn't purposely hidden the fact that he lived in the same complex. It just hadn't seemed important, and he didn't understand why it mattered. The ride back to the newspaper office had been silent and uncomfortable. Emma hadn't been able to get out of the truck fast enough.

Walt slid his gaze to Oliver when he claimed the stool next to him, nodding morosely. The bartender looked over and Oliver motioned toward the beer in Walt's hand. "I'll take one of those. And get another for my friend."

"Thanks," Walt said.

"My pleasure."

Neither spoke again until the beers arrived.

"What's got you so down in the dumps?" Walt asked.

"I don't want to talk about it. What about you?"

Walt shrugged. "Same."

Women were beyond Oliver's comprehension. He had sisters and knew from experience that Emma was probably talking to Phoebe right now, describing every aspect of his many faults. Things had begun to look promising, too. He'd been attracted to Emma from the start and he'd been certain she felt the same way. After this morning, he was no longer sure.

"How's it going with that reporter of mine?" Walt asked, reaching for his cold beer.

"Not bad." Oliver didn't elaborate.

"Emma's got real potential as a journalist, you know."

Oliver believed that, even if he hadn't read anything she'd written. This was her big shot and despite their differences, he wished her well. "She's got a few hang-ups." He didn't mean to say that aloud and was surprised to hear his own voice.

"All women do," Walt said, as if he were an authority on the subject.

"You know this from your vast research, do you?"

Walt laughed and shook his head. "Hey, when it comes to women and relationships, I'm a disaster waiting to happen."

Oliver gave him a second look. Walt had always seemed secure and confident. He knew his stuff, as befitted a man who was the third generation of his family in the newspaper business. Now, however, Walt seemed to feel downright miserable.

Oliver did, too. And it was all because of Emma. It was times like these when he felt like sitting in the dark, listening to Harry Connick Jr., bourbon in hand. Either that, or go and visit his mother. Knowing her, she'd pry out of him what was wrong, give him some common-sense advice and then feed him a huge dinner, as if her cabbage rolls would solve all his problems.

Oliver loved her and her stuffed cabbage, but even his mother wouldn't be able to help him understand Emma Collins.

After a second beer, Oliver slid off the stool and placed a twenty-dollar bill on the bar. "See you around," he mumbled at Walt.

Neither one of them had been very talkative.

"Yeah, sure," Walt responded in the same weary tone. "Thanks for the beer. I'll buy next time."

Oliver nodded, and got up to head back to his truck, where Oscar was waiting impatiently inside the cab.

"You got plans for the evening?" Walt asked unexpectedly.

"Not necessarily." It was either his mother's cabbage rolls or listening to Harry. "What have you got in mind?"

"You are a friend indeed," Emma said as she came out of the bedroom dragging a cardboard box filled with books. She and Phoebe had left work early, once Emma had finished the article, skipping lunch to do it. They'd collected boxes on the way to Emma's place and spent the past two hours packing. Fortunately, Boots was still at the vet's and therefore not underfoot.

Phoebe didn't seem to be listening. "You'd help me move, too, if our circumstances were reversed."

"Something on your mind?" Emma asked. Phoebe hadn't been her usual self since she'd returned from lunch.

Sighing, her friend straightened. "I met Walt for lunch. We left separately and went five miles out of our way in order not to be seen. It's ridiculous! I love Walt, but I told him I was through sneaking around."

Emma didn't blame her.

"I won't do it again." Phoebe sounded firm about her decision. "If he wants to wait until after Christmas, then fine, we'll wait. But I won't see Walt again until he's willing to be open and honest about our relationship."

"You're right." Emma admired her friend's courage and conviction. "What did Walt say?"

Phoebe's shoulders slumped. "He thinks I'm overreacting."

"You aren't!"

"I know. I've been feeling dreadful all afternoon, and when I left, I didn't let him know I was going to help you move. Instead, I let him assume—" a slow smile formed "—that I had…other plans."

"Other plans? Like being with another man?"

Phoebe gave a careless shrug. "Never mind. It'll do him good to wonder where I am."

"I really do appreciate the help," Emma said earnestly as they both walked out to the parking lot with loaded boxes.

"I know. You'd do the same for me," Phoebe said again. "When's the next fruitcake interview?" she asked, although Emma wasn't sure why she'd changed the subject.

"Next week—Tuesday, I think."

Emma didn't welcome the reminder that Oliver was scheduled to fly her into Friday Harbor. She didn't want to think about him—or the fact that she'd soon be in the air again.

"Are you ready to take these over to the new place?" Emma asked in an effort to derail her thoughts. She was eager to show off her apartment. An apartment she wouldn't have if it wasn't for Oliver, her conscience pointed out.

"Sure," Phoebe said. "Let's go." But her enthusiasm seemed forced.

Emma hesitated. "Do you want to talk some more?" This disagreement with Walt had really depressed her friend.

"Not especially," Phoebe murmured, revealing a little more life. "Let's go," she said again.

It was nearly seven and completely dark out. The first thing Emma noticed when she pulled up in front of the complex on Cherry Street was that Oliver's apartment lights were off; only his Christmas lights flashed a festive message. He was probably out on some hot date, she thought glumly. Despite her best efforts, her spirits sank. It shouldn't matter where he was or with whom—and yet, it did.

She stood by her car, fumbling for the door key, as Phoebe's SUV drove up behind her. Carrying a couple of plants she'd transported on the front seat, she joined Emma. "What's wrong, Em?"

Emma looked at her blankly.

"You just growled."

"I did? I was thinking what a bother moving is," she said, inventing an explanation that was also the truth.

"I'll work as long as you want tonight."

Emma nodded her thanks. She wanted out of the old place as quickly as possible. Because she didn't own much, it hadn't taken long to pack. Books, bedding and towels, clothes, kitchen stuff. Her TV and CD player. Odds and ends. Only a few pieces of furniture remained.

They made two trips, with both her car and Phoebe's loaded, rooftop and all. Back at the old apartment, they surveyed the things that still had to be moved.

"We should take the bed over tonight," Phoebe suggested, hands on her hips as she stood in the almost-empty bedroom. "That way you'll be able to sleep at the new place."

The idea appealed to Emma. "Are you sure you're up to this?"

Phoebe nodded.

Oliver's lights were on when they arrived with the bed and nightstand. So he was home. Not that she cared.

The mattress was the most difficult to handle. With Phoebe on one end and Emma on the other, they wrestled it out of the SUV.

"I'm starved," Emma said as she paused to take a breath. She hadn't eaten lunch; her only sustenance had come from a vending-machine pack of peanuts. "When we finish, I'm treating you to dinner. What time is it, anyway?"

Phoebe didn't answer. When Emma looked around the protruding mattress, she saw why.

Oliver's apartment door was open, and Walt Berwald and Oliver stood just outside the doorway, watching them struggle.

Phoebe dropped her end of the mattress. "Walt," she said in a choked voice.

"Oh, could you use some help?" Oliver asked coolly as he stepped forward.

"Phoebe?" Walt sounded nervous.

Even in the dark, Emma swore her friend's cheeks blossomed brighter than the cherry trees across the street ever would. She looked directly at Walt and then—reluctantly—at Oliver. She realized she owed him an apology. Her ungracious and ungrateful behavior toward him had worried her all day, and she needed to make it right.

"I'll take that," he said, hurrying toward her end of the mattress.

"Thank you," she whispered, and moved aside so he could grab the mattress. "For everything."

Oliver nearly stumbled. He dropped his corner of the mattress. "What did you just say?"

"I, ah, was attempting to apologize."

"That's what I thought," he said. "It felt good to hear that. Would you mind saying it again?"

Emma considered refusing, since he just wanted to rub it in. Oh, well, she supposed he deserved to hear her apology twice. Not that she intended to use the word *sorry* even once. She cleared her throat. "I wanted to thank you for all your help," she said more loudly.

He seemed gratified. Nodding his head, he said, "You're welcome." He lifted his end of the mattress again and grappled with it for a moment until he noticed that Walt hadn't taken hold of the other side. He propped the mattress against the back of the vehicle.

Emma saw that Walt and Phoebe were staring at each other. He'd come to stand beside her, ignoring the mattress, Emma, everything.

"When you said you had 'other plans,' you let me think they were with someone else," Walt murmured, frowning.

"It was what you deserved to think."

"What's going on with those two?" Oliver whispered, moving closer to Emma.

"They had a disagreement."

"They're seeing each other?" This seemed news to him. "They're a couple?"

Emma nodded, watching her friend and their boss.

"I wasn't joking, Walt." Phoebe held her ground. She crossed her arms.

Walt exhaled and looked at Oliver. "Did I just hear you ask if Phoebe and I are a couple?"

"That's your business, man."

"No," Walt countered, "I want you to know. I love Phoebe and she loves me." He turned to face her. "There, does that satisfy you?"

Phoebe grinned. "It's a start."

With that, Walt opened his arms and Phoebe walked into his embrace. A second later, they had their arms around each other and were locked in a passionate kiss.

"Hey, about this mattress?" Oliver whispered to Emma.

"Shh," she whispered back. This was a scene normally reserved for the movies; all it lacked was a soundtrack. Emma didn't think she'd seen anything more romantic in her life. "Isn't this just so…so perfect?"

"What?" Oliver demanded, leaning against the mattress.

She scowled up at him, then understood that he really didn't get it.

"Hey, anyone interested in Chinese?" Oliver asked.

Chapter Thirteen

Fruitcake—love it or hate it—is about the ritual of a family recipe. The longer the ritual is repeated, the more it becomes part of what is "done" at the holidays. With that in mind, there are only two fruitcakes that matter to me, and I eat them over the Christmas holidays every year. One is the recipe of my Grandma Prendergast, which my dad now makes at Christmas. It never turns out exactly the same as Grandma's did, but it tastes good because it reminds me of her at the best time of year—when I'm with family. I eat it spread with butter, just the way Grandma served it. The other belongs to my mother-in-law, who labors over her version for weeks on end. In addition to the obvious fact that everyone should eat what their mother-in-law serves, hers are actually moist.

—Kevin Prendergast, executive chef,
New York Marriott Marquis

Bright and early the next Tuesday morning, Oliver pounded on Emma's apartment door. When she didn't immediately answer, he peered inside her front window. He saw her run into the living room and stare back. Smiling, he raised a small white bag and a large cup of coffee.

If she needed any inducement to unlock her door, that was it. She was dying for a latte.

"You sweetheart," she said, letting him into her apartment. Boots was at her feet, the ready protector. She'd been pronounced healthy and was scheduled to be spayed right after Christmas.

Oliver smiled and handed her the take-out latte. "I have another surprise for you."

"Another surprise?"

"More of a Christmas surprise."

"All right." Emma didn't trust that gleam in his eyes, and adding Christmas wasn't a bonus. "Tell me."

"I got us a float plane for the trip to Friday Harbor." He smiled again, as if this was something that should excite her.

"A float plane," she repeated slowly. It'd been difficult enough to deal with an aircraft that landed on the ground. "As in a plane that lands on *water*?"

"Yup." He positively glowed with the news. "You'll love it."

The one small sip of latte she'd taken curdled in her stomach. "I don't think so."

"Sure you do. We're flying out of Lake Union. A friend of mine is letting me use his plane and—"

She felt the sudden urge to sit down, but didn't.

"Now, listen," Oliver said, steering her into the kitchen and placing the white sack on the counter. It contained a large cranberry muffin, but Emma couldn't eat, nauseated as she was by the thought of flying—and worse, landing—in a float plane. "Everything'll be fine," he said soothingly. "Just one thing."

"What?"

"You should wear sensible shoes because those docks can get slippery."

"In other words, there's a chance I could fall in the water?"

"It's not likely, but it's been known to happen, so be extra-cautious when you're climbing into the plane, okay?"

"Is this a trick?"

"Of course not." He marched out of the kitchen, and Emma followed. Boots hung behind, gazing eagerly at the white sack.

"You can bring Boots," Oliver said before she could even ask.

Emma threw on her coat, scooped up Boots and grabbed her briefcase for this last interview, which would be in the San Juan Islands. Emma had spoken to Peggy Lucas by phone, and she sounded like a woman in her thirties, much younger than the other finalists. Emma was looking forward to chatting with her about her No-Bake Fruitcake recipe.

Oliver opened the truck door for her and Boots, and Emma thanked him politely.

"It's all part of being a romantic hero," he reminded her with what she thought was a smirk.

Both dogs were in the truck, and the cab was crowded. "If I slip off the dock, I'm going to blame you," she said as she fastened the seat belt around her and Boots. Before they left, Emma had changed her shoes twice. In the end, she'd decided on tennis shoes with rubber soles, although they didn't do much for her dark-gray pantsuit.

"Why would you blame me?" Oliver asked as they merged into the traffic on Interstate 5.

She tapped her finger against her temple. "You're the one who put the idea in my head." He'd added a brand-new element to her fears, as if she needed more to worry about.

"You can swim, right?"

"Yes." Actually, Emma was a capable swimmer. "Why do you ask?"

"Well, it's only fair to let you know that if you go in the water you're on your own."

She rolled her eyes. "My hero."

"My hero, nothing. The water this time of year is damn cold."

Emma performed some contortions to look at the soles of her shoes once more, checking the treads.

"Don't worry, you'll be fine." His eyes sparkled with delight; Oliver Hamilton was enjoying himself far too much.

Lake Union was situated between Puget Sound and Lake Washington, with canals that connected both. One of Emma's favorite movies was *Sleepless in Seattle,* and she remembered that the houseboat the Tom Hanks character and his son had lived in was situated on Lake Union. She knew these houseboats were *very* expensive, and as Oliver drove closer, Emma saw a number of them in the distance. Cheerful, flashing Christmas lights strung around the decks were reflected on the still surface of the lake. One houseboat had Santa poised on the roof with a sleigh and eight reindeer. Everyone who lived on the lake was apparently serious about observing the holiday spirit. Just like all her new neighbors....

As they continued on the road around the lake, the float planes came into view, and Emma immediately tensed. From her long-ago yoga classes, she knew the best cure for that was to draw in deep, even breaths. In to the count of eight, out to the—

"What's with you?" Oliver asked.

"I'm practicing my breathing exercises."

"I thought that was for when you're in labor."

"You've spent time in labor rooms, have you?"

"No, but my sister has, and she told me all about that breathing thing."

"I'm just trying to remain calm."

"Driving frightens you, too?"

Emma looked out the window. "Never mind."

Once they arrived at the dock where the float planes were tied up, it was immediately apparent that Oliver was well-known and well-liked. He introduced her to his friends and then led her out to the dock. Emma tested her footing with each step.

"You aren't going to fall from the middle of the dock," Oliver said scathingly. Boots and Oscar ran circles around them both, barking and playing.

"Can't be too careful."

He said something under his breath that she couldn't understand, but considering the irritation lining his mouth and eyes, that was probably for the best. Taking slow, careful steps, it took her five minutes to get to the end of the dock. Oliver got there maybe three minutes earlier, and he didn't conceal his impatience for one second of that time.

Stepping onto the pontoon, he opened the door to the cockpit. Then he lifted Oscar and placed the terrier in the back. Next he swooped Boots into his arms and set her inside, as well. Emma stood there frozen, afraid to inch forward.

"Will you put my briefcase and purse in, too?" she asked, pushing them toward Oliver.

Oliver did as she requested and then extended his arm, urging her forward. "You ready?" he asked. He was balancing one foot on the dock and the other on the pontoon.

She nodded anxiously. Her heart was beating so fast she could hear the echo in her ears. Putting all her faith in Oliver, she stretched her arm toward his and stepped off the deck. She made the transition from dock to plane easily and was astonished that she'd allowed his warnings to fill her with dread.

"I did it!" she said, feeling triumphant.

"Yes, you did." Oliver smiled. "I'm proud of you."

Emma crawled into the passenger seat, pulled the seat belt toward her and locked it into place. Both Oscar and Boots were in the back, next to her purse and briefcase.

A boat went past and the wake rocked the plane. Standing on the dock, Oliver untied the craft and pushed off. Not a second later, Emma heard a tremendous splash. She didn't immediately understand what had happened. Then it hit her.

Oliver had slipped and fallen into the lake.

Caught in the boat's wake, the plane drifted toward the middle of Lake Union.

Scrambling out of her seat belt, Emma was on her knees in the pilot's seat. "Oliver! Oliver! What should I do?"

In response, he started swimming out after her. She covered her mouth. With part of her she wanted to laugh, and with the other she was holding back tears.

Oliver reached the plane a moment later. He levered himself up onto the pontoon and glared at her. "Don't you *dare* say a word," he managed from between clenched teeth.

"But Oliver…"

He stood on the pontoon, water streaming off him, and grabbed the plane's wheel, steering the aircraft back toward the dock. A couple of pilots were waiting for him. Oliver tossed them the rope and they efficiently tied down the plane. One handed him a towel as he climbed onto the dock. There was a lot of good-natured teasing, but she noticed that Oliver didn't have a whole lot to say.

"It happens to all of us at one time or another," his friend consoled him.

Oliver threw the towel over his shoulders, shivering visibly.

His lips were blue.

Emma felt terrible.

"I've got an extra set of clothes," she heard one of the other pilots tell him as they led him away.

She stayed where she was, unwilling to risk climbing onto the dock again. Twenty minutes passed before Oliver reappeared. His mood didn't seem to have improved.

"You okay?" she asked tentatively.

"I feel like a damn fool."

"Oh, Oliver, you were wonderful."

Her comment didn't amuse him. "So you enjoyed that spectacle, did you?"

"Well, no, not really, but you swam after me. That was the most romantic thing you've done."

"It was?" He sounded a bit puzzled.

She nodded. "You truly are my hero."

"I knew *that*," he said confidently.

"Oh, for goodness' sake."

They taxied farther onto Lake Union with only a minimum of fuss and took off.

Unexpectedly, Emma enjoyed the flight. She wasn't nearly as afraid as she'd been in the Cessna Caravan. Thinking about it, she realized it was because of the pontoons—if the plane went down, they'd float. That might be false security, of course; if they did crash on the water the plane would probably disintegrate on impact, but she didn't let that destroy her illusions of safety.

While flying, Oliver acted as a tour guide, showing her various points of interest. The San Juan Islands, she learned, were a cluster of 743 rocky islands of different sizes, situated in the Strait of Juan de Fuca and Puget Sound. Only about sixty of the islands were populated, according to Oliver, who seemed to know the area quite well.

The largest of the islands, San Juan Island, was home to the bustling town of Friday Harbor. Emma remembered reading about the annual jazz festival in late summer. The island was also a popular site for whale watching. Emma hoped to join one of the expeditions next summer, since she'd never seen a whale in the wild. She didn't think she could count visiting Sea World.

"I have a confession," Oliver said, frowning. "I'm not as much of a hero as you seem to think."

"You are. You swam out and saved me."

"I hate to disillusion you, Emma, but I wasn't swimming after you. I was going for the plane. Do you know how much one of these is worth?"

"In other words, if I'd been in a canoe you would've let me drift off into the sunset?"

"Well…"

"Come on," she said, "be honest."

"I would've taken a hot shower and changed clothes and then gone looking for you in a speed-boat."

Okay, so maybe he was right. He wasn't as much of a hero as she'd assumed.

He sneezed violently.

"You're catching a cold. You should take care of yourself."

He dismissed her concern. "I'll live."

"You need hot soup and extra vitamin C and—"

He placed his hand on her arm. "And a whole lot of lovin'."

Boy, had she asked for that.

"I'm fine," he said with a smirk. "Go do your interview. I'll be waiting here when you're finished."

Emma had been looking forward to this interview ever since she'd spoken to Peggy on Monday afternoon. Her sudden reluctance to leave Oliver was hard to explain.

He climbed out, tied up the float plane and then helped her out. Clasping his hand, Emma leaped from the plane onto the dock, which rocked gently when she landed.

Oliver retrieved her purse and briefcase and handed them to her.

One of Peggy's neighbors was waiting to drive her to the Lucas home.

"I won't be gone long," she promised.

"The dogs and I will be fine. Now go." For the first time since he'd crashed into the water, Oliver grinned.

Emma couldn't stop herself. Still holding tightly to her purse and briefcase, she kissed Oliver. He slid his arms around her and kissed her back. Soon they were so involved in each other, it was a wonder they both didn't slip off the dock.

That was when Emma knew she'd fallen in love with Oliver Hamilton.

Chapter Fourteen

Those who don't like fruitcake have never had
a white fruitcake.

—Nathalie Dupree,
cookbook author and television personality

Peggy Lucas's matter-of-fact humor had Emma
laughing even before she was in the front door of the
fifties-style tract home in Friday Harbor. The neighbor, Sally, had dropped her off with a cheerful goodbye, after telling her repeatedly how proud everyone
was of Peggy, how delicious her fruitcake was, how
they were all convinced she'd win.

Peggy and her husband, Larry, had four small children. Children's toys littered the lawn surrounding a big-
ger-than-life blow-up snowman that was anchored to
the ground.

The oldest child, Rosalie, was in first grade and the
second daughter, Abby, was a year younger. Two lit-

tle boys, Trevor and Dylan, rushed onto the small front porch to greet her, hiding behind their mother's legs. Emma guessed the boys' ages to be around four and two. The two younger ones seemed to be best buddies, although they were constantly bickering.

"Please excuse the mess," Peggy said as she ushered Emma into the living room. A small Christmas tree stood in the corner, decorated with what appeared to be hand-crafted ornaments. It reminded Emma of the tree in the "Peanuts" cartoons, the Charlie Brown tree—a little skimpy and with a definite homemade quality. The children had made a chain of colored paper loops and strung popcorn and cranberries. A small array of badly wrapped gifts circled the base.

Peggy hurriedly removed clean laundry from the recliner and motioned for Emma to take what was clearly the best seat in the house.

Emma appeared to be the main attraction. All four children gathered around their mother and stared at the stranger in their living room. Rosalie was still dressed in her pajamas.

"She's home from school today because of a cold," Peggy explained. "Abby, too. This is cold and flu season. It's the last week of classes, and I hate to have them miss out, but I can't expose the entire class to their germs."

Emma nodded, sympathizing with the young mother.

"Go and play," Peggy instructed the kids, but they refused to budge. Emma wondered if they feared that the minute they left the room, she'd abscond with the Christmas presents.

Peggy sat down on the ottoman with her children gathered around her like a small herd of lambs.

"Tell me about your fruitcake recipe," Emma said when she'd retrieved pen and pad from her briefcase.

"There's not much to tell. I concocted it myself a little while ago, using several fruitcake recipes I found in one of my mother's old cookbooks. I also found a newspaper clipping that dated back to the 1960s, which must've been mailed to my mom by my grandmother. Everyone in the family loves fruitcake."

"So you grew up with fruitcake?"

Peggy smiled. "Mom bakes it every Christmas. It's a family tradition."

"So you do, too?"

Peggy smiled again. "With some significant differences. My recipe isn't a typical one, although I use all the same ingredients most everyone uses in fruitcake."

"I like Mama's fruitcake," Rosalie whispered, her face averted so she wouldn't have to look at Emma.

"Is it good?"

"*Real* good," Abby added without a hint of shyness. "It's the best, and my mama's going to win. That's what our daddy says."

"What made you submit the recipe to *Good Home-*

making magazine?" This wasn't a question she'd asked the other Washington State finalists, but Emma found she was curious about Peggy's reasons. Both Earleen Williams and Sophie McKay had perfected their recipes through the years. That didn't seem to be the case with Peggy.

The young mother blushed. "My husband encouraged me to enter, so I did. No one was more surprised than me when I found out I was a finalist." She lifted Dylan onto her lap and the little boy leaned his head against her shoulder and promptly placed his thumb in his mouth.

"Exactly how long have you been using this recipe?"

"How long?" Peggy repeated, and the question seemed to fluster her. Her hand went to her hair, as if she was afraid it needed attention. "Actually, the first one I baked was last December—a year ago."

"Wow. It must be good." If this relatively untried recipe was a finalist, it had to be impressive.

"Would you care to taste a slice?" Peggy asked. Setting Dylan aside despite his mumbled protests, she stood.

Emma imagined this young mother wasn't accustomed to sitting down for any length of time. A buzzer went off in the distance, signaling that the dryer had finished its cycle.

"Rosalie, take the sheets out of the dryer, would you?"

The oldest girl left the room, and the three remaining children all stared at Emma, the youngest with his thumb still firmly planted in his mouth.

Rosalie returned a minute later, her arms wrapped around a huge load of fresh laundry. "Where should I put them? The reporter lady is sitting in the chair." Apparently the recliner was the spot for sorting clean laundry.

"I can move," Emma volunteered, although she didn't know where. The one other piece of furniture was a sofa, and that appeared to be functioning as a sickbed for the two girls.

"Go and put them on my bed," Peggy shouted from the kitchen.

"Okay."

"Mama," Abby cried in sudden alarm. "Dylan has to go potty."

Emma hadn't noticed but, sure enough, the youngest boy was holding himself and crossing and uncrossing his legs.

"Where's his blankie?" Peggy asked calmly, coming in from the kitchen.

Peggy and the three children sprang into action, launching what was obviously a familiar and well-rehearsed routine. The two girls hurried out of the room and Trevor scrambled under the coffee table, crawling on all fours. Emma stood, fearing she was in the way.

Peggy grabbed Dylan and, holding the two-year-old at arm's length, carried him from the room. She disappeared into the hallway.

Never having witnessed anything like this, Emma followed and watched with interest as Peggy got her youngest son on the kiddie toilet. Dylan madly waved his arms, resembling a young bird about to take flight. Rosalie leaped into the room with a tattered yellow blanket.

"The duck?" Peggy asked. "Has anyone found the duck?"

Trevor was the hero of the hour. He slid into the tiny bathroom on his stocking feet, then thrust the plush duck at his brother.

As soon as Dylan had both his yellow blanket and his duck, he let out a tremendous sigh. His shoulders relaxed and a slow smile came over his face. Apparently he could now relax enough to concentrate on the job.

"Good boy," Peggy cheered and started to clap.

So did Dylan's three siblings, and because it seemed the thing to do, Emma joined in.

She didn't want to get sidetracked from the interview, but she couldn't help being curious about the minor production she'd just witnessed.

"Dylan's afraid of the potty chair," Abby explained after Emma asked. "The only way he can go is if he has his security blanket and his favorite duck."

"He has more than one?"

"He's got three—white and orange and yellow, but

he only wants the yellow one." Again it was Abby who explained. "It *has* to be that one."

Dylan smiled and his thumb came out of his mouth when he'd finished his task. Peggy pulled up his pants and led the youngster to the sink. Dylan pushed the step stool over, then by himself turned on the water and washed his hands. When he'd finished, he looked to his mother and siblings for another round of applause.

"Sorry for the interruption," Peggy said, lifting the little boy into her arms. The six of them returned to the living room, a ragtag parade.

"Let me get you that fruitcake," Peggy said. "I left it in the kitchen." Still holding Dylan, she retreated to the kitchen and came back with a small plate.

To Emma's surprise the fruitcake was a light brown. The candied fruits liberally spread throughout the slice made her think of a stained glass window. "It's different, all right," she told Peggy. "Very pretty."

"The recipe is no-bake."

Emma nodded. "I know, but what exactly does that mean? The ingredients aren't raw, are they?"

"Oh, no," Peggy said with a laugh. "I use graham cracker crumbs. Not surprisingly, graham crackers are a staple around here. That's the base that holds everything together."

"Oh." She took a small bite. This cake really was unusual, filled with nuts and the brilliantly colored candied fruit and something else—something she couldn't quite identify. Could it be marshmallows? Peggy had kindly agreed to share the recipe.

"I'm not the first person who's come up with this no-bake concept. It's surprising how well it works."

Emma's second bite confirmed her initial opinion. The flavors melded together in a delectable sweet taste. Sweet but not too sweet, Emma decided. At the start of this assignment, she hadn't liked fruitcake, and now she was a connoisseur. Every recipe she'd sampled was unique, although each was based on traditional ingredients. If the three finalists' recipes from Washington State were this innovative, she could only speculate what the other nine recipes must be like.

"With my family, a cake doesn't last more than a day or two," Peggy said, describing what had inspired the revised recipe. "My children don't understand the concept of leaving a cake for several weeks in order to refine the flavors. They want to eat it *now*. The traditional fruitcake my mother makes is excellent. Every year she starts baking right after Thanksgiving. She'll bathe the cake in rum for weeks and then on Christmas Eve we have this ceremony and Dad slices it for the first time. In theory that's great, but it doesn't work around here." She grinned. "And the quantity of booze isn't appropriate for kids, either."

"Trevor ate Mom's cake," Abby said, pointing to her little brother. "Last year. At Grandma's."

"Did not."

"Did, too. And then he fell asleep."

"Enough." Peggy raised her hand and the squabbling ceased. "That convinced me to try something different. So I came up with this idea."

"She doesn't always make it the same, either," Rosalie said proudly. "Sometimes Mom adds different stuff."

"Like what?"

"She put caramels in one time," Trevor said.

Rosalie made a face. "I didn't like that."

"I won't do it again, although I like the version with melted marshmallows."

That sounded interesting, too. "Will you tell me about yourself?" Emma asked, turning to Peggy.

"Me?" Peggy said, sounding surprised. "There's not much to say."

"You married young." That much was obvious.

Peggy nodded. "I met Larry shortly after I graduated from high school. I wasn't sure what I wanted to do with my life and was working at a Starbucks and taking a few college classes. Larry was working for a plumber and had just become certified by the Department of Labor and Industries. He's almost five years older than me, and we both wanted children. We'd been dating for a while and decided to marry." She smiled and looked slightly embarrassed. "We didn't start out wanting four children, but now that we've got them…" Peggy wrapped her arms around her brood. "We wouldn't change a thing."

"What will you do with the prize money if you win?" Emma asked. This was a new question.

"That's easy," Peggy said. "We'd use it as a down payment on a small farm. Larry has always been an animal person and we were hoping to buy an alpaca or two. Eventually I'd like to weave my own yarn. It's something I've always dreamed of doing."

"I hope you do win," Emma said, and meant it. She wished that for all three of the Washington State finalists.

"Would you like another piece?" Peggy asked.

"I would," Trevor volunteered.

"It's almost lunchtime," his mother told him.

The little boy's eyes brightened. "I can have fruit-cake for lunch?"

"We'll see."

"I want it *now*," Trevor said.

That comment could serve as part of the opening paragraph. Emma stayed long enough to have a cup of tea and another slice of fruitcake with Peggy Lucas. While Peggy worked in the kitchen, preparing peanutbutter-and-jelly sandwiches for her children and heating up soup, Emma sat at the kitchen table and they talked. Eventually the children lost interest in her and wandered back to their bedroom to play. All four, Emma noted, slept in the same room. It made for tight quarters but no one seemed to mind.

By the time Sally, Peggy's neighbor, returned her to

the waterfront, ideas for the article were tumbling over each other in Emma's mind.

Oliver stood on the dock next to the plane, waiting. Whatever business had brought him to Friday Harbor seemed to have been completed. Oscar and Boots wandered up and down the pier, sniffing around curiously, but as soon as they saw Emma, both dogs leaped up repeatedly and barked for joy.

"How'd it go?" Oliver asked, walking toward her in his borrowed leather jacket. It was a little too small and his wrists stuck out, looking oddly vulnerable.

Her heart jumped when she saw him, leaping about in a way that reminded her of the dogs' exuberant display.

"Good," she said and then amended, "Very good."

"You liked the fruitcake?"

"Loved it." She opened her purse and brought out a small slice wrapped in plastic. "Peggy insisted I bring this for you."

A cocky grin slid effortlessly into place. "So you mentioned me?"

Emma had, in an offhand manner, during their conversation in the kitchen. Something in her tone must have indicated that Oliver was more to her than a means of transportation, because Peggy picked up on it right away. Despite Emma's protests that it wasn't necessary, Peggy had given her a slice of fruitcake for Oliver, too.

When she didn't immediately respond, he added, "I'll bet you told her you're crazy about me."

Emma had no intention of pandering to his ego. "I didn't say anything of the kind," she told him briskly. "Are you ready to leave?"

Oliver laughed. "You're that eager to fly again?"

"Not really. I just want to get it over with." That was true enough. More importantly, she wanted to sit at her computer and organize her thoughts while they were fresh in her mind.

"One of these days you'll admit you can't live without me." He stepped onto the pontoon and opened the plane's door.

"I just might," she agreed.

Her words appeared to shock him because Oliver nearly slipped. He grabbed hold of the door; otherwise he would've fallen into the icy water a second time.

"*What* did you just say?" he demanded gruffly.

"Never mind," she said, highly amused. "It was a joke."

"Very funny."

As a matter of fact, Emma thought so, too. Even if there was more truth in that remark than she wanted him to know.

Chapter Fifteen

The first time I had fruitcake was as an adult at a coffee shop in Paris. The amount of sherry is simply overwhelming and the cake is too heavy and sweet for my taste. And with so many fruits, there is no specific taste. For my family, the apple-cranberry tart is our traditional holiday cake.

—Jasmine Bojic, executive pastry chef,
Tavern on the Green, New York City

Emma sat at her computer, which she'd set up on the kitchen table, trying to work on her article. When Oliver had finally landed at Lake Union again and they'd started back to Puyallup, it was rush hour. The Seattle traffic inched along Interstate 5; what normally would have been an easy half-hour drive took almost ninety minutes. Emma's nerves were frayed and she didn't even attempt to go to the office.

Oliver had dropped her and Boots off at the apartment. "Would you like to come in and have a hot drink?" she'd asked. It was the first time she'd made such an offer and she'd expected him to accept her invitation instantly.

Oliver hesitated. "Some other time."

His rejection took her by surprise. Not knowing how to respond, she mumbled her thanks for the ride and climbed out of the truck, retrieving Boots and her briefcase. She stood on the sidewalk and watched him drive away. He obviously wasn't going home.

Oliver was out of sight within seconds. Emma had wanted to demand that he tell her where he was going, but she couldn't. It was none of her business. Besides, she reminded herself, she had a dozen things to do, all of which were more important than frittering away time with an unresponsive and ungrateful man. "I have an article to write," she mumbled to no one in particular.

But even now, an hour after he'd left, Emma's mind continually wandered back to Oliver. Boots seemed unsettled, too. Her dog ran back and forth from the kitchen to the front window, hopping onto the chair and peering out at the street. Boots obviously missed her two companions.

Emma shared the feeling. She didn't *want* to care about Oliver, but she did. This was too similar to the way her mother had behaved toward her husband, which Emma had hated. Bret had acted as if Pamela should be grateful for whatever crumbs of his life he offered them.

Emma forced herself to think about the interview with Peggy Lucas. She'd enjoyed meeting Peggy and her children, and...

Oliver was up to something. Emma knew it—there, she'd done it again. No matter how hard she tried, her mind was filled with thoughts of Oliver.

She got up and walked over to the window, petting Boots, who'd jumped into the chair to stand guard. This late in the afternoon, there was little activity outside. The streetlights had come on, casting a warm glow that illuminated the Christmas bells that hung from each lamp post.

Emma drew her sweater more tightly around her. She refused to think about Oliver anymore. No—not for another second. She sat down at the kitchen table again with a cup of tea and read over the opening paragraph she'd drafted. With her interview notes propped next to the monitor, she resumed writing.

Lessons From Fruitcake: Peggy Lucas

Peggy Lucas is the third Washington State resident to place in *Good Homemaking* magazine's national fruitcake contest. Her motto—inspired by her children—is EAT IT NOW. The young wife and mother, who lives in Friday Harbor, married her plumber husband as a teenager, and they have four children ranging in age from two to six.

It was for her children that Peggy created the recipe for this no-bake Christmas fruitcake. Like all kids, her children lacked the patience to wait months for a traditional fruitcake. As four-year-old Trevor said, "I want it now."

His three siblings agreed with him, and Peggy devised this unusual recipe, which can be made overnight and eaten immediately.

As with the two previous finalists, there are lessons to be learned from Peggy's fruitcake. Earleen Williams was determined to bake the perfect fruitcake, a masterpiece, and while it took her many years and three marriages, she discovered that *she* was the masterpiece.

Sophie McKay bakes her fruitcake using unexpected ingredients, including maraschino cherries and semisweet chocolate chips, because those were the ingredients her late husband enjoyed. She blends pineapple and coconut with chocolate liqueur, and her recipe is a compromise between the traditional way of doing something and individual preferences. Her lesson: Use the ingredients you like. Do what you love.

Last, there is Peggy Lucas with her four young children, eager to partake of anything Christmas. She couldn't bear to make them wait even a day for their special cake. Her fruitcake is meant to be enjoyed right away. According to Peggy, life's like that. Enjoy it now.

Three finalists, three valuable lessons that—

Emma sighed and saved her draft, then shut down her computer. She couldn't concentrate on fruitcake anymore, or metaphors for life. Her mind wasn't on Peggy but on Oliver.

In order to distract herself from memories of the man, she phoned Phoebe.

"Hello, Emma," Phoebe said, picking up after five rings, just before the answering machine came on.

"What took you so long to get to the phone?" Emma wanted to know.

"Ah…"

Emma could almost hear her friend blush and suddenly understood. "You're not alone, are you?"

Again the hesitation. "Not at the moment."

"Is it, by chance, anyone I know?"

"Could be."

Her friend's face would be beet-red by now. "Is it…drumroll, please…Walt?"

"Ah…"

"Say no more," Emma murmured. "Call me when you're free."

"Okay. Bye."

"Bye." Emma replaced the telephone receiver, more depressed than before. Everyone she met was in love. Okay, maybe not everyone; it just felt that way. Ever since the night Phoebe had helped Emma move, she and Walt were practically never apart. They hadn't made a big announcement, but everyone at the office knew. Emma didn't understand why Walt had been so concerned. Their romance had barely been a blip on the office gossip monitor. They seemed to suit each other; Phoebe's sense of adventure balanced Walt's caution. Their relationship struck her as natural and healthy, now that it was out in the open.

Emma gave another deep sigh. What did *she* know about healthy relationships, anyway? With her parents as an example, she was destined to mess up. Falling for Oliver Hamilton was a prime example of that.

Emma covered her face with her hands, hating this sense of despair.

The doorbell chimed and her heart kicked into overdrive. It had to be Oliver! She hoped it was him. No, she didn't. Yes, she *did*.

If ever Emma understood her mother's feelings about her father, it was now. She wanted to slam the door in Oliver's face and yet, at the same time, she wanted to hug and kiss him.

The doorbell chimed again.

"Who is it?" she asked, stalling for time.

"Look through your peephole."

It was Oliver's voice. "Uh, is there something you want?" she asked. Should she let him in or not?

"You didn't check the peephole, did you?"

She did, then gasped at what she saw. Oliver stood there with the largest, most beautiful Christmas tree she'd ever seen. It was the kind of tree the White House put up every year. Or Rockefeller Center. Definitely not as big, but about as perfect as a tree could get.

"Are you going to let me in?"

She unlatched the lock and swung open the door.

Boots and Oscar raced toward each other as if it'd been years since their last meeting. Emma had wondered if they'd ever get beyond the stage of sniffing each other's butts. Although she supposed that was like saying "Hello" or "What's new?" in the dog world.

"Well," Oliver said proudly, clutching the tree by its trunk. "What do you think?"

Emma stared. "It's gorgeous. Absolutely gorgeous." She tried to figure out where he planned to put it. In his dining room, perhaps? She recalled catching a glimpse of one in his living room last week, glittering with decorations.

He smiled as he thrust the tree at her. "Merry Christmas."

She backed away a step. "Merry Christmas to you, too."

He cocked his head to one side. "Where do you want it?"

Emma leaned closer in order to hear him better. "*Want* it? This tree is for *me?*"

He nodded. "Yes. Isn't it obvious?"

Emma took another step backward.

He blinked, as if he'd been expecting her to throw her arms around him in gratitude. "You don't like it?"

"Of course I like it. That's the most beautiful Christmas tree I've ever seen."

"It's yours."

Emma froze. He'd been serious about giving her the tree. Her—a woman who didn't have a stand or ornaments or anything else one needed for a Christmas tree.

"It's kind of…big, don't you think?" she asked.

"I might need to take a bit more off the bottom, but no, it's not too big. I thought you could do with a bit of Christmas cheer, and I decided to make a contribution."

"But…"

"You'll thank me later."

Emma wasn't sure about that. Not sure at all.

Chapter Sixteen

"I've never seen anything so big in my life," Emma complained to Phoebe. "He didn't even *ask* me if I wanted a Christmas tree." Thanks to her unenthusiastic response, Oliver hadn't spoken to her in two days. Now Emma was miserable and needed to talk with her friend.

Phoebe frowned. "But don't you think bringing you a Christmas tree was very romantic of Oliver?"

Emma stopped her pacing, deep in The Dungeon, as she considered this. "Oh, my goodness." That hadn't even occurred to her. She pressed her hand to her forehead, then flopped down in her chair. "That's it." She should've realized earlier what had prompted him to buy her a tree. "Oliver thought he was being romantic." They'd had this ongoing conversation about romantic heroes and she'd failed to recognize what he was doing. The tree was his way of being romantic according to his theory of "show, not tell" romance. Action rather than words.

"Yes! Oliver was being romantic," Phoebe insisted. "You've really fallen for him, haven't you?" She smiled—a smile that could only be described as smug.

"I think he's arrogant and dogmatic, opinionated and—"

"Yeah, yeah." Phoebe's smile grew even wider. "I thought so." She returned to work as if there was nothing left to argue about.

Emma felt she couldn't leave her friend with that impression. Phoebe might say something to Walt, and Oliver and Walt were pals. She wasn't ready to acknowledge her feelings for Oliver, wasn't even sure those feelings would last long enough to be worth acknowledging.

"I think Oliver's a good pilot," she said, carefully weighing her words. "We've each made an effort to make the best of an uncomfortable situation."

Phoebe ignored her.

"You're right...." Emma admitted reluctantly, walking over to her friend's desk. She folded her arms and spoke casually. "There *was* a slight attraction in the beginning. We even joked about it." Well...Oliver had joked.

Phoebe turned and looked up at Emma. "Did he or did he not kiss you?"

"He...ah, okay, yes, there were a couple of times when I...that happened. So technically, yes, he did kiss me." This was all she was willing to say on the subject.

"So there was *more* than the one time?" Phoebe probed.

"There might have been." Emma wanted her friend to stop studying her with that appraising light in her eyes. "It wasn't a big deal."

"But you said Oliver's your romantic hero."

"No. I said it looked like Oliver was just proving a point." She wished he wouldn't try so hard, but she didn't know how to make him stop. The entire conversation about romantic heroes had come about by chance. But now he seemed to be going out of his way to prove that he was every bit as romantic as Humphrey Bogart or Cary Grant.

Emma sat at her desk, hardly able to concentrate. She'd be leaving the office in a few minutes to drum up advertisements for the newspaper. During the fruitcake interviews, Walt had excused her from that responsibility. Apparently his arrangement with Oliver had sparked an idea, and Walt was now willing to trade newspaper space for goods and services. Rumor had it that the Subway Express down the street would be catering the company Christmas lunch. Talk around the water cooler was that Walt had worked out some sort of deal with the owner—three weekly ads in exchange for thirty turkey sandwiches, pickles and coleslaw on the side. Thankfully, he hadn't been negotiating with the Mexican restaurant/sushi bar. Cross-cultural restaurants weren't so rare in small towns, but this was a combination Emma found a little bizarre.

"How are things going with you and Walt?" Emma asked, deciding it was her turn to ask personal questions.

Phoebe glowed. "Fabulous."

"Define fabulous."

"He asked me to have Christmas dinner with his family."

This was big, and Emma released a low whistle.

"We're having two dinners that day," Phoebe went on to explain. "First with my mom and dad, and then later with his."

"I hope you like turkey."

"I do," Phoebe assured her. "But my mom's serving prime rib and I don't know about his mother. What are you doing for Christmas?"

Christmas fell on a Sunday this year, and Emma wouldn't be doing anything special. She'd probably do what she had the year before—attend a movie and have buttered popcorn for dinner. It would be a day like any other.

"Emma?"

"I have plans." She hated to lie, so she remained vague. If she mentioned going to a movie, Phoebe would feel sorry for her and then find a way to include her. Emma didn't want to intrude on Phoebe and her family, or on Walt and his.

"What sort of plans?" Phoebe pressed.

Emma didn't want to be rude or arouse her suspicions, so she played it coy. "Private plans," she said, dropping her voice until it was almost a purr.

This was a mistake because Phoebe's curiosity was certainly piqued now. "They involve Oliver, don't they?"

"They could." Emma reached for her coat and purse, anxious to leave.

"You'll tell me later?"

Emma sighed deeply. "Yes, but only if you torture it out of me."

"That could be arranged," a gruff male voice said from behind her.

Both Phoebe and Emma gasped as Walt stepped between their desks. "I should come downstairs more often to see how the two of you spend your time." He frowned at Emma and handed her a sheet of paper printed with a list of businesses. The highlighted ones were the companies he wanted her to approach. Oh joy, The Taco Stand and California Rock & Roll were on the list, the combination ethnic restaurant so recently in her thoughts.

Emma stared at the paper and squelched a groan. She did not consider ad sales her forte.

Half an hour later, Emma was sitting with Mr. Garcia of The Taco Stand and his wife, Suki, who operated the other half of the restaurant. There weren't any lunch customers yet, and they'd chosen a booth on the

Mexican side of the building with its strings of red chili pepper lights proclaiming Christmas cheer. Emma carefully reviewed the newspaper's advertising rates. Suki, whose English was poor, looked to her Hispanic husband to explain what Emma had suggested. Emma glanced from one to the other and realized they had a language all their own.

"Is it for newspaper?" Suki wanted to know for the third time.

Emma smiled and nodded. "Yes," she said. She found herself speaking slowly and deliberately. "Advertise your good food to all the people in Puyallup so they will come in and place many orders." After five minutes of talking to the young Asian woman, Emma sounded as if she were the one struggling with English. It embarrassed her; she didn't want to offend the gentle young woman, but in her effort to make herself understood, she was overemphasizing each word.

Carlos, Suki's husband, nodded. "Very good for business."

Suki brightened. "We talk," she said and smiled softly at her husband.

A bell tinkled in the Japanese half of the restaurant, separated by a doorway. "Suki, where are you?"

Emma would recognize that voice anywhere.

Suki's eyes widened with pleasure. "Mr. Oliver," she said and immediately scooted out of the booth.

Carlos laughed. "She has a big crush on the pilot. It's a good thing she met me first."

Emma didn't doubt Oliver's appeal to the opposite sex for a moment. He had that effect on women; she knew from her own experience.

"Leave the information with me," Carlos said. "I'll call Mr. Walt later."

"So you think you'll buy an ad?" Emma asked hopefully.

Carlos hemmed and hawed. "Maybe. I'll talk it over with Suki."

It happened like this every time. She nearly had a commitment, and then the business owner would back off. She had no idea what she needed to do in order to get businesses to advertise in their local paper. Some of the businesspeople she talked to practically gave her the impression that they were afraid of attracting more customers. She didn't know how else to explain it. Fortunately, she'd had one success— Badda Bing, Badda Boom Pizza. They'd seen an increase in pizza sales and had happily signed a new contract.

She couldn't resist. After thanking Carlos, Emma walked over to the other half of the restaurant. Sure enough, Oliver sat on a stool with his back to her, while Suki worked behind the counter, assembling his order.

"I would never have taken you for someone who enjoys sushi," she said, and slid onto the stool beside him.

Oliver didn't look surprised to see her. "Really? I love it. My guess is you've never tried it."

He was beginning to know her. Then again, he seemed to have that ability from the moment they met. "You're right, I haven't."

"California rolls for the lady," Oliver told Suki.

"Oh, I'm not hungry," she said, which wasn't true.

Oliver didn't allow her to protest. "At least give it a try."

She'd been saying the same thing all afternoon. The least she could do was follow her own advice. "All right, I will."

Oliver gave her a warm smile, and she couldn't help basking in his approval. "See?" he said. "You didn't like fruitcake but you were willing to try it. And look how well that worked out." Emma could have stared into this man's eyes forever; instead, she quickly glanced away.

"I wondered where the name California Rock and Roll came from," she said casually. "Now I know."

Suki placed both orders on the counter and Emma examined hers. On a rectangular plate, Suki had arranged four California rolls. They seemed to be rolled logs of rice around a thin sheet of processed seaweed, with strips of avocado and various vegetables tucked in the center. On the same plate were two small bowls. One held soy sauce and the other was filled with a thin guacamole. Apparently Carlos and Suki had found a way to cross their foods culturally. Emma was intrigued. While Oliver reached for his chopsticks, she spread a liberal portion of the guacamole across the top of one California roll.

Oliver watched her with raised eyebrows.

Emma was about to take her first bite when he stopped her.

"You might want to scrape off some of the wasabi."

"The what?"

"Wasabi."

She must have looked confused, because he dipped the end of his chopstick in her guacamole and offered her a taste. The minute her lips touched it, her mouth was on fire. She grabbed her cup of tea and swallowed the entire contents. Waving her hand in front of her mouth, all she could do was feel grateful for Oliver's intervention.

"Oh, my goodness," she gasped.

"You thought that was guacamole?"

She nodded. "Thank you. Oh, thank you."

His eyes crinkled with a smile as he returned to his sushi.

Once Emma had tasted her first real bite, sans wasabi, she was surprised by how delicious the California roll was. "Hey, this is good."

"Told you."

She merely smiled.

They sat in companionable silence, and Emma had to admit she was thrilled to see him. She wanted to explain why she'd reacted the way she had to his gift of a Christmas tree, but was afraid any attempt would destroy this fragile peace.

"You came here for an early lunch?" Oliver asked.

"No, I was on another of my advertising treks for Walt."

"How's it going?"

She hated to admit how unsuccessful she was at this selling business. It was so much harder than she would've expected. Oliver listened and nodded. Then he told her, "You're doing it all wrong."

"What do you mean, I'm doing it wrong?" *He* wasn't the one hoofing it from business to business, putting on a smile and talking his heart out, only to be shown the door.

"Emma, listen to me. You're an attractive, charming young woman and it should be difficult for people to tell you no."

She scoffed, although she took note of the "attractive" and "charming." "That hasn't been a problem today."

"You've gotten nothing but *no?*" He seemed astonished by that.

She wasn't proud of it, but that was exactly what had happened. If she didn't get a flat rejection, it was "we'll think it over" or "later, maybe."

"Like I said, you must be doing it wrong."

That annoyed her. "*You* turned me down," she reminded him, allowing her temper to flare just a bit.

"I most certainly did not. I couldn't afford you, but I wanted you."

"It was the advertising you wanted, not me," she told him, stiffening at the implication.

"Whatever. I got you in my plane, didn't I? *And* I got advertising in the paper."

"Okay, okay, I'll concede the point." She reached for the teapot and refilled her cup. "If you think it's so easy, you try."

"All right. I'll bet I can prove to you that people can be talked into anything. What do you want me to do?"

Another man had entered the restaurant and sat at a table by the window. Emma pointed at him. "Ask that man to pay for your meal and watch how fast he tells you no."

"Okay, you're on." Oliver slid off the stool and walked toward the gentleman dining alone. He looked like a midlevel bank employee. Possibly a loan officer, judging by the fact that he was smartly but conservatively dressed.

Oliver didn't hesitate. He strolled over to the other man and when he spoke, he made sure it was just loud enough for Emma to overhear the conversation.

"Excuse me," he said in a friendly way.

The other man glanced up from his menu. "Yes?"

"I just ordered lunch for my girlfriend and me, and I've discovered I left my wallet at home. Would you mind paying for our meal? I'll repay you, of course."

The other man didn't say anything for a long moment. "How much is it?"

Emma was shocked he hadn't immediately laughed in Oliver's face and told him to get lost.

In a display of false humility, Oliver shook his head. "I haven't got the bill yet, but I'd guess around ten dollars." He shrugged. "I just assumed I had my wallet."

"You didn't think of that before you ordered?" the man asked.

Oliver gave him a look that said he was absolutely right. "I know I should've but...I didn't."

"You seem like a decent sort," the other man said slowly.

Emma couldn't stand it. She climbed off the stool and hurried to Oliver's side. "You can tell him no," she said eagerly. She'd hate it if Oliver won this bet so easily. Besides, they hadn't decided what the winner would get.

"Now, Emma." Oliver frowned at her. "This is man to man. Don't you worry about it."

Emma wasn't going to let him win this bet without a struggle. "My friend is being irresponsible. It certainly isn't up to you to pay for his mistake. All you have to do is say no."

The gentleman nodded. "True, but it is the holiday season, and ten dollars won't break me."

Oliver grinned triumphantly. He stretched out his hand to the other man. "Thank you very much. I'm Oliver Hamilton, by the way."

"Gary Sullivan. Nice to meet you." Gary stood and reached for his wallet.

"No," Oliver said, refusing the money. "I was just proving a point to my girlfriend. This is Emma Collins, of *The Puyallup Examiner.*"

"I'm not his girlfriend." Emma felt it was important to clarify that. "We're friends...." She let the rest fade, embarrassed to have said anything.

Gary looked confused.

"You could've just said no," Emma repeated, unable to understand why it had been so easy for Oliver and so difficult for her.

"I didn't mind. Like I said, this is Christmas, I could afford it and your boyfriend—Oliver—is very persuasive. The idea of paying for your meal actually made me feel good. Christmas spirit and all."

Emma gave up then and walked back to the counter.

"See," Oliver said as he returned to his stool. "People *want* to help and it's the same in sales. If you just remember that, and remember to show them what *they'll* get out of it, then you'll have a better chance of selling advertising for Walt."

She sighed loudly. "Okay, you win."

"I beg your pardon?"

"You win," she said a little louder this time, although she nearly choked on the words.

"Good. I'll be by for dinner around seven."

"Dinner?"

"Yes. Didn't I mention my prize?"

"I'm afraid you didn't."

"You're going to make me dinner." He grinned. "I hope it's all right if Oscar comes, too."

Chapter Seventeen

As children growing up in Ireland, we would watch our grandmother make fruitcake and she would always let us lick the bowl afterward. I liked fruitcake simply because of the association with Christmas and spending time in the kitchen with my grandmother. However, it always seemed that the cake lasted until the next century and there was always the possibility of broken bones if the cake accidentally fell on you!

—Frank McMahon, executive chef at
Hank's Seafood in Charleston, South Carolina

Oliver was pleased with himself. His spur-of-the-moment experiment couldn't have gone any better. Later, as they left the restaurant, Emma seemed to think she'd been tricked. She claimed Oliver must have known Gary beforehand. He didn't, and she'd eventually believed him.

He hoped his little lesson in sales would help—and not just with her ad quota. The fact was, you had to persuade people that they were going to get something out of the deal. It was more of an emotional thing than it was a practical or financial one. Look at Gary for instance—he felt good about helping someone out. Oliver wanted to convince Emma that there'd be an emotional payoff for her, too, if she bought his sales pitch. Only what *he* was selling was himself.

She'd described them as friends, but he was interested in more than friendship, and if his intuition was right, so was Emma. The problem, and he considered it a minor one, was that she hadn't acknowledged it yet.

After his lunch, Oliver returned to the airfield, did some paperwork and then drove home. Emma had called to say dinner would be ready around seven-thirty and he took that to mean she had some grocery shopping to do before he came by. He was thinking a big, juicy T-bone steak would suit him just fine.

On his way home, Oliver bought a bottle of his favorite merlot. Humming a Christmas carol, he hopped back inside his pickup. Oscar, waiting for him in the passenger seat, yawned ostentatiously.

"So how's it going with you and Boots?" Oliver asked his terrier. "You looking forward to having dinner with her?"

Oscar cocked his head to one side.

His cell rang and when he checked caller ID, he saw that it was his mother. He picked up on the third ring, and they discussed Christmas Day and the dinner she had planned. "Hey, Mom," he said, glancing in his sideview mirror before he changed lanes. "Would it be all right if I brought a guest?"

"For Christmas?"

"Yeah. A…friend of mine." The word *friend* made him feel self-conscious. He hoped that by Christmas Day their relationship would have progressed to something a little more exciting.

His mother knew him far too well. "I'm assuming this guest you want to include is female?"

"Yes."

"Is she someone special?"

He was silent for a moment. "Yes," he finally admitted. "Yeah, she is."

"What's her name?"

"Emma Collins."

"Emma Collins?" his mother repeated. "That sounds familiar."

"No reason it should," Oliver said, changing lanes a second time. "She works for *The Examiner.* I met her earlier in the month when she came down to the airfield to—"

"She works for the newspaper?" his mother said excitedly, cutting him off. "She's that reporter!"

"What reporter?"

"The girl who wrote those articles about fruitcake," she told him, her tone suggesting he must be a simpleton.

"Well, yes, but I didn't know they'd been published." He'd been too busy to read the paper this last week and when he did, he rarely looked past the front page and the sports section.

"She interviewed the three Washington State fruitcake recipe finalists."

"I know." Oliver realized he probably sounded smug. "I was the one who flew her in for the interviews. Don't you remember I told you about that?"

"Yes, but you didn't tell me who you were flying or what for."

"She usually writes obituaries, Mom."

"You haven't read her articles, have you?"

"I've been busy."

"Everyone in town is talking about them," his mother informed him. "At my bridge club luncheon, we all said we were surprised someone that young could be so wise."

"How do you know her age?"

"The paper ran her photo at the bottom of the last article. She's an attractive woman."

Oliver agreed.

"My son is dating Emma Collins."

"She's making dinner for me tonight." He didn't think now was the time to mention that Emma had agreed to this only because she'd lost a bet.

"I can't believe you haven't said anything!"

"Sorry."

"You should be. That girl is gifted. Those articles were *so* good."

"Save them for me, would you?" He'd look through the papers in his recycling bin, but just in case…

"I already used one of the recipes and I'm going to serve it on Christmas Day."

Oliver liked fruitcake, and there always seemed to be plenty of it around his parents' house. "So I can bring Emma?"

"Don't you *dare* show up without her."

"Wouldn't dream of it."

As soon as he arrived home, Oliver collected a week's worth of papers and sat down with them, searching until he located the first article—about the Yakima interview. He studied a picture of Earleen Williams displaying her fruitcake. Emma wasn't a bad photographer. He recalled that first flight and how nervous she'd been. Then he remembered her problem with the television in the motel room and her effort to hear the news that turned out to be nudes. At that he laughed outright.

His mother was right; the article was insightful and well-written. Within a few paragraphs, Oliver felt he knew Earleen. He'd certainly met women like her who didn't recognize their own worth or, as in Earleen's case, recognized it later in life. Emma had characterized her with real sensitivity. Logically but subtly, she led the reader to her own conclusion—that this was a generous woman who'd spent her life loving men who didn't deserve her devotion.

He found the article about Sophie McKay next. Sophie was a woman who enjoyed life. Neither she nor her fruitcake recipe was in any way typical. She took the ingredients she liked best and combined them into a truly unique recipe, just as she'd done with her life. Both she and her beloved husband, Harry, had been willing to compromise on the fruitcake issue and, no doubt, on the more important conflicts within their marriage. After his death, she'd mourned him and continued to love him but also continued to live. Sophie McKay, like her fruitcake, was one of a kind.

As Oliver rummaged through discarded papers for the third and final article, he understood what had intrigued his mother and her friends about Emma. She *was* special, and her understanding of these women's lives was compassionate as well as incisive.

When he found the third article, he smiled at the picture of Peggy Lucas surrounded by her children. He almost wished Emma had been in the photograph. The theme for that article was *eat it now* and the No-Bake Fruitcake recipe followed. With Peggy, too, Emma had found just the right tone.

In all three articles, she'd managed to write about fruitcake—on the surface a rather limited subject—in ways that gave it a larger meaning. Fruitcake as a symbol for life. Hmm…

Emma might not be much good at garnering advertising dollars for Walt, but she shouldn't worry. What she lacked in sales ability she more than compensated for with her writing talent.

Oliver saw that it was almost seven. Rubbing his hand down his cheek, he decided to shave. He was in a good mood and knew he should credit Emma with that. She'd impressed him with her work and she made him laugh. There was a lot to be said for a woman who possessed a sense of humor. After throwing on his leather jacket, which had survived its icy bath in Puget Sound, he reached for the wine bottle, called Oscar and together, man and dog headed out the door.

Striking what he hoped was a sexy Cary Grant pose, Oliver rang the doorbell. He leaned his shoulder against the doorjamb and crossed his ankles, bottle tucked under one arm. It didn't take Emma long to answer. Unlatching the lock, she opened the door and immediately made a fuss over Oscar. She hardly seemed to notice Oliver was even there. Apparently she was immune to his many charms—or wanted him to think she was. Definitely hard on the ego.

"That's all the greeting I get?" he chided.

She wore a towel apron over jeans and looked lovely. He couldn't resist. Slipping his hand behind her neck, Oliver bent forward and kissed her. She tasted wonderful—a little spicy, a little sweet.

She blinked several times when he released her. "Hi," she said in a husky voice, sounding flustered.

When they'd first met, he'd enjoyed teasing her about how much she wanted him. Actually, the reverse was true. *He* wanted *her.* In an effort to derail the direction of his thoughts, he asked, "What's for dinner?"

"If I don't get back to the stove in a hurry, it'll be takeout." She dashed across the room and returned to her kitchen.

Oliver bent down and petted Boots. The two dogs resumed their ritual sniffing.

"Ever heard of puttanesca?" Emma asked, emptying a large can of crushed tomatoes into a pan.

"Putin what?" Oliver asked as he set the wine bottle down on the crowded countertop. "Is it some Russian dish?"

"Puttanesca," Emma repeated. "It's an Italian pasta sauce. My mother used to make it. I have to warn you it's kind of spicy."

The scents in the kitchen were delectable. He smelled garlic and tomatoes and something else he couldn't identify. He saw an empty anchovy can and wondered if that was it. Oliver enjoyed the little fish on his pizza. So far, that was the only time he'd ever eaten anchovies.

Emma stirred the simmering sauce, her back to him. "Mom told me that women of the night would put a pan of this sauce in the window in order to entice men."

"Are you trying to entice *me,* Emma Collins?" Oliver asked softly.

As if she realized what she'd said, Emma whirled around, her eyes wide. "No…you misunderstood. This has nothing to do with you and me."

It was probably wrong of him to find amusement in her obvious discomfort, but he grinned and said, "Pity."

She held his gaze. "Could I?" she asked, her voice hesitant. "Entice you, I mean."

He shrugged carelessly. "You could always give it a try." He grinned again. "In fact, why don't you?"

She smiled in response and the tip of her tongue moistened her lower lip before she turned back to the pasta sauce.

Oliver was convinced she had no idea what an effective job she was doing of enticing him right then and there. He fought the impulse to kiss her again. "Is there anything you'd like me to do?"

She nodded. "You can roll the lemon."

Oliver was sure he'd misheard. "You want me to what?"

"Roll the lemon between your hands," she explained. "I'd normally roll it against the countertop, but as you can see, I don't have much space here."

He pressed the lemon between his hands, then crushed it with all his might. "This is for the pasta?"

"No," she said with a laugh. "The salad. I'm squeezing fresh lemon juice over the greens and then tossing them with a little extra-virgin olive oil."

Extra-virgin, was it? Oliver didn't even want to know what that meant. Then again, maybe he did.

"The bread's warming in the oven."

"Of course." The table was already set, and when he'd finished pulverizing the lemon, he opened the wine. After giving it a couple of minutes to breathe—he'd read about that once in an airline magazine—he poured them each a glass.

Emma certainly seemed to know what she was doing. He asked her about it over dinner as he swallowed every noodle and scraped up every last drop of the delicious sauce.

"My mom was the cook in the family. I miss her so much," she said quietly. "This is the first time I've made puttanesca since she died and I was a little concerned it wouldn't be the same."

"If it isn't, don't change anything. This was fabulous."

Emma smiled and picked up her glass of wine.

She rarely mentioned her mother. Oliver knew the subject was a painful one, but he sensed that she wanted to talk about her now.

"She taught you to cook, right?"

Emma nodded. "Mom insisted I should know my way around a kitchen. Isn't that something in these days of convenience food? I can't remember Mom *ever* resorting to processed food. I didn't taste macaroni and cheese from a box until I was almost an adult." She grimaced comically. "That's what comes of living on a student budget."

"Do you like cooking?" he asked.

She nodded again. "I don't do it often enough. If Mom were alive, I'm afraid I'd be a disappointment to her."

"I'm sure that's not true." He was sincere; her mother would be very proud of Emma and rightly so. "Speaking of mothers, I talked to mine this afternoon and she read your articles."

Emma's eyes brightened. "Did she enjoy them?"

"Mom was very impressed." Oliver was a little disgruntled that Emma hadn't let him know those fruitcake pieces had been published. He'd also been put out over her lack of appreciation for the Christmas tree. She had the tree up, but it didn't have a single strand of lights or even one decoration. It leaned rather forlornly against the corner of her living room. She hadn't bought a stand; she'd just stuck it in a large, dirt-filled flower pot.

"That's great." Emma seemed pleased by his mother's reaction.

"What did Walt say?"

Emma chuckled. "His only comment after he read the final drafts was that I gave him clean copy. Which is high praise from Walt."

Oliver helped himself to the last of the pasta sauce and sopped it up with his bread. "Getting back to my mother, she wants to meet you."

"She does?"

Oliver played this part cool. "Yeah. I told her I could arrange it."

"I'd be delighted to meet her."

"How about Christmas Day?" he asked, again casually.

Emma's smile faded. "Christmas Day," she said slowly.

"Is that a problem?" Oliver felt like smacking his forehead. He should've realized she'd have plans. Everyone did on Christmas.

"I'm sorry, it won't work." At least she had the good grace to look regretful.

"You've already got plans?"

"Sort of," she said after a brief hesitation.

Oliver straightened. "Either you have plans or you don't. Which is it?"

Emma set her napkin on the table, stood up and carried their plates to the sink. "I know you have a hard time understanding this, but I don't 'do' Christmas."

He looked over at the bare tree he'd gotten her. Point taken.

"It isn't anything religious," she explained. "Christmas just hasn't been the same since my mother died. I tried to continue all the traditions we'd done together. It was too sad. So I stopped."

She returned from the kitchen, carrying a pie and a couple of small glass plates. "My…father and I are estranged. He invites me out of obligation, but I can't go to him and his new wife. I just can't."

She sat down at the table again. "Friends invited

me over a couple of years in a row, but it made me feel like a charity case." She lowered her head. "People tend to feel sorry for me and I don't want that. The last two years I've spent the day alone and, really, it isn't so bad. I've come to enjoy it."

Oliver shrugged off her rejection as if it didn't matter. His invitation had been issued in an offhand manner, which he now decided was a mistake. He should've made a big deal of it.

Because it *was* a big deal. Christmas was important to him and to his family, and he wanted Emma to be part of that. He wanted Emma with him.

Now all he had to do was figure out how to convince her.

Chapter Eighteen

Emma knew she'd disappointed Oliver and she felt bad about that. She was quite fond of him and— Okay, that was a mild assessment of her feelings. She was crazy about him.

"I think I blew it with Oliver," she told Phoebe on the phone later that evening.

"What happened?"

Emma sat down and put her feet up as she mentally reviewed their dinnertime conversation. "He invited me to meet his mother."

"That's terrific! Oh, Emma, Oliver's letting you know that you're more than just a friend. He's asking you to meet his family. That's a huge step in a relationship."

"It was all very casual," she murmured.

"Of course it was…." Phoebe paused. "You're not going to tell me you refused, are you?"

"He invited me to Christmas dinner."

The line went silent for a moment. "You mean to tell me that Oliver invited you to meet his parents on Christmas Day and you *turned him down?*"

"Yes." The word was barely audible, even to Emma.

"Don't you understand that's as good as it gets with a guy—his parents *and* Christmas?"

"But…"

"Tell me you're joking."

"Well, no."

Phoebe groaned. "I was afraid of that. I thought you liked Oliver."

"I do," she said in a small voice. Emma was afraid to admit how much. She knew now that he wasn't like her father. Oliver was caring, generous and had a great relationship with his family. He was kind to animals. He had a sense of humor. If she were to make a list of what she wanted in a man, those traits would be at the very top.

"How can you be so smart and so stupid at the same time?" Phoebe muttered.

"It's a gift," Emma said sarcastically.

"What did Oliver say after you told him no?"

Emma closed her eyes and pressed her palm against her forehead. "Hardly anything. I'd made dinner, he offered to help with the dishes, but there weren't that many and—"

"Stop right there," Phoebe commanded. "Oliver offered to help with the dishes and you refused that, too?"

"That was wrong?"

"Never, I repeat—never—turn down a man's offer to do the dishes. Men are like puppies that have to be trained. This training takes place during the courtship period. Men will take their cues from you and if you let them know you're fine with doing all the housework, they'll simply accept it. Who wouldn't? That, my friend, was mistake number two. Okay, now tell me what happened next."

"Nothing much. He said he had an errand to run and he left."

"Did he thank you for dinner?"

"Oh, yes. He really seemed to enjoy it." His enjoyment gratified her. This was a special recipe—a special meal. In her own way, she'd been letting him know he was important to her.

"But he left almost right afterward?"

"Yes." Emma was feeling worse by the minute.

Her friend exhaled slowly. "You're right, you blew it."

Emma swallowed around the lump forming in her throat. "Any suggestions on what I should do now?"

"Call and tell him you've had a change of heart and would love to spend Christmas with him and his family." She gulped in an urgent breath. "And do it soon."

This wasn't what Emma wanted to hear. "But I *haven't* changed my mind."

"Do you love this guy or not?" Phoebe demanded. *Love? Love. Love!* She didn't know. Okay, maybe she did. She loved him. And deep down she knew that if she didn't act quickly, she might lose him.

"But I don't do—"

"Don't say it," Phoebe interrupted. "Do you honestly think this is how your mother wants you to spend Christmas? You told me how much she liked the holidays and all the things you used to do together."

"I know. I'm not opposed to Christmas for other people," Emma said, defending herself. "But it's not for me. Christmas makes me sad and—"

"You didn't answer my question."

When had Phoebe become so dictatorial? "No…"

"No what?"

"Mom would want me to be with people at Christmas," she murmured.

"That's what I thought."

Emma knew Phoebe was right about this. Her mother had always said there was something special about Christmas. Oliver had tried to tell her there was something special about her, too, and she'd brushed him off.

"Okay, you've made your point." Now all she had to do was explain to Oliver that she'd been wrong. That she'd mourned her mother in a negative way instead of a positive one. That she should have celebrated all the things they'd shared—like Christmas. Phoebe was right about something else. This dinner had been a turning point in Emma's relationship with

Oliver. Unfortunately, she'd made the wrong choice once again.

"Call him."

"Okay."

"Tell him you've changed your mind and *mean* it," Phoebe said.

Emma nodded dutifully. "What do you think he'll say?"

Phoebe didn't answer for a long moment. "I don't know. Call me back after you talk to him, okay?"

"I will," Emma promised. This wasn't going to be easy. Before she lost her nerve she punched out his phone number. After three rings, voice mail came on and she left a message. "Hi," she said awkwardly. "This is Emma… Listen, about Christmas. I am so honored that you invited me. I'd love to meet your mother. I was thinking I might've offended you and I'd never want to do that and so—" BEEP.

Emma had been cut off. She dialed the number again, then replaced the receiver before the recorded message began. She wondered if Oliver was screening his calls and preferred not to talk to her. The last thing she wanted to be was a pest.

Sleeping was out of the question. The big office party was the following afternoon. The Subway Express lunch had fallen through—apparently the county Health Department had some concerns about them—and Walt had made another deal with a brand-new catering company. Emma had purchased the requisite gift and dutifully wrapped it for the Secret Santa exchange, but her heart wasn't in it.

The following morning when she showed up at the office, Phoebe met her with a cup of coffee. "Here, you look like you need this. Why didn't you call me back?"

"I didn't talk to Oliver."

"You tried?"

"Yes, twice." She hadn't left a message the second time. One message was enough, she reasoned.

Phoebe frowned. "It's still early."

Two days was all she had. The office closed for the holidays at the end of business hours today. Saturday was Christmas Eve and then Sunday was Christmas Day itself. She had to settle this with Oliver and soon.

Needless to say, Emma wasn't looking forward to the office party, but she was required to attend. No one said as much; it was simply understood. Staff and freelance writers mingled in the upstairs office, and the conference room table was covered with an elaborate culinary display.

Emma wasn't sure how much free advertising Walt had agreed to with the catering company. A lot, she assumed. The spread was gorgeous, with huge shrimp arranged around a bowl of cocktail sauce, smoked salmon and cream cheese on small rounds of rye bread, chicken teriyaki tidbits, veggie trays, cheese and crackers and enough desserts to send the entire staff racing to Weight Watchers on the second of January. To Emma's delight, among the desserts was a large platter of sliced fruitcake.

"You're Emma Collins?" the young female caterer asked when Emma paused to admire it.

"I am."

"I really enjoyed your articles," she said. "My name is Dixie Rogers."

They shook hands. "I enjoyed meeting the finalists—and trying their fruitcake," Emma told her.

"Has the winner been announced?"

Emma nodded. "It was a woman from South Carolina." She'd checked the Web last night, just before she went to bed, and had seen the results.

"Oh. I hope the Washington State finalists aren't too disappointed."

Emma thought that Earleen, Sophie and Peggy were thrilled to have made the final cut. She'd heard from each one after the articles were published and they'd all been pleased.

"As you probably guessed, the no-bake fruitcake is Peggy Lucas's recipe." Dixie pointed to the tray Emma had recently admired. "I think everyone who normally dislikes fruitcake will be eager to give it a second try after reading your articles. I know I was."

The praise felt good. "Thank you again."

"Next year I'm determined to bake all three fruitcakes. The chocolate one especially interests me."

"It's wonderful," Emma assured her. The three finalists had made a believer out of her. Her intense

dislike of fruitcake had come about more because of
its association with Christmas than any aversion to
the cake itself. It was an unreasonable dislike, she
recognized, since she'd only tasted it a couple of
times. Next year, she'd bake one herself. Maybe even
all three.

Emma filled her plate and joined Phoebe while
Walt made the traditional Christmas champagne
toast. The Secret Santa gift exchange turned out, surprisingly, to be a lot of fun, and Emma ended up the
proud possessor of a pair of Christmas tree earrings.
Soon everyone was getting ready to leave for the
night. There were plenty of hugs and holiday greetings as the office staff began to drift away.

Bundled against the cold, Emma walked out of the
office, Phoebe and Walt behind her. Being alone over
the holidays had never troubled Emma this much in
the past. It was the thought of not being with Oliver.
She wanted to be in his life and she wanted him in
hers.

Just before the office party, Walt had sought her
out. He hadn't openly praised her work; that would've
been asking too much. But he'd given her another assignment. Shortly after the first of the year, the big
Bridal Fair would be held at the Tacoma Dome. Walt
seemed to feel she'd find plenty of human interest
stories at an event like that.

It wasn't a random choice, Emma realized. When
Phoebe returned to work after Christmas, Emma ex-

pected to see her wearing an engagement ring. In fact, she was virtually certain that Phoebe had whispered the idea for her new assignment in Walt's ear.

The wind sent icy shivers down Emma's back as she headed toward the parking lot. A dog barked. Could it possibly be Oscar, which meant Oliver would be close by? She scanned the area but didn't see either Oliver or his terrier.

As she drove through town, Emma noticed—as if for the first time—all the street decorations. Wreaths, striped candy canes and snowmen were suspended from light posts, with evergreen boughs stretched from one side of the street to the other. These decorations were truly an expression of the community's spirit. Before, she'd barely glanced at them, viewing it all as evidence of the commercialization of Christmas. Now she looked at the scene in front of her with fresh eyes.

Snowflakes floated down. She caught her breath at the sheer wonder of it. Carolers stood in the center of a roundabout with their songbooks open. Even through the noise of the traffic, Emma could hear the harmonic blend of voices. It was lovely and peaceful and festive—and so was Christmas…. Just like it'd been when she was a kid growing up.

Emma thought about the women she'd met and the articles she'd written. Earleen had taught her to look at her mother and herself in an entirely different way. Pamela Collins had made her own choice, and that choice had been to remain in a failed marriage. Even though she knew Oliver was nothing like her father, Emma had been afraid of repeating her mother's mistakes. But she was her own woman, a masterpiece in her own right. From Sophie she'd learned about the value of compromise and the importance of recognizing what you want and making it part of your life. And Peggy had shown her how to live in the moment.

Fortified with enthusiasm, Emma drove to the local Wal-Mart and, using her Christmas bonus, bought lights and decorations for her tree. While she was there, she loaded up on groceries. Then she went to a local strip mall and did her first real Christmas shopping in years.

Nothing had been resolved with Oliver; still, she felt wonderful. Christmas music played loudly from her car radio as she arrived home and carried all her bags into the apartment. Boots jumped up and down with happiness at her homecoming.

She didn't stop to see if the red light was blinking on her answering machine. It didn't matter if Oliver had tried to return her call or not. Riding on the crest of her newborn appreciation for Christmas—and for him—she went directly to his apartment with Boots in tow. She didn't hesitate before she rang his doorbell.

He looked surprised to see her. He waited for her to speak.

She smiled warmly. "Hi."

"Hi, yourself," he repeated without much animation.

Her smile grew wider. "Merry Christmas."

His eyes widened. "Merry Christmas? The original Ms. Scrooge is wishing me Merry Christmas?"

"Oh, yes." With that, she launched herself into his arms and spread eager kisses over his face. She started with his cheek, gradually working her way to his mouth.

Sliding his arms around her waist, Oliver lifted her from the ground. His mouth hungrily covered hers. Somehow he managed to bring her into his apartment—Boots scurrying past them—and kick the door shut. Emma wrapped her arms around his neck and hung on tight. This was exactly where she wanted to be. If the fervor with which he returned her kisses was any indication, Oliver shared her feeling.

"Did you get my message?" she asked when she could breathe again.

"Did you get mine?"

"No."

His lips went back to hers. "I decided to give you another chance."

"Good." She kissed his jaw, then cradled his face between her hands so she could gaze into his eyes. "Can I still join you and your family for Christmas?"

Oliver's expression grew solemn. "Sorry, I've already asked another girl."

His answer shocked her until she realized he was

teasing. Playfully she punched him in the ribs. "That wasn't funny."

Oliver laughed. Emma had always loved his robust laughter and closed her eyes to hold on to the sound of it as long as possible.

"Do you want to help me decorate the tree?" she asked.

"What?" Oliver pretended to stagger back, hand to his heart. "This is indeed a complete transformation. Sure."

"Also," she said, slipping her arm around his waist. "If I'm going to be joining your family for Christmas dinner, it's only polite that I bring something."

Oliver disagreed. "Mom won't hear of it. You're our guest."

"No, I insist. Besides, I've already been to the grocery store."

"Okay, okay. Bring whatever you want."

She tilted back her head. "Don't you want to know what I intend to make for your family?"

"Okay, tell me."

So she did. "Fruitcake, of course."

Epilogue

I'm not a fruitcake fan generally speaking, but then there's my mother's. She makes a fabulous, upscale fruitcake using a high-quality sherry. She bakes the cakes in November, wraps them in cheesecloth and lets them marinate for a couple of weeks, routinely adding sherry to keep them moist. Each year she sends me a few of her superb fruitcakes and they always disappear surprisingly quickly—especially for fruitcake!

—Robert Carter, executive chef at Peninsula Grill in Charleston, South Carolina

A year later

Her mother had been right; Christmas was good for the human spirit.

"Emma, would you take this out to the table?" Oliver's mother asked, handing her a bowl piled high with fluffy mashed potatoes. She didn't wait for a response before she gave Oliver's sister, Laurel, a second bowl, and picked up a third, filled with Brussels sprouts, herself. Walking in single file, the Hamilton women brought the serving dishes to the huge dining room table for Christmas dinner.

A turkey, roasted to golden perfection, rested on a huge oval platter at the far end of the table for Oliver's father to carve. Nieces and nephews, plus dogs and cats, raced around the house with sounds of glee.

Oliver was talking to his father but glanced up when she entered the room. They exchanged a smile. For the second year in a row, she'd joined his family for the holiday festivities. Only this year, Emma was a member of the family. Oliver and Emma had been married in June, two months after Phoebe and Walt. Following the reception, they flew—yes, flew—to Hawaii for a two-week honeymoon. Thankfully, their flight was aboard a 747 and not Oliver's Cessna Caravan.

With Oliver's urging and support, Emma had called her father. That first conversation had been tense, and she'd realized Bret Collins wished their relationship was different. To her surprise, he showed up for the wedding. He attended the reception, too, and made a point of meeting Emma's in-laws. Though he'd left shortly afterward, they'd talked a number of times since. In fact, he'd called that very morning to wish her and Oliver a merry Christmas.

It was a start.

Emma's journalism career was progressing, and although she was still responsible for her share of obituaries, she routinely wrote feature articles for *The Examiner*. Walt sometimes offered suggestions, but lately he'd allowed her to write whatever she chose. Emma's work had even garnered attention from some of the larger newspapers in the area. For now, she was content to continue writing for *The Examiner*. She enjoyed living in Puyallup, home of the Western Washington Fairgrounds and the Victorian Christmas extravaganza. She'd covered both events for the paper this year.

Oliver's freight business was doing well, too. He'd managed to pick up another exclusive contract with an Alaska fishing company. Five days a week, he flew in fresh salmon and other seafood to restaurants in Washington and Oregon. Emma was proud of his company's success. In November Oliver had hired another pilot and leased a second plane in order to meet demand. He advertised regularly in *The Examiner*, and Emma wrote all his ads.

Oliver's mother stepped out of the kitchen and removed her apron, signaling the start of the Christmas meal. "Ollie, dinner's on the table," she called to her husband. The family migrated to the dining room.

Oliver and Emma stood in front of their chairs as his sisters and brother and their families found their way to the table. Emma smiled, admiring the meal. In addition to turkey and all the fixings, there were a number of salads and vegetable dishes, plus fresh-baked rolls still warm from the oven. Desserts lined the sideboard. For the second year in a row, Emma had brought fruitcake—three varieties this year, all made from the recipes contributed by the three women she'd interviewed last Christmas.

When the family surrounded the table, they all joined hands and Oliver's father offered a simple grace. Emma closed her eyes; at the end of the prayer she whispered a heartfelt "Amen." She was in love, and she felt as though she'd reclaimed herself—and reclaimed the joy of Christmas.

With dinner came a lot of good-natured teasing between Oliver and his younger brother and three younger sisters. Although he was the oldest, he'd been the last to marry.

"I don't know how you put up with him," Laurel said, speaking to Emma.

"You wouldn't believe the stuff he pulled on us as kids," Carrie added.

"Do you remember the time Mom made you babysit, and Donny put a huge hole in the living room wall?" Jenny asked Oliver.

"Remember it?" he said with a groan. "I knew the

minute Mom saw that hole, I'd be grounded my entire senior year."

Oliver's mother waved her fork at him and turned to Emma. "Do you know what he did? My genius son rearranged the living room furniture so the wall was covered."

"I hid the hole," Oliver said in a stage whisper.

"Then he demanded extra pay because he claimed he did housework in addition to babysitting," his mother reminded them.

The whole family laughed.

Laurel spoke to Emma again. "Okay, you've been married to our big brother for six months now."

"Six months," Donny repeated. "Leslie was pregnant a month after our wedding. What's the problem?"

Oliver laughed. "Trust me, there's no problem."

This was her cue, Emma realized. "We're due in July."

Amid cheers and gasps, Oliver's parents rose to their feet and applauded. His siblings and their spouses joined in.

Oliver slipped his arm around her shoulders. "I told you they'd be happy," he murmured.

"You'd think this was their first grandchild," Emma said, overwhelmed by the family's reaction to their news. She'd never known families could be like this.

By the end of a memorable Christmas Day, Emma

was tired and ready to go home. After a series of hugs and promises to meet again soon, Oliver steered her to the car parked out front, his arm protectively around her. The dogs followed obediently in their wake.

"It's a bit overpowering, isn't it?" he said.

"What?" she asked.

"My family, when we're all together."

"They're wonderful, each and every one." Oliver's sisters were among her closest friends. Her circle of family, friends and acquaintances had increased from the day she'd met him.

"They love you, too." He opened the car door for her and helped her inside. Oscar and Boots piled into the back.

As they neared their newly constructed home, Oliver glanced at her. Emma's eyes were closed, her head back against the leather seat. "You've really taken to Christmas," he said. "Hard to believe that just over a year ago you didn't want anything to do with it. Now look at you."

Emma opened her eyes and smiled. Their home was decorated with not one, but two, Christmas trees. The second, a smaller one, was for the dogs. She'd written a series of articles about Christmas customs around the world. And she'd started baking right after Thanksgiving. As Oliver had said last year, the transformation had been complete.

"I don't know what to tell you," she said with a laugh, "except to repeat what my mother told me."

"And what would that be?" he asked, a smile in his voice.

"There's something special about Christmas."

HERE COMES TROUBLE

Prologue

"Tomorrow's Christmas Eve, Mom!" nine-year-old Courtney Adams said.

"Mom, you have my list for Santa, don't you?" seven-year-old Bailey asked anxiously. She knelt on her bed, her large brown eyes beseeching.

This, Maryanne Adams recognized, was a blatant attempt to postpone bedtime. Both girls were supposed to turn out their lights ten minutes ago but, as usual, they were looking for any excuse to delay the inevitable. The one thing Maryanne hoped to avoid was yet another discussion about the top item on both their Christmas lists—a puppy.

"What about *my* list?" Courtney asked from her bed. She, at least, had crawled between the covers, but remained in a sitting position.

"Don't worry, I'm sure Santa has both your lists by now," Maryanne reassured her daughters. She stood in the doorway, her hand poised over the light switch.

Both her daughters slept in canopy beds their Simpson grandparents had insisted on purchasing for them. It was their prerogative to spoil the grandkids, her father had told her so she didn't argue too much. The grandchildren were the delight of their grandparents' lives and could do no wrong.

"Did you read the list before you gave it to Santa?" Courtney asked.

At nine, Courtney was well aware that Santa was actually her mom and dad, but she was generous enough not to spoil the fantasy for her younger sister.

"You said your prayers?" Maryanne asked, wanting to turn the subject away from a dog.

Bailey nodded. "I prayed for a puppy."

"I did, too." Courtney echoed.

They were certainly persistent. "We'll see what happens," Maryanne said.

Bailey glanced at her older sister. "Is 'we'll see' good news?"

Courtney looked uncertain. "I don't know." She turned pleading eyes to her mother. "Mom, we *have* to know."

"Mom, please, I beg of you," Bailey cried dramatically. "We've just got to have a dog. We've *got* to."

Maryanne sighed. "I hate to disappoint you, but I don't think it's a good idea for our family to get a puppy now."

"Why not?" Courtney demanded, her sweet face filling with disappointment.

Instinctively, Maryanne pressed her hand to her stomach. It was time to tell the girls that there'd be a new family member in six months—past time, really, for them to know. She'd wanted to share the news earlier, but this baby was a complete surprise; she and Nolan had needed time to adjust to the idea first.

Stepping all the way into the room, Maryanne sat on the edge of Courtney's bed. She'd prefer to tell the girls with Nolan at her side, but her husband was on deadline and had barricaded himself in his home office, coming out once or twice a day. The last fifty pages of a book were always the most difficult for him to write, winding down the plot and tying up all the loose ends. It was never easy, according to Nolan, to part with the characters he'd lived with for the past number of months. They were as real to him as his own flesh and blood, and because she was a writer, too, she understood that.

"We'll discuss this later." Checking her watch, she frowned. "It's past your bedtime as it is."

"Aw, Mom," Bailey moaned.

"Mom, please," Courtney chimed in. "I won't be able to sleep if you don't tell me now."

"Tell them what?" Nolan asked from the doorway.

At the sight of their father both girls squealed with delight. Bailey was out of bed first, flying across the room at breakneck speed. Anyone would think it'd been weeks since she'd last seen their father, when in fact he'd had breakfast with the girls that morning.

"Daddy!" Courtney leaped off the bed, as well.

Bailey was in Nolan's arms, fiercely hugging his neck, and Courtney clasped her skinny arms around his waist.

"Are you finished the book?" Maryanne asked, her gaze connecting with his. She remained seated on the bed, tired out from a long day of Christmas preparations.

"I typed *The End* about five minutes ago," her husband said, smiling down at her.

"What do you think?" she asked. As a wildly popular suspense author, Nolan generally had an excellent feel for his own work.

"I think it's good, but I'll wait for your feedback."

Maryanne loved the way they worked together as husband and wife and as two professional writers. Nolan wrote his novels, and it was the income he generated from the sales of his books that supported their family. Maryanne tackled nonfiction projects. She wrote a weekly column for the *Seattle Review* and contributed articles to various parenting magazines. One day, she might try her hand at fiction, but for the present she was content.

"Mom says now isn't a good time for us to get a puppy," Courtney whined, and it wasn't long before her younger sister added her own disconsolate cries.

"Why can't we, Daddy?" Bailey cried. "Every kid should have a puppy."

"A puppy," Nolan repeated, locking eyes with

Maryanne. He sat down on the bed beside her and exhaled slowly. "Well, the truth is, there are other considerations."

"Like what?" Courtney asked. It was inconceivable to her that anything should stand in the way of her heart's desire.

Nolan placed his arm around Maryanne's shoulders, indicating that perhaps now was the time to explain. "Well," he began in thoughtful tones. "When a man and a woman fall in love and marry, they sometimes…" He paused and waited for Maryanne to finish.

"They love each other so much that they…" She hesitated, thinking this might not be the right approach.

"They make babies," Nolan supplied.

"You were a baby once," Maryanne continued, reaching out to tickle Bailey's tummy.

"And you, too," Nolan told Courtney.

The girls sat cross-legged on Bailey's bed, their attention on Nolan and Maryanne. Their long brown hair spilled over their shoulders.

"What has this got to do with a puppy?" Courtney asked, cocking her head to one side, a puzzled frown on her face. How like Nolan she looked just then, Maryanne thought. The Nolan she remembered from the days of their courtship, the newspaper reporter who always seemed to be frowning at her for one reason or another.

"What your mother and I are attempting to explain is that…" He paused and a smile crept across his face.

"You're both going to be big sisters," Maryanne said.

Courtney understood the implications before her little sister did. "Mom's going to have a *baby*?"

Maryanne nodded.

The girls screamed with happiness. As if they'd been practicing the move for a week, they leaped off the bed and immediately started jumping up and down. Soon Nolan was laughing at their antics.

"I want another sister," Bailey insisted.

"No, no, a brother," Courtney said.

"Personally I'll be overjoyed with either," Nolan assured them all. His arm tightened around Maryanne's shoulders, and he buried his face in her neck as she hid a smile. While this baby was certainly unexpected, he was most welcome. Yes, he! Earlier in the day Maryanne had been at the doctor's, had her first ultrasound and received the news. How appropriate for Christmas-time… She'd tell Nolan as soon as the kids were asleep.

"Are you excited, Mom?" Courtney asked.

Maryanne nodded and held out her arms to her daughter. "Very much so."

Courtney came into the circle of Maryanne's arms. "A baby is even better than a puppy." She grinned. "But a puppy's good, too!"

"Yeah," Bailey said. She climbed into Nolan's lap, leaning her head against his chest.

"But you girls understand that a baby *and* a puppy at the same time would be too much, don't you?"

"Yes." Both girls nodded.

"Later," Courtney said in a solemn voice. "When the baby's older."

"Yeah," Bailey said again.

"Isn't it bedtime yet?" Nolan asked.

"Not yet," Bailey said. "I can't sleep, I'm too excited."

"I can't either." Courtney gazed up at her mother.

"Tell us a story," Bailey suggested. "A *long* story."

"You should get into bed first," Nolan said, and both girls reluctantly climbed back into their beds, and pulled the covers all the way up to their chins.

"Do you want me to read to you?" Nolan asked.

"Not a book," Courtney said. "Tell us a *real* story."

"About Grandpa and the newspaper business?" Maryanne knew how much her daughters loved to hear about their grandfather Simpson when he'd first started his business.

"No," Courtney shook her head. "Tell us about how you and Daddy met."

"You already know that story," Nolan said.

"We want the unabridged version this time," Bailey piped up.

Unabridged? Only the seven-year-old daughter of a writer would know the meaning of that word.

"What do you think, Annie?" Nolan asked.

Grinning, Maryanne lowered her head. When they'd first met, Nolan had been convinced she was nothing more than a spoiled debutante. From that point on, he'd taken to referring to her as *Deb, Trouble* and, with obvious affection, Annie.

"It was love at first sight," Nolan told his children.

Maryanne smiled again. Despite his sometimes cynical manner, her husband could be a real romantic.

"Your mother was head over heels in love with me the minute we met," he went on.

"I don't remember it quite that way," Maryanne protested.

"You don't?" Nolan feigned surprise.

"No, because you infuriated me no end." She remembered the notorious column he'd written about her—"My Evening with the Debutante."

"Me?" His expression turned to one of exaggerated indignation.

"You thought I was a spoiled rich kid."

"You *were* spoiled."

"I most certainly was not." Although Maryanne could see the gleam in his eye, she wasn't going to let him get away with this. It was true her father owned the newspaper and had arranged for her position, but that didn't mean she didn't deserve the opportunity. She might not have worked her way up through the normal channels, but in time she'd proved herself to the staff at the *Seattle Review*. She'd also proved herself to Nolan—in a rather different way.

Courtney and Bailey exchanged glances.

"Are you fighting?" Bailey asked.

Nolan chuckled. "No, I was just setting your mother straight."

Maryanne raised her eyebrows. "Apparently your father remembers things differently from the way I do."

"Start at the beginning," Bailey urged.

Excitedly clapping her hands, Courtney added, "Don't forget to tell us about the time Daddy embarrassed you in front of the whole city."

Nolan had worked for the *Sun*, the rival paper in town. It wasn't as if Maryanne would ever forget the column he'd written about his evening with her. Even now, after all these years, she bristled at the memory. He'd informed the entire city of Seattle that she was a naive idealist, and worst of all, he'd announced that she was away from home for the first time and lonely.

"I still don't get why that column upset your mother so much," Nolan said, gesturing helplessly toward his daughters. "All I did was thank her for making me dinner."

"Did Daddy kiss you that night?" Bailey asked.

"No, he—"

"Don't tell us," Courtney cried, interrupting

Maryanne. "Start at the *very* beginning and don't leave anything out."

Nolan looked at Maryanne. "Why don't you tell them, sweetheart?"

"I'll tell them everything, then."

"Everything?" Nolan repeated.

Courtney rubbed her hands together. "Oh, boy, this is going to be good."

"It all started fifteen years ago…"

Chapter One

"Maryanne Simpson of the New York Simpsons, I presume?"

Maryanne glared at the man standing across from her in the reception area of the radio station. She pointedly ignored his sarcasm, keeping her blue eyes as emotionless as possible.

Nolan Adams—Seattle's most popular journalist— looked nothing like the polished professional man in the black-and-white photo that headed his daily column. Instead he resembled a well-known disheveled television detective. He even wore a wrinkled raincoat, one that looked as if he'd slept in it for an entire week.

"Or should I call you Deb?" he taunted.

"Ms. Simpson will suffice," she said in her best finishing-school voice. The rival newspaperman was cocky and arrogant—and the best damn journalist Maryanne had ever read. Maryanne was a good columnist herself, or at least she was desperately striving to become one. Her father, who owned the *Seattle Review* and twelve other daily newspapers nationwide, had seen to it that she was given this once-in-a-lifetime opportunity with the Seattle paper. She was working hard to prove herself. Perhaps too hard. That was when the trouble had begun.

"So how's the heart?" Nolan asked, reaching for a magazine and flipping idly through the dog-eared pages. "Is it still bleeding from all those liberal views of yours?"

Maryanne ignored the question, removed her navy-blue wool coat and neatly folded it over the back of a chair. "My heart's just fine, thank you."

With a sound she could only describe as a snicker, he threw himself down on a nearby chair and indolently brought an ankle up to rest on his knee.

Maryanne sat across from him, stiff and straight in the high-backed chair, and boldly met his eyes. Everything she needed to know about Nolan Adams could be seen in his face. The strong well-defined lines of his jaw told her how stubborn he could be. His eyes were dark, intelligent and intense. And his mouth…well, that was another story altogether. It seemed to wrestle with itself before ever breaking into a smile, as if a gesture of amusement went against his very nature. Nolan wasn't smiling now. And Maryanne wasn't about to let him see how much he intimidated her. But some emotion must have shone in her eyes, because he said abruptly, "You're the one who started this, you know?"

Maryanne was well aware of that. But this rivalry between them had begun unintentionally, at least on her part. The very morning that the competition's paper, the *Seattle Sun,* published Nolan's column on solutions to the city's housing problem, the *Review* had run Maryanne's piece on the same subject. Nolan's article was meant to be satirical, while Maryanne's was deadly serious. Her mistake was in stating that there were those in the city who apparently found the situation amusing, and she blasted anyone who behaved so irresponsibly. This was not a joking matter, she'd pointed out.

It looked as if she'd read Nolan's column and set out to reprimand him personally for his cavalier attitude.

Two days later, Nolan's column poked fun at her, asking what Ms. High Society could possibly know about affordable housing. Clearly a debutante had never had to worry about the roof over her head, he'd snarled. But more than that, he'd made her suggestions to alleviate the growing problem sound both frivolous and impractical.

Her next column came out the same evening and referred to tough pessimistic reporters who took themselves much too seriously. She went so far as to make fun of a fictional Seattle newsman who resembled Nolan Adams to a T.

Nolan retaliated once more, and Maryanne seethed. Obviously she'd have to be the one to put an end to this silliness. She hoped that not responding to Nolan's latest attack would terminate their rivalry, but she should've known better. An hour after her column on community spirit had hit the newsstands, KJBR, a local radio station, called, asking Maryanne to give a guest editorial. She'd immediately agreed, excited and honored at the invitation. It wasn't until later that she learned Nolan Adams would also be speaking. The format was actually a celebrity debate, a fact of which she'd been blithely unaware.

The door opened and a tall dark-haired woman walked into the station's reception area. "I'm Liz Walters," she said, two steps into the room. "I produce the news show. I take it you two know each other?"

"Like family," Nolan muttered with that cocky grin of his.

"We introduced ourselves five minutes ago," Maryanne rebutted stiffly.

"Good," Liz said without glancing up from her clipboard. "If you'll both come this way, we'll get you set up in the control booth."

From her brief conversation with the show's host, Brian Campbell, Maryanne knew that the show taped on Thursday night wouldn't air until Sunday evening.

When they were both seated inside the control booth, Maryanne withdrew two typed pages from her bag. Not to be outdone, Nolan made a show of pulling a small notepad from the huge pocket of his crumpled raincoat.

Brian Campbell began the show with a brief introduction, presenting the evening's subject: the growing popularity of the Seattle area. He then turned the microphone over to Maryanne, who was to speak first.

Forcing herself to relax, she took a deep calming breath, tucked her long auburn hair behind her ears and started speaking. She managed to keep her voice low and as well modulated as her nerves would allow.

"The word's out," she said, quickly checking her notes. "Seattle has been rated one of the top cities in the country for several years running. Is it any wonder Californians are moving up in droves, attracted by the area's economic growth, the lure of pure fresh air and beautiful clean waters? Seattle has appeal, personality and class."

As she warmed to her subject, her voice gained confidence and conviction. She'd fallen in love with Seattle when she'd visited for a two-day stopover before flying to Hawaii. The trip had been a college graduation gift from her parents. She'd returned to New York one week later full of enthusiasm, not for the tourist-cluttered islands, but for the brief glimpse she'd had of the Emerald City.

From the first, she'd intended to return to the Pacific Northwest. Instead she'd taken a job as a nonfiction editor in one of her father's New York publishing houses; she'd been so busy that travelling time was limited. That editorial job lasted almost eighteen months, and although Maryanne had thoroughly enjoyed it, she longed to write herself and put her journalism skills to work.

Samuel Simpson must have sensed her restlessness because he mentioned an opening at the *Seattle Review,* a long-established paper, when they met in Nantucket over Labor Day weekend. Maryanne had plied him with questions, mentioning more than once that she'd fallen in love with Seattle. Her father had grinned, chewing vigorously on the end of his cigar, and looked towards his wife of twenty-seven years before he'd casually reached for the telephone. After a single call lasting less than three minutes, Samuel announced that the job was hers. Within two weeks, Maryanne was packed and on her way west.

"In conclusion I'd like to remind our audience that there's no turning back now," Maryanne said. "Seattle sits as a polished jewel in the beautiful Pacific Northwest. Seattle, the Emerald City, awaits even greater prosperity, even more progress."

She set her papers aside and smiled in the direction of the host, relieved to be finished. She watched in dismay as Nolan scowled at her, then slipped his notepad back inside his pocket. He apparently planned to wing it.

Nolan—who needed, Brian declared, no introduction—leaned toward the microphone. He glanced at Maryanne, frowned once more, and slowly shook his head.

"Give me a break, Ms. Simpson!" he cried. "Doesn't anyone realize it *rains* here? Did you know that until recently, if Seattle went an entire week without rain, we sacrificed a virgin? Unfortunately we were running low on those until you moved to town."

Maryanne barely managed to restrain a gasp.

"Why do you think Seattle has remained so beautiful?" Nolan continued. "Why do you think we aren't suffering from the pollution problems so prevalent in Southern California and elsewhere? You seem to believe Seattle should throw open her arms and invite the world to park on our unspoiled doorstep. My advice to you, and others like you, is to go back where you came from. We don't want you turning Seattle into another L.A.—or New York."

The hair on the back of Maryanne's neck bristled. Although he spoke in general terms, his words seemed to be directed solely at her. He was telling her, in effect, to pack up her suitcase and head home to Mommy and Daddy where she belonged.

When Nolan finished, they were each given two minutes for a rebuttal.

"Some of what you have to say is true," Maryanne admitted through clenched teeth. "But you can't turn back progress. Only a fool," she said pointedly, "would try to keep families from settling in Washington state. You can argue until you've lost your voice, but it won't help. The population in this area is going to explode in the next few years whether you approve or not."

"That's probably true, but it doesn't mean I have to sit still and let it happen. In fact, I intend to do everything I can to put a stop to it," he said. "We in Seattle have a way of life to protect and a duty to future generations. If growth continues in this vein, our schools will soon be overcrowded, our homes so overpriced that no one except those from out of state will be able to afford housing—and that's only if they can find it. If that's what you want, then fine, bask in your ignorance."

"What do you suggest?" Maryanne burst out. "Setting up road blocks?"

"That's a start," Nolan returned sarcastically. "Something's got to be done before this area becomes another urban disaster."

Maryanne rolled her eyes. "Do you honestly think you're going to single-handedly turn back the tide of progress?"

"I'm sure as hell going to try."

"That's ridiculous."

"And that's our Celebrity Debate for this evening," Brian Campbell said quickly, cutting off any further argument. "Join us next week when our guests will be City Council candidates Nick Fraser and Robert Hall."

The microphone was abruptly switched off. "That

was excellent," the host said, flashing them a wide enthusiastic smile. "Thank you both."

"You've got your head buried in the sand," Maryanne felt obliged to inform Nolan, although she knew it wouldn't do any good. She dropped her notes back in her bag and snapped it firmly shut, as if to say the subject was now closed.

"You may be right," Nolan said with a grin. "But at least the sand is on a pollution-free beach. If you have your way, it'll soon be cluttered with—"

"If I have my way?" she cried. "You make it sound as though I'm solely responsible for the Puget Sound growth rate."

"You *are* responsible, and those like you."

"Well, excuse me," she muttered sarcastically. She nodded politely to Brian Campbell, then hurried back to the reception room where she'd left her coat. To her annoyance Nolan followed her.

"I don't excuse you, Deb."

"I asked you to use my name," she said furiously, "and it isn't Deb."

Crossing his arms over his chest, Nolan leaned lazily against the doorjamb while she retrieved her wool coat.

Maryanne crammed her arms into the sleeves and nearly tore off the buttons in her rush to leave. The way he stood there studying her did little to cool her temper.

"And another thing…" she muttered.

"You mean there's more?"

"You're darn right there is. That crack about virgins was intolerably rude! I…I expected better of you."

"Hell, it's true."

"How would you know?"

He grinned that insufferable grin of his, infuriating her even more.

"Don't you have anything better to do than follow me around?" she demanded, stalking out of the room.

"Not particularly. Fact is, I've been looking forward to meeting you."

Once she'd recovered from the shock of learning that he'd be her opponent in this radio debate, Maryanne had eagerly anticipated this evening, too. Long before she'd arrived at the radio station, she'd planned to tell Nolan how much she admired his work. This silly rivalry between them was exactly that: silly. She hadn't meant to step on his toes and would've called and cleared the air if he hadn't attacked her in print at the earliest opportunity.

"Sure you wanted to meet me. Hurling insults to my face must be far more fun."

He laughed at that and Maryanne was astonished at how rich and friendly his amusement sounded.

"Come on, Simpson, don't take everything so personally. Admit it. We've been having a good time poking fun at each other."

Maryanne didn't say anything for a moment. Actually he was partially right. She *had* enjoyed their exchanges, although she wouldn't have admitted that earlier. She wasn't entirely sure she wanted to now.

"Admit it," he coaxed, again with a grin.

That uneven smile of his was her undoing. "It hasn't exactly been *fun*," she answered reluctantly, "but it's been…interesting."

"That's what I thought." He thrust his hands into his pockets, looking pleased with himself.

She glanced at him appraisingly. The man's appeal was definitely of the rugged variety: his outrageous charm—Maryanne wasn't sure charm was really the right word—his craggy face and solid compact build. She'd been surprised to discover he wasn't as tall as she'd imagined. In fact, he was probably under six feet.

"Word has it Daddy was the one responsible for landing you this cushy job," he commented, interrupting her assessment.

"Cushy?" she repeated angrily. "You've got to be kidding!" She often put in twelve-hour days, trying to come up with a column that was both relevant and entertaining. In the four weeks since she'd joined the *Seattle Review*, she'd worked damn hard. She had something to prove, not only to herself but to her peers.

"So being a journalist isn't everything it's cracked up to be?"

"I didn't say that," she returned. To be perfectly honest, Maryanne had never tried harder at anything. Her pride and a whole lot more was riding on the outcome of the next few months. Samuel Simpson's daughter or not, she was on probation, after which her performance would be reviewed by the managing editor.

"I wonder if you've ever done anything without Daddy's approval."

"I wonder if you've always been this rude."

He chuckled at that. "Almost always. As I said, don't take it personally."

With her leather purse tucked securely under her arm, she marched to the exit, which Nolan was effectively blocking. "Excuse me, please."

"Always so polite," he murmured before he straightened, allowing her to pass.

Nolan followed her to the elevator, annoying her even more. Maryanne felt his scrutiny, and it flustered her. She knew she was reasonably attractive, but she also knew that no one was going to rush forward with a banner and a tiara. Her mouth was just a little too full, her eyes a little too round. Her hair had been fire-engine red the entire time she was growing up, but it had darkened to a deep auburn in her early twenties, a fact for which she remained truly grateful. Maryanne had always hated her red hair and the wealth of freckles that accompanied it. No one else in her family had been cursed with red hair, let alone freckles. Her mother's hair was a beautiful blonde and her father's a rich chestnut. Even her younger brothers had escaped her fate. If it weren't for the distinctive high Simpson forehead and deep blue eyes, Maryanne might have suspected she'd been adopted. But that wasn't the case. Instead she'd been forced to discover early in life how unfair heredity could be.

The elevator arrived, and both Maryanne and Nolan stepped inside. Nolan leaned against the side— he always seemed to be leaning, Maryanne noticed. Leaning and staring. He was studying her again; she could feel his eyes as profoundly as a caress.

"Would you kindly stop?" she snapped.

"Stop what?"

"Staring at me!"

"I'm curious."

"About what?" She was curious about him, too, but far too civilized to make an issue of it.

"I just wanted to see if all that blue blood showed."

"Oh, honestly!"

"I am being honest," he answered. "You know, you intrigue me, Simpson. Have you eaten?"

Maryanne's heart raced with excitement at the off-hand question. He seemed to be leading up to suggesting they dine together. Unfortunately she'd been around Nolan long enough to realize she couldn't trust the man. Anything she said or did would more than likely show up in that column of his.

"I've got an Irish stew simmering in a pot at home," she murmured, dismissing the invitation before he could offer it.

"Great! I love stew."

Maryanne opened her mouth to tell him she had no intention of asking him into her home. Not after the things he'd said about her in his column. But when she turned to tell him so, their eyes met. His were a deep, dark brown and almost…she couldn't be sure, but she thought she saw a faint glimmer of admiration. The edge of his mouth quirked upward with an unmistakable hint of challenge. He looked as if he expected her to reject him.

Against her better judgment, and knowing she'd live to regret this, Maryanne found herself smiling.

"My apartment's on Spring Street," she murmured.

"Good. I'll follow you."

She lowered her gaze, feeling chagrined and already regretful about the whole thing. "I didn't drive."

"Is your chauffeur waiting?" he asked, his voice and eyes mocking her in a manner that was practically friendly.

"I took a cab," she said, glancing away from him. "It's a way of life in Manhattan and I'm not accustomed to dealing with a car. So I don't have one." She half expected him to make some derogatory comment and was thankful when he didn't.

"I'll give you a lift, then."

He'd parked his car, a surprisingly stylish sedan, in a lot close to the waterfront. The late-September air was brisk, and Maryanne braced herself against it as Nolan cleared the litter off the passenger seat.

She slipped inside, grateful to be out of the chill. It didn't take her more than a couple of seconds to realize that Nolan treated his car the same way he treated his raincoat. The front and back seat were cluttered with empty paper cups, old newspapers and several paperback novels. Mysteries, she noted. The great Nolan Adams read mysteries. A container filled with loose change was propped inside his ashtray.

While Maryanne searched for the seatbelt, Nolan raced around the front of the car, slid inside and quickly started the engine. "I hope there's a place to park off Spring."

"Oh, don't worry," Maryanne quickly assured him, "I've got valet service."

Nolan murmured something under his breath. Had she made an effort, she might've been able to hear, but she figured she was probably better off not knowing.

He turned up the heater and Maryanne was warmed by a blast of air. "Let me know if that gets too hot for you."

"Thanks, I'm fine."

"Hot" seemed to describe their relationship. From the first, Maryanne had inadvertently got herself into scalding water with Nolan, water that came closer to the boiling point each time a new column appeared. "Hot" also described the way they seemed to ignite sparks off each other. The radio show had proved that much. There was another popular meaning of "hot"—one she refused to think about.

Nevertheless, Maryanne was grateful for the opportunity to bridge their differences, because, despite everything, she genuinely admired Nolan's writing.

They chatted amicably enough until Nolan pulled into the crescent-shaped driveway of The Seattle, the luxury apartment complex where she lived.

Max, the doorman, opened her car door, his stoic face breaking into a smile as he recognized her. When Nolan climbed out of the driver's side, Maryanne watched as Max's smile slowly turned into a frown, as though he wasn't certain Nolan was appropriate company for a respectable young lady.

"Max, this is Mr. Adams from the *Seattle Sun*."

"Nolan Adams?" Max's expression altered immediately. "You don't look like your picture. I read your work faithfully, Mr. Adams. You gave ol' Larson hell last month. From what I heard, your column was what forced him to resign from City Council."

Nolan had given Maryanne hell, too, but she refrained from mentioning it. She doubted Max had ever read her work or was even aware that Nolan had been referring to her in some of his columns.

"Would you see to Mr. Adams's car?" Maryanne asked.

"Right away, Ms. Simpson."

Burying his hands in his pockets, Nolan and Maryanne walked into the extravagantly decorated foyer with its huge crystal chandelier and bubbling fountain. "My apartment's on the eleventh floor," she said, pushing the elevator button.

"Not the penthouse suite?" he teased.

Maryanne smiled weakly in response. While they rode upward, she concentrated on taking her keys from her bag to hide her sudden nervousness. Her heart was banging against her ribs. Now that Nolan was practically at her door, she wondered how she'd let this happen. After the things he'd called her, the least of which were Ms. High Society, Miss Debutante and Daddy's Darling, she felt more than a little vulnerable in his company.

"Are you ready to change your mind?" he asked. Apparently, he'd read her thoughts.

"No, of course not," she lied.

She noticed—but sincerely hoped Nolan didn't— that her hand was shaking when she inserted the key.

She turned on the light as she walked into the spacious apartment. Nolan followed her, his brows raised at the sight of the modern white leather-and-chrome-furniture. There was even a fireplace.

"Nice place you've got here," he said, glancing around.

She thought she detected sarcasm in his voice, then decided it was what she could expect from him all evening; she might as well get used to it.

"I'll take your raincoat," she said. Considering the fondness with which he wore the thing, he might well choose to eat in it, too.

To Maryanne's surprise, he handed it to her, then walked over to the fireplace and lifted a family photo from the mantel. The picture had been taken several summers earlier, when they'd all been sailing off Martha's Vineyard. Maryanne was facing into the wind and laughing at the antics of her younger brothers. It certainly wasn't her most flattering photo. In fact, she looked as if she was gasping for air after being underwater too long. The wind had caught her red hair, its color even more pronounced against the backdrop of white sails.

"The two young men are my brothers. My mom and dad are at the helm."

Nolan stared at the picture for several seconds and then back at her. "So you're the only redhead."

"How kind of you to mention it."

"Hey, you're in luck. I happen to like redheads." He said this with such a lazy smile that Maryanne couldn't possibly be offended.

"I'll check the stew," she said, after hanging up their coats. She hurried into the kitchen and lifted the lid of the pot. The pungent aroma of stewing lamb, vegetables and basil filled the apartment.

"You weren't kidding, were you?" Nolan asked, sounding mildly surprised.

"Kidding? About what?"

"The Irish stew."

"No. I put it on this morning, before I left for work. I've got one of those all-day cookers." After living on her own for the past couple of years, Maryanne had become a competent cook. When she'd rented her first apartment in New York, she used to stop off at a deli on her way home, but that had soon become monotonous. Over the course of several months, she'd discovered some excellent recipes for simple nutritious meals. Her father wasn't going to publish a cookbook written by her, but she did manage to eat well.

"I thought the stew was an excuse not to have dinner with me," Nolan remarked conversationally. "I didn't know what to expect. You're my first deb."

"Some white wine?" she asked, ignoring his comment.

"Please."

Maryanne got a bottle from the refrigerator and expertly removed the cork. She filled them each a glass, then gave Nolan his and carried the bottle into the living room, where she set it on the glass-topped coffee table. Sitting down on one end of the white leather sofa, she slipped off her shoes and tucked her feet beneath her.

Nolan sat at the other end, resting his ankle on his knee, making himself at home. "Dare I propose a toast?" he asked.

"Please."

"To Seattle," he said, his mischievous gaze meeting hers. "May she forever remain unspoiled." He reached over and touched the rim of her glass with his.

"To Seattle," Maryanne returned. "The most enchanting city on the West Coast."

"But, please, don't let anyone know," he coaxed in a stage whisper.

"I'm not making any promises," she whispered back.

They tasted the wine, which had come highly recommended by a colleague at the paper. Maryanne had only recently learned that wines from Washington state were quickly gaining a world reputation for excellence. Apparently the soil, a rich sandy loam over a volcanic base, was the reason for that.

They talked about the wine for a few minutes, and the conversation flowed naturally after that, as they compared experiences and shared impressions. Maryanne was surprised by how much she was enjoying the company of this man she'd considered a foe. Actually, they did have several things in common. Perhaps she was enjoying his company simply because she was lonely, but she didn't think that was completely true. Still, she'd been too busy with work to do any socializing; she occasionally saw a few people from the paper, but other than that she hadn't had time to establish any friendships.

After a second glass of wine, feeling warm and relaxed, Maryanne was willing to admit exactly how isolated she'd felt since moving to Seattle.

"It's been so long since I went out on a real date," she said.

"There does seem to be a shortage of Ivy League guys in Seattle."

She giggled and nodded. "At least Dad's not sending along a troupe of eligible men for me to meet. I enjoyed living in New York, don't get me wrong, but every time I turned around, a man was introducing himself and telling me my father had given him my phone number. You're the first man I've had dinner with that Dad didn't handpick for me since I moved out on my own."

"I hate to tell you this, sugar, but I have the distinct impression your daddy would take one look at me and have me arrested."

"That's not the least bit true," Maryanne argued. "My dad isn't a snob, only…only if you do meet him take off the raincoat, okay?"

"The raincoat?"

"It looks like you sleep in it. All you need is a hat and a scrap of paper with 'Press' scrawled on it sticking out of the band—you'd look like you worked for the *Planet* in Metropolis."

"I hate to disillusion you, sugar, but I'm not Ivy League and I'm not Superman."

"Oh, darn," she said, snapping her fingers. "And we had such a good thing going." She was feeling too mellow to remind him not to call her sugar.

"So how old are you?" Nolan wanted to know. "Twenty-one?"

"Three," she amended. "And you?"

"A hundred and three in comparison."

Maryanne wasn't sure what he meant, but she let that pass, too. It felt good to have someone to talk to, someone who was her contemporary, or at least close to being her contemporary.

"If you don't want to tell me how old you are, then at least fill in some of the details of your life."

"Trust me, my life isn't nearly as interesting as yours."

"Bore me, then."

"All right," he said, drawing a deep breath. "My family was dirt-poor. Dad disappeared about the time I was ten and Mom took on two jobs to make ends meet. Get the picture?"

"Yes." She hesitated. "What about women?"

"I've had a long and glorious history."

"I'm not kidding, Nolan."

"You think I was?"

"You're not married."

"Not to my knowledge."

"Why not?"

He shrugged as if it was of little consequence. "No time for it. I came close once, but her family didn't consider my writing career noble enough. Her father tried to fix me up with a job in his insurance office."

"What happened?"

"Nothing much. I told her I was going to work for the paper, and she claimed if I really loved her I'd accept her father's generous offer. It didn't take me long to decide. I guess she was right—I didn't love her."

He sounded nonchalant, implying that the episode hadn't cost him a moment's regret, but just looking at him told Maryanne otherwise. Nolan had been deeply hurt. Every sarcastic irreverent word he wrote suggested it.

In retrospect, Maryanne mused one afternoon several days later, she'd thoroughly enjoyed her evening with Nolan. They'd eaten, and he'd raved about her Irish stew until she flushed at his praise. She'd made them cups of café au lait while he built a fire. They'd sat in front of the fireplace and talked for hours. He'd told her more about his own large family, his seven brothers and sisters. How he'd worked his way through two years of college, but was forced to give up his education when he couldn't afford to continue. As it turned out, he'd been grateful because that decision had led to his first newspaper job. And, as they said, the rest was history.

"You certainly seem to be in a good mood," her coworker, Carol Riverside, said as she strolled past Maryanne's desk later that same afternoon. Carol was short, with a pixielike face and friendly manner. Maryanne had liked her from the moment they'd met.

"I'm in a fabulous mood," Maryanne said, smiling. Nolan had promised to pay her back by taking her out to dinner. He hadn't set a definite date, but she half expected to hear from him that evening.

"In that case, I hate to be the bearer of bad tidings, but someone has to tell you, and I was appointed."

"Tell me? What?" Maryanne glanced around the huge open office and noted that several faces were staring in her direction, all wearing sympathetic looks. "What's going on?" she demanded.

Carol moved her arm out from behind her and Maryanne noticed that she was holding a copy of the rival paper's morning edition. "It's Nolan Adams's column," Carol said softly, her eyes wide and compassionate.

"W-what did he say this time?"

"Well, let's put it this way. He titled it, 'My Evening with the Debutante.'"

Chapter Two

Maryanne was much too furious to stand still. She paced her living room from one end to the other, her mind spitting and churning. A slow painful death was too good for Nolan Adams.

Her phone rang and she went into the kitchen to answer it. She reached for it so fast she nearly ripped it off the wall. Rarely did she allow herself to become this angry, but complicating her fury was a deep and aching sense of betrayal. "Yes," she said forcefully.

"This is Max," her doorman announced. "Mr. Adams is here. Shall I send him up?"

For an instant Maryanne was too stunned to speak. The man had nerve, she'd say that much for him. Raw courage, too, if he knew the state of mind she was in.

"Ms. Simpson?"

It took Maryanne only about a second to decide. "Send him up," she said with deceptive calm.

Arms hugging her waist, Maryanne continued pacing. She was going to tell this man in no uncertain terms what she thought of his duplicity, his treachery. He might have assumed from their evening together that she was a gentle, forgiving soul who'd quietly overlook this. Well, if that was his belief, Maryanne was looking forward to enlightening him.

Her doorbell chimed and she turned to glare at it. Wishing her heart would stop pounding, she gulped in a deep breath, then walked calmly across the living room and opened the door.

"Hello, Maryanne," Nolan said, his eyes immediately meeting hers.

She stood exactly where she was, imitating his tactic of leaning against the door frame and blocking the threshold.

"May I come in?" he asked mildly.

"I haven't decided yet." He was wearing the raincoat again, which looked even more disreputable than before.

"I take it you read my column?" he murmured, one eyebrow raised.

"Read it?" she nearly shouted. "Of course I read it, and so, it seems, did everyone else in Seattle. Did you really think I'd be able to hold my head up after that? Or was that your intention—humiliating me and…and making me a laughingstock?" She stabbed her index finger repeatedly against his solid chest. "And if you think no one'll figure out it was me just because you didn't use my name, think again."

"I take it you're angry?" He raised his eyebrows again, as if to suggest she was overreacting.

"Angry! Angry? That isn't the half of it, buster!" The problem with being raised in a God-fearing, flag-loving family was that the worst thing she could think of to call him out loud was *buster*. Plenty of other names flashed through her mind, but none she dared verbalize. No doubt Nolan would delight in revealing this in his column, too.

Furious, she grabbed his tie and jerked him into the apartment. "You can come inside," she said.

"Thanks. I think I will," Nolan said wryly. He smoothed his tie, which drew her attention to the hard defined muscles of his chest. The last thing Maryanne wanted to do was notice how virile he looked, and she forced her gaze away from him.

Because it was impossible to stand still, she resumed her pacing. With the first rush of anger spent, she had no idea what to say to him, how to make him realize the enormity of what he'd done. Abruptly, she paused at the edge of her living room and pointed an accusing finger at him. "You have your nerve."

"What I said was true," Nolan stated, boldly meeting her glare. "If you'd bothered to read the column all the way through, objectively, you'd have noticed there were several complimentary statements."

"'A naive idealist, an optimist…'" she said, quoting what she remembered, the parts that had offended her the most. "You made me sound like Mary Poppins!"

"Surprisingly unspoiled and gentle," Nolan returned, "and very much a lady."

"You told the entire city I was *lonely*," she cried, mortified to even repeat the words.

"I didn't say you were lonely," Nolan insisted, his voice all too reasonable and controlled. That infuriated her even more. "I said you were away from your family for the first time."

She poked his chest again, punctuating her speech. "But you made it sound like I should be in a day-care centre!"

"I didn't imply anything of the kind," he contended. "And I did mention what a good cook you are."

"I'm supposed to be grateful for that? As I recall you said, I was 'surprisingly adept in the kitchen'— as if you were amazed I knew the difference between a goldfish bowl and an oven."

"You're blowing the whole thing out of proportion."

Maryanne barely heard him. "The comment about my being insecure was the worst. You want security, buster, you're looking at security. My feet could be molded in cement, I'm that secure." Defiant angry eyes flashed to him as she pointed at her shoes.

Nolan didn't so much as blink. "You work twice as hard as anyone else at the *Review*, and twice as many hours. You push yourself because you've got something to prove."

A strained silence followed his words. She *did* work hard, she *was* trying to prove herself, and Nolan knew it. Except for high school and college, she'd had no experience working at a newspaper.

"Did you wake up one morning and decide to play Sigmund Freud with my life?" she demanded. "Who, may I ask, gave you that right?"

"What I said is true, Maryanne," he told her again. "I don't expect you to admit it to me, but if you're honest you'll at least admit it to yourself. Your family is your greatest asset and your weakest link. From everything I've read about the Simpsons, they're good people, but they've cheated you out of something important."

"Exactly what do you mean by that?" she snapped, ready to defend her father to the death, if need be. How dared this pompous, arrogant, argumentative man insult her family?

"You'll never know if you're a good enough journalist to get a job like this without your father's help. He handed you this plum position, and at the same time cheated you out of a just reward."

Maryanne opened her mouth, an argument on the tip of her tongue. Instead, she lowered her gaze, since she couldn't deny what he'd just said. From the moment she arrived at the *Seattle Review,* she'd known that Carol Riverside was the one who'd earned the right to be the local-affairs columnist, not her. And yet Carol had been wonderfully supportive and kind.

"It wasn't my intention to insult you or your family," Nolan continued.

"Then why did you write that column?" she asked, her voice quavering. "Did you think I was going to be flattered by it?"

He'd been so quick with the answers that his silence caught her attention more effectively than anything he could've said. She watched as he started pacing. He drew his fingers through his hair and his shoulders rose in a distinct sigh.

"I'm not sure. In retrospect, I believe I wanted to set the record straight. At least that was my original intent. I wrote more than I should have, but the piece was never meant to ridicule you. Whether you know it or not, you impressed the hell out of me the other night."

"Am I supposed to be grateful you chose to thank me publicly?"

"No," he answered sharply. Once more he jerked his fingers roughly through his hair. He didn't wince, but Maryanne did—which was interesting, since only a few minutes earlier she'd been daydreaming about the joy she'd experience watching this man suffer.

"Inviting myself to dinner the other night was an impulse," he admitted grudgingly. "The words slipped out before I realized what I was saying. I don't know who was more surprised, you or me. I tried to act like I knew what I was doing, play it cool, that sort of thing. The fact is, I discovered I like you. Trust me, I wasn't in any frame of mind to talk civilly to you when you got to the radio station. All along I'd assumed you were a spoiled rich kid, but I was wrong. Since I'd published several pieces that suggested as much, I felt it was only fair to set the record straight. Besides, for a deb you aren't half-bad."

"Why is it every time you compliment me I feel a knife between my shoulder blades?"

"We certainly don't have a whole lot in common," Nolan said thoughtfully. "I learned most everything I know on the streets, not in an expensive private school. I doubt there's a single political issue we can agree on. You're standing on one side of the fence and I'm way over on the other. We're about as far apart as any two people could ever be. Socially. Economically. And every other way I could mention. We have no business even speaking to each other, and yet we sat down and shared a meal and talked for hours."

"I felt betrayed by that column today."

"I know. I apologize, although the damage is already done. I guess I wasn't aware it would offend you. Like I said, that wasn't what I intended at all." He released a giant sigh and paused, as though collecting his thoughts. "After I left your place, I felt good. I can't remember a time I've enjoyed myself more. You're a charming, interesting—"

"You might have said *that* in your column!"

"I did, only you were obviously too upset to notice it. When I got home that night, I couldn't sleep. Every time I'd drift off, I'd think of something you'd said, and before I knew it I'd be grinning. Finally I got up and sat at my desk and started writing. The words poured out of me as fast as I could type them. The quality that impressed me the most about you was your honesty. There's no pretense in you, and the more I thought about that, the more I felt you've been cheated."

"And you decided it was your duty to point all this out—for everyone in town to read?"

"No, it wasn't. That's why I'm here. I admit I went further than I should have and came over to apologize."

"If you're telling me this to make me feel better, it isn't working." Her ego was rebounding somewhat, but he still had a lot of apologizing to do.

"To be honest, I didn't give the column a second thought until this afternoon, when someone in the office said I'd really done it now. If I was hoping to make peace with you, I'd failed. This friend said I was likely to get hit by the wrath of a woman scorned and suggested I run for cover."

"Rightly so!"

"Forgive me, Maryanne. It was arrogant in the extreme of me to publish that piece. If it'll make you feel any better, you can blast me to kingdom come in your next column. I solemnly promise I'll never write another word about you."

"Don't be so humble—it doesn't suit you," she

muttered, gnawing on her lower lip. "Besides, I won't be able to print a rebuttal."

"Why not?"

"I don't plan on working for the *Review* any more, or at least not after tomorrow." The idea seemed to emerge fully formed; until that moment she hadn't known what she was going to say.

The silence following her words was fraught with tension. "What do you mean?"

"Don't act so surprised. I'm quitting the paper."

"What? Why?" Nolan had been standing during their whole conversation, but he suddenly found it necessary to sit. He lowered himself slowly to the sofa, his face pale. "You're overreacting! There's no need to do anything so drastic."

"There's every need. You said so yourself. You told me I've been cheated, that if I'm even half as good a reporter as I think I am I would've got this 'plum position' on my own. I'm just agreeing with you."

He nodded stiffly.

"As painful as this is to admit, especially to you," she went on, "you're right. My family is wonderful, but they've never allowed me to fall on my face. Carol Riverside is the one who deserved the chance to write that column. She's been with the paper for five years— I'd only been there five minutes. But because my name is Simpson, and because my father made a simple phone call, I was given the job. Carol was cheated. She should've been furious. Instead, she was kind and helpful." Maryanne sat down next to Nolan and propped her feet on the coffee table. "And maybe worse than what happened to Carol is what happened to me as a result of being handed this job. What you wrote about me wondering if I had what it takes to make it as a journalist hit too close to home. All my life my father's been there to tell me I can be anything I want to be and then he promptly arranges it."

"Quitting the *Review* isn't going to change that," Nolan argued. "Come on, Maryanne, you're taking this too seriously."

"Nothing you say is going to change my mind," Maryanne informed him primly. "The time has come for me to cut myself loose and sink or swim on my own."

Her mind was galloping ahead, adjusting to the coming changes. For the first time since she'd read Nolan's column that afternoon, she experienced the beginnings of excitement. She glanced around the apartment as another thought struck her. "Naturally I'll have to move out of this place."

"Are you going back to New York?"

"Heavens, no!" she declared, unaccountably thrilled at the reluctance she heard in his voice. "I love Seattle."

"Listen to me, would you? You're leaping into the deep end, you don't know how to swim and the lifeguard's off duty."

Maryanne hardly heard Nolan, mainly because she

didn't like what he was saying. How like a man to start a bonfire and then rush to put out the flames. "The first thing I need to worry about is finding another job," she announced. "A temporary one, of course. I'm going to continue writing, but I don't think I'll be able to support myself on that, not at first, anyway."

"If you insist on this folly, you could always freelance for the *Sun*."

Maryanne discounted that suggestion with a shake of her head. "I'd come off looking like a traitor."

"I suppose you're right." His eyebrows drew together as he frowned.

"You know what else I'm going to do?" She shifted her position, tucking her legs beneath her. "I've got this trust fund that provides a big interest payment every month. That's what I've been using to pay my bills. You and I both know I couldn't afford this place on what I make at the paper. Well, I'm not going to touch those interest payments and I'll live solely on what I earn."

"I…wouldn't do that right away, if I were you."

"Why not?"

"You just said you were quitting your job." Nolan sounded uneasy. "I can see that I've set off an avalanche here, and I'm beginning to feel mildly concerned."

"Where do you live?"

"Capitol Hill. Listen, if you're serious about moving, you need to give some thought as to what kind of neighborhood you're getting into. Seattle's a great town, don't get me wrong, but like any place we have our problem areas." He hesitated. "Annie, I don't feel comfortable with this."

"No one's ever called me Annie before." Her eyes smiled into his. "What do you pay in rent?"

With his hands buried deep in his pants pockets, he mumbled something under his breath, then mentioned a figure that was one-third of what she was currently dishing out every month.

"That's more than reasonable."

Maryanne saw surprise in his eyes, and smiled again. "If you're so concerned about my finding the right neighborhood, then you pick one for me. Anyplace, I don't care. Just remember, you're the one who got me into this."

"Don't remind me." Nolan's frown darkened.

"I may not have appreciated what you said about me in your column," Maryanne said slowly, "but I'm beginning to think good things might come of it."

"I'm beginning to think I should be dragged to the nearest tree and hanged," Nolan grumbled.

"Hi." Maryanne slipped into the booth opposite Nolan at the greasy spoon called Mom's Place. She smiled, feeling like a child on a grand adventure. Perhaps she *was* going off the deep end, as Nolan had so adamantly claimed the day before. Perhaps, but she doubted it. Everything felt so *right*.

Once the idea of living on her own—on income she earned herself, from a job she'd been hired for on her own merits—had taken hold in her mind, it had fast gained momentum. She could work days and write nights. That would be perfect.

"Did you do it?"

"I handed in my notice this morning," she said, reaching for the menu. Nolan had insisted on meeting her for a late lunch and suggested this greasy spoon with its faded neon sign that flashed Home Cooking. She had the impression he ate there regularly.

"I talked to the managing editor this morning and told him I was leaving."

"I don't imagine he took kindly to that," Nolan muttered, lifting a white ceramic mug half-full of coffee. He'd been wearing a frown from the moment she'd entered the diner. She had the feeling it was the same frown he'd left her apartment with the night before, but it had deepened since she'd last seen him.

"Larry wasn't too upset, but I don't think he appreciated my suggestion that Carol Riverside take over the column, because he said something I'd rather not repeat about how he was the one who'd do the hiring and promoting, not me, no matter what my name was."

Nolan took a sip of coffee and grinned. "I'd bet he'd like my head if it could be arranged, and frankly I don't blame him."

"Don't worry, I didn't mention your name or the fact that your column was what led to my decision."

Maryanne doubted Nolan even heard her. "I'm regretting that column more with each passing minute. Are you sure I can't talk you out of this?"

"I'm sure."

He sighed and shook his head. "How'd the job hunting go?"

The waitress came by, automatically placing a full mug of coffee in front of Maryanne. She fished a pad from the pocket of her pink apron. "Are you ready to order?"

"I'll have a turkey sandwich on rye, no sprouts, a diet soda and a side of potato salad," Maryanne said with a smile, handing her the menu.

"You don't need to worry, we don't serve sprouts here," she said, scribbling down the order.

"I'll have the chili, Barbara," Nolan said. The waitress nodded and strolled away from the booth. "I was asking how your job hunting went," Nolan reminded Maryanne.

"I found one!"

"Where? What will you be doing? And for how much?"

"You're beginning to sound like my father."

"I'm beginning to *feel* like your father. Annie, you're a babe in the woods. You don't have a clue what you're getting involved in. Heaven knows I've tried to talk some sense into you, but you refuse to listen. And, as you so delight in reminding me, I'm the one responsible for all this."

"Stop blaming yourself." Maryanne leaned across the table for her water glass. "I'm grateful, I honestly am—though, trust me, I never thought I'd be saying that. But what you wrote was true. By insulting me, you've given me the initiative to make a name for myself without Dad's help and—"

He closed his eyes. "Just answer the question."

"Oh, about the job. It's for a…service company. It looks like it'll work out great. I didn't think I'd have any chance of getting hired, since I don't have much experience, but they took that into consideration. You see, it's a new company and they can't afford to pay much. Everyone seems friendly and helpful. The only drawback is my salary and the fact that I won't be working a lot of hours at first. In fact, the money is a lot less than I was earning at the paper. But I expect to be able to sell a couple of articles soon. I'll get along all right once I learn to budget."

"How much less than the paper?"

"If I tell you, you'll only get angry." His scowl said he'd be even angrier if she didn't tell him. From the way he was glaring at her, Maryanne knew she'd reached the limits of his patience. She muttered the amount and promptly lowered her gaze.

"You aren't taking the job," Nolan said flatly.

"Yes, I am. It's the best I can do for now. Besides, it's only temporary. It isn't all that easy to find work, you know. I must've talked to fifteen companies today. No one seemed too impressed with my double degree in Early American History and English. I wanted to find employment where I can use my writing skills, but that didn't happen, so I took this job."

"Annie, you won't be able to live on so little."

"I realize that. I've got a list of community newspapers and I'm going to contact them about freelance work. I figure between the writing and my job, I'll do okay."

"Exactly *what* will you be doing?" he demanded.

"Cleaning," she mumbled under her breath.

"What did you say?"

"I'm working for Rent-A-Maid."

"Dear Lord," Nolan groaned. "I hope you're kidding."

"Get your mind out of the gutter, Adams. I'm going to work six hours a day cleaning homes and offices and I'll spend the rest of the time doing research for my articles. Oh, and before I forget, I gave your name as a reference."

"You're going to go back and tell whoever hired you that you're terribly sorry, but you won't be able to work there, after all," Nolan said, and the hard set of his mouth told her he brooked no argument.

Maryanne was saved from having to say she had no intention of quitting, because the waitress, bless her heart, appeared with their orders at precisely that moment.

"Now what about an apartment?" Maryanne asked. After his comment about living in a safe neighborhood, she was more than willing to let him locate one for her. "Have you had a chance to check into that for me?"

"I hope you didn't give your notice at The Seattle."

Swallowing a bite of her sandwich, Maryanne nodded eagerly. "First thing this morning. I told them I'd be out by the fifteenth, which, in case you were unaware of it, happens to be early next week."

"You shouldn't have done that."

"I can't afford the place! And I won't be able to eat in restaurants everyday or take cabs or buy things whenever I want them." She smiled proudly as she said it. Money had never been a problem in her life—it had sometimes been an issue, but never a problem. She felt invigorated just thinking about her new status.

"Will you stop grinning at me like that?" Nolan burst out.

"Sorry, it's sort of a novelty to say I can't afford something, that's all," she explained. "It actually feels kind of good."

"In a couple of weeks it's going to feel like hell." Nolan's face spelled out apprehension and gloom.

"Then I'll learn that for myself." She noticed he hadn't touched his meal. "Go ahead and eat your chili before it gets cold."

"I've lost my appetite." He immediately contradicted himself by grabbing a small bottle of hot sauce and dousing the chili with several hard shakes.

"Now did you or did you not find me a furnished studio apartment to look at this afternoon?" Maryanne pressed.

"I found one. It's nothing like you're used to, so be prepared. I'll take you there once we're finished lunch."

"Tell me about it," Maryanne said eagerly.

"There's one main room, small kitchen, smaller bathroom, tiny closet, no dishwasher." He paused as if he expected her to jump to her feet and tell him the whole thing was off.

"Go on," she said, reaching for her soda.

"The floors are pretty worn but they're hardwood."

"That'll be nice." She didn't know if she'd ever lived in a place that didn't have carpeting, but she'd adjust.

"The furniture's solid enough. It's old and weighs a ton, but I don't know how comfortable it is."

"I'm sure it'll be fine. I'll be working just about every day, so I can't see that there'll be a problem," Maryanne returned absently. As soon as she'd spoken, she realized her mistake.

Nolan stabbed his spoon into the chili. "You seem to have forgotten you're resuming your job hunt. You won't be working for Rent-A-Maid, and that's final."

"You sound like a parent again. I'm old enough to know what I can and can't do, and I'm going to take that job whether you like it or not, and *that's final*."

His eyes narrowed. "We'll see."

"Yes, we will," she retorted. Nolan might be an astute journalist, but there were several things he had yet to learn about her, and one of them was her stubborn streak. The thought produced a small smile as she realized she was thinking of him in a way that suggested a long-term friendship. He was right when he said they stood on opposite sides of the fence on most issues. He was also right when he claimed they had no business being friends. Nevertheless, Nolan Adams was the most intriguing man she'd ever met.

Once they'd finished their meal, Nolan reached for the bill, but Maryanne insisted on splitting it. He clearly wasn't pleased about that but let it pass. Apparently he wasn't going to argue with her, which suited Maryanne just fine. He escorted her to his car, parked outside the diner, and Maryanne slid inside, absurdly pleased that he'd cleaned up the front seat for her.

Nolan hesitated when he joined her, his hands on the steering wheel. "Are you sure you want to go through with this?"

"Positive."

"I was afraid you were going to say that." His mouth twisted. "I can't believe I'm aiding and abetting this nonsense."

"You're my friend, and I'm grateful."

Without another word, he started the engine.

"Where's the apartment?" Maryanne asked as the

car progressed up the steep Seattle hills. "I mean, what neighborhood?"

"Capitol Hill."

"Oh, how nice. Isn't that the same part of town you live in?" It wasn't all that far from The Seattle, either, which meant she'd still have the same telephone exchange. Maybe she could even keep her current number.

"Yes," he muttered. He didn't seem to be in the mood for conversation and kept his attention on his driving, instead. He pulled into a parking lot behind an eight-storey post-World War II brick building. "The apartment's on the fourth floor."

"That'll be fine." She climbed out of the car and stared at the old structure. The Dumpster was backed against the wall and full to overflowing. Maryanne had to step around it before entering by a side door. Apparently there was no elevator, and by the time they reached the fourth floor she was so winded she couldn't have found the breath to complain, anyway.

"The manager gave me the key," Nolan explained as he paused in the hallway and unlocked the second door on the right. Nolan wasn't even breathing hard, while Maryanne was leaning against the wall, dragging deep breaths into her oxygen-starved lungs.

Nolan opened the door and waved her in. "As I said, it's not much."

Maryanne walked inside and was struck by the sparseness of the furnishings. One overstuffed sofa and one end table with a lamp on a dull stained-wood floor. She blinked, squared her shoulders and forced a smile to her lips. "It's perfect."

"You honestly think you can live here after The Seattle?" He sounded incredulous.

"Yes, I do," she said with a determination that would've made generations of Simpsons proud. "How far away is your place?"

Nolan walked over to the window, his back to her. He exhaled sharply before he announced, "I live in the apartment next door."

Chapter Three

"I don't need a baby-sitter," Maryanne protested. She had some trouble maintaining the conviction in her voice. In truth, she was pleased to learn that Nolan's apartment was next door, and her heart did a little jig all its own.

Nolan turned away from the window. His mouth was set in a thin straight line, as if he was going against his better judgment in arranging this. "That night at the radio station," he mumbled softly. "I knew it then."

"Knew what?"

Slowly, he shook his head, apparently lost in his musings. "I took one look at you and deep down inside I heard a small voice cry out, 'Here comes trouble.'"

Despite his fierce expression, Maryanne laughed.

"Like a fool I ignored it, although Lord only knows how I could have."

"You're not blaming me for all this, are you?" Maryanne asked, placing her hands on her hips, prepared to do battle. "In case you've forgotten, you're the one who invited yourself to dinner that night. Then you got me all mellow with wine—"

"You were the one who brought out the bottle. You can't blame me for *that*." He was muttering again and buried his hands deep in the pockets of his raincoat.

"I was only being a good hostess."

"All right, all right, I get the picture," he said through clenched teeth, shaking his head again. "I was the one stupid enough to write that column afterward. I'd give a week's pay to take it all back. No, make that a month's pay. This is the last time," he vowed, "that I'm ever going to set the record straight. Any record." He jerked his hand from his pocket and stared at it.

Maryanne crossed to the large overstuffed sofa covered with faded chintz fabric and ran her hand along the armrest. It was nearly threadbare in places and nothing like the supple white leather of her sofa at The Seattle. "I wish you'd stop worrying about me. I'm not as fragile as I look."

Nolan snickered softly. "A dust ball could bowl you over."

A ready argument sprang to her lips, but she quickly swallowed it. "I'll take the apartment, but I want it understood, right now, that you have no responsibilities toward me. I'm a big girl and I'll manage perfectly well on my own. I have in the past and I'll continue to do so in the future."

Nolan didn't respond. Instead he grumbled something she couldn't hear. He seemed to be doing a lot of that since he'd met her. Maybe it was a long-established habit, but somehow she doubted it.

Nolan drove her back to The Seattle, and the whole way there Maryanne could hardly contain a feeling of delight. For the first time, she was taking control of her own life. Nolan, however, was obviously experiencing no such enthusiasm.

"Do I need to sign anything for the apartment? What about a deposit?"

"You can do that later. You realize this studio apartment is the smallest one in the entire building? My own apartment is three times that size."

"Would you stop worrying?" Maryanne told him. A growing sense of purpose filled her, and a keen exhilaration unlike anything she'd ever felt. .

Nolan pulled into the circular driveway at her building. "Do you want to come up for a few minutes?" she asked.

His dark eyes widened as if she'd casually suggested they play a round of Russian roulette. "You've got to be kidding."

She wasn't.

He held up both hands. "No way. Before long, you'll be serving wine and we'll be talking like old friends. Then I'll go home thinking about you, and before I know how it happened—" He stopped abruptly. "No, thanks."

"Goodbye, then," she said, disappointed. "I'll see you later."

"Right. Later." But the way he said it suggested that if he didn't stumble upon her for a decade or two it would be fine with him.

Maryanne climbed out of his car and was about to close the door when she hesitated. "Nolan?"

"Now what?" he barked.

"Thank you," she said softly.

Predictably, he started mumbling and drove off the instant she closed the door. In spite of his sour mood, Maryanne found herself smiling.

Once inside her apartment, she was immediately struck by the contrast between this apartment at The Seattle and the place Nolan had shown her. One was grey, cramped and dingy, the other polished and spacious and elegant. Her mind's eye went over the dreary apartment on Capitol Hill, and she felt a growing sense of excitement as she thought of different inexpensive ways to bring it color and character. She'd certainly faced challenges before, but never one quite like this. Instinctively she knew there'd be real satisfaction in decorating that place with her newly limited resources.

Turning her new apartment into a home was the least of her worries, however. She had yet to tell her parents that she'd quit her job. Their reaction would be as predictable as Nolan's.

The phone seemed to draw her. Slowly she walked across the room toward it, sighing deeply. Her fingers closed tightly around the receiver. Before she could change her mind, she closed her eyes, punched out the number and waited.

Her mother answered almost immediately.

"I was sitting at my desk," Muriel Simpson explained. She seemed delighted to hear from Maryanne. "How's Seattle? Are you still as fascinated with the Northwest?"

"More than ever," Maryanne answered without a pause; what she didn't say was that part of her fascination was now because of Nolan.

"I'm pleased you like it so well, but I don't mind telling you, sweetie, I miss you terribly."

"I haven't lived at home for years," Maryanne reminded her mother.

"I know, but you were so much closer to home in Manhattan than you are now. I can't join you for lunch the way I did last year."

"Seattle's lovely. I hope you'll visit me soon." But not too soon, she prayed.

"Sometime this spring, I promise," Muriel said. "I was afraid once you settled there all that rain would get you down."

"Mother, honestly, New York City has more annual rainfall than Seattle."

"I know, dear, but in New York the rain all comes in a few days. In Seattle it drizzles for weeks on end, or so I've heard."

"It's not so bad." Maryanne had been far too busy to pay much attention to the weather. Gathering her courage, she forged ahead. "The reason I called is that I've got a bit of exciting news for you."

"You're madly in love and want to get married."

Muriel Simpson was looking forward to grand-children and had been ever since Maryanne's graduation from college. Both her brothers, Mark and Sean, were several years younger, so Maryanne knew the expectations were all focused on her. For the past couple of years they'd been introducing her to suitable young men.

"It's nothing that dramatic," Maryanne said, then, losing her courage, she crossed her fingers behind her back and blurted out, "I've got a special assignment...for the—uh—paper." The lie nearly stuck in her throat.

"A special assignment?"

All right, she was stretching the truth about as far as it would go, and she hated doing it. But she had no choice. Nolan's reaction would look tame compared to her parents' if they ever found out she was working as a janitor. Rent-A-Maid gave it a fancy name, but basically she'd been hired to clean. It wasn't a glamorous job, nor was it profitable, but it was honest work and she needed something to tide her over until she made a name for herself in her chosen field.

"What kind of special assignment?"

"It's a research project. I can't really talk about it

yet." Maryanne decided it was best to let her family assume the "assignment" was with the newspaper. She wasn't happy about this; in fact, she felt downright depressed to be misleading her mother this way, but she dared not hint at what she'd actually be doing. The only comfort she derived was from the prospect of showing them her published work in a few months.

"It's not anything dangerous, is it?"

"Oh, heavens, no," Maryanne said, forcing a light laugh. "But I'm going to be involved in it for several weeks, so I won't be mailing you any of my columns, at least not for a while. I didn't want you to wonder when you didn't hear from me."

"Will you be travelling?"

"A little." Only a few city blocks, as a matter of fact, but she couldn't very well say so. "Once everything's completed, I'll get in touch with you."

"You won't even be able to phone?" Her mother's voice carried a hint of concern.

Not often, at least not on her budget, Maryanne realized regretfully.

"Of course I'll phone," she hurried to assure her mother. She didn't often partake in subterfuge, and being new to the game, she was making everything up as she went along. She hoped her mother would be trusting enough to take her at her word.

"Speaking of your columns, dear, tell me what happened with that dreadful reporter who was harassing you earlier in the month."

"Dreadful reporter?" Maryanne repeated uncertainly. "Oh," she said with a flash of insight. "You mean Nolan Adams."

"That's his name?" Her mother's voice rose indignantly. "I hope he's stopped using that column of his to irritate you."

"It was all in good fun, Mother." All right, he *had* irritated her, but Maryanne was willing to forget their earlier pettiness. "We're friends now. As it happens, I like him quite a lot."

"Friends," her mother echoed softly. Slowly. "Your newfound friend isn't married, is he? You know your father and I started our own relationship at odds with each other, don't you?"

"Mother, honestly. Stop matchmaking."

"Just answer me one thing. Is he married or not?"

"Not. He's in his early thirties and he's handsome." A noticeable pause followed the description. "Mother?"

"You're attracted to him, aren't you?"

Maryanne wasn't sure she should admit it, but on the other hand she'd already given herself away. "Yes," she said stiffly, "I am...a little. There's a lot to like about him, even though we don't always agree. He's very talented. I've never read a column of his that didn't make me smile—and think. He's got this—er—interesting sense of humor."

"So it seems. Has he asked you out?"

"Not yet." *But he will,* her heart told her.

"Give him time." Muriel Simpson's voice had lowered a notch or two. "Now, sweetie, before we hang up, I want you to tell me some more about this special assignment of yours."

They talked for a few minutes longer, and Maryanne was astonished at her own ability to lie by omission—and avoid answering her mother's questions. She hated this subterfuge, and she hated the guilt she felt afterward. She tried to reason it away by reminding herself that her motives were good. If her parents knew what she was planning, they'd be sick with worry. But she couldn't remain their little girl forever. She had something to prove, and for the first time she was going to compete like a real contender—without her father standing on the sidelines, bribing the judges.

Maryanne didn't hear from Nolan for the next three days, and she was getting anxious. At the end of the week, she'd be finished at the *Review;* the following Monday she'd be starting at Rent-A-Maid. To her delight, Carol Riverside was appointed as her replacement. The look the managing editor tossed Maryanne's way suggested he'd given Carol the job not because of her recommendation, but despite it.

"I'm still not convinced you're doing the right thing," Carol told her over lunch on Maryanne's last day at the paper.

"But *I'm* convinced, and that's what's important,"

Maryanne returned. "Why is everyone so afraid I'm going to fall flat on my face?"

"It's not that, exactly."

"Then what is it?" she pressed. "I don't think Nolan stopped grumbling from the moment I announced I was quitting the paper, finding a job and moving out on my own."

"And well he should grumble!" Carol declared righteously. "He's the one who started this whole thing. You're such a nice girl. I can't see you getting mixed up with the likes of him."

Maryanne had a sneaking suspicion her friend wasn't saying this out of loyalty to the newspaper. "Mixed up with the likes of him? Is there something I don't know about Seattle's favorite journalist?"

"Nolan Adams may be the most popular newspaper writer in town, but he's got a biting edge to him. Oh, he's witty and talented, I'll give him that, but he has this scornful attitude that makes me want to shake him till he rattles."

"I know he's a bit cynical."

"He's a good deal more than cynical. The problem is, he's so darn entertaining that his attitude is easy to overlook. I'd like two minutes alone with that man just so I could set him straight. He had no business saying what he did about you in that 'My Evening with the Debutante' piece. Look where it's led!"

For that matter, Maryanne wouldn't mind spending two minutes alone with Nolan, either, but for an entirely different reason. The speed with which the thought entered her mind surprised her enough to produce a soft smile.

"Only this time his words came back to bite him," Carol continued.

"Everything he wrote was true," Maryanne felt obliged to remind her friend. She hadn't been all that thrilled when he'd decided to share those truths with the entire western half of Washington state, but she couldn't fault his perceptions.

"Needless to say, I'm not as concerned about Nolan as I am about you," Carol said, gazing down at her sandwich. "I've seen that little spark in your eye when you talk about him, and frankly it worries me."

Maryanne immediately lowered her betraying eyes. "I'm sure you're mistaken. Nolan and I are friends, but that's the extent of it." She wasn't sure Nolan would even want to claim her as a friend; she rather suspected he thought of her as a nuisance.

"Perhaps it's friendship on his part, but it's a lot more on yours. I'm afraid you're going to fall in love with that scoundrel."

"That's crazy," Maryanne countered swiftly. "I've only just met him." Carol's gaze narrowed on her like a diamond drill bit and Maryanne sighed. "He intrigues me," she admitted, "but that's a long way from becoming emotionally involved with him."

"I can't help worrying about you. And, Maryanne, if you're falling in love with Nolan, that worries me more than the idea of you being a Rent-a-Maid or finding yourself an apartment on Capitol Hill."

Maryanne swallowed tightly. "Nolan's a talented, respected journalist. If I was going to fall in love with him, which I don't plan to do in the near future, but if I *did* fall for him, why would it be so tragic?"

"Because you're sweet and caring and he's so..." Carol paused and stared into space. "Because he's so scornful."

"True, but underneath that gruff exterior is a heart of gold. At least I think there is," Maryanne joked.

"Maybe, but I doubt it," Carol went on. "Don't get me wrong—I respect Nolan's talent. It's his devil-may-care attitude that troubles me."

But it didn't trouble Maryanne. Not in the least. Perhaps that was what she found most appealing about him. Yet everything Carol said about Nolan was true. He did tend to be cynical and a bit sardonic, but he was also intuitive, reflective and, despite Carol's impression to the contrary, considerate.

Since it was her last day at the paper, Maryanne spent a few extra minutes saying goodbye to her co-workers. Most were sorry to see her go. There'd been a fair amount of resentment directed at her when she arrived, but her hard work seemed to have won over all but the most skeptical doubters.

On impulse, Maryanne stopped at the diner where Nolan had met her earlier in the week, hoping he'd be there. Her heart flew into her throat when she saw him sitting in a booth by the window, a book propped open in front of him. He didn't look up when she walked in.

Nor did he notice her when she approached his booth. Without waiting for an invitation, she slid in across from him.

"Hi," she murmured, keeping her voice low and secretive. "Here comes trouble to plague you once more."

Slowly, with obvious reluctance, Nolan dragged his gaze from the novel. Another mystery, Maryanne noted. "What are you doing here, Trouble?"

"Looking for you."

"Why? Have you thought up any other ways to test my patience? How about walking a tightrope between two skyscrapers? That sounds right up your alley."

"I hadn't heard from you in the past few days." She paused, hoping he'd pick up the conversation. "I thought there was something I should do about the apartment. Sign a lease, give the manager a deposit, that sort of thing."

"Annie—"

"I hope you realize I don't even know the address. I only saw it that one time."

"I told you not to worry about it."

"But I don't want anyone else to rent it."

"They won't." He laid the book aside just as the waitress appeared carrying a glass of water and a menu. Maryanne recognized her from the other day.

"Hello, Barbara," she said, reading the woman's name tag. "What's the special for the day? Mr. Adams owes me a meal and I think I'll collect it while I've got the chance." She waited for him to ask her what she was talking about, but apparently he remembered his promise of dinner to pay her back for the Irish stew he'd eaten at her house the first evening they'd met.

"Cabbage rolls, with soup or salad," Barbara said, pulling out her pad and pencil while Maryanne quickly scanned the menu.

"I'll have a cheeseburger and a chocolate shake," Maryanne decided.

Barbara grinned. "I'll make sure it comes up with Mr. Adams's order."

"Thanks," she said, handing her back the menu. Barbara sauntered off toward the kitchen, scribbling on her order pad as she walked.

"It was my last day at the paper," Maryanne said.

"I'll ask you one more time—are you *sure* you want to go through with this?" Nolan demanded. "Hell, I never thought for a moment you'd want that apartment. Damn it all, you're a stubborn woman."

"Of course I'm taking the apartment."

"That's what I thought." He closed his eyes briefly. "What did the Rent-A-Maid agency say when you told them you wouldn't be taking the job?"

Maryanne stared purposely out the window. "Nothing."

He cocked an eyebrow. "Nothing?"

"What could they say?" she asked, trying to ignore the doubt reflected in his eyes. Maybe she was getting good at this lie-telling business, which wasn't a comforting thought. The way she'd misled her mother still bothered her.

Nolan drew one hand across his face. "You didn't tell them, did you? Apparently you intend to play the Cinderella role to the hilt."

"And you intend to play the role of my wicked stepmother to perfection."

He didn't say anything for a long moment. "Is there a part in that fairy tale where Cinderella gets locked in a closet for her own good?"

"Why?" she couldn't resist asking. "Is that what you're going to do?"

"Don't tempt me."

"I wish you had more faith in me."

"I do have faith in you. I have faith that you're going to make my life hell for the next few months while you go about proving yourself. Heaven knows what possessed me to write that stupid column, but, trust me, there hasn't been a minute since it hit the streets that I haven't regretted it. Not a single minute."

"But—"

"Now you insist on moving into the apartment next to mine. That's just great. Wonderful. Whatever peace I have in my life will be completely and utterly destroyed."

"That's not true!" Maryanne cried. "Besides, I'd

like to remind you, you're the one who found that apartment, not me. I have no intention of pestering you."

"Like I said, I figured just seeing the apartment would be enough to put you off. Now I won't have a minute to myself. I know it, and you know it." His eyes were darker and more brooding than she'd ever seen them. "I wasn't kidding when I said you were trouble."

"All right," Maryanne said, doing her best to disguise her crushing sense of defeat. "It's obvious you never expected me to take the place. I suppose you arranged it to look as bleak as you could. Don't worry, I'll find somewhere else to live. Another apartment as far away from you as I can possibly get." She was out of the booth so fast, so intent on escaping, that she nearly collided with Barbara.

"What about your cheeseburger?" the waitress asked.

Maryanne glanced at Nolan. "Wrap it up and give it to Mr. Adams. I've lost my appetite."

The tears that blurred her eyes only angered her more. Furious with herself for allowing his words to wound her, she hurried down the street, headed in the direction of the Seattle waterfront. It was growing dark, but she didn't care; she needed to vent some of her anger, and a brisk hike would serve that purpose nicely.

She wasn't concerned when she heard hard quick

footsteps behind her. As the wind whipped at her, she shivered and drew her coat closer, tucking her hands in her pockets and hunching her shoulders forward.

Carol and Nolan both seemed to believe she needed a keeper! They apparently considered her incompetent, and their doubts cut deeply into her pride.

Her head bowed against the force of the wind, she noticed a pair of male legs matching steps with her own. She looked up and discovered Nolan had joined her.

For the longest time, he said nothing. They were halfway down a deserted pier before he spoke. "I don't want you to find another apartment."

"I think it would be for the best if I did." He'd already told her she was nothing but trouble, and if that wasn't bad enough, he'd implied she was going to be a constant nuisance in his life. She had no intention of bothering him. As far as she was concerned, they could live on opposite sides of town. That was what he wanted and that was what he was going to get.

"It isn't for the best," he argued.

"It is. We obviously rub each other the wrong way."

Nolan turned and gripped her by the shoulders. "The apartment's been cleaned. It's ready for you to move into anytime you want. The rent is reasonable and the neighborhood's a good one. As I recall, this whole ridiculous business between us started over an article about the lack of affordable housing. You're not going to find anyplace else, not with what you intend to live on."

"But you live next door!"

"I'm well aware of that."

Maryanne bristled. "I won't live beside a man who considers me a pest. And furthermore, you still owe me dinner."

"I said you were trouble," he pointed out, ignoring her claim. "I didn't say you were a pest."

"You did so."

"I said you were going to destroy my peace—"

"Exactly."

"—of mind," he went on. He closed his eyes briefly and expelled a sharp frustrated sigh, then repeated, "You're going to destroy my peace of mind."

Maryanne wasn't sure she understood. She stared up at him, intrigued by the emotion she saw in his intense brown eyes.

"Why the hell should it matter if you live next door to me or in The Seattle?" he exclaimed. "My serenity was shot the minute I laid eyes on you."

"I don't understand," she said, surprised when her voice came out a raspy whisper. She continued to look up at him, trying to read his expression.

"You don't have a clue, do you?" he whispered. His fingers found their way into her hair as he lowered his mouth with heart-stopping slowness toward hers. "Heaven keep me from redheaded innocents."

But heaven apparently didn't receive the message, because even as he whispered the words Nolan's arms were pulling her toward him. With a sigh of regret—

or was it pleasure?—his mouth settled over hers. His kiss was light and undemanding, and despite her anger, despite his words, Maryanne felt herself melting.

With a soft sigh, she flattened her hands on his chest and slid them up to link behind his neck. She leaned against him, letting his strength support her, letting his warmth comfort her.

He pulled her even closer, wrapped his arms around her waist and half lifted her from the pier. Maryanne heard a low hungry moan; she wasn't sure if it came from Nolan or from her.

It didn't matter. Nothing mattered except this wonderful feeling of being cherished and loved and protected.

Over the years, Maryanne had been kissed by her share of men. She'd found the experience pleasant, but no one had ever set her on fire the way Nolan did now.

"See what I mean," he whispered unsteadily. "We're in trouble here. Big trouble."

Chapter Four

Maryanne stood in the doorway of her new apartment, the key held tightly in her hand. She was embarking on her grand adventure, but now that she'd actually moved out of The Seattle her confidence was a bit shaky.

Carol joined her, huffing and puffing as she staggered the last few steps down the narrow hallway. She sagged against the wall, panting to catch her breath.

"This place doesn't have an elevator?" she demanded, when she could speak.

"It's being repaired."

"That's what they always say."

Maryanne nodded, barely hearing her friend. Her heart in her throat, she inserted the key and turned the lock. The door stuck, so she used the force of one hip to dislodge it. The apartment was just as she remembered: worn hardwood floors, the bulky faded furniture, the kitchen appliances that would soon be valuable antiques. But Maryanne saw none of that.

This was her new life.

She walked directly to the window and gazed out. "I've got a great view of Volunteer Park," she announced to her friend. She hadn't noticed it the day Nolan had shown her the apartment. "I had no idea the park was so close." She turned toward Carol, who was still standing in the threshold, her expression one of shock and dismay. "What's wrong?"

"Good heavens," Carol whispered. "You don't really intend to live here, do you?"

"It isn't so bad," Maryanne said with a smile, glancing around to be sure she hadn't missed anything. "I've got lots of ideas on how to decorate the place." She leaned back against the windowsill, where much of the dingy beige paint was chipped away to reveal an even dingier grey-green. "What it needs is a fresh coat of paint, something light and cheerful."

"It's not even half the size of your other place."

"There was a lot of wasted space at my apartment." That might be true, Maryanne thought privately, but she wouldn't have minded bringing some of it with her.

"What about your neighbor?" Carol asked in a grudging voice. "He's the one who started this. The least he could do is offer a little help."

Straightening, Maryanne brushed the dust from her palms and looked away. "I didn't ask him to. I don't think he even knows when I was planning to move in."

Nolan was a subject Maryanne wanted to avoid. She hadn't talked to him since the night he'd followed her to the waterfront…the night he'd kissed her. He'd stopped off at The Seattle to leave the apartment key and a rental agreement with the doorman. Max had promptly delivered both. The implication was obvious; Nolan didn't want to see her and was, in fact, doing his best to avoid her.

Clearly he disapproved of the way things had developed on the pier that night. She supposed he didn't like kissing her. Then again, perhaps he did. Perhaps he liked it too much for his oft-lamented "peace of mind."

Maryanne knew how *she* felt about it. She couldn't sleep for two nights afterward. Every time she closed her eyes, the image of Nolan holding her in his arms danced through her mind like a waltzing couple from a 1940s movie. She remembered the way he'd scowled down at her when he'd broken off the kiss and how he'd struggled to make light of the incident. And she remembered his eyes, so warm and gentle, telling her another story.

"Hey, lady, is this the place where I'm supposed to bring the boxes?" A lanky boy of about fourteen stood in the doorway, carrying a large cardboard box.

"Y-yes," Maryanne said, recognizing the container as one of her own. "How'd you know to bring it up here?"

"Mr. Adams. He promised a bunch of us guys he'd play basketball with us if we'd help unload the truck."

"Oh. How nice. I'm Maryanne Simpson," she said, her heart warming at Nolan's unexpected thoughtfulness.

"Nice to meet you, lady. Now where do you want me to put this?"

Maryanne pointed to the kitchen. "Just put it in the corner over there." Before she finished, a second and third boy appeared, each hauling boxes.

Maryanne slipped past them and ran down the stairs to the parking area behind the building. Nolan was standing in the back of Carol's husband's pickup, noisily distributing cardboard boxes and dire warnings. He didn't see her until she moved closer. When he did, he fell silent, a frown on his face.

"Hi," she said, feeling a little shy. "I came to thank you."

"You shouldn't have gone up and left the truck unattended," he barked, still frowning. "Anyone could've walked off with this stuff."

"We just arrived."

"We?"

"Carol Riverside and me. She's upstairs trying to regain her breath. How long will it be before the elevator's fixed?"

"Not soon."

She nodded. Well, if he'd hoped to discourage her, she wasn't going to let him. So what if she had to walk up four flights of stairs every day! It was wonderful aerobic exercise. In the past she'd paid good money to attend a health club for the same purpose.

Nolan returned to his task, lifting boxes and handing them to a long line of teenage boys. "I'm surprised you didn't have a moving company manage this for you."

"Are you kidding?" she joked. "Only rich people use moving companies."

"Is this all of it, or do you need to make a second trip?"

"This is it. Carol and I put everything else in storage earlier this morning. It's only costing me a few dollars a month. I have to be careful about money now, you know."

He scowled again. "When do you start with the cleaning company?"

"Monday morning."

Nolan placed his hands on his hips and glared down at her. "If you're really intending to take that job—"

"Of course I am!"

"Then the first thing you'll need to do is ask for a raise."

"Oh, honestly, Nolan," she protested, walking backward. "I can't do that!"

"What you can't do is live on that amount of money, no matter how well you budget," he muttered. He leapt off the back of the truck as agilely as a cat. "Will you listen to me for once?"

"I am listening," she said. "It just so happens I don't agree. Quit worrying about me, would you? I'm going to be perfectly all right, especially once I start selling articles."

"I'm not a knight in shining armor, understand?" he shouted after her. "If you think I'll be racing to your rescue every time you're in trouble, then you need to think again."

"You're insulting me by even suggesting I'd accept your help." She tried to be angry with him but found it impossible. He might insist she was entirely on her own, but all the while he was lecturing her he was doling out her boxes so she wouldn't have to haul them up the stairs herself. Nolan might claim not to be a knight riding to her rescue, but he was behaving suspiciously like one.

Two hours later, Maryanne was alone in her new apartment for the first time. Standing in the middle of her living room, she surveyed her kingdom. As she'd told Carol, it wasn't so bad. Boxes filled every bit of available space, but it wouldn't take her long to unpack and set everything in order.

She was grateful for the help Carol, Nolan and the neighborhood teenagers had given her, but now it was up to her. And she had lots of plans—she'd paint the walls and put up her pictures and buy some plants—to make this place cheerful and attractive. To turn it into a home.

It was dark before she'd finished unpacking, and

by that time she was both exhausted and hungry. Actually *famished* more adequately described her condition. Her hunger and exhaustion warred with each other: she was too tired to go out and buy herself something to eat, but too hungry to go to bed without eating. Making the decision about which she should do created a dilemma of startling proportions.

She'd just decided to make do with a bowl of cornflakes, without milk, when there was a loud knock at her door. She jerked it open to find Nolan there, wearing grey sweatpants and a sweat-soaked T-shirt. He held a basketball under one arm and clutched a large white paper sack in his free hand.

"Never open the door without knowing who's on the other side," he warned, walking directly into the apartment. He dropped the basketball on the sofa and placed his sack—obviously from a fast-food restaurant—on the coffee table. "That security chain's there for a reason. Use it."

Maryanne was still standing at the door, inhaling the aroma of french fries and hamburgers. "Yes, your majesty."

"Don't get testy with me, either. I've just lost two years of my life on a basketball court. I'm too old for this, but luckily what I lack in youth I make up for in smarts."

"I see," she said, closing the door. For good measure she clipped the chain in place and turned the lock.

"A little show of appreciation would go a long way

toward soothing my injuries," he told her, sinking on to the sofa. He rested his head against the cushion, eyes drifting shut.

"You can't be that smart, otherwise you'd have managed to get out of playing with boys twenty years younger than you," she said lightly. She had trouble keeping her eyes off the white sack on the scratched mahogany coffee table.

Nolan straightened, wincing as he did so. "I thought you might be hungry." He reached for the bag and removed a wrapped hamburger, which he tossed to her before taking a second for himself. Next he set out two cardboard cartons full of hot french fries and two cans of soda.

Maryanne sat down beside him, her hand pressed against her stomach to keep it from growling. "You'd better be careful," she said. "You're beginning to look suspiciously like that knight in shining armor."

"Don't kid yourself."

Maryanne was too hungry to waste time arguing. She devoured the hamburger and fries within minutes. Then she relaxed against the back of the sofa and sighed, content.

"I came to set some ground rules," Nolan explained. "I think you and I need to get a few things straight."

"Sure," she agreed, although she was fairly certain she knew what he wanted to talk about. "I've already promised not to pester you."

"Good. I intend to stay out of your way, too."

"Perfect." It didn't really sound all that wonderful, but it seemed to be what he wanted, so she didn't have much choice. "Anything else?"

Nolan hesitated. Then he leaned forward, resting his forearms on his knees. "Yes, one other thing." He turned to her with a frown. "I don't think we should…you know, kiss again."

A short silence followed his words. At first Maryanne wasn't sure she'd heard him correctly.

"I realize talking about this may be embarrassing," Nolan continued, sounding as detached as if he'd introduced the subject of football scores. "I want you to know I'm suggesting this for your own good."

"I'm pleased to hear that." It was an effort not to mock him by rolling her eyes.

He nodded and cleared his throat, and Maryanne could see he wasn't nearly as indifferent as he wanted her to believe.

"There appears to be a certain amount of physical chemistry between us," he said, avoiding even a glance in her direction. "I feel that the sooner we settle this, the less likelihood there'll be for misunderstandings later on. The last thing I need is for you to fall in love with me."

"That's it!" she cried, throwing up her arms. The ridiculousness of his comment revived her enough to indulge in some good-natured teasing. "If I can't have your heart and soul, then I'm leaving right now!"

"Damn it, Annie, this is nothing to joke about."

"Who's joking?" she asked. She made her voice absurdly melodramatic. "I knew the minute I walked into the radio station for the Celebrity Debate that if I couldn't taste your lips there was nothing left to live for."

"If you're going to make a joke out of this, then you can forget the whole discussion." He vaulted to his feet and stuffed the wrappers from their burgers and fries into the empty sack. "I was hoping we could have a mature talk, one adult to another, but that's obviously beyond you."

"Don't get so bent out of shape," she said, trying not to smile. "Sit down before you do something silly, like leave in a huff. We both know you'll regret it." She didn't know anything of the sort, but it sounded good.

He complied grudgingly, but he stared past her, training his eyes on the darkened window.

Maryanne got stiffly to her feet, every muscle and joint protesting. "It seems to me that you're presuming a great deal with this hands-off decree," she said with all the dignity she could muster. "What makes you think I'd even *want* you to kiss me again?"

A slow cocky grin raised the corners of his mouth. "A man can tell. My biggest fear is that you're going to start thinking things I never meant you to think. Eventually you'd end up getting hurt. I intend to make damn sure nothing romantic develops between us. Understand?"

"You're saying my head's in the clouds when it comes to you?"

"That's right. You're a sweet kid, stubborn and idealistic, but nonetheless naive. One kiss told me you've got a romantic soul, and frankly I don't want you fluttering those pretty blue eyes at me and dreaming of babies and a white picket fence. You and I are about as different as two people can get."

"Different?" To Maryanne's way of thinking, she had more in common with Nolan Adams than with any other man she'd ever dated.

"That's right. You come from this rich upstanding family—"

"Stop!" she cried. "Don't say another word about our economic differences. They're irrelevant. If you're looking for excuses, find something else."

"I don't need excuses. It'd never work between us and I want to make sure neither of us is ever tempted to try. If you want someone to teach you about being a woman, go elsewhere."

His words were like a slap in the face. "Naturally a man of your vast romantic experience gets plenty of requests." She turned away, so angry she couldn't keep still. "As for being afraid I might fall in love with you, let me assure you right now that there's absolutely no chance of it. In fact, I think you should be more concerned about falling for me!" Her voice was gaining strength and conviction with every word. The man had such colossal nerve. At one time she might have found herself attracted to him, but that possibility had disappeared the minute he walked in her door and opened his mouth.

"Don't kid yourself," he argued. "You're halfway in love with me already. I can see it in your eyes."

Carol had said something about her eyes revealing what she felt for Nolan, too.

Maryanne whirled around, intent on composing a suitably sarcastic retort, away from his searching gaze. But before any mocking words could pass her lips, a sharp pain shot through her neck, an ache so intense it brought immediate tears to her eyes. She must have moved too quickly, too carelessly.

Her hands flew to the back of her neck.

Nolan was instantly on his feet. "What's wrong?"

"Nothing," she mumbled, easing her way back to the sofa. She sat down, hand still pressed to her neck, waiting a moment before slowly rotating her head, wanting to test the extent of her injury. Quickly, she realized her mistake.

"Annie," Nolan demanded, kneeling in front of her, "what is it?"

"I...don't know. I moved wrong, I guess."

His hands replaced hers. "You've got a crick in your neck?"

"If I do, it's all your fault. You say the most ridiculous things."

"I know." His voice was as gentle as his hands. He

began to knead softly, his fingers tenderly massaging the tight muscles.

"I'm all right."

"Of course you are," he whispered. "Just close your eyes and relax."

"I can't." How could he possibly expect her to do that when he was so close, so warm and sensual? He was fast making a lie of all her protestations.

"Yes, you can," he said, his voice low and seductive. He leaned over her, his face, his lips, scant inches from hers. His hands were working the tightness from her neck and shoulders and at the same time creating a dizzying heated sensation that extended to the tips of her fingers and the soles of her feet.

She sighed and clasped his wrist with both hands, wanting to stop him before she made a fool of herself by swaying toward him or doing something equally suggestive. "I think you should stop. Let me rephrase that. I *know* you should stop."

"I know I should, too," he admitted quietly. "Remember what I said earlier?"

"You mean the hands-off policy?"

"Yes." She could hardly hear him. "Let's delay it for a day—what do you think?"

At that moment, clear organized thought was something of a problem. "W-whatever you feel is best."

"Oh, I know what's best," he whispered. "Unfortunately that doesn't seem to make a damn bit of difference right now."

She wasn't sure exactly when it happened, but her hands seemed to have left his wrists and were splayed across the front of his T-shirt. His chest felt rigid and muscular; his heart beneath her palms pounded hard and fast. She wondered if her own pulse was keeping time with his.

With infinite slowness, Nolan lowered his mouth to hers. Maryanne's eyes drifted closed of their own accord and she moaned, holding back a small cry of welcome. His touch was even more compelling than she remembered. Nolan must have felt something similar, because his groan followed, an echo of hers.

He kissed her again and again. Maryanne wanted more, but he resisted giving in to her desires—or his own. It was as if he'd decided a few kisses were of little consequence and wouldn't seriously affect either one of them.

Wrong. Maryanne wanted to shout it at him, but couldn't.

His mouth left hers and blazed a fiery trail of kisses across her sensitized skin. His lips brushed her throat, under her chin to the vulnerable hollow. Only minutes earlier, moving her neck without pain had been impossible; now she did so freely, turning it, arching, asking—no, demanding—that he kiss her again the way he had that night at the waterfront.

Nolan complied, and he seemed to do it willingly,

surrendering the battle. He groaned anew and the sound came from deep in his throat. His fingers tangled in the thick strands of her hair as his mouth rushed back to hers.

Maryanne was experiencing a renewal of her own. She felt as if she had lain dormant and was bursting to life, like a flower struggling out of winter snows into the light and warmth of spring.

All too soon, Nolan pulled away from her. His eyes met and held hers. She knew her eyes were filled with questions, but his gave her no answers.

He got abruptly to his feet.

"Nolan," she said, shocked that he would leave her like this.

He looked back at her and she saw it then. The regret. A regret tinged with compassion. "You're so exhausted you can barely sit up. Go to bed and we'll both forget this ever happened. Understand?"

Too stunned to reply, she nodded. Maybe Nolan could forget it, but she knew she wouldn't.

"Lock the door after me. And next time don't be so eager to find out who's knocking. There isn't any doorman here."

Once more she nodded. She got up and followed him to the door, holding it open.

"Damn it, Annie, don't look at me like that."

"Like what?"

"Like that," he accused, then slowly shook his head as if to clear his thoughts. He rubbed his face and sighed, then pressed his knuckle under her chin. "The two of us are starting over first thing tomorrow. There won't be any more of this." But even as he was speaking, he was leaning forward to gently brush her mouth with his.

It was the sound of Nolan pounding furiously away on his electric typewriter—a heavy, outdated office model—that woke Maryanne the next morning. She yawned loudly, stretching her arms high above her head, arching her back. Her first night in her new apartment, and she'd slept like a rock. The sofa, which opened into a queen-size sleeper, was lumpy and soft, nearly swallowing her up, but she'd been too exhausted to care.

Nolan's fierce typing continued most of the day. Maryanne hadn't expected to see him, so she wasn't disappointed when she didn't. He seemed determined to avoid her and managed it successfully for most of the week.

Since she'd promised not to make a nuisance of herself, Maryanne kept out of his way, too. She started work at the cleaning company and wrote three articles in five days, often staying up late into the night.

The work for Rent-A-Maid was backbreaking and arduous. She spent three afternoons a week picking up after professional men who were nothing less than slobs. Maryanne had to resist the urge to write them each a note demanding that they put their dirty dishes in the sink and their soiled clothes in the laundry basket.

Rent-A-Maid had made housekeeping sound glamorous. It wasn't. In fact, it was the hardest, most physically exhausting job she'd ever undertaken.

By the end of the week, her nails were broken and chipped and her hands were red and chapped.

It was by chance rather than design that Maryanne bumped into Nolan late Friday afternoon. She was carrying a bag of groceries up the stairs when he bounded past her, taking the steps two at a time.

"Annie." He paused on the landing, waiting for her to catch up. "How's it going?"

Maryanne didn't know what to say. She couldn't very well inform him that the highlight of her week was scraping a crusty patch off the bottom of an oven at one of the apartments she cleaned. She'd had such lofty expectations, such dreams. Nor could she casually announce that the stockbroker she cleaned for had spilled wine on his carpet and she'd spent an hour trying to get the stain out and broken two nails in the process.

"Fine," she lied. "Everything's just wonderful."

"Here, let me take that for you."

"Thanks." She handed him the single bag, her week's allotment of groceries. Unfortunately it was all she could afford. Everything had seemed so exciting when she started out; her plans had been so promising. The reality was proving to be something else again.

"Well, how do you like cleaning?"

"It's great, really great." It was shocking how easily the lie came. "I'm finding it…a challenge."

Nolan smiled absently. "I'm glad to hear it. Have you got your first paycheck yet?"

"I cashed it this afternoon." She used to spend more each week at the dry cleaners than she'd received in her first paycheck from Rent-A-Maid. The entire amount had gone for food and transportation, and there were only a few dollars left. Her budget was tight, but she'd make it. She'd have to.

Nolan paused in front of her door and waited while she scrabbled through her bag, searching for the key. "I hear you typing at night," she said. "Are you working on anything special?"

"No."

She eyed him curiously. "How fast do you type? Eighty words a minute? A hundred? And for heaven's sake, why don't you use a computer like everyone else?"

"Sixty words a minute on a good day. And for your information, I happen to like my electric. It may be old, but it does the job."

She finally retrieved her key, conscious of his gaze on her hands.

Suddenly he grasped her fingers. "All right," he demanded. "What happened to you?"

Chapter Five

"Nothing's happened to me," Maryanne insisted hotly, pulling her hand free of Nolan's.

"Look at your nails," he said. "There isn't one that's not broken."

"You make it sound like I should be dragged before a firing squad at dawn. So I chipped a few nails this week. I'll survive." Although she was making light of it, each broken fingernail was like a small loss. She took pride in her perfect nails, or at least she once had.

His eyes narrowed as he scrutinized her. "There's something you're not telling me."

"I didn't realize you'd appointed yourself my father confessor."

Anger flashed in his dark eyes as he took the key from her unresisting fingers. He opened the door and, with one hand at her shoulder, urged her inside. "We need to talk."

"No, we don't." Maryanne marched into the apartment, plunked her bag of groceries on the kitchen counter and spun around to confront her neighbor. "Listen here, buster, you've made it perfectly clear that you don't want anything to do with me. That's your choice, and I'm certainly not going to bore you with the sorry details of my life."

He ignored her words and started pacing the small living area, pausing in front of the window. His presence filled the apartment, making it seem smaller than usual. He pivoted sharply, pointing an accusatory finger in her direction. "These broken nails came from swinging a dust mop around, didn't they? What the hell are you doing?"

Maryanne didn't answer him right away. She was angry, and his sudden concern for her welfare made her even angrier. "I told you before, I don't need a guardian."

"Against my advice, you took that stupid job. Anyone with half a brain would know it wasn't going to—"

"Will you stop acting like you're responsible for me?" Maryanne snapped.

"I can't help it. I *am* responsible for you. You wouldn't be here if I hadn't written that damn column. I don't want to intrude on your life any more than you want me to, but let's face it, there's no one else to look out for you. Sooner or later someone's going to take advantage of you."

That did it. Maryanne stalked over to him and jabbed her index finger into his chest with enough force to bend what remained of her nail. "In case you need reminding, I'm my own woman. I make my own decisions. I'll work any place I damn well please. Furthermore, I can take care of myself." She whirled around and opened her front door. "Now kindly leave!"

"No."

"No?" she repeated.

"No," he said again, returning to the window. He crossed his arms over his chest and sighed impatiently. "You haven't eaten, have you? I can tell, because you get testy when you're hungry."

"If you'd leave my apartment the way I asked, that wouldn't be a problem."

"How about having dinner with me?"

The invitation took Maryanne by surprise. Her first impulse was to throw it back in his face. After an entire week of pretending she didn't exist, he had a lot of nerve even asking.

"Well?" he prompted.

"Where?" As if that made a difference. Maryanne was famished, and the thought of sharing her meal with Nolan was more tempting than she wanted to admit, even to herself.

"The diner."

"Are you going to order chili?"

"Are you going to ask them to remove the non-existent bean sprouts from your sandwich?"

Maryanne hesitated. She felt confused by all her contradictory emotions. She was strongly attracted to Nolan and every time they were together she caught herself hoping they could become friends—more than friends. But, equally often, he infuriated her or left her feeling depressed. He made the most outlandish remarks to her. He seemed to have appointed himself her guardian. When he wasn't issuing decrees, he neglected her as if she were nothing more than a nuisance. And to provide a finishing touch, she was lying to her parents because of him! Well, maybe that wasn't quite fair, but...

"I'll throw in dessert," he coaxed with a smile.

That smile was her Waterloo, yet she still struggled. "A la mode?"

His grin widened. "You drive a hard bargain."

Maryanne's eyes met his and although Nolan could make her angrier than anyone she'd ever known, a smile trembled on her own lips.

They agreed to meet a half-hour later. That gave Maryanne time to unpack her groceries, change clothes and freshen her make-up. She found herself humming as she applied lip gloss, wondering if she was reading too much into this impromptu dinner date.

When Nolan came to her door to pick her up, Maryanne noted that he'd changed into jeans and a fisherman's sweater. It was the first time she'd seen him without the raincoat, other than the day he'd played basketball with the neighborhood boys. He looked good. All right, she admitted grudgingly, he looked fantastic.

"You dressed up," she said before she could stop herself, grateful she'd understated her attraction to him.

"So did you. You look nice."

"Thanks."

"Before I forget to tell you, word has it the elevator's going to be fixed Monday morning."

"Really? That's the best news I've heard all week." Goodness, could she take all these glad tidings at once? First Nolan had actually invited her out on a date, and now she wouldn't have to hike up four flights of stairs every afternoon. Life was indeed treating her well.

They were several blocks from the apartment building before Maryanne realized Nolan was driving in the opposite direction of the diner. She said as much.

"Do you like Chinese food?" he asked.

"I love it."

"The diner's short-staffed—one of the waitresses quit. I thought Chinese food might be interesting, and I promise we won't have to wait for a table."

It sounded heavenly to Maryanne. She didn't know how significant Nolan's decision to take her to a different restaurant might be. Perhaps it was foolish, but Maryanne hoped it meant she was becoming special to him. As if he could read her mind, Nolan was un-usually quiet on the drive into Seattle's International District.

So much for romance. Maryanne could almost hear his thoughts. If she were a betting woman, she'd place odds on the way their dinner conversation would go. First Nolan would try to find out exactly what tasks had been assigned to her by Rent-A-Maid. Then he'd try to convince her to quit.

Only she wasn't going to let him. She was her own woman, and she'd said it often enough to convince herself. If this newsman thought he could sway her with a fancy dinner and a few well-spoken words, then he was about to learn a valuable lesson.

The restaurant proved to be a Chinese version of the greasy spoon where Nolan ate regularly. The minute they walked into the small room, Maryanne was greeted by a wide variety of tantalizing scents. Pungent spices and oils wafted through the air, and the smells were so appealing it was all she could do not to follow them into the kitchen. She knew before sampling a single bite that the food would be some of the best Asian cuisine she'd ever tasted.

An elderly Chinese gentleman greeted Nolan as if he were a long-lost relative. The two shared a brief ex-change in Chinese before the man escorted them to a table. He shouted into the kitchen, and a brightly painted ceramic pot of tea was quickly delivered to their table.

Nolan and Maryanne were never given menus. Almost from the moment they were seated, food began appearing on their table. An appetizer plate came first, with several items Maryanne couldn't readily identify. But she was too hungry to care. Everything was delicious and she happily devoured one after another.

"You seem well acquainted with the waiter," Maryanne commented, once the appetizer plate was empty. She barely had time to catch her breath before a bowl of thick spicy soup was brought to them by the same elderly gentleman. He paused and smiled proudly at Nolan, then glanced at Maryanne, before nodding in a profound way.

"Wong Su's the owner. I went to school with his son."

"Is that where you picked up Chinese?"

"Yes. I only know a few words, just enough to get the gist of what he's saying," he answered brusquely, reaching for his spoon.

"What was it he said when we first came in? I noticed you seemed quick to disagree with him."

Nolan dipped his spoon into the soup, ignoring her question.

"Nolan?"

"He said you're too thin."

Maryanne shook her head, immediately aware that he was lying. "If he really thought that, you'd have agreed with him."

"All right, all right," Nolan muttered, looking severely displeased. "I should've known better than to bring a woman to Wong Su's place. He assumed there was something romantic between us. He said you'd give me many fine sons."

"How sweet."

Nolan reacted instantly to her words. He dropped his spoon beside the bowl with a clatter, planted his elbows on the table and glared at her heatedly. "Now don't go all sentimental on me. There's nothing between us and there never will be."

Maryanne promptly saluted. "Aye, aye, Captain," she mocked.

"Good. Well, now that's settled, tell me about your week."

"Tell me about yours," she countered, unwilling to change the subject to herself quite so easily. "You seemed a whole lot busier than I was."

"I went to work, came home…"

"…worked some more," she finished for him. Another plate, heaped high with sizzling hot chicken and crisp vegetables, was brought by Wong Su, who offered Maryanne a grin.

Nolan frowned at his friend and said something in Chinese that caused the older man to laugh outright. When Nolan returned his attention to Maryanne, he was scowling again. "For heaven's sake, don't encourage him."

"What did I do?" To the best of her knowledge she was innocent of any wrongdoing.

Nolan thought it over for a moment. "Never mind, no point in telling you."

Other steaming dishes arrived—prawns with cashew nuts, then ginger beef and barbecued pork, each accompanied by small bowls of rice until virtually every inch of the small table was covered.

"You were telling me about your week," Maryanne reminded him, reaching for the dish in the centre of the crowded table.

"No, I wasn't," Nolan retorted.

With a scornful sigh, Maryanne passed him the chicken. "All right, have it your way."

"You're going to needle me to death until you find out what I'm working on in my spare time, aren't you?"

"Of course not." If he didn't want her to know, then fine, she had no intention of asking again. Acting as nonchalant as possible, she helped herself to a thick slice of the pork. She dipped it into a small dish of hot mustard, which proved to be a bit more potent than she'd expected; her eyes started to water.

Mumbling under his breath, Nolan handed her his napkin. "Here."

"I'm all right." She wiped the moisture from her eyes and blinked a couple of times before picking up her water glass. Once she'd composed herself, she resumed their previous discussion. "On the contrary,

Mr. Adams, whatever project so intensely occupies your time is your own concern."

"Spoken like a true aristocrat."

"Obviously you don't care to share it with me."

He gave an exaggerated sigh. "It's a novel," he said. "There now, are you satisfied?"

"A novel," she repeated coolly. "Really. And all along, I thought you were taking in typing jobs on the side."

He glared at her, but the edges of his mouth turned up in a reluctant grin. "I don't want to talk about the plot, all right? I'm afraid that would water it down."

"I understand perfectly."

"Damn it all, Annie, would you stop looking at me with those big blue eyes of yours? I already feel guilty as hell without you smiling serenely at me and trying to act so blasé."

"Guilty about what?"

He expelled his breath sharply. "Listen," he said in a low voice, leaning toward her. "As much as I hate to admit this, you're right. It's none of my business where you work or how many nails you break or how much you're paid. But damn it all, I'm worried about you."

She raised her chopsticks in an effort to stop him. "It seems to me I've heard this argument before. Actually, it's getting downright boring."

Nolan dropped his voice even lower. "You've been sheltered all your life. I know you don't want me to feel responsible for what you're doing—or for you.

And I wish I didn't. Unfortunately I can't help it. Believe me, I've tried. It doesn't work. Every night I lie awake wondering what trouble you're going to get into next. I don't know what's going to happen first—you working yourself to death, or me getting an ulcer."

Maryanne's gaze fell to her hands, and the uneven length of her once perfectly uniform fingernails. "They are rather pitiful, aren't they?"

Nolan glanced at them and grimaced. "As a personal favor to me would you consider giving up the job at Rent-A-Maid?" He ran his fingers through his hair, sighing heavily. "It doesn't come easy to ask you this, Annie. If for no other reason, do it because you owe me a favor for finding you the apartment. But for heaven's sake, quit that job."

She didn't answer him right away. She wanted to do as he asked, because she was falling in love with him. Because she craved his approval. Yet she wanted to reject his entreaties, flout his demands. Because he made her feel confused and contrary and full of unpredictable emotions.

"If it'll do any good, I'll promise not to interfere again," he said, his voice so quiet it was almost a whisper. "If you'll quit Rent-a-Maid."

"As a personal favor to you," she repeated, nodding slowly. So much for refusing to be swayed by dinner and a few well-chosen words.

Their eyes met and held for a long moment. Deliberately, as though it went against his will, Nolan reached out and brushed an auburn curl from her cheek. His touch was light yet strangely intimate, as intimate as a kiss. His fingers lingered on her cheek and it was all Maryanne could do not to cover his hand with her own and close her eyes to savor the wealth of sensations that settled around her.

Nolan's dark eyes narrowed, and she could tell he was struggling. She could read it in every line, every feature of his handsome face. But struggling against what? She could only speculate. He didn't want to be attracted to her; that much was obvious.

As if he needed to break contact with her eyes, he lowered his gaze to her mouth. Whether it was intentional or not, Maryanne didn't know, but his thumb inched closer to her lips, easing toward the corner. Then, with an abrupt movement, he pulled his hand away and returned to his meal, eating quickly and methodically.

Maryanne tried to eat, but her own appetite was gone. Wong Su refused payment although Nolan tried to insist. Instead the elderly man said something in Chinese that sent every eye in the place straight to Maryanne. She smiled benignly, wondering what he could possibly have said that would make the great Nolan Adams blush.

The drive back to the apartment was even more silent than the one to the restaurant had been. Maryanne considered asking Nolan exactly what

Wong Su had said just before they'd left, but she thought better of it.

They took their time walking up the four flights of stairs. "Will you come in for coffee?" Maryanne asked when they arrived at her door.

"I can't tonight," Nolan said after several all-too-quiet moments.

"I don't bite, you know." His eyes didn't waver from hers. The attraction was there—she could feel it as surely as she had his touch at dinner.

"I'd like to finish my chapter."

So he was going to close her out once again. "Don't work too hard," she said, opening the apartment door. Her disappointment was keen, but she managed to disguise it behind a shrug. "Thank you for dinner. It was delicious."

Nolan thrust his hands into his pockets. It might have been her imagination, but she thought he did it to keep from reaching for her. The idea comforted her ego and she smiled up at him warmly.

She was about to close the door when he stopped her. "Yes?" she asked.

His eyes were as piercing and dark as she'd ever seen them. "My typing. Does it keep you awake nights?"

"No," she told him and shook her head for emphasis. "The book must be going well."

He nodded, then sighed. "Listen, would it be possible…" He paused and started again. "Are you busy tomorrow night? I've got two tickets to the Seattle Repertory Theatre and I was wondering…"

"I'd love to go," she said eagerly, before he'd even finished the question.

Judging by the expression on his face, the invitation seemed to be as much a surprise to him as it was to her. "I'll see you tomorrow, then."

"Right," she answered brightly. "Tomorrow."

The afternoon was glorious, with just the right mixture of wind and sunshine. Hands clasped behind her back, Maryanne strolled across the grass of Volunteer Park, kicking up leaves as she went. She'd spent the morning researching an article she hoped to sell to a local magazine and she was taking a break.

The basketball court was occupied by several teenage boys, a couple of whom she recognized from the day she'd moved. With time on her hands and an afternoon to enjoy, Maryanne paused to watch the hotly contested game. Sitting on a picnic table, she swung her legs, content to laze away the sunny afternoon. Everything was going so well. With hardly any difficulty she'd found another job. Nolan probably wasn't going to approve of this one, either, but that was just too bad.

"Hi." A girl of about thirteen, wearing a jean jacket and tight black stretch leggings, strolled up to the picnic table. "You're with Mr. Adams, aren't you?"

Maryanne would've liked to think so, but she didn't

feel she could describe it quite that way. "What makes you ask that?"

"You moved in with him, didn't you?"

"Not exactly. I live in the apartment next door."

"I didn't believe Eddie when he said Mr. Adams had a woman. He's never had anyone live with him before. He's just not the type, if you know what I mean."

Maryanne did know. She was learning not to take his attitude toward her personally. The better acquainted she became with Nolan, the more clearly she realized that he considered all women a nuisance. The first night they met, he'd mentioned that he'd been in love once, but his tone had been so casual it implied this romance was merely a long-ago mistake. He'd talked about the experience as if it meant little or nothing to him. Maryanne wasn't sure she believed that.

"Mr. Adams is a really neat guy. All the kids like him a lot." The girl smiled, suggesting she was one of his legion of admirers. "I'm Gloria Masterson."

Maryanne held out her hand. "Maryanne Simpson."

Gloria smiled shyly. "If you don't live with him, are you his girlfriend?"

"Not really. We're just friends."

"That's what he said when I asked him about you."

"Oh." It wasn't as though she could expect him to admit anything more.

"Mr. Adams comes around every now and then and talks to us kids in the park. I think he's checking up on us and making sure no one's into drugs or gangs."

Maryanne smiled. That sounded exactly like the kind of thing Nolan would do.

"Only a few kids around here are that stupid, but you know, I think a couple of the boys might've been tempted to try something if it wasn't for Mr. Adams."

"Hey, Gloria." A lanky boy from the basketball court called out. "Come here, woman."

Gloria sighed loudly, then shouted. "Just a minute." She turned back to Maryanne. "I'm really not Eddie's woman. He just likes to think so."

Maryanne smiled. She wished she could say the same thing about her and Nolan. "It was nice to meet you, Gloria. Maybe I'll see you around."

"That'd be great."

"Gloria," Eddie shouted, "are you coming or not?"

The teenage girl shook her head. "I don't know why I put up with him."

Maryanne left the park soon afterward. The first thing she noticed when she got home was an envelope taped to her door.

She waited until she was inside the apartment to open it, and as she did a single ticket and a note slipped out. "I'm going to be stuck at the office," the note read. "The curtain goes up at eight—don't be late. N."

Maryanne was mildly disappointed that Nolan wouldn't be driving her to the play, but she decided to splurge and take a taxi. By seven-thirty, when the cab arrived, she was dressed and ready. She wore her best evening attire, a long black velvet skirt and matching blazer with a cream-colored silk blouse. She'd even put on her pearl earrings and cameo necklace.

The theatre was one of the nicest in town, and Maryanne's heart sang with excitement as the usher escorted her to her seat. Nolan hadn't arrived yet and she looked around expectantly.

The curtain was about to go up when a man she mentally categorized as wealthy and a bit of a charmer settled in the vacant seat next to hers.

"Excuse me," he said, leaning toward her, smiling warmly. "I'm Griff Bradley. Nolan Adams sent me."

It didn't take Maryanne two seconds to figure out what Nolan had done. The low-down rat had matched her up with someone he considered more appropriate. Someone he assumed she had more in common with. Someone wealthy and slick. Someone her father would approve of.

"Where's Nolan?" Maryanne demanded. She bolted to her feet and grabbed her bag, jerking it so hard the gold chain strap threatened to break.

Griff looked taken aback by her sharp question. "You mean he didn't discuss this with you?"

"He invited me to this play. I assumed...I believed the two of us would be attending it together. He didn't say a word about you. I'm sorry, but I can't agree to this arrangement." She started to edge her way out of the row just as the curtain rose.

To her dismay, Griff followed her into the aisle. "I'm sure there's been some misunderstanding."

"You bet there has," Maryanne said, loudly enough to attract the angry glares of several patrons sitting in the aisle seats. She rushed toward the exit with Griff in hot pursuit.

"If you'll give me a moment to explain—"

"It won't be necessary."

"You are Maryanne Simpson of the New York Simpsons?"

"Yes," she said, walking directly outside. Moving to the curb, she raised her hand and shouted, "Taxi!"

Griff raced around to stand in front of her. "There isn't any need to rush off like this. Nolan was just doing me a good turn."

"And me a rotten one. Listen, Mr. Bradley, you look like a very nice gentleman, and under any other circumstances I would've been more than happy to make your acquaintance, but there's been a mistake."

"But—"

"I'm sorry, I really am." A cab raced toward her and squealed to a halt.

Griff opened the back door for her, looking more charming and debonair than ever. "I'm not sure my heart will recover. You're very lovely, you know."

Maryanne sighed. The man was overdoing it, but he certainly didn't deserve the treatment she was giving him. She smiled and apologized again, then swiftly turned to the driver and recited her address.

Maryanne fumed during the entire ride back to her apartment. Rarely had she been more furious. If Nolan Adams thought he could play matchmaker with her, he was about to learn that everything he'd ever heard about redheads was true.

"Hey, lady, you all right?" the cabbie asked.

"I'm fine," she said stiffly.

"That guy you were with back at the theatre didn't try anything, did he?"

"No, some other man did, only he's not going to get away with it." The driver pulled into her street. "That's the building there," Maryanne told him. She reached into her bag for her wallet and pulled out some of her precious cash, including a generous tip. Then she ran into the apartment building, heedless of her clothes or her high-heeled shoes.

For the first time since moving in, Maryanne didn't pause to rest on the third-floor landing. Her anger carried her all the way to Nolan's apartment door. She could hear him typing inside, and the sound only heightened her temper. Dragging breath through her lungs, she slammed her fist against the door.

"Hold on a minute," she heard him grumble.

His shocked look as he threw open the door would have been comical in different circumstances. "Maryanne, what are you doing here?"

"That was a rotten underhanded thing to do, you deceiving, conniving, low-down…rat!"

Nolan did an admirable job of composing himself. He buried his hands in his pockets and smiled nonchalantly. "I take it you and Griff Bradley didn't hit it off?"

Chapter Six

Maryanne was so furious she couldn't find the words to express her outrage. She opened and closed her mouth twice before she collected herself enough to proceed.

"I told you before that I don't want you interfering in my life, and I meant it."

"I was doing you a favor," Nolan countered, clearly unmoved by her angry display. In fact, he yawned loudly, covering his mouth with the back of his hand. "Griff's a stockbroker friend of mine and one hell of a nice guy. If you'd given him half a chance, you might have found that out yourself. I could see the two of you becoming good friends. Why don't you give it a try? You might hit it off, after all."

"The only thing I'd consider hitting is *you*." To her horror, tears of rage flooded her eyes. "Don't ever try that again. Do you understand?" Not waiting for his reply, she turned abruptly, stalked down the hall to her apartment and unlocked the door. She flung it shut with sufficient force to rattle the windows on three floors.

She paced back and forth several times, blew her nose once and decided she hadn't told him nearly enough. Throwing open her door, she rushed down the hall to Nolan's apartment again. She banged twice as hard as she had originally.

Nolan opened the door, wearing a martyr's expression. He cocked one eyebrow expressively. "What is it this time?"

"And furthermore you're the biggest coward I've ever met. If I still worked for the newspaper, I'd write a column so all of Seattle would know exactly what kind of man you are." Her voice wobbled just a little, but that didn't diminish the strength of her indignation.

She stomped back to her own apartment and she hadn't been there two seconds before there was a pounding on her door. It didn't surprise her to find Nolan Adams on the other side. He might have appeared calm, but his eyes sparked with an angry fire. They narrowed slightly as he glowered at her.

"What did you just say?" he asked.

"You heard me. You're nothing but a coward. Coward, coward, coward!" With that she slammed her door so hard that a framed family photo hanging on the wall crashed to the floor. Luckily the glass didn't break.

Her chest heaving, Maryanne picked up the photo, wiped it off and carefully replaced it. But for all her outward composure, her hands were trembling. No sooner had she completed the task than Nolan beat on her door a second time.

"Now what?" she demanded, whipping open the door. "I would have thought you got my message."

"I got it all right. I just don't happen to like it."

"Tough." She would have slammed the door again, but before she could act, a loud banging came from the direction of the floor. Not knowing what it was, Maryanne instinctively jumped back.

Nolan drew a deep breath, and Maryanne could tell he was making an effort to compose himself. "All right, Mrs. McBride," Nolan shouted at the floor, "we'll hold it down."

"Who's Mrs. McBride?"

"The lady who lives in the apartment below you."

"Oh." Maryanne had been too infuriated to realize she was shouting so loudly half the apartment building could hear. She felt ashamed at her loss of control and guilty for disturbing her neighbors—but she was still furious with Nolan.

The man in question glared at her. "Do you think it's possible to discuss this situation without involving any more doors?" he asked sharply. "Or would you rather wait until someone phones the police and we're both arrested for disturbing the peace?"

She glared back at him defiantly. "Very funny," she

said, turning around and walking into her apartment. As she knew he would, Nolan followed her inside.

Maryanne moved into the kitchen. Preparing a pot of coffee gave her a few extra minutes to gather her dignity, which had been as abused as her apartment door. Mixed with the anger was a chilling pain that cut straight through her heart. Nolan's thinking so little of her that he could casually pass her on to another man was mortifying enough. But knowing he considered it a favor only heaped on the humiliation.

"Annie, please listen—"

"Did it ever occur to you that arranging this date with Griff might offend me?" she cried.

Nolan seemed reluctant to answer. "Yes," he finally said, "it did. I tried to catch you earlier this afternoon, but you weren't in. This wasn't the kind of situation I felt comfortable explaining in a note, so I took the easy way out and left Griff to introduce himself. I didn't realize you'd take it so personally."

"How else was I supposed to take it?"

Nolan glanced away uncomfortably. "Let's just say I was hoping you'd meet him and the two of you would spend the evening getting to know each other. Griff comes from a well-established family and—"

"That's supposed to impress me?"

"He's the type of man your father would arrange for you to meet," Nolan said, his voice sandpaper-gruff.

"How many times do I have to tell you I don't need a second father?" His mention of her family reminded her of the way she was deceiving them, which brought a powerful sense of remorse.

He muttered tersely under his breath, then shook his head. "Obviously I blew it. Would it help if I apologized?"

An apology, even a sincere one, wouldn't dissolve the hurt. She looked up, about to tell him exactly that, when her eyes locked with his.

He stood a safe distance from her, his expression so tender that her battered heart rolled defencelessly to her feet. She knew she ought to throw him out of her home and refuse to ever speak to him again. No one would blame her. She tried to rally her anger, but something she couldn't explain or understand stopped her.

All the emotion must have sharpened her perceptions. Never had she been more aware of Nolan as a man. The space separating them seemed to close, drawing them toward each other. She could smell the clean scent of the soap he used and hear the music of the rain as it danced against her window. She hadn't even realized, until this moment, that it was raining.

"I am sorry," he said quietly.

Maryanne nodded and wiped the moisture from her eyes. She wasn't a woman who cried easily, and the tears were a surprise.

"What you said about my being a coward is true," Nolan admitted. He sighed heavily. "You frighten me, Annie."

"You mean my temper?"

"No, I deserved that." He grinned that lazy insolent grin of his.

"What is it about me you find so unappealing?" She had to know what was driving him away, no matter how much the truth damaged her pride.

"Unappealing?" His abrupt laugh was filled with irony. "I wish I could find something, *anything,* unappealing about you, but I can't." Dropping his gaze, he stepped back and cleared his throat. When he spoke again, his words were brusque, impatient. "I was a lot more comfortable with you before we met."

"You thought of me as a debutante."

"I assumed you were a pampered immature…girl. Not a woman. I expected to find you ambitious and selfish, so eager to impress your father with what you could do that it didn't matter how many people you stepped on. Then we did the Celebrity Debate, and I discovered that none of the things I wanted to believe about you were true."

"Then why—"

"What you've got to understand," Nolan added forcefully, "is that I don't *want* to become involved with you."

"That message has come through loud and clear." She moistened her lips and cast her gaze toward the floor, afraid he'd see how vulnerable he made her feel.

Suddenly he was standing directly in front of her, so close his breath warmed her face. With one gentle finger, he lifted her chin, raising her eyes to his.

"All evening I was telling myself how noble I was," he said. "Griff Bradley is far better suited to you than I'll ever be."

"Stop saying that!"

He wrapped his arms around her waist and pulled her against him. "There can't ever be any kind of relationship between us," he said, his voice rough. "I learned my lesson years ago, and I'm not going to repeat that mistake." But contrary to everything he was saying, his mouth lowered to hers until their lips touched. The kiss was slow and familiar. Their bottom lips clung as Nolan eased away from her.

"That wasn't supposed to happen," he murmured.

"I won't tell anyone if you won't," she whispered.

"Just remember what I said," he whispered back. "I don't do well with rich girls. I already found that out. The hard way."

"I'll remember," she said softly, looking up at him.

"Good." And then he kissed her again.

It was three days before Maryanne saw Nolan. She didn't need anyone to tell her he was avoiding her. Maybe he thought falling in love would wreak havoc with his comfortable well-ordered life. If he'd given her a chance, Maryanne would've told him she didn't expect him to fill her days. She had her new job, and she was fixing up her apartment. Most importantly, she had her writing, which kept her busy the rest of the time. She'd recently queried a magazine about doing a humorous article on her experiences working for Rent-A-Maid.

"Here's Nolan now," Barbara whispered as she hurried past Maryanne, balancing three plates.

Automatically Maryanne reached for a water glass and a menu and followed Nolan to the booth. He was halfway into his seat when he saw her. He froze and his narrowed gaze flew across the room to the middle-aged waitress.

Barbara didn't appear in the least intimidated. "Hey, what did you expect?" she called out. "We were one girl short, and when Maryanne applied for the job she gave you as a reference. Besides, she's a good worker."

Nolan didn't bother to look at the menu. Standing beside the table, Maryanne took her green order pad out of her apron pocket.

"I'll have the chili," he said gruffly.

"With or without cheese?"

"Without," he bellowed, then quickly lowered his voice. "How long have you been working here?"

"Since Monday morning. Don't look so angry. You were the one who told me about the job. Remember?"

"I don't want you working here!"

"Why not? It's a respectable establishment. Honestly, Nolan, what did you expect me to do? I had to find another job, and fast. I can't expect to sell any articles for at least a month, if then. I've got to have some way of paying the bills."

"You could've done a hell of a lot better than Mom's Place if you wanted to be a waitress."

"Are we going to argue? Again?" she asked with an impatient sigh.

"No," he answered, grabbing his napkin just in time to catch a violent sneeze.

Now that she had a chance to study him, she saw his nose was red and his eyes rheumy. In fact he looked downright miserable. "You've got a cold."

"Are you always this brilliant?"

"I try to be. And I'll try to ignore your rudeness. Would you like a glass of orange juice or a couple of aspirin?"

"No, Florence Nightingale, all I want is my usual bowl of chili, *without* the cheese. Have you got that?"

"Yes, of course," she said, writing it down. Nolan certainly seemed to be in a rotten mood, but that was nothing new. Maryanne seemed to bring out the worst in him.

Barbara met her at the counter. "From the looks your boyfriend's been sending me, he'd gladly cut off my head. What's with him, anyway?"

"I don't think he's feeling well," Maryanne answered in a low worried voice.

"Men, especially sick ones, are the biggest babies on earth," Barbara said wryly. "They get a little virus and think someone should rush in to make a documentary about their life-threatening condition. My advice to you is let him wallow in his misery all by himself."

"But he looks like he might have a fever," Maryanne whispered.

"And he isn't old enough to take an aspirin all on his own?" The older woman glanced behind her. "His order's up. You want me to take it to him?"

"No…"

"Don't worry, if he gets smart with me I'll just whack him upside the head. Someone needs to put that man in his place."

Maryanne picked up the large bowl of chili. "I'll do it."

"Yes," Barbara said, grinning broadly. "I have a feeling you will."

Maryanne got home several hours later. Her feet hurt and her back ached, but she felt a pleasant glow of satisfaction. After three days of waitressing, she was beginning to get the knack of keeping orders straight and remembering everything she needed to do. It wasn't the job of her dreams, but she was making a living wage, certainly better money than she'd been getting from Rent-A-Maid. Not only that, the tips were good. Maryanne didn't dare imagine what her family would say if they found out, though. She suffered a stab of remorse every time she thought about the way she was deceiving them. In fact, it was simpler not to think about it at all.

After his initial reaction, Nolan hadn't so much as mentioned her working at Mom's Place. He clearly wasn't thrilled, but that didn't surprise her. Little, if anything, she'd done from the moment she'd met him had gained his approval.

Maryanne had grown accustomed to falling asleep most nights to the sound of Nolan's typing. She found herself listening for it when she climbed into bed. But she didn't hear it that night or the two nights that followed.

"How's Nolan?" Barbara asked her on Friday afternoon.

"I don't know." Maryanne hadn't seen him in days, but then, she rarely did.

"He must have got a really bad bug."

Maryanne hated the way her heart lurched. She'd tried not to think about him. Not that she'd been successful...

"His column hasn't been in the paper all week. The *Sun's* been running some of his old ones—Nolan's Classics. Did you read the one last night?" Barbara asked, laughing. "It was about how old-fashioned friendly service has disappeared from restaurants today." She grinned. "He said there were a few exceptions, and you know who he was talking about."

As a matter of fact, Maryanne had read the piece and been highly amused—and flattered, even though the column had been written long before she'd even come to Seattle, let alone worked at Mom's Place. As always she'd been impressed with Nolan's dry wit. They often disagreed—Nolan was too much of a pessimist to suit her—but she couldn't help admiring his skill with words.

Since the afternoon he'd found her at Mom's, Nolan hadn't eaten there again. Maryanne didn't consider that so strange. He went to great lengths to ensure that they didn't run into each other. She did feel mildly guilty that he'd decided to stay away from his favorite diner, but it *was* his choice, after all.

During the rest of her shift, Maryanne had to struggle to keep Nolan out of her mind. His apartment had been unusually quiet for the past few days, but she hadn't been concerned about it. Now she was.

"Do you think he's all right?" she asked Barbara some time later.

"He's a big boy," the older woman was quick to remind her. "He can take care of himself."

Maryanne wasn't so sure. After work, she hurried home, convinced she'd find Nolan hovering near death, too ill to call for help. She didn't even stop at her own apartment, but went directly to his.

She knocked politely, anticipating all kinds of disasters when there was no response.

"Nolan?" She pounded on his door and yelled his name, battling down a rising sense of panic. She envisioned him lying on his bed, suffering—or worse. "Nolan, please answer the door," she pleaded, wondering if there was someone in the building with a passkey.

She'd waited hours, it seemed, before he yanked open the door.

"Are you all right?" she demanded, so relieved to see him she could hardly keep from hurling herself into his arms. Relieved, that was, until she got a good look at him.

"I was feeling just great," he told her gruffly, "until I had to get out of bed to answer the stupid door. Which, incidentally, woke me up."

Maryanne pressed her fingers over her mouth to hide her hysterical laughter. If Nolan felt anywhere near as bad as he looked, then she should seriously consider phoning for an ambulance. He wore grey sweatpants and a faded plaid robe, one she would guess had been moth fodder for years. His choice of clothes was the least of her concerns, however. He resembled someone who'd just surfaced from a four-day drunk. His eyes were red and his face ashen. He scowled at her and it was clear the moment he spoke that his disposition was as cheery as his appearance.

"I take it there's a reason for this uninvited visit?" he growled, then sneezed fiercely.

"Yes…" Maryanne hedged, not knowing exactly what to do now. "I just wanted to make sure you're all right."

"Okay, you've seen me. I'm going to live, so you can leave in good conscience." He would have closed the door, but Maryanne stepped forward and boldly forced her way into his apartment.

In the weeks they'd lived next door to each other, she'd never seen his home. The muted earth colors, the rich leather furniture and polished wood floors appealed to her immediately. Despite her worry about his condition, she smiled; this room reminded her of Nolan, with papers and books littering every available space. His apartment seemed at least twice the size of hers. He'd once mentioned that it was larger, but after becoming accustomed to her own small rooms, she found the spaciousness of his a pleasant shock.

"In case you haven't noticed, I'm in no mood for company," he informed her in a surly voice.

"Have you been to a doctor?"

"No."

"Do you need anything?"

"Peace and quiet," he muttered.

"You could have bronchitis or pneumonia or something."

"I'm perfectly fine. At least, I was until you arrived." He walked across the carpet—a dark green-and-gold Persian, Maryanne noted automatically—and slumped onto an overstuffed sofa piled with blankets and pillows. The television was on, its volume turned very low.

"Then why haven't you been at work?"

"I'm on vacation."

"Personally, I would've chosen a tropical island over a sofa in my own apartment." She advanced purposefully into his kitchen and stopped short when she caught sight of the dirty dishes stacked a foot high in the stainless-steel sink. She was amazed he could cram so much into such a tight space.

"This place is a mess!" she declared, hands on her hips.

"Go ahead and call the health department if you're so concerned."

"I probably should." Instead, she walked straight to the sink, rolled up her sleeves and started stacking the dishes on the counter.

"What are you doing now?" Nolan shouted from the living room.

"Cleaning up."

He muttered something she couldn't hear, which was probably for the best.

"Go lie down, Nolan," she instructed. "When I'm done here, I'll heat you some soup. You've got to get your strength back in order to suffer properly."

At first he let that comment pass. Then, as if she was taxing him to the limit of his endurance, he called out, "The way you care is truly touching."

"I was hoping you'd notice." For someone who'd been outraged at the sight of her dishpan hands a week earlier, he seemed oddly unconcerned that she was washing his dirty dishes. Not that Maryanne minded. It made her feel good to be doing something for him.

She soon found herself humming as she rinsed the dishes and set them in his dishwasher.

Fifteen minutes passed without their exchanging a word. When Maryanne had finished, she looked in the living room and wasn't surprised to find him sound asleep on the sofa. A curious feeling tugged at her heart as she gazed down at him. He lay on his back with his left hand flung across his forehead. His features were relaxed, but there was nothing remotely angelic about him. Not about the way his thick dark lashes brushed the arch of his cheek—or about the slow hoarse breaths that whispered through his half-open mouth.

Maryanne felt a strong urge to brush the hair from his forehead, to touch him, but she resisted. She was afraid he'd wake up. And she was even more afraid she wouldn't want to stop touching him.

Moving about the living room, she turned off the television, picked up things here and there and straightened a few piles of magazines. She should leave now; she knew that. Nolan wouldn't welcome her staying. She eyed the door regretfully, looking for an excuse to linger. She closed her eyes and listened to the sound of Nolan's raspy breathing.

More by chance than design, Maryanne found herself standing next to his typewriter. Feeling brave, and more than a little foolish, she looked down at the stack of paper resting beside it. Glancing over her shoulder to make sure he was still asleep, Maryanne carefully turned over the top page and quickly read the last couple of paragraphs on page 212. The story wasn't finished, but she could tell he'd stopped during a cliff-hanger scene.

Nolan had been so secretive about his project that she dared not invade his privacy any more than she already had. She turned the single sheet back over, taking care to place it exactly as she'd found it.

Once again, she reminded herself that she should go back to her own apartment, but she felt strangely reluctant to end these moments with Nolan. Even a sleeping Nolan who would certainly be cranky when he woke up.

Seeking some way to occupy herself, she moved down the hall and into the bathroom, picking up several soiled towels on the way. His bed was unmade. She would've been surprised to find it in any other condition. The sheets and blankets were sagging onto the floor, and two or three sets of clothing were scattered all about.

Without questioning the wisdom of her actions, she bundled up the dirty laundry to take to the coin-operated machine in the basement. She loaded it into a large garbage bag, then set about vigorously cleaning the apartment. Scrubbing, scouring and sweeping were skills she'd perfected in her Rent-A-Maid days. If nothing else, she'd had lots of practice cleaning up after messy bachelors.

Studying the contents of his refrigerator, more than an hour later, proved to be a humorous adventure. She found an unopened bottle of wine, a carton of broken egg shells and one limp strand of celery. Concocting anything edible from that would be impossible, so she searched the apartment until she found his keys. Then, with his garbage bag full of laundry in her arms, she let herself out the door, closing it softly.

She returned a half-hour later, clutching two bags of groceries bought with her tip money. Then she went down to put his laundry in the dryer. To her relief, Nolan was still asleep. She smiled down at him indulgently before she began preparing his dinner. After another forty-five minutes she retrieved his clean clothes and put them neatly away.

She was in the kitchen peeling potatoes when she heard Nolan get up. She continued her task, knowing he'd discover she was there soon enough. He stopped cold when he did.

"What are you doing here?"

"Making your dinner."

"I'm not hungry," he snapped with no evidence of appreciation for her efforts.

His eyes widened as he glanced around. "What happened here? Oh, you've cleaned the place up."

"I didn't think you'd notice," she answered sweetly, popping a small piece of raw potato in her mouth. "I'll get soup to the boiling stage before I leave you to your...peace of mind. It should only take another ten or fifteen minutes. Can you endure me that much longer?"

He made another of his typical grumbling replies

before disappearing. No more than two seconds had passed before he let out a bellow loud enough to shake the roof tiles.

"What did you do to my bed?" he demanded as he stormed into the kitchen.

"I made it."

"What else have you been up to? Damn it, a man isn't safe in his own home with you around."

"Don't look so put out, Nolan. All I did was straighten up the place a bit. It was a mess."

"I happen to like messes. I thrive in messes. The last thing I want or need is some neat-freak invading my home, organizing my life."

"Don't exaggerate," Maryanne said serenely, as she added a pile of diced carrots to the simmering broth. "All I did was pick up a few things here and there and run a load of laundry."

"You did my laundry, too?" he exploded, jerking both hands through his hair. Heaven only knew, she thought, what would happen if he learned she'd read a single word of his precious manuscript.

"Everything's been folded and put away, so you needn't worry."

Nolan abruptly left the kitchen, only to return a couple of moments later. He circled the table slowly and precisely, then took several deep breaths.

"Listen, Annie," he began carefully, "it isn't that I don't appreciate what you've done, but I don't need a nurse. Or a housekeeper."

She looked up, meeting his eyes, her own large and guileless. "I quite agree," she answered.

"You do?" Some of the stiffness left his shoulders. "Then you aren't going to take offence?"

"No, why should I?"

"No reason," he answered, eyeing her suspiciously.

"I was thinking that what you really need," she said, smiling at him gently, "is a wife."

Chapter Seven

"A wife," Nolan echoed. His dark eyes widened in undisguised horror. It was as if Maryanne had suggested he climb to the roof of the apartment building and leap off.

"Don't get so excited. I wasn't volunteering for the position."

With his index finger pointing at her like the barrel of a shotgun, Nolan walked around the kitchen table again, his journey made in shuffling impatient steps. He circled the table twice before he spoke.

"You cleaned my home, washed my clothes and now you're cooking my dinner." Each word came at her like an accusation.

"Yes?"

"You can't possibly look at me with those baby-blues of yours and expect me to believe—"

"Believe what?"

"That you're not applying for the job. From the

moment we met, you've been doing all these...these sweet *girlie* things to entice me."

"Sweet girlie things?" Maryanne repeated, struggling to contain her amusement. "I don't think I understand."

"I don't expect you to admit it."

"I haven't the foggiest idea what you're talking about."

"You know," he accused her with an angry shrug.

"Obviously I don't. What could I possibly have done to make you think I'm trying to *entice* you?"

"Sweet girlie things," he said again, but without the same conviction. He chewed on his bottom lip for a moment while he mulled the matter over. "All right, I'll give you an example—that perfume you're always wearing."

"Windchime? It's a light fragrance."

"I don't know the name of it. But it hangs around for an hour or so after you've left the room. You know that, and yet you wear it every time we're together."

"I've worn Windchime for years."

"That's not all," he continued quickly. "It's the way I catch you looking at me sometimes."

"*Looking* at you?" She folded her arms at her waist and rolled her eyes toward the ceiling.

"Yes," he said, sounding even more peevish. He pressed his hand to his hip, cocked his chin at a regal angle and fluttered his eyelashes like fans.

Despite her effort to hold in her amusement,

Maryanne laughed. "I can only assume that you're joking."

Nolan dropped his hand from his hip. "I'm not. You get this innocent look and your lips pout just so… Why, a man—any man—couldn't keep from wanting to kiss you."

"That's preposterous." But Maryanne instinctively pinched her lips together and closed her eyes.

Nolan's arm shot out. "That's another thing."

"What now?"

"The way you get this helpless flustered look and it's all a simpleminded male can do not to rush in and offer to take care of whatever's bothering you."

"By this time you should know I'm perfectly capable of taking care of myself," Maryanne felt obliged to remind him.

"You're a lamb among wolves," Nolan said. "I don't know how long you intend to play out this silly charade, but personally I think you've overdone it. This isn't your world, and the sooner you go back where you belong, the better."

"Better for whom?"

"Me!" he cried vehemently. "And for you," he added with less fervor, as though it was an afterthought. He coughed a couple of times and reached for a package of cough drops in the pocket of his plaid robe. Shaking one out, he popped it in his mouth with barely a pause.

"I don't think it's doing you any good to get so excited," Maryanne said with unruffled patience. "I was merely making an observation and it still stands. I believe you need a wife."

"Go observe someone else's life," he suggested, sucking madly on the cough drop.

"Aha!" she cried, waving her index finger at him. "How does it feel to have someone interfering in *your* life?"

Nolan frowned and Maryanne turned back to the stove. She lifted the lid from the soup to stir it briskly. Then she lowered the burner. When she was through, she saw with a glimmer of fun that Nolan was standing as far away from her as humanly possible, while still remaining in the same room.

"That's something else!" he cried. "You give the impression that you're in total agreement with whatever I'm saying and then you go about doing exactly as you damn well please. I've never met a more frustrating woman in my entire life."

"That's not true," Maryanne argued. "I quit my job at Rent-A-Maid because you insisted." It had worked out for the best, since she had more time for her writing now, but this wasn't the moment to mention that.

"Oh, right, bring *that* up. It's the only thing you've ever done that I wanted. I practically had to get down on my knees and beg you to leave that crazy job before you injured yourself."

"You didn't!"

"Trust me, it was a humbling experience and not one I intend to repeat. I've known you how long? A month?" He paused to gaze at the ceiling. "It seems like an eternity."

"You're trying to make me feel guilty. It isn't going to work."

"Why should you feel anything of the sort? Just because living next door to you is enough to drive a man to drink."

"You're the one who found me this place. If you don't like living next door to me, then I'm not the one to blame!"

"Don't remind me," he muttered.

The comment about Nolan finding himself a wife had been made in jest, but he'd certainly taken it seriously. In fact, he seemed to have strong feelings about the entire issue. Realizing her welcome had worn extremely thin, Maryanne headed for his apartment door. "Everything's under control here."

"Does that mean you're leaving?"

She hated the enthusiastic lift in his voice, as if he couldn't wait to be rid of her. Although he wasn't admitting it, she'd done him a good turn. Fair exchange, she supposed; Nolan had been generous enough to her over the past month.

"Yes, I'm leaving."

"Good." He didn't bother to disguise his delight.

"But I still think you'd do well to consider what I said." Maryanne had the irresistible urge to heap coals on the fires of his indignation. "A wife could be a great help to you."

Nolan frowned heavily, drawing his eyebrows into a deep V. "I think the modern woman would find your suggestion downright insulting."

"What? That you marry?"

"Exactly. Haven't you heard? A woman's place isn't in the home anymore. It's out there in the world, forging a career for herself. Living a fuller life, and all that. It's not doing the mundane tasks you're talking about."

"I wasn't suggesting you marry for the convenience of gaining a live-in housekeeper."

His brown eyes narrowed. "Then what *were* you saying?"

"That you're a capable talented man," she explained. She glanced surreptitiously at his manuscript, still tidily stacked by the typewriter. "But unfortunately, that doesn't mean a whole lot if you don't have someone close—a friend, a companion, a…wife—to share it with."

"Don't you worry about me, Little Miss Muffet. I've lived my own life from the time I was thirteen. You may think I need someone, but let me assure you, I don't."

"You're probably right," she said reluctantly. She opened his door, then hesitated. "You'll call if you want anything?"

"No."

She released a short sigh of frustration. "That's what I thought. The soup should be done in about thirty minutes."

He nodded, then, looking a bit chagrined, added, "I suppose I should thank you."

"I suppose you should, too, but it isn't necessary."

"What about the money you spent on groceries? You can't afford acts of charity, you know. Wait a minute and I'll—"

"Forget it," she snapped. "I can spend my money on whatever I damn well please. I'm my own person, remember? You can just owe me. Buy me dinner sometime." She left before he could say anything else.

Maryanne's own apartment felt bleak and lonely after Nolan's. The first thing she did was walk around turning on all the lights. No sooner had she finished when there was a loud knock at her door. She opened it to find Nolan standing there in his disreputable moth-eaten robe, glaring.

"Yes?" she inquired sweetly.

"You read my manuscript, didn't you?" he boomed in a voice that echoed like thunder off the apartment walls.

"I most certainly did not," she denied vehemently. She straightened her back as if to suggest she found the very question insulting.

Without waiting for an invitation, Nolan stalked into her living room, then whirled around to face her. "Admit it!"

Making each word as clear and distinct as possible, Maryanne said, "I did not read your precious manuscript. How could I possibly have cleaned up, done the laundry, prepared a big kettle of homemade soup, and still had time to read 212 pages of manuscript?"

"How did you know it was 212 pages?" Sparks of reproach shot from his eyes.

"Ah—" she swallowed uncomfortably "—it was a guess, and from the looks of it, a good one."

"It wasn't any guess."

He marched toward her and for every step he took, she retreated two. "All right," she admitted guiltily, "I did look at it, but I swear I didn't read more than a few lines. I was straightening up the living room and…it was there, so I turned over the last page and read a couple of paragraphs."

"Aha! Finally, the truth!" Nolan pointed directly at her "You did read it!"

"Just a few lines," she repeated in a tiny voice, feeling completely wretched.

"And?" His eyes softened.

"And what?"

"What did you think?" He looked at her expectantly, then frowned. "Never mind, I shouldn't have asked."

Rubbing her palms together, Maryanne took one step forward. "Nolan, it was wonderful. Witty and terribly suspenseful and… I would have given anything to read more. But I knew I didn't dare because, well, because I was invading your privacy...which I didn't want to do, but I did and I really didn't want...that."

"It is good, isn't it?" he asked almost smugly, then his expression sobered as quickly as it had before.

She grinned, nodding enthusiastically. "Tell me about it."

He seemed undecided, then launched excitedly into his idea. "It's about a Seattle newspaperman, Leo, who stumbles on a murder case. Actually, I'm developing a series with him as the main character. This one's not quite finished yet—as I'm sure you know."

"Is there a woman in Leo's life?"

"You're kidding, aren't you?"

Maryanne wasn't. The few paragraphs she'd read had mentioned a Maddie who was apparently in danger. Leo had been frantic to save her.

"You had no business going anywhere near that manuscript," Nolan reminded her.

"I know, but the temptation was so strong. I shouldn't have peeked, I realize that, but I couldn't help myself. Nolan, I'm not lying when I say how good the writing was. Do you have a publisher in mind? Because if you don't, I have several New York editor friends I could recommend and I know—"

"I'm not using you or any influence you may have in New York. I don't want anything to do with your father's publishing company. Understand?"

"Of course, but you're overreacting." He seemed to

be doing a lot of that lately. "My father wouldn't stay in business long if he ordered the editors to purchase my friends' manuscripts, would he? Believe me, it would all be on the up and up, and if you've got an idea for a series using Leo—"

"I said no."

"But—"

"I mean it, Annie. This is my book and I'll submit it myself without any help from you."

"If that's what you want," she concurred meekly.

"That's the way it's going to be." The stern unyielding look slipped back into place. "Now if you don't mind, I'll quietly go back to my messy little world, sans wife and countless interruptions from a certain neighbor."

"I'll try not to bother you again," Maryanne said sarcastically, since he was the one who'd invaded *her* home this time.

"It would be appreciated," he said, apparently ignoring her tone.

"Your apartment is yours and mine is mine, and I'll uphold your privacy with the utmost respect," she continued, her voice still faintly mocking. She buried her hands in her pockets and her fingers closed around something cold and metallic.

"Good." Nolan was nodding. "Privacy, that's what we need."

"Um, Nolan…" She paused. "This is somewhat embarrassing, but it seems I have…" She hesitated again, then resolutely squared her shoulders. "I suppose you'd appreciate it if I returned your keys, right?"

"My keys?" Nolan exploded.

"I just found them. They were in my pocket. You see, all you had in your refrigerator was one limp strand of celery and I couldn't very well make soup out of that, so I had to go to the store and I didn't want to leave your door unlocked and—"

"You have my keys?"

"Yes."

He held out his palm, casting his eyes toward the ceiling. Feeling like a pickpocket caught in the act, Maryanne dropped the keys into his hand and stepped quickly back, almost afraid he was going to grab her by the shoulders and shake her. Which, of course, was ludicrous.

Nolan left immediately and Maryanne followed him to the door, staring out into the hallway as he walked back to his own apartment.

The next Thursday, Maryanne was hurrying to get ready for work when the phone rang. She frowned and stared at it, wondering if she dared take the time to answer. It might be Nolan, but every instinct she possessed told her otherwise. They hadn't spoken all week. Every afternoon, like clockwork, he'd arrived at Mom's Diner. More often than not, he ordered chili. Maryanne waited on him most of the time, but she might have been a robot for all the attention he paid her. His complete lack of interest dented her pride; still, his attitude shouldn't have come as any surprise.

"Hello," she said hesitantly, picking up the receiver.

"Maryanne," her mother responded, her voice rising with pleasure. "I can't believe I finally got hold of you. I've been trying for the past three days."

Maryanne immediately felt swamped by guilt. "You didn't leave a message on my machine."

"You know how I hate those things."

Maryanne did know that. She also knew she should have phoned her parents herself, but she wasn't sure how long she could continue with this farce. "Is everything all right?"

"Yes, of course. Your father's working too hard, but that's nothing new. The boys are busy with soccer and growing like weeds." Her mother's voice fell slightly. "How's the job?"

"The job?"

"Your special assignment."

"Oh, that." Maryanne had rarely been able to fool her mother, and she could only wonder how well she was succeeding now. "It's going...well. I'm learning so much."

"I think you'll make a terrific investigative reporter, sweetie, and the secrecy behind this assignment makes it all the more intriguing. When are your father and I going to learn exactly what you've been doing? I wish we'd never promised not to check up on your progress at the paper. We're both so curious."

"I'll be finished with it soon." Maryanne glanced at her watch and was about to close the conversation when her mother asked, "How's Nolan?"

"Nolan?" Maryanne's heart zoomed straight into her throat. She hadn't remembered mentioning him, and just hearing his name sent a feverish heat through her body.

"You seemed quite enthralled with him the last time we spoke, remember?"

"I was?"

"Yes, sweetie, you were. You claimed he was very talented, and although you were tight-lipped about it I got the impression you were strongly attracted to this young man."

"Nolan's a friend. But we argue more than anything."

Her mother chuckled. "Good."

"How could that possibly be good?"

"It means you're comfortable enough with each other to be yourselves, and that's a positive sign. Why, your father and I bickered like old fishwives when we first met. I swear there wasn't a single issue we could agree on." She sighed softly. "Then one day we looked at each other, and I knew then and there I was going to love this man for the rest of my life. And I have."

"Mom, it isn't like that with Nolan and me. I...I don't even think he likes me."

"Nolan doesn't like you?" her mother repeated. "Why, sweetie, that would be impossible."

Maryanne started to laugh then, because her mother was so obviously biased, yet sounded completely objective and matter-of-fact. It felt good to laugh again, good to find something amusing. She hadn't realized how melancholy she'd become since her last encounter with Nolan. He was still making such an effort to keep her at arm's length for fear... She didn't know exactly *what* he feared. Perhaps he was falling in love with her, but she'd noticed precious little evidence pointing to that conclusion. If anything, Nolan considered her an irritant in his life.

Maryanne spoke to her mother for a few more minutes, then rushed out the door, hoping she wouldn't be late for her shift at Mom's Place. Some investigative reporter she was!

At the diner, she slipped the apron around her waist and hurried out to help with the luncheon crowd. Waiting tables, she was learning quite a lot about character types. This could be helpful for a writer, she figured. Some of her customers were pretty eccentric. She observed them carefully, wondering if Nolan did the same thing. But she wasn't going to think about Nolan....

Halfway through her shift, she began to feel light-headed and sick to her stomach.

"Are you feeling all right?" Barbara asked as she slipped past, carrying an order.

"I—I don't know."

"When was the last time you ate?"

"This morning. No," she corrected, "last night. I didn't have much of an appetite this morning."

"That's what I thought." Barbara set the hamburger and fries on the counter in front of her customer and walked back to Maryanne. "Now that I've got a good look at you, you do seem a bit peaked."

"I'm all right."

Hands on her hips, Barbara continued to study Maryanne as if memorizing every feature. "Are you sure?"

"I'm fine." She had the beginnings of a headache, but nothing she could really complain about. It probably hadn't been a good idea to skip breakfast and lunch, but she'd make up for it when she took her dinner break.

"I'm not sure I believe you," Barbara muttered, dragging out a well-used phone book. She flipped through the pages until she apparently found the number she wanted, then reached for the phone.

"Who are you calling?"

She held the receiver against her shoulder. "Nolan Adams, who else? Seems to me it's his turn to play nursemaid."

"Barbara, no!" She might not be feeling a hundred per cent, but she wasn't all that sick, either. And the last person she wanted running to her rescue was Nolan. He'd only use it against her, as proof that she should go back to the cosy comfortable world of her parents. She'd almost proved she could live entirely on her own, without relying on interest from her trust fund.

"Nolan's not at the office," Barbara said a moment later, replacing the receiver. "I'll talk to him when he comes in."

"No, you won't! Barbara, I swear to you I'll personally give your phone number to every trucker who comes into this place if you so much as say a single word to Nolan."

"Honey," the other waitress said, raising her eyebrows, "you'd be doing me a favor!"

Grumbling, Maryanne returned to her customers.

By closing time, however, she was feeling slightly worse. Not exactly sick, but not exactly herself, either. Barbara was watching Maryanne closely, regularly feeling her cheeks and forehead and muttering about her temperature. If there was one thing to be grateful for, it was the fact that Nolan hadn't shown up. Barbara insisted Maryanne leave a few minutes early and shooed her out the door. Had she been feeling better, Maryanne would have argued.

By the time she arrived back at her apartment, she knew beyond a doubt that she was coming down with some kind of virus. Part of her would've liked to blame Nolan, but she was the one who'd let herself into his apartment. She was the one who'd lingered there, straightening up the place and staying far longer than necessary.

After a long hot shower, she put on her flannel pyjamas and unfolded her bed, climbing quickly beneath the covers. She'd turned the television on for company and prepared herself a mug of soup. As she took her first sip, she heard someone knock at her door.

"Who is it?" she called out.

"Nolan."

"I'm in bed," she shouted.

"You've seen me in my robe. It's only fair I see you in yours," he yelled back.

Maryanne tossed aside her covers and sat up. "Go away."

A sharp pounding noise came from the floor, followed by an equally loud roar that proclaimed it time for "Jeopardy". Apparently Maryanne's shouting match with Nolan was disrupting Mrs. McBride's favorite television show.

"Sorry." Maryanne cupped her hands over her mouth and yelled at the hardwood floor.

"Are you going to let me in, or do I have to get the passkey?" Nolan demanded.

Groaning, Maryanne shuffled across the floor in her giant fuzzy slippers and turned the lock. "Yes?" she asked with exaggerated patience.

For the longest moment, Nolan said nothing. He shoved his hands deep into the pockets of his beige raincoat. "How are you?"

Maryanne glared at him with all the indignation she could muster, which at the moment was considerable. "Do you mean to say you practically pounded down my door to ask me that?"

He didn't bother to answer, but walked into her apartment as though he had every right to do so. "Barbara phoned me."

"Oh, brother! And what exactly did she say?" She continued to hold open the door, hoping he'd get the hint and leave.

"That you caught my bug." His voice was rough with ill-disguised worry.

"Wrong. I felt a bit under the weather earlier, but I'm fine now." The last thing she wanted Nolan motivated by was guilt. He'd succeeded in keeping his distance up to now; if he decided to see her, she wanted to be sure his visit wasn't prompted by an overactive sense of responsibility.

"You look…"

"Yes?" she prompted.

His gaze skimmed her, from slightly damp hair to large fuzzy feet. "Fine," he answered softly.

"As you can see I'm really not sick, so you needn't concern yourself."

Her words were followed by a lengthy silence. Nolan turned as though to leave. Maryanne should have felt relieved to see him go, instead, she experienced the strangest sensation of loss. She longed to reach out a hand, ask him to stay, but she didn't have the courage.

She brushed the hair from her face and smiled, even though it was difficult to put on a carefree facade.

"I'll stop by in the morning and see how you're doing," Nolan said, hovering by the threshold.

"That won't be necessary."

He frowned. "When did you get so prickly?"

"When did you get so caring?" The words nearly caught in her throat and escaped on a whisper.

"I *do* care about you," he said.

"Oh, sure, the same way you'd care about an annoying younger sister. Believe me, Nolan, your message came through loud and clear. I'm not your type. Fine, I can accept that, because you're not my type, either." She didn't really think she had a type, but it sounded philosophical and went a long way toward salving her badly bruised ego. Nolan couldn't have made his views toward her any plainer had he rented a billboard. He'd even said he'd taken one look at her and immediately thought, "Here comes trouble."

She'd never been more attracted to a man in her life, and here she was, standing in front of him lying through her teeth rather than admit how she truly felt.

"So I'm not your type, either?" he asked, almost in a whisper.

Maryanne's heartbeat quickened. He studied her as intently as she studied him. He gazed at her mouth, then slipped his hand behind her neck and slowly, so very slowly, lowered his lips to hers.

He paused, their mouths a scant inch apart. He seemed to be waiting for her to pull away, withdraw from him. Everything inside her told her to do exactly that. He was only trying to humiliate her, wasn't he? Trying to prove how powerful her attraction to him was, how easily he could bend her will to his own.

And she was letting him.

Her heart was beating so furiously her body seemed to rock with the sheer force of it. Every throb seemed to drive her directly into his arms, right where she longed to be. She placed her palms against his chest and sighed as his mouth met hers. The touch of his lips felt warm and soft. And right.

His hand cradled her neck while his lips continued to move over hers in the gentlest explorations, as though he feared she was too delicate to kiss the way he wanted.

Gradually his hands slipped to her shoulders. He drew a ragged breath, then put his head back as he stared up at the ceiling. He exhaled slowly, deliberately.

It took all the restraint Maryanne possessed not to ask him why he was stopping. She wanted these incredible sensations to continue. She longed to explore the feelings his kiss produced and the complex responses she experienced deep within her body. Her pulse hammered erratically as she tried to control her breathing.

"Okay, now we've got that settled, I'll leave." He backed away from her.

"Got what settled?" she asked swiftly, then realized she was only making a bigger fool of herself. Naturally he was talking about the reason for this impromptu visit, which had been her health. Hadn't it? "Oh, I see."

"I don't think you do," Nolan said enigmatically. He turned and walked away.

Chapter Eight

"Whose turn next?" Maryanne asked. She and her two friends were sitting in the middle of her living room floor, having a "pity party."

"I will," Carol Riverside volunteered eagerly. She ceremonially plucked a tissue from the box that rested in the centre of their small circle, next to the lit candle. Their second large bottle of cheap wine was nearly empty, and the three of them were feeling no pain.

"For years I've wanted to write a newspaper column of my own," Carol said, squaring her shoulders and hauling in a huge breath. "But it's not what I thought it'd be like. I ran out of ideas for things to write about after the first week."

"Ah," Maryanne sighed sympathetically.

"Ah," Barbara echoed.

"That's not all," Carol said sadly. "I never knew the world was so full of critics. No one seems to agree with me. I—I didn't know Seattle had so many cantankerous readers. I try, but it's impossible to make everyone happy. What happens is that some of the people like me some of the time and all the rest hate everything I write." She glanced up. "Except the two of you, of course."

Maryanne nodded her head so hard she nearly toppled over. She spread her hands out at either side in an effort to maintain her balance. The wine made her yawn loudly.

Apparently in real distress, Carol dabbed at her eyes. "Being a columnist is hard work and nothing like I'd always dreamed." The edges of her mouth turned downward. "I don't even like writing anymore," she sobbed.

"Isn't that a pity!" Maryanne cried, ritually tossing her tissue into the centre of the circle. Barbara followed suit, and then they both patted Carol gently on the back.

Carol brightened once she'd finished. "I don't know what I'd do without the two of you. You and Betty are my very best friends in the whole world," she announced.

"Barbara," Maryanne corrected. "Your very best friend's name is Barbara."

The three of them looked at each other and burst into gales of laughter. Maryanne hushed them by waving her hands. "Stop! We can't allow ourselves to become giddy. A pity party doesn't work if all we do is laugh. We've got to remember this is sad and serious business."

"Sad and serious," Barbara agreed, sobering. She grabbed a fresh tissue and clutched it in her hand, waiting for the others to share their sorrows and give her a reason to cry.

"Whose idea was the wine?" Maryanne wanted to know, taking a quick sip.

Carol blushed. "I thought it would be less fattening than the chocolate ice-cream bars you planned to serve."

"Hey," Barbara said, narrowing her eyes at Maryanne. "You haven't said anything about your problem."

Maryanne suddenly found it necessary to remove lint from her jeans. Sharing what disturbed her most was a little more complicated than being disappointed in her job or complaining about fingernails that cracked all too easily, as Barbara had done. She hadn't sold a single article since she'd quit the paper, or even received a positive response to one of her queries. But worst of all she was falling in love with Nolan. He felt something for her, too—she knew that—but he was fighting her every step of the way. Fighting her and fighting himself.

He was attracted to her, he couldn't deny it, although he'd tried to, more than once. When they were alone together, the tension seemed to throb between them.

He was battling the attraction so hard he'd gone as far as arranging a date for her with another man. Since the evening they'd met, Nolan had insulted her, harangued her and lectured her. He'd made it plain that he didn't want her around. And yet there were times he sought out her company. He argued with her at every opportunity, took it upon himself to be her guardian, and yet...

"Maryanne?" Carol said, studying her with concern. "What's wrong?"

"Nolan Adams," she whispered. Lifting her wineglass, she took a small swallow, hoping that would give her the courage to continue.

"I should have guessed," Carol muttered, frowning. "From the moment you moved in here, next door to that madman, I just knew he'd cause you nothing but problems."

Her friend's opinion of Nolan had never been high and Maryanne had to bite back the urge to defend him.

"Tell us everything," Barbara said, drawing up her knees and leaning against the sofa.

"There isn't much to tell."

"He's the one who got you into this craziness in the first place, remember?" Carol pointed out righteously—as if Maryanne needed reminding. Carol then turned to Barbara and began to explain to the older woman how it had all started. "Nolan wrote a derogatory piece about Maryanne in his column a while back, implying she was a spoiled debutante, and she took it to heart and decided to prove him wrong."

"He didn't mean it. In fact, he's regretted every word of that article." This time Maryanne did feel obliged to defend him. As far as she was concerned, all of that was old business, already resolved. It was the unfinished business, the things happening between them now, that bothered her the most.

The denial. The refusal on both their parts to accept the feelings they shared. Only a few days earlier, Maryanne had tried to convince Nolan he wasn't her type, that nothing about them was compatible. He'd been only too eager to agree.

But they'd been drawn together, virtually against their wills, by an attraction so overwhelming, so inevitable, they were powerless against it. Their sensual and emotional awareness of each other seemed more intense every time they met. This feeling couldn't be anything except love.

"You're among friends, so tell us everything," Barbara pressed, handing Maryanne the entire box of tissues. "Remember, I've known Nolan for years, so nothing you say is going to shock me."

"For one thing, he's impossible," Maryanne whispered, finding it difficult to express her thoughts.

"He deserves to be hanged from the closest tree," Carol said scornfully.

"And at the same time he's wonderful," Maryanne concluded, ignoring Carol's comment.

"You're not…" Carol paused, her face tightening as if she was having trouble forming the words. "You don't mean to suggest you're falling in—" she swallowed "—*love* with him, are you?"

"I don't know." Maryanne crumpled the soggy tissue. "But I think I might be."

"Oh, no," Carol cried, covering her mouth with both hands, "you've got to do something quick. A man like Nolan Adams eats little girls like you for breakfast. He's cynical and sarcastic and—"

"Talented and generous," Maryanne finished for her.

"You're not thinking clearly. It probably has something to do with that fever you had. You've got to remember the facts. Nolan insulted you in print, seriously insulted you, and then tried to make up for it. You're mistaking that small attack of conscience for something more—which could be dangerous." Awkwardly, Carol rose to her feet and started pacing.

"He's probably one of the most talented writers I've ever read," Maryanne continued, undaunted by her friend's concerns. "Every time I read his work, I can't help being awed."

"All right," Carol said, "I'll concede he does possess a certain amount of creative talent, but that doesn't change who or what he is. Nolan Adams is a bad-tempered egotistical self-centred…grouch."

"I hate to say this," Barbara said softly, shaking her head, "but Carol's right. Nolan's been eating at Mom's

Place for as long as I've worked there, and that's three years. I feel I know him better than you do, and he's everything Carol says. But," she said thoughtfully, "underneath it all, there's more to him. Oh, he'd like everyone to believe he's this macho guy. He plays that role to the hilt, but after you've been around him awhile, you can tell it's all a game to him."

"I told you he's wonderful!" Maryanne exclaimed.

"The man's a constant," Carol insisted. "Constantly in a bad mood, constantly making trouble, constantly getting involved in matters that are none of his business. Maryanne here is the perfect example. He should never have written that column about her." Carol plopped back down and jerked half a dozen tissues from the box in quick succession. She handed them to Maryanne. "You've got blinders on where he's concerned. Take it from me, a woman can't allow herself to become emotionally involved with a man she plans to change."

"I don't want to change Nolan."

"You don't?" Carol echoed, her voice low and disbelieving. "You mean to say you like him as he is?"

"You just don't know him the way I do," Maryanne said. "Nolan's truly generous. Did either of you know he's become sort of a father figure to the teenagers in this neighborhood? He's their friend in the very best sense. He keeps tabs on them and makes sure no one gets involved in drugs or is lured into gang activities. The kids around here idolize him."

"Nolan Adams does that?" Carol sounded skeptical. She arched her brows as though she couldn't completely trust Maryanne's observations.

"When Barbara told him I was coming down with a virus, he came over to check on me and—"

"As well he should!" Barbara declared. "He was the one who gave you that germ in the first place."

"I'm not entirely sure I caught it from him."

Carol and Barbara exchanged a look. Slowly each shook her head, and then all three shared a warm smile.

"I think we might be too late," Barbara said theatrically, speaking from the side of her mouth.

"She's showing all the signs," Carol agreed solemnly.

"You're right, I fear," Barbara responded in kind. "She's already in love with him."

"Good grief, no," Carol wailed, pressing her hands to her mouth. "Say it isn't so. She's too young and vulnerable."

"It's a pity, such a pity."

"I can't help but agree. Maryanne is much too sweet for Nolan Adams. I just hope he appreciates her."

"He won't," Carol muttered, reverting to her normal voice, "but then no man ever fully appreciates a woman."

"It's such a pity men act the way they do." Barbara said in a sad voice.

"Some men," Maryanne added.

Carol and Barbara dabbed their eyes and solemnly tossed the used tissues into the growing heap in the middle of their circle.

The plan had been to gather all the used tissues and ceremonially dump them in the toilet, flush their "pity pot", and then celebrate all the good things in their lives.

The idea for this little party had been an impromptu one of Maryanne's on a lonely Friday night. She'd been feeling blue and friendless and decided to look for a little innocent fun. She'd phoned Carol and learned she was a weekend widow; her husband had gone fishing with some cronies. Barbara had thought the idea was a good one herself, since she'd just broken her longest fingernail and was in the mood for a shoulder to cry on.

A pity party seemed just the thing to help three lonely women make it through a bleak Friday night.

Maryanne awoke Saturday morning with a humdinger of a headache. Wine and the ice cream they'd had at the end of the evening definitely didn't mix.

If her head hadn't been throbbing so painfully, she might have recognized sooner that her apartment had no heat. Her cantankerous radiator was acting up again. It did that some mornings, but she'd always managed to coax it back to life with a few well-placed whacks. The past few days had been unusually cold for early November—well below freezing at night.

She reached for her robe and slippers, bundling herself up like a December baby out in her first snowstorm. Cupping her hands over her mouth, she blew until a frosty mist formed.

A quickly produced cup of coffee with two extra-strength aspirin took the edge off her headache. Maryanne shivered while she slipped into jeans, sweatshirt and a thick winter coat. She suspected she resembled someone preparing to join an Arctic expedition.

She fiddled with the radiator, twisting the knobs and slamming her hand against the side, but the only results were a couple of rattles and a hollow clanking.

Not knowing what else to try, she got out her heavy cast-iron skillet and banged it against the top of the rad in hopes of reviving the ageing pipes.

The noise was deafening, vibrating through the room like a jet aircraft crashing through the sound barrier. If that wasn't enough, Maryanne's entire body began to quiver, starting at her arm and spreading outward in a rippling effect that caused her arms and legs to tremble.

"What the hell's going on over there?" Nolan shouted from the other side of the wall. He didn't wait for her to answer and a couple of seconds later came barreling through her front door, wild-eyed and dishevelled.

"What... Where?" He was carrying a baseball bat,

and stalked to the middle of her apartment, scanning the interior for what Maryanne could only assume were invaders.

"I don't have any heat," she announced, tucking the thin scarf more tightly around her ears.

Nolan blinked. She'd apparently woken him from a sound sleep. He was barefoot and dressed in pyjama bottoms, and although he wore a shirt, it was unbuttoned, revealing a broad muscular chest dusted with curly black hair.

"What's with you? Are you going to a costume party?"

"Believe me, this is no party. I'm simply trying to keep warm."

His gaze lowered to the heavy skillet in her hand. "Do you plan to cook on that radiator?"

"I might if I could get it to work. In case you hadn't noticed, there isn't any heat in this place."

Nolan set the baseball bat aside and moved to the far wall to look at the radiator. "What's wrong with it?"

How like a man to ask stupid questions! If Maryanne had *known* what was wrong with it, she wouldn't be standing there shivering, with a scarf swaddling her face like an old-time remedy for toothache.

"How in heaven's name am I supposed to know?" she answered testily.

"What went on here last night, anyway? A wake?"

She glanced at the mound of tissues and shrugged. He was scanning the area as if it were a crime scene and he should take caution not to stumble over a dead body.

Walking across the living room, he picked up the two empty wine bottles and held them aloft for her inspection, pretending to be shocked.

"Very funny." She put the skillet down and removed the bottles from his hands, to be deposited promptly in the garbage.

"So you had a party and I wasn't invited." He made it sound as though he'd missed the social event of the year.

Maryanne sighed loudly. "If you must know, Carol, Barbara and I had a pity party."

"A what? You're kidding, right?" He didn't bother to hide his mocking grin.

"Never mind." She should've realized he'd only poke fun at her. "Can you figure out how to get this thing working before the next ice age?"

"Here, give me a shot at it." He gently patted the top of the radiator as he knelt in front of it. "Okay, ol' Betsy, we're trusting you to be good." He began fiddling with knobs, still murmuring ridiculous endearments—like a cowboy talking to his horse.

"It doesn't do any good to talk to an inanimate object," she advised primly, standing behind him.

"You want to do this?"

"No," she muttered. Having Nolan in her home,

dressed in his night clothes, did something odd to her, sent her pulse skittering erratically. She deliberately allowed her attention to wander to the scene outside her window. The still-green lawns of Volunteer Park showed in the distance and she pretended to be absorbed in their beauty.

"I thought I told you to keep that door chain in place," he said casually as he worked. "This isn't The Seattle."

"Do you honestly think you need to remind me of that now?" She rubbed her hands together, hoping to generate some warmth before her fingers went numb.

"There," he said, sounding satisfied. "All she needed was a little loving care."

"Thanks," Maryanne said with relief.

"No problem, only the next time something like this happens don't try to fix it yourself."

"Translated, that means I shouldn't try to fix the radiator again while *you're* trying to sleep."

"Right."

She smiled up at him, her eyes alive with appreciation. He really had been good to her from the day she'd moved in—before then, too. Discounting what he'd written about her in his column, of course. And even that had ended up having a positive effect.

It'd been a week since she'd seen him. A long week. A lonely week. Until now, she'd hardly been able to admit, even to herself, how much she'd missed him. Standing there as he was, Maryanne was struck by just how attractive she found him. If only he'd taken the time to button his shirt! She reveled in his lean strength and his aura of unquestionable authority—and that chest of his was driving her to distraction.

She wasn't the only one enthralled. Nolan was staring at her, too. The silence lingered between them, lengthening moment by moment as they gazed into each other's eyes.

"I have to go," he finally said, breaking eye contact by glancing past her, out the window.

"Right. I—I understand," she stammered, stepping back. Her hands swung at her sides as she followed him to the door. "I really do appreciate this." Already she could feel the warmth spilling into her apartment. And none too soon, either.

"Just remember to keep the door locked."

She grinned and mockingly saluted him. "Aye, aye, sir."

He left then. Maryanne hated to see him go, hated to see him walk away from her, and yet it seemed he was always doing exactly that.

Later that same afternoon, after she'd finished her errands, Maryanne was strolling through the park when a soft feminine voice spoke from behind her.

Maryanne turned around and waved when she discovered Gloria, the teenager she'd met here earlier. But this time Gloria wasn't alone.

"This is my little sister, Katie, the pest," Gloria explained. "She's three."

"Hello, Katie," Maryanne said, smiling.

"Why am I a pest?" Katie asked, gazing at Gloria, but apparently not offended that her older sister referred to her that way.

"Because." Looking annoyed, the teenager shrugged in the same vague manner Maryanne had so often seen in her younger brothers. "Katie's three and every other word is 'why'. Why this? Why that? It's enough to drive a person straight to the loony bin."

"I have brothers, so I know what you mean."

"You do?"

"They're several years younger than I am. So trust me, I understand what you're talking about."

"Did your brothers want to go every place you did? And did your mother make you take them even if it was a terrible inconvenience?"

Maryanne tried to disguise a smile. "Sometimes."

"Eddie asked me to come and watch him play basketball this afternoon with Mr. Adams, and I had to drag Katie along because she wanted to come to the park, too. My mom pressured me into bringing her. I didn't even get a chance to say no." Gloria made it sound as if she were being forced to swim across Puget Sound with the three-year-old clinging to her back.

"I'm not a pest," Katie insisted now, flipping her braid over one shoulder in a show of defiance. Look-

ing up at Maryanne, the little girl carefully manipu-
lated her fingers and proudly exclaimed, "I'm three."

"Three?" Maryanne repeated, raising her eyebrows,
feigning surprise. "Really? I would've thought you
were four or five."

Katie grinned delightedly. "I'm nearly four, you
know."

"Mr. Adams is already here," Gloria said, bright-
ening. She frowned as she glanced down at her little
sister and jerked the small arm in an effort to hurry
her along. "Come on, Katie, we have to go. Eddie
wants me to watch him play ball."

"Why?"

Gloria groaned. "See what I mean?"

"You go on," Maryanne said, offering Katie her
hand. The youngster obediently slipped her small
hand into Maryanne's much larger one, willingly
abandoning her cranky older sister. "Katie and I will
follow behind."

Gloria looked surprised by the offer. "You mean you
don't mind? I mean, Katie's my responsibility and it
wouldn't be fair to palm her off on you. You're not
going to kidnap her or anything, are you? I mean, I
know you're not—you're Mr. Adams's friend. I
wouldn't let her go with just anyone, you know. But if
anything happened to her, my mother would kill me."

"I promise to take the very best care of her."

Gloria grinned, looking sheepish for having suggested anything else. "You're sure you don't mind?"

"I don't mind in the least. I don't think Katie does, either. Is that right, Katie?"

"Why?"

"Are you *really* sure? Okay, then…" Once she'd made a token protest Gloria raced off to join her friends.

Katie was content to skip and hop at Maryanne's side until they reached a huge pile of leaves under a chestnut tree, not far from the basketball court. Almost before Maryanne realized it, Katie raced toward the leaves, bunching as many as she could in her small arms and carrying them back to Maryanne as though presenting her with the rarest of jewels.

"Look," she cried happily. "Leafs."

"Leaves," Maryanne corrected, bending over and grabbing an armful herself. She tossed them in the air and grinned as Katie leapt up to catch as many as she could and in the process dropped the armload she was holding.

Laughing, Maryanne clasped the child by the waist and swung her around, while Katie shrieked with delight. Dizzy, Maryanne leaned against the tree in an effort to regain her equilibrium and her breath.

It was then that she saw Nolan had stopped playing and was standing in the middle of the basketball court, staring at her. The game was going on all around him, boys scattering in one direction and then another, racing to one end of the court and back again.

Nolan seemed oblivious to them and to the game—to everything but her.

A tall boy bumped into him from behind and Nolan stumbled. Maryanne gasped, fearing he might fall, but he caught himself in time. Without a pause, he rejoined the game, racing down the court at breakneck speed. He stole the ball and made a slam dunk, coming down hard on the pavement.

Gloria ran back toward Maryanne and Katie. "I thought you said you and Mr. Adams were just friends?" she teased. She was grinning in a way that suggested she wasn't about to be fooled again. "He nearly got creamed because he couldn't take his eyes off you."

With Katie on her lap, Maryanne sat beside the teenage girls watching the game. Together she and the three-year-old became Nolan's personal cheering squad, but whether or not he appreciated their efforts she didn't know. He didn't give a single indication that he heard them.

When the game was finished, Nolan walked breathlessly off the court. His grey sweatshirt was stained with perspiration, and his face was red and damp from the sheer physical exhaustion of keeping up with kids half his age.

For an anxious moment, Maryanne assumed he was planning to ignore her and simply walk away. But after he'd stopped at the water fountain, he came over to the bench where she and Katie were sitting.

He slumped down beside her, dishevelled and still breathing hard. "What are you doing here?" he grumbled.

"I happened to be in the park," she answered, feeling self-conscious now and unsure. "You don't need to worry, Nolan. I didn't follow you."

"I didn't think you had."

"You look nice in blue," he said hoarsely, then cleared his throat as if he hadn't meant to say that, as if he wanted to withdraw the words.

"Thanks." The blue sweater was one of her favorites. She'd worn her long wool coat and was surprised he'd even noticed the periwinkle-blue sweater beneath.

"Hello, Katie."

Katie beamed, stretching out both arms for Nolan to lift her up, which he did. The little girl hugged him quickly, then leapt off the bench and ran to her sister, who stood talking to her boyfriend.

"You're good with children," Nolan said. His voice fell slightly, as though the fact surprised him.

"I do have a knack with them. I always have." She'd been much-sought as a baby-sitter by her parents' friends and for a time had considered becoming a teacher. If she'd pursued that field of study she would have preferred to teach kindergarten. She found five-year-olds, with their eagerness to learn about the world, delightful. A couple of articles she'd written the week

-before were geared toward children's magazines. If only she'd hear something soon. It seemed to take so long.

"How many years of your life did you lose this time?" Maryanne asked teasingly.

"Another two or three, at least."

He smiled at her and it was that rare special smile he granted her only in those brief moments when his guard was lowered. His resistance to the attraction he felt to her was at its weakest point, and they both knew it.

Maryanne went still, almost afraid to move or speak for fear of ruining the moment. His eyes, so warm and gentle, continued to hold hers. When she tried to breathe, the air seemed to catch in her lungs.

"Maryanne." Her name was little more than a whisper.

"Yes?"

He raked his hand through his hair, then looked away. "Nothing. Never mind."

"What is it?" she pressed, unwilling to let the matter drop.

The muscles along the side of his jaw clenched. "I said it was nothing," he answered gruffly.

Maryanne gazed down at her hands, feeling an overwhelming sense of frustration and despair. The tension between them was so thick she could practically touch it, but nothing she could say or do would make any difference. If anything, her efforts would only make it worse.

"Hey, Nolan," Eddie called out, loping toward

them. "What's with you, man?" He laughed, tossing his basketball from one hand to the other. "You nearly lost that game 'cause you couldn't take your eyes off your woman."

Nolan scowled at him. "You looking for a rematch?"

"Any time you want."

"Not today." Shaking his head, Nolan slowly pushed the sleeves of his sweatshirt past his elbows.

"Right," Eddie said with a knowing laugh. "I didn't think so, with your woman here and all."

"Maryanne isn't my woman," Nolan informed him curtly, his frown darkening.

"Right," Eddie responded. "Hey, dude, this is me, Eddie. Can't fool me! You practically went comatose when you saw her. I don't blame you, though. She ain't bad. So when are you two getting married?"

Chapter Nine

"I've changed my mind," Barbara announced at closing time Monday evening.

Maryanne was busy refilling the salt and pepper shakers and reloading the napkin holders. "About what?" she asked absently, stuffing napkins into the small chrome canisters.

"You and Nolan."

If Barbara hadn't had Maryanne's attention earlier, she did now. Nolan had left the restaurant about forty minutes earlier, after having his customary meal of chili and coffee. He'd barely said two words to Maryanne the whole time he was there. He'd buried his face in the evening edition of the *Sun* and done a brilliant job of pretending he didn't know her.

"What about us?" Maryanne's expression might have remained aloof, but her heart was pounding furiously.

"Since the night of our pity party, I've had a change of heart. You're exactly the right kind of woman for

Nolan. The two of you…balance each other. At first I agreed with Carol. My opinion of Nolan isn't as negative as hers, but you have to remember that those two work for rival papers. At any rate, I was concerned. You *are* really sweet."

Maryanne winced at the "sweet." It rather sounded as though friendship with her was like falling into a jar of honey.

"And now?"

"I don't know exactly what changed my mind. Partly it was watching Nolan when he was here. I got quite a kick out of him."

"How do you mean?"

Barbara's grin was broad as she continued to wipe the counter. "I swear that man couldn't keep his eyes off you."

Maryanne was puzzled. "What are you talking about? Nolan didn't look my way even once."

"Oh, he'd scowl every time you were close, but behind that cross expression of his was an intensity I've never seen in him before. It was like he had to come in and get his daily fix of you."

Maryanne's heart couldn't decide whether to lift with happiness or sink with doubt. "You're wrong. Other than ordering his meal, he didn't speak to me at all. I might as well have been a robot."

"That's what he'd like you to believe."

"He was reading the paper," Maryanne said. "The same way he reads it every time he comes here."

"Correction," Barbara said, and her face broke into a spontaneous smile. "He *pretended* to be reading the paper, but when you weren't looking his eyes were following you like a hawk."

"Oh, Barbara, really?" It seemed almost more than she dared hope for. He'd hardly spoken to her in the past few days, and he seemed to be avoiding her. The kids in the park had taken to teasing them about being "in love" and asking pointed questions, and Nolan had practically fallen all over himself denying that they were anything other than friends.

"It's more than just the way he was watching you," Barbara said, slipping on to a stool. "Have you read his columns the past couple of weeks?"

Naturally Maryanne had, more impressed by his work every time she did. The range of his talent and the power of his writing were unmistakable. Within a few years, if not sooner, she expected his newspaper column to be picked up for syndication.

"Lately, I've noticed something unusual about his writing," Barbara said, still clutching the dishrag. "That cynical edge of his—it isn't quite as sharp. His writing's less sarcastic now. I heard one of my customers comment earlier today that Nolan's going soft on us. I hadn't thought about it much until then, but Ernie's right. I don't know what's made the difference, but I figure it must be love. Oh, I doubt there's much in this life that's going to change Nolan Adams. He'll always be stubborn as a mule, headstrong and temperamental. That's just part of his nature. But mark my words, he's in love."

"What you said earlier, about us being so different…"

"You are, with you so nice and all, and Nolan such a grouch. At least he likes to pretend he's one. You and I know better, but most folks don't."

"And?" Maryanne probed.

"And, well, it seems to me the two of you fit together perfectly. Like two pieces of a puzzle."

It seemed that way to Maryanne, too.

"You heard, didn't you?" Barbara muttered, abruptly changing the subject.

Maryanne nodded. Mom's Place was going to close in a month for remodelling.

"What are you going to do?"

Maryanne didn't know yet. "Find a temporary job, I suppose. What about you?" By then, she should have sold a few of the articles she'd submitted. At least she hadn't been rejected yet. She should be hearing any time.

"I'm not that worried about taking a month or so off work," Barbara returned, her look thoughtful. "I could use a vacation, especially over the holidays. I was thinking of staying home and baking Christmas gifts this year. My fudge is out of this world."

"I suppose I should start looking for another job now." Maryanne was already worried about meeting expenses. Mom's Place couldn't have chosen a worse time to close.

* * *

A half hour later, she was waiting for the bus, her mind spinning with what Barbara had said. The diner's closing was a concern, but Barbara's comments about Nolan gladdened Maryanne's heart.

Nolan did feel something for her, something more powerful than he'd let on.

She supposed she should confront him with it, force him to acknowledge his feelings. A brief smile crossed her lips as she envisioned what would happen if she actually did such a thing. She nearly laughed out loud at the thought.

Nolan would deny it, of course, loudly and vehemently, and she'd have to counteract with a loud argument of her own. The smile appeared again. Her decision was made.

Feeling almost light-headed, Maryanne glanced down the street, eager for the bus to arrive so she could get home. The first thing she intended to do was march into Nolan's apartment and demand the truth. If he tried to ignore her, as he usually did, then she had the perfect solution.

She'd kiss him.

A kiss would silence his protests in the most effective way she could imagine. Maryanne almost melted at the memory of being kissed by Nolan, being held in his arms. It was like walking through the gates of an undiscovered paradise. Just remembering those moments made her feel faint with desire, weak with excitement. He seemed to experience the same emotions, Maryanne remembered hopefully.

Cheered by the thought, she nearly applauded when her bus arrived. The ride passed quickly and she hurried into the building, eager to see Nolan.

Consumed by her sense of purpose, she went directly to his apartment. She stood in front of his door, took several deep breaths, then knocked politely. No answer. She tried again, harder this time.

"Who is it?" Nolan growled from the other side.

"Maryanne. I want to talk to you."

"I'm busy."

She was only a little discouraged by his unfriendliness. "This'll just take a minute."

The door was yanked opened with excessive force. Nolan stood before her, dressed in a black tuxedo and white cummerbund, looking so handsome that he caught her completely by surprise. Her mouth sagged open.

"Yes?" he asked crossly.

"Hello, Nolan," she said, aware that her mission had been thwarted. Nothing he could've said or done would have affected her as profoundly as finding him dressed like this. Because it meant he was going out on a date.

"Hello," he said, tugging at the cuffs of his jacket, adjusting the fit. He frowned, apparently waiting for her to say something.

"Uh…" She tried to gather her scattered composure, and finally managed to squeak, "You're going out?"

He scowled. "I don't dress like this for a jaunt to the corner store."

"No, I don't suppose you do."

"You wanted something?"

She'd been so confident, so sure she was doing the right thing. But now, seeing Nolan looking more dressed up and formal than he'd ever looked for *her*, she found herself speechless.

She couldn't help wondering where he was going— and with whom. The "with whom" part bothered her the most.

He glanced pointedly at his wristwatch. "How long is this going to take?" he asked coolly. "I'm supposed to pick up Prudence in fifteen minutes."

"Prudence?" His face, tight with impatience, drew her full attention. *Prudence,* her mind repeated. Who was this woman?

Then in a flash, Maryanne knew. It was all she could do not to laugh and inform him that his little plan just wasn't working. No imaginary date was going to make *her* jealous.

He wasn't seeing anyone named Prudence. Good grief, if he had to invent a name, the least he could've done was come up with something a little more plausible than Prudence.

In fact, Maryanne remembered Nolan casually mentioning a week or so earlier that he'd been asked to speak at a Chamber of Commerce banquet. There had also been a notice in the paper. Who did he think he was kidding?

Of course he wanted her to believe he was dating another woman. That was supposed to discourage her, she guessed. Except that it didn't.

"It wasn't important…" she said, gesturing vaguely. "The radiators were giving me trouble this morning, but I'll manage. I was planning to go out tonight myself."

His eyes connected with hers. "Another pity party?"

"Not this time." She considered announcing she had a hot date herself, but that would have been carrying this farce a little too far. "Barbara and I will probably go to a movie."

"Sounds like fun."

"I'm sure it will be." She smiled up at him, past the square cut of his jaw to his incredibly dark eyes. "Have a good time with… Prudence," she said with a bright knowing smile.

Holding back a laugh, she returned to her own apartment. The rat. The low-down dirty rat! He was pretending to escort some imaginary woman to a fancy affair. Oh, he'd like nothing better than for Maryanne to think he considered her a pest. But she knew that wasn't quite the case.

Where was the man who'd rushed to her rescue when the pipes needed a little coaxing? Where was the man who'd nearly been run over on a basketball court when he saw her standing on the sidelines? Where was the man who'd tried to set her up with someone else he thought more suitable? Nolan Adams had just proved what she'd suspected all along. He was a coward—at least when it came to love.

Suddenly depressed, Maryanne slowly crossed the living room and sank on to her sofa, trying to gather her wits. Ten minutes later, she still sat there, mulling things over and feeling sorry for herself, when she heard Nolan's door open and close. She immediately perked up, wondering if he'd had a change of heart. He seemed to pause for a moment outside her door, but any second thoughts he might be having didn't last long.

Barbara phoned soon after, full of apologies, to cancel their movie plans, so Maryanne spent the evening drowning her sorrows in television reruns and slices of cold pizza.

She must have fallen asleep because a harsh ringing jolted her awake a couple of hours later. She leapt off the sofa and stumbled dazedly around before she realized the sound came from the phone. She rushed across the room.

A greeting had barely left her lips when her father's booming voice assailed her.

"Where the hell are you?"

"Hello, Dad," she muttered, her heart sinking. How like him to get to the subject at hand without anything in the way of preliminaries. "How are you, too?"

"I want to know where you're living and I want to know right now!"

"I beg your pardon?" she asked, stalling for time. Obviously her father had discovered her small deception.

"I talked to the managing editor of the *Seattle Review* this morning and he told me you haven't worked there in weeks. He said you'd quit! Now I want to know what this craziness is you've been feeding your mother and me about a special assignment."

"Uh..." By now, Maryanne was awake enough to know her father wasn't in any mood to listen to excuses.

"You lied to us, girl."

"Not exactly..." She paused, searching for the right words. "It was more a case of omission, don't you think?"

"You've had us worried sick. We've been trying to get hold of you all afternoon. Where were you? And who the hell is Nolan Adams?"

"Nolan Adams?" she echoed, playing dumb, which wasn't all that difficult at the moment.

"Your mother mentioned his name, and when I called the paper, some woman named...Riverside, Carol Riverside, claimed this was his fault."

"Dad, listen, it's all rather complicated, so I think—"

"I don't want excuses, I want facts. You decided to work on the other side of the country. Against my better judgment, I arranged it for you with the promise that I wouldn't intrude—and look where it's gotten me! To have you deceive us by—"

"Dad, please, just settle down."

He seemed to be making an effort to calm himself, but more than likely the effort was thanks to her mother. Maryanne could hear her arguing softly in the background.

"Can I explain?" she asked, waiting a minute for the tension to ease, although she wasn't sure what to say, what excuses she could possibly offer.

"You can try to explain, but I doubt it'll do any good," he answered gruffly.

Now that she had the floor, Maryanne floundered.

"I take it this all revolves around that columnist friend of yours from the *Sun*?" her father asked. "That Adams character?"

"Well, yes," Maryanne admitted reluctantly. But she didn't feel she could place the whole blame on him. "Leaving the paper was my decision—"

"Where are you living?"

That was one of several questions Maryanne was hoping to avoid. "I—I rented an apartment."

"You were in an apartment before. It doesn't make the least bit of sense for you to move. The Seattle has a reputation for excellence."

"Yes, Dad, I know, but moving was necessary." She didn't go on to explain why. She didn't want to mislead her father more than she already had. But at the same time, if she told him she couldn't afford to continue living at The Seattle, he'd certainly demand to know why.

"That doesn't explain a damn thing," Samuel Simpson boomed.

Maryanne held the phone away from her ear and sighed heavily. She was groggy from her nap and discouraged by her relationship with Nolan. To complicate matters, she was truly in love for the first time in her life. Loving someone shouldn't be this difficult!

"I insist you tell me what's going on," her father said, in the tone she remembered from childhood confrontations about missed curfews and other transgressions.

She tried again. "It's not that easy to explain."

"You have three seconds, young lady, to tell me why you've lied to your parents."

"I apologize for that. I've felt horrible about it, I really have, but I didn't want to say anything for fear you'd worry."

"Of course we'd worry! Now tell me exactly what it is we should be worrying about."

"Dad, honestly, I'm over twenty-one. I should be able to live and work where I please. You can't keep me your little girl forever." This conversation was not only reminiscent of several she'd had with Nolan, it was one she should have had with her father years ago.

"I demand to know why you quit the paper!"

Maryanne refused to be intimidated. "I already explained that. I had another job."

"Obviously you're doing something you're too ashamed to tell your parents."

"I'm not ashamed! It's nothing illegal. Besides, I happen to like what I do, and I've managed to live entirely on what I make, which is no small feat. I'm happy, Dad, really happy." She tried to force some cheerful enthusiasm into her voice, but unfortunately she didn't entirely succeed. How she wished she could brag about selling her articles. Surely she'd receive word soon!

"If you're so pleased about this change in jobs, then why do you seem upset?" her mother asked reasonably, joining the conversation from an extension.

"I—I'm fine, really I am."

"Somehow, sweetie, that just doesn't ring true—"

"I don't like the sound of this," her father interrupted impatiently. "I made a mistake in arranging this Seattle assignment for you. It seems to me it'd be best if you quit whatever you're doing and moved back to—"

"Dad, I refuse to quit now."

"I want you to move back home. As far as I can see, you've got one hell of a lot of explaining to do."

"It seems to me," Maryanne said after a moment of strained silence, "that we should both take time to cool down and think this over before one of us says or does something we're all going to regret."

"I'm calm." The voice that roared over the long-distance wires threatened to impair Maryanne's hearing.

"Daddy, I love you and Mom dearly, but I think it would be best if we both slept on this. I'm going to hang up now, not to be rude, but because I don't think this conversation is accomplishing anything. I'll call you first thing in the morning."

"Maryanne...Maryanne, don't you dare—"

She didn't allow him to finish, knowing it would do no good to argue with him when he was in this frame of mind. Her heart was heavy with regret as she replaced the receiver. Knowing her father would immediately call again, she unplugged the phone.

Now that her family had discovered she wasn't working at the *Review*, everything would change. And not for the better. Her father would hound her until she was forced to tell him she'd taken a job as a waitress. Once he discovered that, he'd hit the roof.

Still thinking about what had happened, she put on her flannel pyjamas and pulled out her bed. With the demanding physical schedule she kept, sleeping had never been a problem. Tonight, she missed the clatter of Nolan's typing. She'd grown accustomed to its comforting familiarity, in part because it was a sign of his presence. She often lay awake wondering how his mystery novel was developing. Some nights she even fantasized that he'd let her read the manuscript, which to her represented the ultimate gesture of trust.

But Nolan wasn't at his typewriter this evening. He

was giving a speech. Closing her eyes, she imagined him standing before the large dinner crowd. How she would have enjoyed being in the audience! She knew beyond a doubt that his eyes would have sought her out....

Instead she was spending the night alone. She lay with her eyes wide open; every time she started to drift off, some small noise would jerk her into wakefulness. She finally had to admit that she was waiting to hear the sounds of Nolan's return.

Some time in the early morning hours, Maryanne did eventually fall asleep. She woke at six to the familiar sound of Nolan pounding on his typewriter.

She threw on her robe, thrust her feet into the fuzzy slippers and began pacing, her mind whirling.

When she could stand it no longer, she banged on the wall separating their two apartments.

"Your typing woke me up!" Which, of course, wasn't fair or even particularly true. But she'd spent a fretful night thinking about him, and that was excuse enough.

Her family had found out she'd quit her job and all hell was about to break loose. Time was running out for her and Nolan. If she was going to do something— and it was clear she'd have to be the one—she'd need to do it soon.

"Just go back to bed," Nolan shouted.

"Not on your life, Nolan Adams!" Without questioning how wise it was to confront him now,

Maryanne stormed out of her apartment dressed as she was, and beat hard on his door.

Nolan opened it almost immediately, still wearing the tuxedo from the night before, without the jacket and cummerbund. The sleeves of his shirt were rolled past his elbows and the top three buttons were open. His dishevelment and the shadows under his eyes suggested he hadn't been to bed.

"What now?" he demanded. "Is my breathing too loud?"

"We need to talk," she stated calmly as she marched into his apartment.

Nolan remained standing at the door. "Why don't you come in and make yourself at home?" he muttered sarcastically.

"I already have." She sat on the edge of his sofa and waited until he turned to face her. "So?" she asked with cheerful derision. "How'd your hot date go?"

"Fine." He smiled grimly. "Just fine."

"Where'd you go for dinner? The Four Seasons? Fullers?" She named two of the best restaurants in town. "By the way, do I know Prudence?"

"No," he answered with sharp impatience.

"I didn't think so."

"Maryanne—"

"I don't suppose you have coffee made?"

"It's made." But he didn't offer her any. The fact that he was still standing by the door suggested he wanted her out of his home. But when it came to dealing with

Nolan, Maryanne had long since learned to ignore the obvious.

"Thanks, I'll get myself a cup." She walked into the kitchen and found two clean mugs in the dishwasher. "You want one?"

"I have some," he said pointedly, stationing himself in the kitchen doorway. He heaved a long-suffering sigh. "Maryanne, I'm busy, so if you could get on with—"

"My father knows," she said calmly, watching him closely for some sort of reaction. If she'd been looking for evidence of concern or regret, he showed neither. The only emotion she was able to discern was a brief flicker of what she could only assume was relief. That wasn't encouraging. He appeared all too willing to get her out of his life.

"Well?" she probed. "Say something."

"What the hell have you been telling him?"

"Nothing about you, so don't worry. I did mention you to my mother, but you don't need to worry about that, either. She thinks you and I… Never mind."

"*What* does your father know?" Nolan asked.

She sipped from the edge of the mug and shrugged. "He found out I wasn't on special assignment for the paper."

"Special assignment? What does that have to do with anything?"

"That's what I told my mother when I moved."

"Why the hell would you tell her something like that?"

"She was expecting me to send her my columns, and call every other day. I couldn't continue to do either of those things. I had to come up with some excuse."

He cocked an eyebrow. "You might have tried the truth."

Maryanne nodded her agreement. If she'd bungled any part of this arrangement, it had been with her parents. However, there wasn't time for regrets now.

"Dad learned I moved out of The Seattle. I didn't tell him where I was living, but that won't deter him. Knowing Dad, he'll have all the facts by noon today. To put it mildly, he isn't pleased. He wants me to return to the East Coast."

"Are you going?" Nolan's question was casual, as though her response was of little concern to him.

"No."

"Why not?" The impatient look was back. "For the love of heaven, Annie, will you kindly listen to reason? You don't belong here. You've proved your point. If you're waiting for me to admit I was wrong about you, then fine, I'll admit it, and gladly. You've managed far better than I ever dreamed you would, but it's time to get on with your life. It's time to move back into the world where you belong."

"I can't do that now."

"Why the hell not?"

"Because…I've fallen—"

"Look, Annie, it's barely seven and I have to go to

work," he said brusquely, cutting her off. "Shouldn't you be getting dressed? Walking around the hallway in your pyjamas isn't wise—people might think something."

"Let them."

He rubbed his face wearily, shaking his head.

"Nolan," Maryanne said softly, her heart in her throat. "I know you didn't go out with anyone named Prudence. You made the whole thing up. This game of yours isn't going to work. It's too late. I'm…already in love with you."

The whole world seemed to come to an abrupt halt. Maryanne hadn't intended to blurt out her feelings this way, but she didn't know how else to cut through the arguments and the denial.

For one wild-eyed moment Nolan didn't say anything. Then he raised his hand, as though fending off some kind of attack, and retreated from the kitchen.

"You can't be in love with me," he insisted, slowly sinking to the sofa, like a man in the final stages of exhaustion. "I won't allow it."

Chapter Ten

"Unfortunately it's too late," Maryanne told him again, no less calmly. "I'm already in love with you."

"Now just a minute," Nolan said, apparently regaining his composure. "You're a nice kid, and to be honest I've been impressed—"

"I am not a kid," she corrected with quiet authority, "and you know it."

"Annie…Maryanne," he said, "listen to me. What you feel for me isn't love." His face revealed a bitterness she hadn't seen before. He walked toward her, gripped her shoulders and gazed down at her.

"That won't work, either," she said in the same quiet voice. She wasn't a poor little rich girl who'd only recently discovered who she was. Nor had she mistaken admiration for love. "I know what I feel."

She slipped her arms around his neck and stood on tiptoe, wanting to convince him of her sincerity with a kiss.

But before her mouth could meet his, Nolan jerked his head back, preventing the contact. He dropped his arms and none too gently pushed her away.

"Are you afraid to kiss me?"

"You're damn right I am," he said, burying his hands in his pockets as he hastily moved even farther away.

Maryanne smiled softly. "And with good reason. We both know what would happen if you did. You've done a good job of hiding your feelings, I'll grant you that much. I was nearly fooled."

"Naturally I'm flattered." His expression was darkening by the second. He stalked across the room, his shoulders hunched forward. He didn't say anything else, and Maryanne strongly suspected he was at a loss for words. Nolan was *never* at a loss for words. Words were his stock-in-trade.

But he was confronting emotions now, not words or concepts, and she knew him well enough to realize how uncomfortable that made him.

He'd hidden his feelings behind a mask of gruff annoyance, allowing her to believe she'd become a terrible nuisance in his life. He needed to disguise what he felt for her—to prevent her from learning what everyone else already knew.

Nolan was in love with her.

The mere thought thrilled her and gave her more courage than she'd ever possessed in her life.

"I fully expect you to be flattered," she said gently,

"but I'm not telling you this to give your ego a boost. I honestly love you, and nothing my parents say is going to convince me to leave Seattle."

"Maryanne, please…"

He was prepared to push her away verbally, as he had so often. This time she wouldn't let him. This time she walked over to him, threw both arms around his waist and hugged him close.

He raised his hands to her shoulders, ready to ease her from him, but the moment they came to rest on her he seemed to lose his purpose.

"This is ridiculous," she heard him mumble. He held himself rigid for a moment or two, then with a muttered curse buried his face in her hair. A ragged sigh tore through his body.

Experiencing a small sense of triumph, Maryanne pressed her ear to his chest and smiled contentedly when she heard his racing uneven heartbeat.

"You shouldn't let me hold you like this." His voice was low and hushed. "Tell me not to," he breathed as his lips moved through her hair and then lower to the pulse point behind her ear and the slope of her neck.

"I don't want you to stop…" She turned her head, begging him to touch and kiss her.

"Annie, please."

"I want to be in your arms more than anywhere. More than anything."

"You don't know what you're saying…."

She lifted her head enough for their eyes to meet.

Placing her finger on his lips, she shook her head. "I'm a woman, a grown woman, and there's no question of my not knowing what I want."

His hands gently grazed her neck, as though he was still hesitant and unsure. Kissing her was what *he* wanted—she could read it clearly in his dark eyes— but he was holding himself back, his face contorted with indecision.

"Go ahead, kiss me," she urged softly, wanting him so much her whole body seemed to ache. "I dare you to."

His breathing was labored, and Maryanne could sense the forces raging within him. A fresh wave of tenderness filled her.

"You make it so hard to do what's right," he groaned.

"Loving each other is what's right."

"I'd like to believe that, but I can't." He placed his hand on her cheek and their eyes locked hungrily. He searched her face.

"I love you," she whispered, smiling up at him. She didn't want him to question her feelings. She'd say it a thousand times a day if that was what it took to convince him.

Flattening her hands against his hard chest, she leaned into his strength and offered him her mouth. Only moments earlier he'd pushed her away, but not now. His gaze softened and he closed his eyes tightly. He was losing the battle.

It was while his eyes were closed that Maryanne claimed the advantage and kissed him. He moaned and seemed about to argue, but once their mouths met, urgency took hold and Nolan was rendered speechless.

To her delight, he responded with the full-fledged hunger she'd witnessed in his eyes. He slid his hands through her hair, his fingers tangling with the thick auburn mass as he angled her head to one side. Maryanne felt herself savoring the taste of his kiss. It was so long since he'd held her like this, so long since he'd done anything but keep her at arm's length. She wanted to cherish these moments, delight in the rush of sensations.

So many thoughts crowded her mind. So many ideas. Plans for their future.

He tore his mouth from hers and nestled his face in the hollow of her neck as he drew in several deep breaths.

Maryanne clung to him, hugging him as close as humanly possible. "Nolan—"

"It isn't going to work—you and me together…it isn't right," he whispered.

"It's more right than anything I've ever known."

"Oh, Annie, the things you do to me."

She smiled gently. "You know what I think?" She didn't give him the opportunity to answer. "I love you and you love me and when two people feel that way about each other, they usually—" she paused and swallowed once "—get married."

"*What?*" Nolan exploded, leaping away from her as though he'd received an electrical shock.

"You heard me," she said.

"You're a crazy woman. You know that, don't you? Downright certifiable." Nolan backed away from her, eyes narrowed. He began pacing rapidly in one direction, then another.

"Marriage was just a suggestion," she said mildly. "I am serious, though, and if you're at all interested we should move fast. Because once my father gets wind of it there'll be hell to pay."

"I have no intention of even considering the idea! In fact, I think it's time you left."

"Nolan, okay, I'm sorry. I shouldn't have mentioned marriage. I was just thinking, hoping actually, that it was something you wanted, too. There's no need to overreact." He had already ushered her across the living room toward the door. She tried to redirect his efforts, turning in his arms, but he wouldn't allow it.

"We need to talk about this," she insisted.

"Oh, no, you don't," he said, opening the door and steering her into the hallway. "Your idea of talking doesn't seem to coincide with mine. Before I figure out how it happens, you're in my arms and we're—"

"Maryanne!" Her father's voice came like a high-intensity foghorn from behind her.

Maryanne whirled around to discover both her parents standing in the hallway outside her apartment door. "Mom…Dad…" Frantic, she looked at Nolan, hoping he'd do the explaining part.

"Mr. and Mrs. Simpson," Nolan said formally, straightening. He removed his arms from around Maryanne, stepped forward and held out his hand to her father. "I'm Nolan Adams."

"How do you do?" Muriel Simpson said in a brittle voice as the two men exchanged brief handshakes. Her mother's troubled gaze moved from the men to Maryanne, surveying her attire with a single devastating look.

Until that moment, Maryanne had forgotten she was still in her pyjamas. She closed her eyes and groaned.

"Samuel," Muriel Simpson said in a shocked voice. "Maryanne's coming out of…his apartment."

"It's not what it looks like," Maryanne rushed to tell them. "Mom and Dad, please, you've got to listen to me. I didn't spend the night at Nolan's, honest. We just happened to get into a tiff this morning and instead of shouting through the walls and—"

"Samuel." Her mother reached for her father's sleeve, gripping it hard. "I feel faint."

Samuel Simpson clamped his arm about his wife's waist and with Nolan's assistance led her through his open apartment door. Maryanne hurried ahead of them to rearrange pillows on the sofa.

Crouched in front of her mother, Maryanne gently patted her hand. Muriel wasn't given to fainting spells; clearly, she'd been worried sick about her daughter, which increased Maryanne's guilt a hundredfold.

"My little girl is safe, and that's all that matters," Muriel whispered.

"Listen here, young man," Maryanne's father said sternly to Nolan. "It seems you two have some explaining to do."

"Daddy, please." Jumping to her feet, Maryanne stood between her father and Nolan, loving them both so much and not sure which one to confront first. She took a deep breath and blurted out, "I'm in love with Nolan."

"Sir, I know the circumstances look bad, but I can assure you there's nothing between me and your daughter."

"What do you mean there's nothing between us?" Maryanne cried, furious with him. Good grief, she'd just finished spilling out her heart to the man! The least he could do was acknowledge what they shared, what they both felt. Well, if he wasn't so inclined, she was. "That's a bold-faced lie," she announced to her father, hearing Nolan groan behind her as she spoke.

Samuel Simpson, so tall and formidable, so distinguished and articulate, seemed to find himself dumbstruck. He slumped onto the sofa next to his wife and rested his face in both hands.

"Maryanne," Nolan said from between gritted teeth. "Your parents appear to think the worst. Don't you agree it would be more appropriate to assure them that—"

"I don't care what they think. Well, I do, of course," she amended quickly, "but I'm more interested in settling things between you and me."

Nolan's frowned impatiently. "This is neither the time nor the place."

"I happen to think it is."

"Maryanne, please," her mother wailed, holding out one hand. "Your father and I have spent a long sleepless night flying across the country. We've been worried half to death about you."

"She didn't answer her phone," Samuel muttered in dire tones, his eyes narrowing suspiciously on the two of them. "If Maryanne had been at her apartment, the way she claims, then she would have picked up the receiver. We must've called fifteen or twenty times. If she was home, why didn't she answer the phone?"

The question seemed to be directed at Nolan, but it was Maryanne who answered. "I unplugged it."

"Why would you do that?" Muriel asked. "Surely you know we'd try to reach you. We're your parents. We love you!"

"That's it, young lady. You're moving back with us."

"You can't force me to leave Seattle. I refuse."

"This place..." Muriel was looking around as though the building was likely to be condemned any minute. "Why would you want to live here? Have you rejected everything we've given you?"

"The answer is obvious," her father bellowed. "She's living here to be close to *him*."

"But why didn't her…friend move into her apartment building?"

"Isn't it obvious?" Samuel stood abruptly and stalked to the other side of the room. "Adams couldn't afford to live within a mile of The Seattle." He stopped short, then nodded apologetically at Nolan. "I didn't mean that in a derogatory way. You seem like a fine young man, but frankly…"

"I wouldn't care where Nolan lived," Maryanne informed them both, squaring her shoulders righteously. Any man she fell in love with didn't need to head a financial empire or be related to someone who did. "I'd live anywhere if it meant we could be together." Her eyes softened at her mother's shocked look.

"Don't you remember what it's like to be young and in love, Mom?" Maryanne asked her. "Remember all those things you told me about you and Dad? How you used to argue and everything? It's the same with Nolan and me. I'm crazy about him. He's so talented and—"

"That's enough," Nolan interrupted harshly. "If you're looking for someone to blame for Maryanne's living in this building and working at Mom's Place—"

"What's Mom's Place?"

"A very nice diner," Maryanne inserted quickly. "We do a brisk lunch trade and carry a limited dinner menu."

Her mother let out a cry of dismay. "You're...you're working as a waitress?"

Miserable, Maryanne nodded. "But I'm doing lots of freelance work. None of the feature articles I've written have sold yet, but it's too soon for that. I just found out the community newspaper's buying a couple of my shorter pieces, and I plan on selling them lots more."

"You might have warned me they didn't know about your being a waitress," Nolan muttered under his breath.

Samuel drew a hand across his eyes, as if that would erase the image of his daughter waiting on tables. "Why would you choose to quit the newspaper to work as a waitress?" Asking the question seemed to cause him pain.

"It's honest work, Dad. I don't understand why you're acting like this. You're making it sound like I'm doing something that'll bring disgrace to the family name."

"But your education is being wasted," her mother said, shaking her head. "You could have any job in publishing you wanted."

That much was true when it was her family doing the hiring, but when she was looking on her own her employers were more interested in her job skills than who her father was.

"I'm afraid I'm the one who started this," Nolan interrupted. "I wrote a column about Maryanne," he said bluntly. "It was unfortunate, because I was out of line in some of the things I said, but—"

"Nolan didn't write anything that wasn't true," Maryanne hastened to say. "He made me stop and think about certain aspects of my life, and I decided it was time to prove I could make it on my own."

"By denouncing your family!"

"I never did that, Dad."

Samuel's shoulders sagged with defeat. The long hours her parents had spent travelling were telling on them both. They looked at her blankly, as though they couldn't quite believe, even now, what she'd been doing for the past month and a half.

"I did it for another reason, too." All three of them were staring at her as if they suspected she'd lost her mind. "I'd met Nolan and we had dinner together and I discovered how much I liked him." She glanced at the man in question and saw him frown, knitting his brow, obviously searching for a way to stop her. "I'm sorry, Mom and Dad. I hated lying to you, but I couldn't see any way around it. I didn't want to worry you," she said, stepping next to Nolan and wrapping her arm around his waist. "I belong here with Nolan." There, she'd said it! "I won't be returning to New York with you."

"Maryanne, sweetie, you can't go on living like this!"

"I have a wonderful life."

Her father was pacing again. "You're in love with this man?"

"Yes, Daddy. I love him so much—enough to defy you for the first time in my life."

Her father's eyes slowly moved from his only daughter to Nolan. "What about you, young man? How do you feel about my daughter?"

Nolan was quiet for so long it was all Maryanne could do not to answer for him. Finally she couldn't stand it any longer and did exactly that. "He loves me. He may not want to admit it, but he does—lock, stock and barrel."

Her father continued to look at Nolan. "Is that true?"

"Unfortunately," he said, gently removing Maryanne's arm, "I don't return her feelings. You've raised a wonderful daughter—but I don't love her, not the way she deserves to be loved."

"Nolan!" His name escaped on a cry of outrage. "Don't lie. Not now, not to my family."

He took her by the shoulders, his face pale and expressionless. She searched his eyes, looking for something, anything to ease the terrible pain his words had inflicted.

"You're sweet and talented, and one day you'll make some man very proud—but it won't be me."

"Nolan, stop this right now. You love me. You're intimidated because of who my father is. But don't you understand that money doesn't mean anything to me?"

"It rarely does to those who have it. Find yourself a nice rich husband and be happy."

She found his words insulting. If she hadn't been so desperate to straighten out this mess, she would have confronted him with it. "I won't be happy without you. I refuse to be happy."

His face was beginning to show signs of strain. "Yes, you will. Now, I suggest you do as your family wants and leave with them."

Every word felt like a kick in the stomach, each more vicious than the one before.

"You don't mean that!"

"Damn it, Maryanne," he said coldly, "don't make this any more difficult than it already is. We don't belong together. We never have. I live in one world and you live in another. I've been telling you that from the first, but you wouldn't listen to me."

Maryanne was too stunned to answer. She stared up at him, hoping, praying, for some sign that he didn't mean what he was saying.

"Sweetie." Her mother tucked an arm around Maryanne's waist. "Please, come home with us. Your friend's right, you don't belong here."

"That's not true. I'm here now and I intend to stay."

"Maryanne, damn it, would you listen to your parents?" Nolan barked. "What do you intend to do once Mom's Place closes for remodeling?"

"Come home, sweetie," her mother pleaded.

Too numb to speak, Maryanne stared at Nolan. She wouldn't leave if he gave the slightest indication he wanted her to stay. Anything. A flicker of his eye, a twitch of his hand, anything that would show her he didn't mean the things he'd said.

There was nothing. Nothing left for her. She couldn't go back to the newspaper, not now. Mom's Place was closing, but the real hardship, the real agony, came from acknowledging that Nolan didn't want her around. Nolan didn't love her.

She turned her back on him and walked to her own apartment. Her mother and father joined her there a few minutes later, trying to hide their dismay at its bleakness.

"I won't need to give my notice," she told them, sorting through the stack of folded clothes for a fresh uniform. "But I'll stay until Mom's closes. I wouldn't want to leave them short-staffed."

"Yes, of course," her mother answered softly, then suggested, "If you like, I can stay with you here in Seattle."

Maryanne declined with a quick shake of her head, trying to conceal how badly Nolan's rejection had hurt. "I'll be fine." She paused, then turned to her family. "He really is a wonderful man. It's just that he's terribly afraid of falling in love—especially with someone like me. I have everything he doesn't—an education, wealth, and perhaps most importantly, parents who love me as much as you do."

Maryanne hadn't known it was possible for two weeks to drag by so slowly. But finally her last day of work arrived.

"The minute I set eyes on Nolan Adams again, I swear I'll give him a piece of my mind," Barbara declared, hands on her hips.

Nolan hadn't eaten at Mom's once in the past two weeks. That didn't surprise Maryanne; in fact, she would've been shocked if he'd decided to show up.

"You keep in touch, you hear? That Nolan Adams—he's got a lot to answer for," Barbara said, her eyes filling. "I'm gonna miss you, girl. Are you sure you have to leave?"

"I'm sure," Maryanne whispered, swallowing back her own tears.

"I suppose you're right. That's why I'm so furious with Nolan."

"It isn't all his fault." Maryanne hadn't told anyone the embarrassing details that had led to her leaving Seattle.

"Of course it is. He should stop you from going. I don't know what's got into that man, but I swear, for two cents I'd give him—"

"A piece of your mind," Maryanne finished for her.

They both laughed, and hugged each other one last time. Although they'd only worked together a short while, they'd become good friends. Maryanne would miss Barbara's down-to-earth philosophy and her reliable sense of humor.

When she arrived home, her apartment was dark and dismal. Cardboard boxes littered the floor. Her packing was finished, except for the bare essentials. She'd made arrangements with a shipping company to come for her things in the morning. Then she'd call a taxi to take her to Sea-Tac Airport in time to catch the noon flight for New York.

The next morning, dressed in jeans and a loose red sweatshirt, Maryanne was hauling boxes out of her living room and stacking them in the hallway when she heard Nolan's door open. She quickly moved back into her own apartment.

"What are you doing?" he demanded, following her in. He was wearing the ever-present beige raincoat, his mood as sour as his look.

"Moving," she responded flippantly. "That was what I thought you wanted."

"Then leave the work to the movers."

"I'm fine, Nolan." Which was a lie. How could she possibly be fine when her heart was broken?

"I guess this is goodbye, then," he said, glancing around the room, looking everywhere but at her.

"Yes. I'll be gone before you get back this afternoon." She forced a trembling smile to her lips as she brushed the dust from her palms. "It's been a pleasure knowing you."

"You, too," he said softly.

"Some day I'll be able to tell my children I knew the famous Nolan Adams when he was a columnist for the *Seattle Sun*." But those children wouldn't be his....

"I wish you only the best." His eyes had dimmed slightly, but she was too angry to see any significance in that.

She didn't reply and the silence stretched, tense and awkward.

"So," she finally said, with a deep sigh, "you're really going to let me go."

"Yes." He spoke without hesitation, but she noticed that his mouth thinned, became taut.

"It may come as a surprise to learn you're not the only one with pride." She spoke as clearly and precisely as she could. "I'm going to do what you asked and leave Seattle. I'll walk away without looking back. Not once will I look back," she repeated, her throat constricting, making speech difficult. She waited a moment to compose herself. "Someday you'll regret this, Nolan. You'll think back to what happened and wish to hell you'd handled the situation differently. Don't you know it's not what you've done that will fill you with regret, but what you haven't done?"

"Annie—"

"No, let me finish. I've had this little talk planned for days and I'm going to deliver it. The least you can do is stand here and listen."

He closed his eyes and nodded.

"I've decided to haunt you."

"What?" His eyes flew open.

"That's right. You won't be able to go into a restaurant without believing you see me there. I'll be hiding behind every corner. I'll follow you down every street. And as for enjoying another bowl of chili, you can forget that, as well." By now her voice was trembling.

"I never meant to hurt you."

She abruptly turned away from him, wiping the tears from her cheeks with both hands.

"Be happy, Annie."

She would try. There was nothing else to do.

Chapter Eleven

"Have you had a chance to look over those brochures?" Muriel asked Maryanne two weeks later. They were sitting at the breakfast table, savoring the last of their coffee.

"I was thinking I should find myself another job." It was either that or spend the rest of her life poring over cookbooks. Some people travelled to cure a broken heart, some worked—but not Maryanne. She hadn't written a word since she'd left Seattle. Not one word.

She'd planned to send out new queries, start researching new articles for specialty magazines. Somehow, that hadn't happened. Instead, she'd been baking up a storm. Cookies for the local day-care center, cakes for the senior citizens' home, pies for the clergy. She figured she'd gone through enough flour in the past week to take care of the Midwest wheat crop. Since the holiday season was fast approaching, baking seemed the thing to do.

"But, sweetie, Europe this time of year is fabulous."

"I'm sorry, Mom, I don't mean to be ungrateful, but travelling just doesn't interest me right now."

Her mother's face softened with concern. "Apparently, baking does. Maryanne, you can't bake cookies for the rest of your life."

"I know, I know. If I keep this up I'll look like the Goodyear blimp by Christmas."

Her mother laughed. "That obviously isn't true. If anything, you've been losing weight." She hesitated before adding, "And you've been so quiet."

When she was in pain, Maryanne always withdrew into herself, seeking what comfort she could in routine tasks—such as baking. She was struggling to push every thought of Nolan from her mind. But as her mother said, she had to get out of the kitchen and rejoin the world. Soon she'd write again. Maybe there was a magazine for bakers—she could submit to that, she thought wryly. It would be a place to start, anyway, to regain her enthusiasm. Soon she'd find the strength to face her computer again. Even the sale of three articles hadn't cheered her. She'd stared at the checks and felt a vague sense of disappointment. If only they'd arrived before she left Seattle; then she might have considered staying.

"Is it still so painful?" Muriel asked unexpectedly. Nolan and Maryanne's time in Seattle, were subjects they all avoided, and Maryanne appreciated the opportunity to talk about him.

"I wish you and Dad had known him the way I did," she said wistfully. "He's such a contradiction. Rough and surly on the outside, but gentle and compassionate on the inside."

"It sounds as though you're describing your father."

She pondered her mother's words. "Nolan *is* a lot like Daddy. Principled and proud. Independent to a fault. I didn't realize that in the beginning, only later." She laughed softly. "No man could ever make me angrier than Nolan." Nor could any man hope to compete when it came to the feelings he evoked as he kissed her. She came to life in his arms.

"He drove me crazy with how stubborn he could be. At first all I could see was his defensiveness. He'd scowl at me and grumble—he always seemed to be grumbling, as if he couldn't wait to get me out of his hair. He used to look at me and insist I was nothing but trouble. Then he'd do these incredibly considerate things." She was thinking of the day she'd moved into the apartment and how he'd organized the neighborhood teens to haul her boxes up four flights of stairs. How he'd brought her dinner. The morning he'd fixed her radiator. Even the time he'd tried to find her a more "suitable" date.

"There'll be another man for you, sweetie, someone who'll love you as much as you love him."

A bittersweet smile crossed Maryanne's lips. That was the irony of it all.

"Nolan does love me. I know it now, in my heart. I believed him when he said he didn't, but he was lying. It's just that he was in love with someone else a long time ago and he was badly hurt," she said. "He's afraid to leave himself open to that kind of pain again. To complicate matters, I'm Samuel Simpson's daughter. If I weren't, he might've been able to let go of his insecurities and make a commitment."

"He's the one who's losing out."

Maryanne understood that her mother's words were meant to comfort her, but they had the opposite effect. Nolan wasn't the only one who'd lost. "I realize that and I think in some sense he does, too, but it's not much help."

Her mother was silent.

"You know, Mom," Maryanne said, surprising herself with a sudden streak of enthusiasm. "I may not feel like flying off to Paris, but I think a shopping expedition would do us both a world of good. We'll start at the top floor of Sak's and work our way straight down to the basement."

They spent a glorious afternoon Christmas shopping. They arrived home at dinnertime, exhausted yet rejuvenated.

"Where was everyone after school?" Mark, the older of the Simpson boys, complained. At sixteen, he was already as tall as his father and his dark eyes shone brightly with the ardor of youth. "I had a rotten day."

"What happened?"

Every eye was on him. Mark sighed expressively. "There's this girl—"

"Susie Johnson. Mark's bonkers over her," four-teen-year-old Sean supplied, grinning shrewdly at his older brother.

Mark ignored him. "I've been trying to get Susie's attention for a long time. At first I thought she'd notice me because of my brains."

"What brains? Why would she do anything as dumb as that?"

Samuel tossed his son a threatening glare and Sean quickly returned to his meal.

"Some girls really go for that intelligent stuff. You, of course—" he looked down his nose at Sean "—wouldn't know that, on account of only being in junior high. Which is probably where you'll stay for the rest of your life."

Samuel frowned again.

"Go on," Maryanne urged Mark, not wanting the conversation to get sidetracked by her two brothers trading insults.

"Unfortunately Susie didn't even seem to be aware I was in three of her classes, let alone that I was working my head off to impress her. So I tried out for the soccer team. I figured she'd have to notice me because she's a cheerleader."

"Your skills have been developing nicely," Samuel said, nodding proudly at his eldest son.

"Susie hasn't noticed."

"Don't be so sure," Maryanne said.

"No, it's true." Mark signed melodramatically, as if the burden of his problem was too heavy to bear. "That was when I came up with the brilliant idea of paying someone—another girl, one I trust—to talk to Susie, ask her a few questions. I figured if I could find out what she really wants in life then I could go out of my way to—" he paused "—you know."

"What you were hoping was that she'd say she wanted to date a guy who drove a red Camaro so you could borrow your mother's to take to school for the next week or so." Samuel didn't succeed in disguising his smile as he helped himself to salad.

"Well, you needn't worry," Mark muttered, rolling his eyes in disgust. "Do you know what Susie Johnson wants most in this world?"

"To travel?" his mother suggested.

Mark shook his head.

"To date the captain of the football team?" Maryanne tried.

Mark shook his head again.

"What then?" Sean demanded.

"She wants thinner thighs."

Maryanne couldn't help it; she started to smile. Her eyes met her younger brother's, and the smile grew into a full-fledged laugh.

Soon they were all laughing.

The doorbell chimed and Maryanne's parents exchanged brief glances. "Bennett will get it," Samuel said before the boys could vault to their feet.

Within a couple of minutes, Bennett appeared. He whispered something to Maryanne's father, who excused himself and hurried out of the dining-room.

Maryanne continued joking with her brothers until she heard raised voices coming from the front of the house. She paused as an unexpected chill shot down her spine. One of the voices sounded angry, even defensive. Nevertheless Maryanne had no difficulty recognizing whose it was.

Nolan's.

Her heart did a slow drumroll. Without hesitating, she tossed down her napkin and ran to the front door.

Nolan was standing just inside the entryway, wearing his raincoat. Everything about him, the way he stood, the way he spoke and moved, conveyed his irritation.

Maryanne went weak at the sight of him. She noticed things she never had before. Small things that made her realize how much she loved him, how empty her life had become without him.

"I've already explained," her father was saying. Samuel managed to control his legendary temper, but obviously with some difficulty.

Nolan's expression showed flagrant disbelief. He looked tired, Maryanne saw, as if he'd been working nights instead of sleeping. His face was gaunt, his eyes shadowed. "You don't expect me to believe that, do you?"

"You're damn right I do," Maryanne's father returned.

"What's going on here?" she asked, stepping forward, her voice little more than a whisper. She was having trouble dealing with the reality that he was here, in New York, in her family's home. But from the look of things, this wasn't a social call.

"My newspaper column's been picked up nationally," Nolan said, his gaze narrowing on her. "Doesn't that tell you something? Because it damn well should!"

Maryanne couldn't conceal how thrilled she was. "But, Nolan, that's wonderful! What could possibly be wrong with that? I thought it was a goal you'd set yourself."

"Not for another two years."

"Then you must be so pleased."

"Not when it was arranged by your father."

Before Maryanne could whirl around to confront her father, he vehemently denied it.

"I tell you, I had nothing to do with it." Samuel's eyes briefly met Maryanne's and the honesty she saw there convinced her that her father was telling the truth. She'd just opened her mouth to comment when Nolan went on.

"I don't suppose you had anything to do with the sale of my novel, either," he said sarcastically.

Samuel Simpson shook his head. "For heaven's sake, man, I didn't even know you were writing one."

"Your novel sold?" Maryanne shrieked. "Oh, Nolan, I knew it would. The little bit I read was fabulous. Your idea was wonderful. I could hardly force myself to put it down and not read any more." She had to restrain the impulse to throw her arms around his neck and rejoice with him.

"For more money than I ever thought I'd see in my life," he added, his voice hard with challenge. Although he was speaking to Samuel, his eyes rested on Maryanne—eyes that revealed a need and a joy he couldn't disguise.

"Oh, Nolan, I'm so happy for you."

He nodded absently and turned to her father again. "Do you honestly expect me to believe you had nothing to do with that?" he asked, more mildly this time.

"Yes," Samuel answered impatiently. "What possible reason would I have for furthering your career, young man?"

"Because of Maryanne, of course."

"What?" Maryanne couldn't believe what she was hearing. It was ridiculous. It made no sense.

"Your father's attempting to buy you a husband," Nolan growled. Then he turned to Samuel. "Frankly, that upsets me, because Maryanne doesn't need any help from you."

Her father's eyes were stern, and he seemed about to demand that Nolan leave his home.

Maryanne stepped directly in front of Nolan, her hands on her hips. "Trust me, Nolan, if my father was going to buy me a husband, it wouldn't be you! Dad had nothing to do with your success. Even if he did, what would it matter? You've already made it clear you don't want anything to do with me."

His only response was silence.

"I may have spoken a bit…hastily about not loving you," Nolan said a moment later, his voice hoarse.

Samuel cleared his throat, murmuring something about giving the two of them time to talk and promptly left the room.

Maryanne stood gazing up at Nolan, her heart shining through her eyes. Nolan *did* love her; she'd known that for a long time. Only he didn't love her enough to discard the burden of his self-doubts. The boy from the wrong side of the tracks. The self-educated, self-made newsman who feared he'd never fit in with the very people who were awed by his talent.

"You were right," he grumbled, the way he always grumbled, as if he felt annoyed with her.

"About what?"

His smile was almost bitter. "About everything. I love you. Heaven knows I tried not to."

Maryanne closed her eyes, savoring the words she'd never expected to hear. Her heart was pounding so furiously that her head spun. Only…only he didn't say he loved her as though it pleased him.

"Is that such a terrible thing?" she asked. "To love me?"

"No…yes."

He seemed trapped by indecision, dragged down by their differences, yet buoyed by the need to see her again, hear the sound of her voice, gaze at her freckle-dotted nose and run his fingers through her hair. Nolan didn't have to say the words for Maryanne to realize what he was thinking.

"When everything started happening in my life, I thought—I assumed—your father was somehow involved."

"Did you really?" she asked skeptically. The excuse was all too convenient.

Nolan lowered his gaze. "No, I guess I didn't believe he really had anything to do with the sale of my book. But having my columns picked up nationally came as a surprise. For a while I tried to convince myself your family had to be behind that, but I knew it wasn't true. What *really* happened is exactly what you said would happen. You haunted me, Annie. Every time I turned around I could've sworn you were there. I've never missed anyone in my life the way I've missed you."

She smiled shakily. "That's the most beautiful thing you've ever said to me."

Nolan's look was sheepish. "I tried to tell myself your father was out to buy you a husband. Namely me. Think about it, Annie. He got you that job with the *Review,* and for all I knew he could've made it his primary purpose in life to give you everything you want."

"I thought I'd proved otherwise," she said. "My parents went out of their way to make sure none of us was spoiled. I was hoping I'd convinced you of that."

"You did." He slid his hands into the wide pockets of his raincoat. "I guess what I'm trying to say is that if your father's willing to have me in the family, I'd be more than happy to take you off his hands."

"Take me off his hands. How very kind of you," Maryanne snapped, crossing her arms in annoyance. She was looking for romance, declarations of love and words that came straight from his heart. Instead he was handing out insults.

"Don't get all bent out of shape," he said and the smile that stole across his lips was so devastating Maryanne's breath caught. "The way I figure it," he continued, "you need someone…"

Maryanne turned to walk away from him. Not any great distance, of course, just far enough for him to know he wasn't getting anywhere with this argument.

"All right," he amended, catching her by the hand and urging her around to face him again. "*I* need someone."

"Someone?"

"You!" he concluded with a wide grin.

"You're improving. Go on."

"Nothing seemed right after you left. There was this giant hole inside me I couldn't seem to fill. Work didn't satisfy me any more. Nothing did. Gloria and Eddie asked about you and I didn't know what to say. I was grateful Mom's Place was closed, because I couldn't have eaten there."

A part of her longed for all the romantic words a woman wanted to hear from the man she loved. But it wasn't too likely she'd get them from Nolan. He wasn't telling her he'd heard her name whispered in the wind or seen it written in his heart. Nolan would never say things like that.

"You want me to move back to Seattle so I'll quit haunting you," she finally said.

"No. I want you to come back because I love you."

"And need me?"

He nodded. "I still think you could do a hell of a lot better than marrying an ornery guy like me. I promise to be a good husband—that is, if you're willing to put up with me…" He let the rest fade. His eyes grew humble as he slowly, uncertainly, pulled her into his arms. "Would you…be willing?"

She smiled, and hot tears gathered in the corners of her eyes. She nodded jerkily. "Yes. Oh, you idiot. I could slap you for putting us through all of this."

"Wouldn't a kiss do just as well?"

"I suppose, only…"

But the thought was left unspoken. His kiss was

long and thorough and said all the tender words, the fanciful phrases she'd never hear.

It was enough.

More than enough to last her a lifetime.

Epilogue

It was Christmas morning in the Adams household.

The wrapping paper had accumulated in a small mountain on the living-room carpet. The Christmas tree lights twinkled and "Silent Night" played in the background.

Maryanne sat on the sofa next to Nolan with her feet up, her head on her husband's shoulder. The girls were busy sorting through their stash of new toys and playing their favorite game—"being grown-ups." Bailey was pretending to be a young college graduate determined to make a name for herself in the newspaper business. Courtney played a jaded reporter from a rival newspaper, determined to thwart her. It was Maryanne and Nolan's romance all over again. The girls had loved hearing every detail of their courtship.

"They don't seem *too* disappointed about not getting a puppy," he said.

"I'm so proud of them," Maryanne smiled. Both Courtney and Bailey were thrilled about the new baby, and although it had been hard, they'd accepted that there wouldn't be a puppy in the family, after all. Not for a few years, anyway.

"They're adorable," Nolan agreed and kissed the top of her head. "Just like their mother."

"Thank you," she whispered.

"When did you say your parents would—" Nolan didn't get a chance to finish the question before the doorbell rang. "Is that them?" Samuel and Muriel Simpson had come from New York to spend Christmas week with the family.

Maryanne nodded. Sitting up, she called to her oldest daughter, "Courtney, could you please answer the door?"

Both girls raced to the front door, throwing it open. They were silent for just a second, then squealed with delight. "Grandma! Grandpa Simpson!"

"Merry Christmas. Merry Christmas."

Maryanne's parents stepped into the house, carrying a large wicker basket. Inside slept a small black-and-white puppy.

"A puppy?" Courtney said in a hushed voice. She stared at her grandparents, who grinned and nodded.

"We think every family needs a dog," Maryanne's father said.

"Oh, he's *so* cute," Bailey whispered, covering her mouth with both hands.

"He's perfect," Courtney said, lifting the squirming puppy from his bed. "Is he ours? Can we keep him?"

"Oh, yes, this is a special-delivery Christmas gift for my two beautiful granddaughters."

Maryanne came over to take the puppy from Courtney. She cuddled the small, warm body and looked into sleepy brown eyes." I guess you've come a long way, haven't you?" she murmured. The puppy gazed up at her, unblinking, and Maryanne fell in love. Just like that, all her concerns disappeared. At least this baby would be house-trained well before their son was born. And the girls could help look after him. She looked up to meet Nolan's eyes, and he nodded. So, despite everything, there's be *two* new additions to the family this next year.

Nolan ushered her parents inside and took their coats. "Sit down and make yourselves comfortable. Maryanne and I have a Christmas surprise, too."

"As good as a new puppy?" her father asked.

"Oh, yes," Courtney told him after a whispered consultation with her sister. She stroked the puppy, still cradled in her mother's arms. "I don't know what we're naming *that* surprise, but we're calling this one Jack."

DEBBIE MACOMBER

32334	6 RAiNIER DRIVE	___ $7.99 U.S.	___ $9.50 CAN.
32208	50 HARBOR STREET	___ $7.50 U.S.	___ $8.99 CAN.
32160	THE SHOP ON BLOSSOM STREET	___ $7.50 U.S.	___ $8.99 CAN.
32110	ON A SNOWY NIGHT	___ $6.99 U.S.	___ $8.50 CAN.
32073	44 CRANBERRY POINT	___ $7.50 U.S.	___ $8.99 CAN.
32028	CHANGING HABITS	___ $7.50 U.S.	___ $8.99 CAN.
66674	BETWEEN FRIENDS	___ $7.50 U.S.	___ $8.99 CAN.
66930	A GIFT TO LAST	___ $6.99 U.S.	___ $8.50 CAN.
66929	204 ROSEWOOD LANE	___ $7.50 U.S.	___ $8.99 CAN.
66891	THURSDAYS AT EIGHT	___ $7.50 U.S.	___ $8.99 CAN.
66830	16 LIGHTHOUSE ROAD	___ $6.99 U.S.	___ $8.50 CAN.
66800	ALWAYS DAKOTA	___ $6.99 U.S.	___ $8.50 CAN.
66719	311 PELICAN COURT	___ $7.50 U.S.	___ $8.99 CAN.
66974	MOON OVER WATER	___ $6.99 U.S.	___ $8.50 CAN.
66976	PROMISE, TEXAS	___ $6.99 U.S.	___ $8.50 CAN.
66975	MONTANA	___ $6.99 U.S.	___ $8.50 CAN.
66973	THIS MATTER OF MARRIAGE	___ $6.99 U.S.	___ $8.50 CAN.
32295	A GOOD YARN	___ $7.99 U.S.	___ $9.50 CAN.
32239	HOME FOR THE HOLIDAYS	___ $7.50 U.S.	___ $8.99 CAN.

(limited quantities available)

TOTAL AMOUNT	$ _____
POSTAGE & HANDLING	$ _____
($1.00 FOR 1 BOOK, 50¢ for each additional)	
APPLICABLE TAXES*	$ _____
TOTAL PAYABLE	$ _____

(check or money order—please do not send cash)

To order, complete this form and send it, along with a check or money order for the total above, payable to MIRA Books, to: **In the U.S.:** 3010 Walden Avenue, P.O. Box 9077, Buffalo, NY 14269-9077; **In Canada:** P.O. Box 636, Fort Erie, Ontario, L2A 5X3.

Name: _____

Address: _____ City: _____

State/Prov.: _____ Zip/Postal Code: _____

Account Number (if applicable): _____

075 CSAS

*New York residents remit applicable sales taxes.
*Canadian residents remit applicable GST and provincial taxes.

MIRA®

www.MIRABooks.com

MDM1106BL